J.G. Austin

A nameless nobleman

J.G. Austin

A nameless nobleman

ISBN/EAN: 9783743303249

Manufactured in Europe, USA, Canada, Australia, Japa

Cover: Foto ©Andreas Hilbeck / pixelio.de

Manufactured and distributed by brebook publishing software
(www.brebook.com)

J.G. Austin

A nameless nobleman

ROUND-ROBIN SERIES.

A

Nameless Nobleman

BOSTON

JAMES R. OSGOOD AND COMPANY

1881

_Stereotyped and Printed by Rand, Avery, & Co.,
117 Franklin Street, Boston._

Mother! For love of thee it was begun ;
In thy most honored name to-day 'tis done.
And though all earthly cares must cease
In that fair land of everlasting peace,
Love aye is one, and they who love are one ;
Time cannot end what God in Time begun ;
And thou wilt joy e'en in thine endless rest,
To know thy child obeys thy last behest.

CONTENTS.

CHAPTER.		PAGE.
I.	Louis the Great and Louis the Little,	1
II.	Provence Roses	11
III.	A Blight upon the Roses	20
IV.	Between Two Days	25
V.	Cain and Abel	33
VI.	Valerie's Choice	42
VII.	Molly	54
VIII.	The Spinning-Wheel	64
IX.	Molly accepts the Consequences	74
X.	The Consequences	81
XI.	The French Invasion	85
XII.	The Rosy Dawn	95
XIII.	The Dagger of Reginald de Montarnaud	102
XIV.	Mrs. Hetherford takes Pity on Molly,	110
XV.	The Priest's Chamber	116
XVI.	The Search-Warrant	127
XVII.	And Valerie?	134
XVIII.	Dr. Schwarz	142
XIX.	Loyalism and Loyolaism	151
XX.	The Doctor Probes a Little	157
XXI.	The Joy of Meeting	160

CONTENTS.

CHAPTER.		PAGE.
XXII.	And the Pain of Parting	171
XXIII.	The Betrothal	179
XXIV.	Grandmother Ames's Curtains	190
XXV.	The Whole Truth, and Nothing but the Truth	201
XXVI.	The Mail-Bag of the "Circé"	209
XXVII.	The Bunch of Grapes	221
XXVIII.	Dame Tilley's Leg	233
XXIX.	The Dark Hour before the Dawn	237
XXX.	A Bridal Procession	247
XXXI.	The Value of a Doctor	254
XXXII.	A Treaty Offensive and Defensive	263
XXXIII.	The Rose-Garden of Provence	268
XXXIV.	The Restorations of the Chapel	275
XXXV.	The Doctor's Dressing-Room	283
XXXVI.	Dead Things that will not Sleep	293
XXXVII.	A Crucial Test	302
XXXVIII.	The "Belle Isle"	316
XXXIX.	Marquises are Unlucky to Me	324
XL.	Molly Holds the Fort	328
XLI.	Letter from the Abbé Despard	340
XLII.	On Burying-Hill	343
XLIII.	A Provence Rose	349
XLIV.	When the Fog Lifted	354
XLV.	Good-by	368

A NAMELESS NOBLEMAN.

CHAPTER I.

LOUIS THE GRAND, AND LOUIS THE LITTLE.

THE Montespan is in great beauty to-night," said the Marquis de Vannes to the Comte de Chablais, as the two stood waiting with all the rest of the world for the entrance of the royal party. It was the grand gallery of Versailles where they stood; and from the lofty ceiling the grim warriors depicted there by LeBrun looked down in surly admiration upon the beauties of the world, so notably assembled at the French court during the first half of the reign of Louis XIV.; for Anne of Austria, always a Spaniard, loved to see herself surrounded by the dark eyes and to hear the lisping accents of her native land; nor did she fail to encourage her poor, timid daughter-in-law in the same tastes, if, indeed, Maria Thérèsa can be said to have had any thing so decisive as a taste, except in the direction of chocolate. Differing subtly from the Spaniards, and yet resembling them in race-marks, came a troop of Italy's fairest and best-born, following the Mancinis and Martinozzis, all hoping fortune and preferment from Mazarin. Poor, charming, doomed Henrietta of England was the magnet of a bevy of fair aristocrats, whose blonde loveliness contrasted, to their mutual advantage, with the brown beauties of Spain, Italy, and France, and surpassed in refinement that of the Germans who had already appeared at the court of France, heralding, perhaps, the advent of their queer countrywoman, the second Duchess of Orleans. But we return to the two gallants themselves, no mean personages at court, who stood discussing the scene with the gay cynicism of their age.

"In beauty, yes," replied De Chablais, glancing across the gallery at the Marquise de Montespan, who stood surrounded by flatterers, rivals, imitators, enemies, every thing but friends: "she looks as content as the cat who has just lapped up the cream, and is still singing jubilate over the fall of poor dear La Vallière."

"Don't be uncharitable, *mon cher*," replied De Vannes maliciously. "Madame de Montespan was the friend of the Duchess de la Vallière, and proved it by dragging an earthly crown from between her hands and giving her an heavenly one instead. No doubt Sister Louise de la Miséricorde feels deeply grateful."

"Oh, of course! especially as this devoted friend prevents any danger of a lapse from grace by herself monopolizing the peril formerly shared by both."

"While the widow Scarron meekly offers herself as a

monument of pious peace set in the very whirlpool of these contending passions."

Monsieur de Chablais turned, and looked keenly at his friend, then breathlessly asked, —

"What do you say, De Vannes? Surely this prude of a *gouvernante* will not presume to supersede her mistress, as her mistress did her friend and equal!"

"If by mistress you mean Madame de Montespan, my friend, I beg to contradict you. Madame de Maintenon, as we are now to style the widow Scarron, is the governess, not of Madame de Montespan's children, but of the king's."

"A distinction, I perceive; but where is the difference?"

"The difference of serving a master or — a mistress."

"I perceive; but allow me to observe it is a dangerous *bon-mot*, since that master is also our master, and possesses sharp ears, keen eyes, and remarkably long arms."

"All which will presently exercise themselves, unless he is the more careful, upon that handsome youth devoting himself so frankly to the fair marquise."

"I see. He seems about to devour her bodily, and she conquers in his behalf that timid and shrinking reserve we all recognize as her distinctive charm. Who is he?"

"Son of that poor old Count de Montarnaud, I believe."

"What, the courtier of King Clovis? Is he still extant?"

"Oh, yes! and is forever in the king's path, asking

him to make this boy generalissimo of the French army."

"Is that all? The young fellow is making out a better road to advancement for himself, if he plays his cards well."

"If the king surprises him making eyes at madame, he is likely to be advanced with a vengeance, — advanced to the front ranks of the next forlorn-hope, against some Dutch. city with an unpronounceable name."

"Gentlemen, gentlemen! the king!" announced an usher passing in front of the speakers, who immediately fell back into the formal line adopted by the courtiers about to be passed in review by the monarch, at this moment appearing in the folding-doors thrown open at his approach. A slight murmur of adulation and delight replaced the busy hum of conversation in the *grande galerie,* a sort of courtly paraphrase of the song issuing from the lips of Memnon as the first rays of morning sunlight touched them; and then Louis, followed by several members of the royal family, passed slowly down the hall, pausing at almost every step to address now one and then another of the rustling and glittering ranks of courtiers, who bent before his look as a parterre of tulips bends before the west wind.

"Did you mark the glance his Majesty shot at the Montespan and her new *breloque?*" murmured De Vannes to De Chablais without turning his head. "I would not be in the shoes of that captain of cavalry for something, unless the marquise puts him in her pocket before his Majesty reaches that spot."

"My Barbary horse against your Damascus sword that she don't, and that Montarnaud is either banished, imprisoned, or punished in some manner."

"Done, although I shall lose my sword."

"You will if *he* does." And as the king's sonorous and measured accents drew nearer, the courtiers became mute and expectant.

It was in fact true, that the Grande Monarque, who, like all potent rulers, had microscopic as well as telescopic powers of vision, had, upon his first entrance into the hall, singled his favorite from among the glittering throng, and at once perceived that she was carrying on one of those audacious and sudden flirtations which some women toss off as others do a glass of champagne, or a full inhalation of volatile salts, — a brief exhilaration and stimulus, only fitting them for more serious and systematic efforts in some other direction.

Already the stimulus told ; for never had Madame de Montespan looked more magnificently handsome than to-night, with her great dark eyes overflowing with brilliancy, her cheeks and lips burning with color, her wonderful hands and arms showing like those of a statue against the garnet-colored velvet of her robe, her shoulders and bust rising invincible from a sea-foam border of priceless lace. Arms and bosom and head glittered with the jewels this woman loved so much better than she did soul or honor, and which her royal lover lavished upon her with such princely munificence that she boasted of owning a richer collection than any queen could claim as private property. To be sūre, they were not all paid for in that reign; but the bill was brought in to Louis XVI. about a century later, and he, poor scapegoat, settled for all.

Yes, the Montespan was in great beauty to-night; and so evidently thought the handsome young man in the uniform of a captain of cavalry, who stood beside her, devouring her with his bold black eyes, and bending more confidentially than deferentially to catch the words murmured for his ear alone. At the entrance of the king he drew himself up, and made a movement of adieu: but the marquise, not appearing to notice the gesture, continued the conversation in a yet more familiar tone; and the Vicomte de Montarnaud, bred in the school of reckless gallantry, whether of love or war, so popular in that day, followed her lead without further hesitation or comment, so that in point of fact a more patient and humble man than Louis Dieu-donné might have felt a little annoyed at the slight to himself involved in this absorbing interest in another, displayed by his haughty mistress. A slight but ominous frown gathered upon the Olympian brow; and the courteous phrases scattered hither and thither among the expectant crowd by the "lips of fate," as some people called the royal mouth, grew scanter and more mechanical, so that several courtiers, not sure of favor, skilfully contrived to melt away behind their companions, preferring not to risk the compliments their royal master was quite capable of bestowing when in an ill humor.

Suddenly the king's eyes lightened wrathfully, and yet unaccountably; for the figure upon which they rested was as harmless an one as could be imagined, and surely a very familiar one, for the Comte de Montarnaud had been longer at court by many years than Louis himself. An old man, wigged, painted, padded, decrepit, and courtly, — a man whose face nature had made handsome and noble, and seventy years of court life had rendered insignificant, crafty, and cringing. As he perceived that the king would address him, the wizened face lighted with servile joy, and the poor old back bent in a bow so profound that one knew not whether to fear the vertebræ should become dislocated or the peruke tumble off; misfortunes about equal, since one meant death, and the other the royal displeasure. Before either danger was fully overpast the king spoke coldly and haughtily : —

"Monsieur de Montarnaud, you asked permission some time since to marry your eldest son to Mademoiselle de Rochenbois, your ward."

"I had thought of it, your Majesty ; but, when your Majesty deigned to remark that you did not like your officers to marry too young, I relinquished " —

"I withdraw my opposition, and permit the marriage. Nay, more : as you have been a faithful servant of my august father as well as of myself, the marriage may take place in the royal chapel ; and we shall see if some position about the court can be found for the bride, who will remain here while the vicomte returns to his duty. Where is she now?"

"At the Château de Montarnaud, your Majesty."

"In Provence, I believe."

"Yes, your Majesty, near Marseilles."

"Ah, near Marseilles! And what family have you there, Monsieur le Comte? You are a widower, I believe."

"Since fifteen years, your Majesty. My family consists, besides my ward, of only two sons."

"Two? where is the other? I never heard of him."

"Oh! your Majesty, he is but a boy yet, hardly twenty years old, and still with his tutor. He inherits a little property from his mother, and with it the title of le Baron de " —

"But where is he, I ask? At Montarnaud, near Marseilles, with Mademoiselle de Rochenbois?"

"Yes, your Majesty," replied the poor old courtier, feeling that the prolonged conversation, which at first had overwhelmed him with delight, was assuming a tone of menace and aggression any thing but indicative of royal favor to the house of Montarnaud. Nor was the king's parting speech calculated to assuage the cruel forebodings of the old man's heart ; for, with a very pronounced sneer upon his Austrian lips, Louis passed on, saying, —

"Really, Monsieur de Montarnaud, you are a man of resource. Since it was not permitted to marry your elder son to this wealthy ward, you shut her up in a country-house with the younger one, trusting to the chapter of accidents for a marriage, public or private, before there should be time to prevent it. I shall, however, expect to receive Madame la Vicomtesse de Montarnaud, *née* de Rochenbois, within the month."

"Your Majesty shall be obeyed," stammered the

count, trembling upon his infirm legs as the chill breath of the royal displeasure swept over his head, like the first frost of autumn over the parterre of tulips, to which but now we likened the ranks of courtiers.

Passing on, the king reached the station of the marquise and her coterie; and while graciously acknowledging her careless salute, and the profound reverences of her companions, he gayly said to the former, —

"Madame, by the pleased expression upon this young gentleman's face, I suspect that you are congratulating him upon his approaching marriage and the already renowned beauty of his bride."

A slight and angry color rose to the haughty beauty's brow; and turning her eyes upon the startled, almost alarmed, face of the young man, she coldly said, —

"Monsieur had not informed me of his happiness."

"His Majesty is pleased to jest. I am not so unfortunate as to be in bondage as yet," stammered the captain of cavalry, divided between the impossibility of contradicting the king or of speaking to any one else in his presence, and the desire to retain his place in the favor of the imperious beauty, to whom he had just vowed to carry her colors triumphantly through the next battle in which he should be called to engage, and of whom he had begged and obtained permission to present himself at her apartments the next day, and there receive from her own hands the scarf to be thus borne. And although neither the social nor the moral code of those days, nor above all the code Montespan, objected to the devotion of anybody's husband to anybody else's wife, it was nevertheless, as both the marquise and her admirer felt, a little out of taste that a man should in the same breath ask permission of the king to marry a charming young girl, and of the king's mistress to carry her colors through the wars.

Louis glanced from the one face to the other, and took a pinch of snuff with uncommon zest.

"The good news is nevertheless true, monsieur," said he, in his most *débonnaire* and gracious tone. "I love to reward the good soldiers who win so many laurels for me; and, as monsieur your father tells me your heart is set upon this marriage, I have consented, not only that it shall take place in the royal chapel, but that Madame de Montarnaud shall be entertained at court during your absence in the approaching campaign in Holland. The nuptials may be, I fear, a little hurried; but you shall have permission to fly to Montarnaud at the earliest possible hour to-morrow."

The king passed on; Madame de Montespan stifled a yawn, and turned her back upon the young man, who with a brow as black as night made his way to the lower end of the hall, where his father awaited him with a pale and frightened face.

CHAPTER II.

PROVENCE ROSES.

IT was a garden deep in the heart of Provence, Provence the fair, Provence the intoxicating, Provence of the Provençals, neighbor of Languedoc and Dauphiny; that region redolent of the traditions of poet and troubadour, of the court of Love and Beauty, of Blondel and his lion-master, of the dear, prolix, impossible, inconsequent romances that drove Don Quixote mad, but whose flavor, like a drop of attar, has been found sufficient to perfume half the more modern works of fiction.

It was a garden innocent of the chilling and formal science just coming into vogue in France under the auspices of Le Notre, the impress of whose style is still to be seen, not only in the gardens of Versailles, but all over France, and even England; a garden left very much to Nature, who, sweet prodigal, in this her beloved summer land, had pleased herself by heaping together in this little hidden nook a wealth of color and perfume, of riotous bloom, of glowing sunlight and alluring shadow, of food for every sensuous capacity of eye and ear, and that subtlest of senses, the sense of smell, enough in this one garden to gild all Switzerland with a charm her grandeur has never attained.

The place was old and irregular, and succeeding generations of Montarnauds had left the impress of their taste in now a dense mass of evergreen forming a background to a great clump of gorgeous bloom; now a fountain, again an arbor, a winding labyrinth leading to a hidden nook of shaded and perfumed rest; again a broad, glowing expanse of massed flowers, geranium, salvia, calceolaria, hydrangea, dahlias, every thing that is positive and imperious of color and form, all weltering in the thick yellow sunshine that seemed to sink into every open pore like wine into the lips of a thirsty man; around these lay borders of pansy and mignonette, and all that is fragrant and unobtrusive, and ready to lend perfume to the beauty of their soulless neighbors; and anon broad ribbons of tulip-beds, and trellises where passion-flower and jasmine and scarlet cypress climbed tumultuously over each other to the very topmost hold, and then waved their long slender arms hither and yon in the effort to grasp at something more. Lilies were there, queen lilies such as the Angel of the Annunciation bears, their milk-white chalices powdered with the gold-dust of promise; lilies of the valley at their feet; lilies from Japan, that land still locked in mystery, yet flinging from her half-opened door this or that object of art and wonder to the French who stood knocking, louis d'or in hand; lilies of Palestine, Solomon lilies, flaunting beneath the Provençal sun robes whose marvel was selected as the type of gorgeous apparel by Him who was born among their glory. And the roses! at the roses we pause: for he who has not seen Provence roses in Provence knows not the meaning of those five letters, knows not why the rose is queen of flowers, knows not why the rose is the type of love, knows not why the dear old mediæval legend changed Bohemian Elizabeth's hidden charity to roses rather than to another flower. The color, oh the impossible color! for the heart of the summer pulsated in its glow, the soul of the sun burned in its intensity, the deep rich light permeated every vein of the petals sumptuous in their substance, and marvellous in their size. No, no! we cannot describe the roses of Provence: but they are there, and you may see them; pass by Paris, and go, if you are wise.

Besides the evergreens, the olive, the pepper-trees, the ilex, the flowers, and the labyrinth, there were the birds who made bridal journeys from all the rest of France to this garden; the butterflies who floated over the flower-beds like blossoms detached and drawn upward by the sun-god; and there was Valerie! Valerie, who all day long flitted through the garden, embodying flower, and bird, and butterfly, and Provençal summer, all in her own mignonne figure; Valerie who loved them all, and was beloved by all, and had feasted all her life upon their beauty, and whose beauty was a feast and daily food to them. A slip of a girl, hardly seventeen: lissome as a passion-flower vine; her clear skin pale and dark with the passionate colorless glow of the South, her purple-black hair hanging in two shining braids from a head fit to be modelled for Hebe; her smooth, low forehead based by two straight black brows, beautiful and threatening as a just-defined thunder-cloud; her great lustrous eyes full of slumberous passion, full of the joy of happy girlhood, full of pride and courage, and with a power of pathos nascent in their depths which the birds and the butterflies and the roses had never yet seen called out, had never demanded or dreamed of. But her mouth! there was perhaps the keystone of Valerie's beauty. Yes, the petals of the roses were velvety, and pulsating with fire, were of a color impossible to define or reproduce, were fragrant, and delicious to the touch; but the rose-leaves were not alive, they did not curve, and pout, and suddenly part in dazzling smiles above little pearls of teeth: they were not the lips of Valerie, nor could they by movement produce those little wells of mirth and caresses, and possible tears, the *fossettes*, the dimples which came and went as Valerie smiled. It was after all the mouth, François said to himself as he stood gazing at her while she played with El Moro her Spanish greyhound, forcing him to eat the purple and amber grapes she pulled from the vine above her head, while she sat throned upon a seat formed in the lowest branches of an oak near the borders of the garden. Flecks of sunlight pierced the foliage and lay like golden ornaments upon the whiteness of her dress, glowed in the ruby bracelet upon her arm, and lighted the dusky masses of her hair to purple sheen. Yes, it was her mouth, that mouth whose coy kisses had grown so rare within the last year, but had become so much more precious than the soulless caresses of childhood. Last night, when they quarrelled and were reconciled, she kissed him twice. and —

"Well, Monsieur le Baron," broke in the ringing voice of Valerie, "are you envying El Moro his feast, or are you composing a Latin poem for your tutor, or have you gone to sleep? You stand there leaning against that tree, and looking at me as if you never had seen me before."

"Perhaps I wish I never had," replied François a little moodily, as he sauntered across the space of sunlight between the cork-tree and the oak, and stood leaning against the latter, his arm resting upon the footstool of the rustic seat.

"Perhaps you, — there, run away, *mon* Moro : run and catch a cricket to take the flavor of the grapes out of your mouth, — perhaps you wish you had never seen me, François? And why?"

She leaned one cheek upon her hand, as she stooped smiling toward him, and the other hand rested lightly and caressingly upon his head. He caught it in his own, and, raising his face, looked long and ardently up into hers. And it is a pity some great painter had not been hidden among the roses to catch that picture, and make himself immortal by it ; for the baron François was as nearly handsome as a manly man should be, and had inherited from his Norman mother all the high and haughty characteristics of her race, — the cold, clear eyes, blue as steel, and betimes as trenchant and as cruel, the fair complexion, proud, thin-lipped mouth, and tawny golden hair. His figure, too, differed largely from the delicate elegance lapsing into sensuous roundness of his Provençal sires, and was tall, large-boned, powerful, and soldierly, like those companions who followed William the Conquerer to the field of Hastings. But just now the steely eyes were dim with tender fears, and the severe mouth was tremulous with loving words; and the hand fit to wield a battle-axe was clasped in timid constraint over the tiny fingers of the Provençal girl, as he slowly answered : —

"Because, if you do not love me, and love me always, you will be the misfortune of my life."

"What, I, little I? I who can never learn the fine things you and the abbé try to teach me? Little frivolous, childish I, who am fit for nothing but to play with El Moro, and pelt Mademoiselle Salerne with roses, and tease old Marie's life out, and sing *chansons* to my guitar, and " —

"And make the joy of my poor life, Valerie."

"I again? What ! poor little I, the present joy and possible misfortune of life to so very grave and learned a youth as François, le Baron de " —

"François, the lover of Valerie !" interposed the young baron, catching in his own the other little hand, and covering them both with kisses, beneath whose breath a dusky crimson crept slowly up into the girl's cheek, and lighted its pallor as fire shows through cream-white porcelain.

"Mamzelle ! Mamzelle Valerie ! *Ma petite* ! where, then, do you hide? Answer, for the love of the Virgin ! Mamzelle, I say !"

"Now what does Marie want, do you suppose?" exclaimed Marie's nursling, in a tone of comic vexation. "Has she found another egg in my canary-bird's nest? or has the cat turned over in her sleep? or — oh, horrors! has she discovered the fearful rent I made in my new dress last night, by running against a rose-bush in the dark? Now that was your fault, François, and "—

"Here she is! I was just going to propose escaping into the labyrinth; but it is too late. Well, Marie, here is Mademoiselle Valerie."

"So I see, Monsieur le Baron," panted the old woman, holding on to her fat sides, and casting reproachful glances up into the tree, where Valerie's bright and glowing face laughed down at her.

"If you had but answered me, mademoiselle, you would have had the news sooner."

"And saved your poor old legs, nursey," replied the child with a burst of tinkling laughter. "Well, now you have found me, what is it? Has the king come to ask me to marry monseigneur the dauphin? He is a thought young for me, but still "—

"You might have guessed farther afield, my poppet," replied the nurse with a sagacious nod of the head; "for it is, if not the king, one of the king's gentlemen; and, as for his errand, who knows?"

"One of the king's gentlemen! What do you mean, nurse?" demanded François, turning so suddenly that the old woman uttered an affected little shriek.

"Mercy, Monsieur le Baron! you need not eat me up alive with your sharp way, so like madame the comtesse, whom you do not remember."

And Marie crossed herself with a very expressive

shake of the head, as if she were not sorry that the Norman countess was at rest and quiet.

"But who is it? Speak, will you, you provoking creature?" demanded Valerie petulantly, as she put one foot down to the lower branch of the tree in preparation for descent.

"Well then," replied the old woman with evident enjoyment of the consternation she was about to evoke, — "well, then, Monsieur le Comte has arrived, and with him Monsieur le Vicomte Gaston."

"My father and Gaston!" exclaimed François in great astonishment ; while Valerie sprang lightly to the ground, and passed her hand over her hair, adjusted her necklace and bracelets, and plumed herself like a bird.

"Yes, as I tell you, and here they are," replied Marie, pointing to the terrace leading down from the château, where now appeared the mean and insignificant figure of the Comte de Montarnaud, his handsome scowling son Gaston, and two or three attendants, the latter apparently offering explanations and apologies which the count waved impatiently and contemptuously aside.

"Valerie !" murmured François, as the two hastened to meet the new-comers ; and Marie kept as close as possible upon their heels, not to lose the explanation and possible scene impending.

"Valerie, I am sure that ill fortune is upon us. Promise me that you will always love me ; promise that you will never marry another man ; promise" —

"Oh, hush, François ! you make me nervous with

your tragic air, and your ' Promise, promise ! ' Who speaks of marrying anybody? See, your father is already frowning at you ; hold up your head, and look like a man instead of a schoolboy. How handsome Gaston has grown ! "

" Frivolous and trifling ! " muttered François bitterly, and he dropped a step behind his companion, who ran eagerly forward, both hands extended, eyes and lips bright with smiles, exclaiming joyfully, —

" Ah, monsieur my god-papa, how glad we are to receive you ! Monsieur Gaston also ! But why did not you let us know that you were coming? We would have received you more worthily."

" Truth to tell, mademoiselle," replied the count, whose brow showed a decided cloud, " the château seems but carelessly kept, considering it holds so rare a treasure as yourself. I found Monsieur l'Abbé Despard, my son's tutor, confessing Mademoiselle Salerne, my ward's governess, while their two charges were hidden, — who knows where ? "

CHAPTER III.

A BLIGHT UPON THE ROSES.

AS the master of the house thus publicly proclaimed his discontent with his reception, a small tumult of defence arose from the parties accused. The abbé, a handsome young priest, whom François had for a considerable period governed as he would, bowed humbly and exclaimed, —

"Pardon, a thousand pardons, monsieur, but" — while Mademoiselle Salerne the governess, an equally good-looking young woman with whom Valerie seldom had any trouble since she had clearly established their relative positions, clasped both hands, bent her knee as if about to prostrate herself, and shrieked, —

"But can monsieur suspect me of neglect of duty! Me! Oh, no, no! never, it can never be; for mademoiselle will explain, that we had but just now finished our lessons, and" —

"Of course, Salerne," interposed Valerie, with good-humored contempt, — "of course monsieur understands that you are all which is faithful and trustworthy; and if I am idle, and like to rest in the garden rather than to work in the house, it is my own fault."

"Or mine, since I asked you to come out this afternoon, not supposing that my father intended that I should be kept at my task like a schoolboy, now that I am old enough to wear a sword, and "—

"There, there, there, there ! " exclaimed the count, raising both hands to his ears : "I had no idea of rousing such a hornet's nest by my idle remark. Mademoiselle, let me lead you to the house."   And, offering his hand to Valerie with all the stately dignity of the court, he led her on between the beds of roses, which seemed suddenly to lose their color and their fragrance, and up the broken, shallow steps to the terrace, and so into the old château, with its sparse and antique furniture, its mouldering tapestries and tarnished gildings ; for the counts of Montarnaud had spent many a fair fortune coming to them in the hand of the heiresses they loved to marry, spent it in war, sometimes for and sometimes against their liege lord, the king ; spent it in mad revelry, in gaming, in luxury, in every form of self-delight, until when Raoul, the present count, came to his dignities, he found them so shorn of the means of maintenance that he had spent very nearly all of what remained in dancing attendance first at the court of Louis XIII., that is to say, at the court of Cardinal Richelieu, and then at that of the Regent Anne of Austria, that is to say, at that of Mazarin.   Finally he was at present bending his aged knees at the shrine of the young King Louis XIV., who, so far from being the shadow of a prime minister, had given to the ministers, who desired to know upon the death of Mazarin to whom they were to apply for orders, the truly royal answer, —

" *Moi-même !* "

But this devotion, bringing no especial pleasure or advantage to either the cardinals, the queen-regent, the young king or his mistresses, naturally brought no profit to the aged courtier, whose influence was stretched to its utmost limit in procuring the appointment of captain of cavalry for his eldest son, and the privilege for himself of winning a few louis d'or now and again at the royal card-tables.

The causes thus accreted had to-day produced two effects: the first, that the Château de Montarnaud was very poorly furnished and very meagrely kept; the second, that the count would not have failed to obey any command the king had deigned to lay upon him, if it had involved carrying Mademoiselle de Rochenbois to Paris in fetters, and obtaining a *lettre-de-cachet* for François if he opposed the movement.

Such extreme measures were not, however, likely to prove necessary in the opinion of the count, who knew his world as well as Monsieur de Meaux knew his Bible, or Louis XIV. his own importance. So, in leading the young girl into the château, he dropped the imperious and fault-finding tone he had assumed among his dependents and toward his son, and spoke of the gayeties of the court, of the magnificence of the young king and the splendors of his entertainments, of the new-born beauties of Versailles, the new comedies of Molière performed in the royal theatre of that palace, and of the charms of several of the court ladies; ending with a significant glance and bow, as he added, —

"Not but what I think we might rival even the dazzling beauty of the Marquise de Montespan, not to mention inferior charms, by the importation into the capital of attractions quite as aristocratic and cultivated, and infinitely fresher. In fact, mademoiselle, the king himself has been good enough to inquire why you were not presented already, and to give orders that the ceremony should no longer be delayed. Does that please you?"

The color mounted swiftly to the young girl's face, and before replying she cast a glance through the glass-door by which they had just entered the saloon. Upon the terrace stood François with his brother Gaston; and, although their conversation was inaudible, the looks and gestures of both indicated annoyance on the part of the younger, insolence on the part of the elder, and a most unfraternal state of feeling on the part of both. The count's eyes followed those of his ward, and rested upon the two young men with a look of dissatisfaction for a moment; then he said, —

"François is nothing but a boy, and needs to see the world. I think I will close the château now that you are about to leave it, and send him to travel with the abbé for a while. He will come home a man."

"It is quite determined, then, that I should go to Paris!" exclaimed Valerie in a startled tone.

"The king himself invites you to do so," replied the count smoothly. "And what is more, my dear, he wishes you to be presented as Madame the Vicomtesse de Montarnaud."

"Monsieur! I the wife of Gaston! Impossible!"

"And why impossible, mademoiselle?   Gaston s
not an ill-looking fellow ; he has a good position in the
army, with prospects of promotion, since his Majesty
deigns to notice him ; he loves you romantically ; I,
his father, and your guardian, beg you to listen favora-
bly to his suit ; and, most important of all, the king
commands you to do so."

"O monsieur !" and choking with anger, grief,
and terror, the young girl hid her face in her hands,
and rushed from the room.

The Count de Montarnaud looked after her, wrinkled
his leathern cheeks in a smile of marvellous cunning,
and slowly inhaled a pinch of snuff.

"*Une ingénue !*" murmured he, dusting some grains
of the fragrant dust from his jabot ; "but it is a fault
that cures itself, and will make her none the less
attractive at court.   It was poor La Vallière's road to
success."

CHAPTER IV

BETWEEN TWO DAYS.

THE conversation of the brothers, meantime, was no more amicable than it looked. Truth to tell, no great affection had ever subsisted between them since early childhood, when the mother's undisguised partiality for the son who inherited her physique, very much of her character, and the family title she had reluctantly abandoned in assuming that of Montarnaud, had sown the seeds of jealousy in the ardent Southern temperament of the elder, and had given François a certain independence and assurance of manner ill fitting him in later days to submit to the domination of a brother. Another cause of annoyance to Gaston was the fact that while himself remaining dependent upon his father's very slender resources, his title of vicomte being but an empty honor, his brother inherited, with his mother's family name and title, a very pretty little property, whose modest income was paid directly into his own hands, and added, perhaps unnecessarily, to the independence of his manner, and reticence as to his movements. The perils of excessive riches were, however, greatly lessened by the policy of the young baron's father, who during his non-age exacted so large a proportion of his revenue toward the maintenance of the household, that there was no great danger of extravagant habits growing up in the young man's life, especially as he had always lived in the Château de Montarnaud, and never visited any city larger than Marseilles. This seclusion had induced a certain rusticity of dress, speech, and manner, affording infinite amusement of an unamiable nature to the elder brother, who had, since boyhood, lived mostly with his father in Paris, and later had mingled in the army with the gay gallants of the court who either for their sins, or from ambitious motives, had sought the variety of killing a few Dutchmen or Spaniards, as the case might be, or at least of airing the ribbons, scarfs, and favors of their lady-loves upon the field of battle. In every folly, every new affectation or whimsical device, Gaston de Montarnaud suffered not even De Lauzun or De Guiche to surpass him so far as his revenues would permit ; and, as insolence and flippancy are but cheap luxuries, he possessed them in abundance.

As the Count de Montarnaud led his ward toward the château, and the brothers followed, François pale and disturbed, Gaston in unusually high spirits, the latter opened the conversation by remarking, —

"That is a wonderfully happy effort of old Marie's in your doublet, François. It is a great economy for you that she can fashion them from the old bedhangings, is it not?"

"My doublet was fashioned by the best tailor in Marseilles, from his best piece of stuff; and, which will perhaps strike you as incredible, vicomte, it is paid for," replied François sententiously.

"It does seem incredible that any man in his senses should pay for such a garment as that. But you had nothing to pay for that dagger and sheath, my prudent brother; for I recognize it as the one our ancestor Count Paul wore at Cressy."

"Not of quite so old a fashion as that, brother, although not new," replied François tranquilly. "It is the dagger with which about a century ago Reginald de Montarnaud, who was a Catholic, slew his elder brother who was a Huguenot, and had, moreover, stolen the promised bride of the younger."

"The younger brothers of our house have ever been envious of their elders; but in these days it is the elder who is the soldier, while the younger weaves daisy-chains in the gardens of Montarnaud," retorted Gaston with a sneer. "But, unhappily, for the future, my dear boy, you must pursue your sports alone. Your playmate goes to Paris with me to-morrow."

"With you, indeed!"

"With my father and me, since you are so precise, Monsieur Huguenot; and, by the way, you had better look up a suit of our great-grandfather's court clothes, in which to dance at my wedding a week or so hence."

"And whom do you marry, if I may inquire?" demanded François, turning pale as death, and clinching his hand upon the pommel of his dagger.

"What, has not my little Valerie told you? oh the pretty coquetries of these timid darlings!" exclaimed Gaston in a coxcombical tone; but François was too much affected by the matter to attend much to the manner of his speech, and could only repeat "Valerie!" in a tone of dismay and terror that delighted Gaston beyond measure.   He twirled his mustache, smiled insufferably, set his left arm akimbo, and replied, —

"Yes, Valerie, my little baron.   The king himself commands the nuptials, I have consented, the lady is delighted, and my father hastens on the affair.   Mademoiselle de Rochenbois with her servants, and escorted by my father and myself, sets out for Paris to-morrow morning; and the marriage will be celebrated in the royal chapel of Versailles immediately upon our arrival.   You knew, of course, that I was so happy as to possess Mademoiselle Valerie's approval, and that the marriage was in process of arrangement?"

"I knew that you were a liar when you were a boy, and I have no reason to imagine you improved since," replied François, staring steadily into the eyes of his brother, who, returning the look more fiercely if less fixedly, slowly replied, —

"Among gentlemen, Monsieur le Baron de" —

"Gaston! Gaston, I say!" chimed in the shrill voice of the Count de Montarnaud, whose subtle instinct warned him that the quarrel of the brothers was at a point where interference without apparent suspicion was his most appropriate *rôle*, and, advancing as he spoke, he ended by linking his arm in that of his elder son, and leading him away; while François with a furious gesture rushed into the château, and vainly sought through all its precincts for Valerie, who was closely shut in her own room, refusing to admit even Marie or Mademoiselle Salerne. This state of things continued until nine o'clock, the hour for supper, when Marie appeared to report that mademoiselle had a headache, and required nothing, but wished her guardian and the young gentlemen a very good night. As the old woman a few moments later passed through a dark corridor between the dining-saloon and the staircase, she was frightened nearly out of her senses by a cold hand grasping her own, into which it pressed a paper and a silver piece, while a voice hoarsely muttered, —

"Give the paper to your mistress without delay."

"Oh, Monsieur le Baron, oh! I took you for, I know not what! Oh, such a fright as you have given me!"

"Never mind: silver will cure it, old woman. How is mademoiselle? What is she doing?"

"Doing! She is doing nothing, nor will she allow me to do any thing, although monsieur tells me to be all ready to set out with mademoiselle for Paris in the morning, to come back perhaps never. And there she sits at this blessed moment, I dare say, in the great *fauteuil* that was madame the countess's, her elbow on its arm, her pretty chin in her hand, her great eyes fixed on the black square of sky outside her casement (for I am sure she can see nothing else); and never a word can I get from her except, 'Hold your tongue,' and 'I want nothing,' and 'Let me alone, good Marie!' Not so much as to say which of her dresses is to be packed, and whether she will carry El Moro and the canary-birds."

"Well, go, good Marie, go and give her my note, and perhaps there will be a change," whispered François hurriedly, for footsteps were approaching; and while the nurse clambered wearily up the stair, the lover strode out into the night, leaving his father and brother to take their supper, and mature their plans for the morrow, without his help.

Two hours or so later the château was quiet, its lights extinguished, its inmates supposed to be asleep in preparation for the fatigues of the morrow; but, whether in houses or their inmates, great apparent calms occasionally cover intensity of emotion or action.

The count, to be sure, slept on principle; for he, too, had principles, logical outgrowth of his religion, a comfortable faith comprised in one tenet, viz.: To gain the utmost personal advantage at the least possible personal sacrifice.

One of the leading principles of this faith was care of the digestive organs, and the securing of that amount of rest and sleep essential to a person no longer young, who desires to retain the appearance of youth. So the count having supped artistically, gently ruminated sufficiently, and gone to bed cheerfully, now slept peacefully, and was out of the question.

Valerie de Rochenbois, on the contrary, was perhaps more widely awake than she had ever been in all her life, for she was thinking more deeply. The few words dropped by her guardian, and the expressive glances of his elder son, had conveyed to her quick intuition the whole story of their visit and intentions in her behalf; her facile fancy already pictured existence at the gorgeous court of Versailles, herself one of those admired and fortunate beings of whose elegance, beauty, and luxury she had heard so much: and the picture was very alluring to the pleasure-loving fancy of the girl. True, the figure of Gaston de Montarnaud, whom she did not very much like, made an unpleasant shadow in the scene; but Valerie had a grand capacity for closing her eyes upon things she did not wish to see, and, like many another girl called to a similar decision, she was too maidenly a maid to know how important an item the husband is in a woman's married life.

Contrasting with Gaston to whom she was indifferent, stood François whom she loved,—no, liked with a promise of love,—and toward whom just now she felt a species of resentment for having, by his declaration of that afternoon, evoked certain feelings in her own heart interfering with the single-sighted delight she otherwise would have felt in the brilliant prospect opened to her by Gaston and his father.

To sum up this most contrarious and yet essentially feminine state of mind, she foresaw that she should hate the man she wished to marry, and she already began to love him whose fortunes she did not wish to share; and she was vexed at François that he could not give her what Gaston offered, and felt a cold repulsion toward Gaston, in that he coupled himself with what he offered.

No wonder, plunged into this conflict of two tides, and not knowing into what maelström they would soon whirl her, that Valerie's great dark eyes ached with the intensity of their wakefulness, or that she declined, both sharply and briefly, to decide upon the merits of the pink paduasoy, or the somewhat frayed brocade, or to give directions for the conveyance of her canary-birds. Poor old Marie, in fact, had suffered so many and such severe repressions, that it was in a silence most unwonted that she entered the chamber after her brief interview with the baron, and laid his note upon the lap of her young mistress, still seated in the deep fauteuil, still staring fixedly at the blackness beyond her window. Valerie, half-eagerly, half-angrily, caught up the paper, and approached the candles burning upon the dressing-table : its contents were brief, and to her fancy somewhat peremptory : —

"I must see you before the morning, that you may reply distinctly to my offer of hand and heart and name, before you are called upon to answer a similar offer from my brother. I shall be under your window as the clock strikes midnight, and hope you will be there ready to answer simply and truthfully the question I have asked, and ask again: Will you be mine, Valerie, my wife, and my beloved? It is the most solemn utterance of my whole life : do not play with it, do not trifle with your reply.

FRANÇOIS."

As the young girl read these words, a blush, a smile, a frown, passed in rapid alternation across her face ; and then she stood meditating, folding and re-folding the paper between her fingers, and finally holding it in the flame of the candle until it fell a floating cinder upon the polished floor.

CHAPTER V.

CAIN AND ABEL.

THE count slept, Valerie meditated, François waited, and Gaston prowled.. The fact was, that this young man, although half a century before the time of Voltaire and Rousseau, was a bit of a philosopher on his own account, and, banished from the polished circles of the court and the smiles of Madame de Montespan, could solace himself very tolerably with certain village companions, not as re-fined certainly, but perhaps quite as edifying to his moral character, as the cavaliers and *grandes dames* of Versailles. When, therefore, the Count de Montarnaud left the salon to secure his beauty-sleep, Monsieur le Vicomte, throwing a dark cloak about him, strolled down through the garden and over a field or two by a way quite familiar to his feet since boyhood, to the *auberge* of the wretched village of Montarnaud, where he knew that a little circle of flatterers and vassals would hail his appearance with slavish delight.

But oh, the wheels within the wheels of even so tiny a microcosm as the Château de Montarnaud !

Mademoiselle Salerne, aged twenty-six, and not ill-looking, had allowed her heart as she would have said, her fancy as we will call it, to go astray, secretly to be

sure, but none the less violently, in the direction of the
vicomte, whose sinister face and supple form seemed
to her those of a Antinous, whose insolent and affected
manners were in her estimation the ideal of dignity
and high-breeding, and whose careless compliments,
flung at her from time to time merely because Gaston
de Montarnaud knew no other mode of addressing a
good-looking young woman, stood for so many avowals
of love.

When, therefore, Mademoiselle Salerne discovered,
in some occult fashion of her own, that the object of
her idol's present visit to Montarnaud was to woo her
pupil for his wife, and was informed that she as gouvernante to Mademoiselle de Rochenbois would on the
morrow accompany her to Paris, the state of mingled
jealousy, pleasure, doubt, and agitation taking possession of her mind was something as terrific as the
proverbial tempest in a teapot, and quite sufficient to
banish slumber from the beady black eyes of the victim, even had she not found the night too short to
furbish up her dilapidated wardrobe, and prepare for
her journey.

Hence it came, that, as Gaston quietly left the château, Adèle Salerne first peeped out of her window
after his retreating figure, and then, moved by some
vague impulse of jealousy and suspicion, seized a
mantle, and, flinging it round her head and shoulders, ran swiftly through the corridor and down the
stairs in pursuit, or at least in espial, of the nocturnal
rambler. Now, it so happened that the Abbé Despard, although not in love, was as wakeful and as dis-

turbed in mind as the governess ; for not only did the note of preparation and change in the château forebode the breaking-up of a happy home to him, with the return to laborious and subservient duty. in the cathedral at Marseilles ; but his conscience, a good, strong, serviceable young conscience, troubled him with suggestions that the hatred, the despair, and the jealousy he had read during the last few hours upon the face of his pupil were, in good measure, referable to the perfect freedom in which the young man had ruled his own life, and pursued the love-affair whose interruption now threatened such disaster to all concerned.

"I have been a false steward, an unfaithful guardian. Monsieur le Comte has every right to send me back to my bishop in disgrace, a dishonored priest ! I have been weak, timid, cowardly : I have allowed my pupil to lead me, instead of I him ; and now — I know his temper ; I know that of the vicomte ; and mademoiselle, how will she choose ?"

Half muttering, half thinking these, and a thousand phrases like them, the chaplain paced up and down the long half-lighted library, whither he had retreated from the frigid and insolent companionship of his master, and his master's son ; his tall figure clad in the black *soutane*, now vanishing into the gloom at either end of the gallery, now showing spectrally in the vague circle of light shed by the two candles, which, mounted upon quaint twisted branches of lacquered brass, only served to make the gloomy hall more gloomy than total darkness. At one end of the library a door stood ajar, — a side-door, giving upon a

small lobby whence a narrow staircase led to the upper
stories of the château; opposite this staircase a door
led to the terrace, and so to the gardens; and it was
by this quiet staircase, lobby, and portal, that Mademoiselle Salerne had chosen to set forth upon her
voyage of observation; and, as the moment of her
arrival at the foot of the stair was also the moment in
which the chaplain reached the end of the library next
this staircase, it fell out that his eyes, accustomed
to the darkness, discerned the outline of a slender
female figure flitting across the lobby, and out at the
door, and his ears assured him that the light footfall,
and gentle rustle of garments, were not those of old
Marie, or Pauline the inferior woman-servant.

"Mademoiselle Valerie! François has persuaded
her to meet him in the garden! What imprudence!
If Monsieur le Comte or Monsieur Gaston hear them!
My fault again, always my fault, — miserable that I
am! I should have foreseen, I should have prevented!" And with these broken exclamations, proving that the good abbé's conscience was more acute
than his knowledge of the world, and the art of man-
aging lovers, he threw his *biretta* upon his head, and
left the house by the same path as the governess. But
Adèle, light of foot and lithe of motion, was already
far down the garden path in the direction she had seen
Gaston take; and, in fact, pursued him so closely, that,
as he passed through the wicket at the lower end of
the garden, Adèle, hidden in a great clump of laurel,
could almost have touched him. Not daring to follow
farther, the governess slowly retraced her steps toward

the house, but in a dark alley ran almost into the arms of a tall, black-clad figure, who first seized his opponent mechanically, but, releasing her immediately, bowed low in the darkness, murmuring reproachfully, —

"O mademoiselle, what imprudence!"

"Imprudence, father!" exclaimed a hard and shrill voice, differing as much from Valerie's cooing tones as a cat-bird's from a linnet's: "I only ran down the garden for a breath of fresh air, after stitching away in my own room all the evening. What imprudence, *mon père?*"

"It is always imprudent to take the night air, and you need your rest for the journey to-morrow," replied the abbé composedly as he passed on, leaving the perplexed and somewhat indignant governess to her own meditations.

"Is he also following Monsieur Gaston?" murmured she: "he never would dare upbraid him, no matter in what peccadillo he discovered him! Can it be that Monsieur François is astray to-night? Is Mademoiselle Valerie safely housed? Truly this is a night of adventure, a night of interest, a night such as does not often come to this stupid old château! I will stay out until the priest and Monsieur Gaston return: they must pass this way."

Wrapping herself more closely in her mantle as she whispered this resolve, Adèle accordingly settled herself upon a well-shaded garden-bench, and remained motionless; quite unconscious that the priest, after passing her by a few yards, had stopped, and bent his acute ear to listen for her return into the house. Finding that this return did not take place, he crept a little nearer, and soon distinguished the deeper shadow against the green of the ilex behind the bench. Again noiselessly withdrawing, the abbé retreated to a safe distance, and, sternly staring up at the walls of the château, seemed to question them of their secrets.

"Mademoiselle Salerne is posted as a spy there, or as a vidette to watch against surprises! That means that her mistress is out here with François! Shall I return, and force the truth from her by my authority as her confessor? or shall I wait and watch? Ha! what is that?"

It was a light in Valerie's window: it was Valerie herself looking down into the garden. Still moving noiselessly upon the soft mould of the garden-beds, the abbé crept in that direction, uncertain even yet as to the course proper for him to pursue; but infinitely relieved to perceive that Mademoiselle de Rochenbois was safe, and not in the commission of imprudences for which he might feel himself more or less accountable.

Truth to tell, Valerie had seldom passed so *mauvais un quart d'heure* as after reading François' note, nor had by any means resolved what to reply to it, when the town-clock struck twelve; and she felt, as Godiva did, as Cinderella did, that the moment of meditation was past, the moment of action had arrived. But what action? Godiva was governed by a grand motive, Cinderella by a grand passion and a fairy godmother; but poor little Valerie possessed neither grand motive, nor passion, nor godmother, in fact, nothing as guide but a very pronounced desire to please, first herself, then François, then everybody; and no amount of meditation showed her how all these objects were to be combined. To be sure, the Snark tells us of a mind so equably divided that when it would call upon Richard or William, it could decide upon neither, and so summoned Rilchiam; but the Snark was not composed in those days, and it is unkind to play with Valerie's feelings in this manner, so let us resume serious history.

The clock struck twelve: a handful of sand thrown against Valerie's window announced a visitor below; and, opening the casement, the young lady was startled to find the top of her lover's blonde head upon a level with the sill.

"Why, how came you there, François?" exclaimed she.

"The fruit-ladder. I was afraid they would hear if we spoke aloud. There is not a moment to spare, for everybody but my father is up and about. I went to see if all was safe, and nearly ran over your governess. But never mind all that. Tell me, Valerie, tell me like a brave and honest girl, tell me that you love me as I love you."

"Certainly, I love you, François: I am very fond of you; but "—

"But what? Speak out, Valerie, be honest."

"How can I speak out when I don't know what to say?" demanded Valerie pettishly. François uttered an exclamation as of physical pain.

"O Valerie! You do not know! You are trifling

with me : you know that this is life and death to me, and you hesitate and toy as if with the choice of a ribbon."

"But you see, François," retorted the young girl with vivacity, "if it is life or death to you, so it is to me ; and I can't tell, all in a minute, which is life and which is death. If it were a ribbon it wouldn't matter : but it's the court and the king, and all the gay, beautiful life there, with Gaston, whom I don't love ; or it's this stupid old château, and poverty, and disgrace, and rust and mould, with you, whom I am fond of, no doubt, and yet " —

"And yet not enough fond of to choose instead of the court and the king and Gaston," suggested François.

"That's the very question," replied Valerie naïvely. "And I'm really afraid, that, whichever I choose, I shall spend all the rest of my life regretting the other."

"Then by all means, mademoiselle," began the baron in a rage ; but was interrupted by a loud and mocking voice from below : —

"What, what ! A robber ! An assassin ! Thieves ! Murderers !   An attack upon the château ! "

And with a well-directed kick the vicomte drove the fruit-ladder from its position, and brought it with its burden to the ground.   François, considerably hurt by the fall, but a good deal more humiliated than hurt, jumped up with a furious exclamation, and, seizing his brother by the throat, bore him to the ground.

"Oh, it is you, you wretched animal ! " gasped the vicomte, —no match for his brawny brother in any thing but courage, of which he had plenty. "How dare you insult my affianced wife? Take that, then!"

"Ugh!" growled the stricken man, smarting from a blow across the eyes nearly blinding him, and returning it with a tremendous thrust. "You lie! She is my affianced wife!"

"Lie, do I?" hissed Gaston, his bad blood fully roused; and Cain and Abel clutched each other in mortal fray. A moment, and the slighter form toppled against the wall, and fell a crumpled heap at its foot; while the other, oppressed with the sudden horror of completed crime, turned and fled into the darkness and the night; and Valerie, bending low from her window, wrung her hands, and shrieked for help, moaning in her poor little selfish heart, —

"François has murdered Gaston, and I have lost them both."

CHAPTER VI.

VALERIE'S CHOICE.

A LITTLE way down the garden-path François paused in his headlong flight, stood still, and began slowly to retrace his steps. Having yielded to two impulses of the wild beast caged in most men's natures, Fight and Flight, he now submitted to the tardier but in the main stronger coercion of education, civilization, or, if you please, honor, the legitimate child of education and civilization.

Three steps of retrogression, and the young man felt his arm grasped from behind, and an eager voice demanded, —

"What is it, Monsieur le Baron? You have fought with your brother? You have killed him? Is he dead?"

"We fought? I do not know. God forbid! I am going to see. Come, *mon père.*"

"Come! Go, I should rather say. Fly while there is time. The house will be roused in a moment: the governess is flying along the terrace already, shrieking like a sea-gull, and Mademoiselle Valerie" —

"What are you thinking of, abbé? Fly! Escape! What words are these for a gentleman to hear? If I have by sore mischance killed my brother, I will abide the consequences of my deed. God knows I never meant more than an angry blow."

"Then no justice of God or man demands your life as forfeit; and yet the count in his first anger — At any rate, wait here for a moment or two, until I discover the real state of the case. If the vicomte is not dead, you ought all the more to keep out of your father's sight for a day or two. Will you wait here five minutes until I go up there and make a report?"

"Well, yes, I will wait five minutes here; not, mind you, that I fear my father's wrath, but that I will not intrude upon the grief of Mademoiselle de Rochenbois, whom even from this distance I can hear calling so piteously upon her Gaston."

The abbé had not paused for more than the first clause of this reply, but was already springing up the steps to the terrace, where all the inhabitants of the château were now assembled; and presently François, himself invisible beneath the dense shadows of the garden, perceived that his father, the abbé, and two men-servants were lifting, and heavily carrying in at the open doors, a something — what was it? — a corpse, or a wounded man? Was he, standing there in that fragrant garden, where so few hours before he had sported like a child with his cousin, — was he a murderer? His brother's blood was on his hand indeed, but was it life-blood?

And the young baron, asking himself this question, facing this possibility, made in those five minutes one of those strides in life which eventless years may not measure, as the Alpine adventurer, losing his hold upon the ice, whirls in a moment down the steep descent whereon by choice he had painfully crept for hours. Perhaps he survives, perhaps he does not; but, at the best, such plunges leave some aches and scratches behind.

"Will he never come?" exclaimed François, and on the instant heard the *soutane* of the priest brushing along the rose-hedged walk.

"Well, *mon père!*"

"Well, my son! He is not dead, and may not be mortally hurt: they cannot yet tell. But Mademoiselle Salerne accuses you of the murder, as she calls it; and your father is in a white rage because the king will be displeased at him. He has sent one man into Marseilles for a surgeon, another for the police to arrest you. He speaks, too, of his seigneurial rights, and of cutting off the hand which has shed the blood of an elder brother. If he finds you to-night he will do some mad thing, not to be remedied to-morrow. You must hide for a day or so at least."

François made a haughty gesture of dissent, and twisted his arm from the hold of the priest, who reluctantly produced his last argument, —

"Mademoiselle Valerie wishes it."

"Wishes me to fly?"

"Yes. She gave me this note, and whispered, 'For God's sake bid him keep out of the way!'"

"A note! How shall I read it? All depends upon what she says. *Mon père*, have you some of that magical stuff you were showing me this morning, that which makes light in the dark? Can you make light for me now?"

"Yes: come into the garden-house." And the abbé, smiling a little to himself at seeing the dependence of the pupil suddenly overtopping the self-assertion of the young noble, led the way into the tool-house, and produced from his pocket a phial of phosphorus, in those days as valuable an adjunct of wonder-work as in our time are cabinets with sliding-doors, wires, magnets, darkened rooms, and boundless credulity.

Dipping a splint of prepared wood in this phial, the abbé procured a light, at which François glanced rather apprehensively, but soon forgot in reading these few words, very badly written upon a crumpled bit of paper : —

"Gaston is not dead, and I am sure I hope he will not die ; but until one knows, you must not be seen here. Hide yourself ; efface yourself thoroughly. The abbé may tell me where. For *my* sake, François. Valerie."

It was not very loving, it was not very definite : but it ended with "for my sake," and surely Valerie would never so enforce her behest unless she meant more than met the eye ; and if, being his, she desired him to save himself for her sake — So far did François untangle the maze of his emotions, and then, turning to the impatient priest, said with a sigh, —

"Well then, *mon père*, I will depart for a while : but whither? To my estates in Normandy?"

"The messengers of Monsieur le Comte would arrive there as soon as yourself, *mon* baron," replied the tutor, in a tone of more authority as he felt himself becoming master of the occasion. "No : you shall come with me to Marseilles; and I will show you a very poor but a very safe refuge, where you may lie securely hid until your brother's fate is disclosed. Then we shall see."

"As well there as anywhere, if I must indeed hide."

"Let us set out at once, and on foot, since to bring horses from the stable would declare our intention."

"Very well." And François, absorbed in thought, set forth at so round a pace that the priest, less used to physical exertion, although well fitted for it, was more than once obliged to beg for consideration.

Two hours later the young men halted in a quiet street of Marseilles, before a small house largely devoted to a grocer's shop, bearing upon the door-posts the name of Jacques Despard.

"It is my father's house and shop, monsieur," said the abbé with quiet dignity, and led the way up a staircase built on the outside at the end, as was the fashion of that day, unlocked a door upon the landing, looked in, beckoned the baron to follow, and, unlocking a second door, ushered him into a small bedroom, sparsely but neatly furnished, and very tidy.

"There, Monsieur le Baron," said the abbé, closing the door, and drawing a long breath, "here you are safe, and welcome for as long as you choose to stay. This is my own room, always kept ready for my arrival by day or night, and never entered by any member of the household save my sister, who loves to keep it in order because she loves me. I will go now, and tell her that I have here a guest who desires to remain in secret; and she will attend you without curiosity and without stupidity. Then I must hasten back to the château before the family are about, lest my absence should suggest your place of retreat."

He left the room, and presently returned with a brisk, brown little maiden, whom he presented as,—

"My sister Clotilde, monsieur, and your hostess."

François bowed gravely and courteously; and Clotilde dropped a respectful courtesy, saying shyly, yet eagerly,—

"Monsieur is very welcome; and I have already told the abbé how discreet and how attentive I will try to be to his friend. Monsieur will excuse the poor place, I am sure."

"I am most grateful for its shelter, mademoiselle, and only sorry to make you trouble," replied François in his grand, grave fashion; and Clotilde, dropping another courtesy, followed her brother from the room, saying,—

"As soon as old Nannette has gone to mass, and my father and Henri are in the shop, I will bring monsieur some breakfast."

"Any time, any thing," replied François wearily; and, as the door closed, he threw himself into a chair, and laid his head upon his folded arms on the table. After all, he was only a boy.

That evening with his supper Clotilde brought her prisoner a note which she handed to him saying,—

"It is a billet, monsieur, which I found in a parcel of linen sent me by my brother the abbé; and I think it must be for you, since Vincent knows I do not read writing, although I can make out print very well."

" It is for me, mademoiselle," said François eagerly ; and Clotilde left the room murmuring, —

" He calls me mademoiselle, which is very nice ; but he is as solemn as if we assisted at his father's funeral."

The abbé's note ran thus : —

" MONSIEUR MY HONORED PUPIL, — I have the pleasure of announcing that the Vicomte de Montarnaud is not so dangerously wounded as was at first feared, and bids fair to recover under the careful tendance of Mademoiselle Valerie, her governess, and old Marie, all of whom are constant at his bedside. But I cannot advise you to return hither at present ; for the comte is far more enraged at the delay in presenting himself, with his son and Mademoiselle de Rochenbois, before the king, than at the danger to his son's life ; and would, could he lay hands upon you, make you suffer severely for his annoyance, and possible disgrace at court.

" Nor have I any better news to give you of Mademoiselle Valerie, who seems in a state of mingled grief and irritability very difficult to encounter. I ventured to ask this morning if she had a message for you ; and she only replied, ' Bid him keep out of the way, if he wishes to please me ; ' and when I again asked if she would not write a line to comfort you in your exile, she sharply inquired, since when priests had made it their duty to act as go-betweens for lovers? The question touched me sharply, monsieur, and I turned away without reply.

" In conclusion, I can only recommend you on all accounts, — your own, Monsieur le Comte's, Mademoiselle Valerie's, and even my own, if you will allow me to mention it, — to remain strictly hidden, at least until I come to you, which will be in two or three days at latest. I send you a packet containing some clothes, your dressing-case, your own table-service, and some books, among them the Satires of Horace which we were lately reading, and which you may find congenial to your present mood ; also the ' Imitation of Christ,' a work more edifying in its spirit than the first, but not nearly so good Latin.

"Until our meeting I remain

"Your faithful tutor and servant,

"VINCENT DE PAUL DESPARD."

The third evening after this, just as François, who had read a good deal of Horace and a little of Thomas à Kempis, had counted all the stones of the dead wall opposite his window, and made some progress in taming the sparrows, which he fed with crumbs on his window-sill, was putting on his plumed hat with the intention of sallying forth to meet his tutor upon the road, or, failing this, to push on to the château, and end this miserable suspense, — the door was hurriedly opened, and Père Vincent entered with a face so full of ill news, that the young baron exclaimed, —

"My brother is worse, — is dead !"

"No monsieur, but" —

"Valerie is betrothed to him?"

"I do not know, monsieur, but—"

"Has not she written to me?"

"Yes, monsieur, but" —

"Give it me, please, then, and in pity do not say 'but' again to-night."

"But, Monsieur le Baron" —

"But, *mon père !*"

And half petulant, half laughing, François snatched the letter from the abbé's tardy fingers, and, tearing it open, hastily read, —

"I have not written to you before, François, because I knew not what to say, and also because I was busy in attending Gaston, whom you hurt very much: and it is a horrible thing for a brother to try to kill his brother, especially the younger the elder; for, as my guardian says, some persons might say you wished to secure the title and estates of Montarnaud in addition to your own. And it was all a mistake too; for Gaston was wandering in the garden, to look at the light in my window, and vexing himself with fears that I should not accept his suit, and really took you for a robber. He is much better now, so much that to-morrow, or even to-night if possible, we are to set out for Paris, carrying him in a litter, and travelling by easy stages; for my guardian will no longer delay obeying the king's command, and says he would risk the lives of all belonging to him, and after all the rest his own, rather than further tempt the royal displeasure.

"Ah, François! my heart is not in what I have written, and you will again call me frivolous and heartless, — I know you will; but, dear, what can I do? My uncle would take me by main force if I resisted; he would kill me sooner than seem to disobey the king; and I, — well, then, I will be brave, at least, and say the truth, — I want to go. I do not love Gaston, — I do not love, not really *love*, anybody; but I must see Versailles; I must breathe the air of the court; I must wave my wings like those great painted butterflies of our fair garden, in the perfumed sunshine of the royal presence. I shall be sorry, I know it already, but — I go!"

There was more of it; but at this last word the lover, muttering a black and bitter malediction, rent the sheet into twenty fragments, crushed them in his hand, and, flinging them upon the hearth, turned a ghastly face upon his tutor, saying, —

"So it is decided. She has gone with him to Paris!"

"Monsieur le Comte, with Mademoiselle de Rochenbois her attendants and Monsieur Gaston, left the château about an hour before I did," said the abbé gently, for the pain upon his pupil's white face stirred his very heart.

"Will you kindly leave me alone, *mon père*, for half an hour or so? Or, no, I will walk for a while. There is now no motive for concealment. In half an hour I will return."

"God be with you, my son, and give you strength!"

"Amen, my father."

Half an hour later the baron, returning to his little room, found an inviting supper spread, and the abbé cheerfully superintending Clotilde's last arrangements.

"Come, my son!" exclaimed he as the young girl withdrew. "Let us first of all eat; since Clotilde tells me you sent away your dinner untasted, and I have taken nothing since morning."

"As you will, *mon père*," replied François carelessly; but even so the priest noted that the voice had a sturdier ring and a more manly tone than he yet had heard in it, and was further rejoiced by seeing his pupil partake of Clotilde's delicacies, not with any great enjoyment certainly, but with the honest appetite of a healthy young fellow of one and twenty.

"And now, *mon abbé*," began the baron, pushing back his chair, "I have to bid you good-by, with many thanks for your kind hospitality here, and your greater kindness in the days past, — the days of my youth as they already seem, for the life of Montarnaud is past."

"And whither go you now, Monsieur le Baron? What are your plans, if I may ask?" inquired the abbé somewhat incredulously; for truly the transition from a runaway schoolboy to a self-reliant young noble was a little sharp, a little incredible. But François, proving his new manhood by failing to resent the other's unbelief in it, quietly answered, —

"I hardly know, except that I go to-morrow into Normandy, to sell my possessions there to this rich contractor who wishes so much to become a proprietor. My one and twentieth birthday is past since yesterday."

"You will sell" — began the abbé aghast. But François interrupted him : "Do not let us argue, *mon père*," said he quietly, but with the air of the *grand seigneur* which had so lately come upon him. "I have no longer a country, a home, or a name. The king of France has stolen my father's honor and my *fiancée's* faith. He shall not rank me among his subjects, lest I, too, become a traitor and a coward. I renounce all that makes me a Frenchman ; and, so soon as this business is concluded, I leave the country of Louis XIV., of Raoul de Montarnaud, of Gaston his son, and of Valerie de Rochenbois, — never, so help me God ! to set foot upon its soil again."

"And where will you go? and how will you live?" asked the abbé, a tinge of excitement rising to his sallow cheek, and kindling his fervent eyes.

"I have hardly considered as yet," replied his pupil. "There is good fighting to be had in the Netherlands, and I am not an ill swordsman."

"I have a thought ! You were lamenting that birth and fortune prevented your pursuing your surgical and anatomical studies. The army hospitals are rough but rapid schools ; and to save life, and ameliorate human suffering, is a nobler and a rarer art than slaughter. Then, too, I might find work as chaplain."

"What !" exclaimed the young man, his fair face flushing eagerly. "You will go with me ! You, too, will expatriate yourself, and for my sake, *mon père !* I wished it so much, but would not ask it for fear I should seem to claim pity and help."

"Pride, my son," quietly suggested the abbé ; and then, the young man's nature suddenly overtopping the priest's, he grasped François by the hand, crying,—

"Courage, *mon ami !* we will go out together to conquer the world, and win for ourselves the place she does not wish to grant us. The sword of the Lord and of Gideon shall prevail over more formidable enemies than yet have assailed us. *Va !*"

CHAPTER VII.

MOLLY.

QUEEN ELIZABETH, of various memory, com-
manded her portrait to be painted without
shadow; and the idea was so little wise that we may
fairly conclude it to have been all her own, and that
Burleigh and the rest of the councillors who made
the greatness and the goodness of the maiden queen
(probably wife of Essex) thought this one of the
occasions when their royal charge might be left to
her own guidance, without danger to any one but
herself.

And why was it so absurd an idea? Simply because
it ignored one of the primal laws of creation, the law
of contrasts. Why is coming day so lovely? Because
it is so strong a contrast to the darkness, colorlessness,
repose, of night. Why is night so lovely when its
soft and perfumed darkness falls between us and the
world which has wearied us all day? Because of the
contrast to that day we welcomed so blithely, and
shall again welcome on the morrow.

Why did the God of beauty make the skies and sea
blue, the forests green, the birds, the flowers, the rain-
bow, the gems and minerals, of every tint into which
light may be divided, if not to teach us the refresh-

ment and delight of contrast? So Elizabeth was, after all, a more pretentious autocrat than her father. He only aspired to reform and rule the Church: she would have reformed and governed creation.

In another reign Madame de Pompadour held power for twenty years. How? By studying and utilizing the science of contrasts. The chief memorial she has left upon earth is that combination of sky-blue and carnation-pink still known by her name, — that soft and vivid contrast adapted from Nature's azure eyes and softly tinted cheeks; and one can hardly help weeping to-day over the memoirs of the poor wretch as one reads of her piteous efforts to maintain her bad eminence, exerting herself day by day to hold the sated voluptuary, at once her slave and her master, by ever freshly linked chains, largely forged at the anvil of contrast. To-day she moved before him in all the grandeur of jewels, cloth of gold, lace, embroidery, all that composed the *grande toilette* of that age; to-morrow she was the artless peasant-maid, with her snow-white linen, scarlet bodice, and brief kirtle, showing the pretty feet and ankles in their gay hose and shoon; now she swam in the postures of an Eastern dance, clad in the gold-shot tissues, the transparent veil, and tinkling ornaments, of a bayadère; and again she drooped meekly before her lord in the costume of a nun, coiffed and wimpled, her bold eyes modestly down-dropt, her white unjewelled fingers clasping a rosary.

Ah, poor wretch, indeed! How she must have longed at times to dare to be herself, to be gloomy or

angry, or tearful or silent, as the mood seized her, — to
know the liberty of Jeanne Poisson once more.   And,
after all, she was a Catholic, and must at least have
been taught the superstitions of her faith : she must
by times have thought of death and judgment and
hell ; she was not "advanced" enough to doubt the
existence of both God and the Devil as real persons,
and suppose the thought of them took possession of
her imagination while the king waited to see her in
the bayadère dress.   Well, she reigned by the power
of contrasts, and achieved her last *coup* of this sort
when she was carried from her lodgings in the royal
palace, from her pink and blue, her jewels, her costumes, her magnificence, to the sordid hearse, quite
good enough to-day for her whose word a few months
earlier could shake the world ; and Louis XV., standing at his window to watch the wretched funeral and
the dismal, rainy November day, took snuff, and
laughed, and said, —

"The marquise has rather poor weather for her
journey."

Is the digression a trifle long?   Pardon it ; for it is
to make you in love with contrast, and to lead you
from Versailles, with its Montespans and Pompadours,
and the rose-garden of Provence, with Valerie, summoned by a king to grace his court, to a desolate
winter sea-coast, its sparse vegetation cut down by
unremitting frosts, its few and scattered dwellings
cowering before the winds that contemptuously hurl
handfuls of sand in their blinking eyes, or tear the
thatch from their roofs like hair from a dishonored

head ; or, growing more furious than contemptuous, shake the whole sturdy frame until it rocks upon its foundations, yet meekly holds its own at last, as the Wat Tylers generally do.

It is with one of these houses that we have to do, — a low but comfortably large farmhouse, set down in the sand with a sort of apologetic uncertainty, as if it hesitated to turn its back, either upon the faint wheel-track denoting a highway, or upon the sea sullenly sliding up a shallow beach about a hundred rods away. The wheel-track meant agriculture and commerce, the sea stood for fisheries and driftwood ; and the question evidently vexing the mind of the undecided house was, whether Humphrey Wilder, its master and owner, was a farmer or fisherman, and so had most need to conciliate land or sea. The house never found out, nor shall we ; so let it pass. As for the man, see him as he stands beside the stout gray horse harnessed to the farm-wagon, wherein he has already bestowed sundry bales and boxes suggestive of provender for man and beast, and an abundance of wraps, fit for an arctic exploration at the least. Perhaps Wilder wishes it were arctic, rather than as hot as he is like to find the end of his journey : for he is bound with Deborah, his wife, to the quarterly meeting of Friends at New Bedford ; and Deborah, like her who dwelt beneath her palm-tree near Ramah, was a prophetess, and ruled in Israel, yet never had been able to so rule the quiet spirit of her husband as to induce him to join the society wherein she was a powerful and favorite speaker and guide. This was a great grief, also a great surprise and discomfiture, to Deborah, who had married in calm opposition to all her relatives and fellow-religionists, because she admired Humphrey's stalwart form and honest English face and manly ways, and fully expected to add to these natural graces all those spiritual ones in which she so abundantly rejoiced.   But, greatly to her astonishment, the good-tempered, placid fellow, so ready to yield to her in most matters, so impossible to quarrel with, although not hard to wound, developed in some few directions a will as immovable, as silent, and as positive as the Peak o' Derby, in whose shadow it had its early growth.   One of these directions was religious: Humphrey did not especially cling to the Church of England, wherein he had been bred, but he distinctly refused to belong to any other; and the only offensive weapon he ever used, in the discussions he could not always avoid with Deborah, was the Book of Common Prayer, which he sometimes brought out, and read aloud wherever it happened to open, in a sonorous voice, around and through whose diapason the wife's shrill and thin tones harmlessly wandered, like the twitter of sparrows around the organ of a cathedral.

Fancy, if you please, Deborah of Ramah's emotions if Lapidoth had declined all sympathy with Barak, and had quite refused to admire Jael, or to listen to his wife's song of triumph!

Another blank wall against which Dame Wilder presently ran her head was her husband's determination that Molly, the first and only child, should be christened in the parish church where her forbears had been for centuries before she was born, and should be educated as they had been in catechism and church-service.

Deborah submitted simply because she couldn't help it: but she wrung from the conqueror a reluctant consent to join a party of emigrants about leaving Old England for New; for, as she pathetically re-marked, —

"She could better bear her disgrace in the wilder-ness than among her own folk."

"If it's disgrace to wed an honest man, that's stanch to State and Church, and will have his child so trained, why didst do it, dame?" asked Humphrey calmly; and Deborah found no reply but tears, and a renewed petition to join the emigrants, to which her husband finally consented; pleasing himself in select-ing a site for his new dwelling so far from any gather-ing place of Friends that it was only on stated occasions, like the quarterly-meetings, that Deborah could find an audience for the grief and shame she never failed to put in evidence before she finished speaking, how-ever she might begin. Wilder invariably attended these occasions, probably because his British pluck suggested that it would be cowardly to shirk any thing so disagreeable; but Molly always remembered how, as she sat one Sunday afternoon on her father's knee, and looked with him at the ghastly prints in "Fox's Book of Martyrs," he muttered over one of them, —

"Maybe that chap didn't witness for his faith any stronger in his half-hour with the lions, than another may do in a dozen years or so of pin-pricks."

"Who pricked him, father? Show me the picture," demanded Molly; but, putting her off his knee, the father answered with a short laugh, —

"Never mind, my little maid; never mind. Come now, say thy catechism and the collect for this day."

And so they came to America, and settled near some Old-World neighbors named Hetherford, hard by the village of Falmouth at the beginning of Cape Cod; and here, nourished by the salt Atlantic breeze, and the plenteous freedom of out-door life, as she followed her father around his fields or out in his fishing-boat, Molly Wilder grew from a fragile, lily-white child to a stately maiden, inheriting her father's finely-developed figure and fair English coloring, deepened in the eyes from the honest blue of Wilder's to a deep grey, suiting well with their steadfast and earnest expression, and with the black lashes and brows which nature had capriciously borrowed from the mother's dark face to bestow upon her fair daughter. But Molly's mouth and chin were all her own, resembling neither the somewhat rough-hewn and bovine features of her father, nor the thin-lipped shrewish mouth and pointed chin of her mother; for Molly's chin was wide and soft and creamy-white, with just the faintest depression in its midst, as if Love had been about to set a dimple there, but had been frightened away by the cold purity of the lips above, so bright of tint, so exquisite of moulding, so soft and sweet in their rare smiles, but ordinarily so grave. If Valerie de Rochenbois' mouth was made for kisses, surely Mary Wilder's was made for prayer; and if still the kisses came, they would be like benedictions, rather than the light caresses Valerie so freely bestowed.

One of the minor crosses of Deborah Wilder's life (and she lived, so to speak, in a forest of crosses large and small) was her daughter's hair. It was so abundant in quantity, so bright in its chestnut tint, so wavy in its growth, mutinously breaking into little burnished curls on the temples, and in the nape of the columnar neck, especially after an encounter with the sweet strong wind, so often Molly's playmate, that it could neither be hidden nor disregarded; and although the girl herself seemed to take no especial thought of it, beyond brushing it smoothly behind her ears, and knotting it in a great coil at the back of her head, whence it too often slipped, and fell a great burnished serpent, almost to her heels, Deborah was always worrying lest this rare abundance and rich coloring should prove a snare, either to the child herself, or some admirer yet to appear; and more than once she would have shorn her like a lamb, but that Humphrey sternly forbade; and at last Molly took the matter into her own hands, and quietly met her mother's last proposition to shorten it, with, —

" Nay, mother, father has said he will have my hair as it is, and I shall never touch scissors to it again."

"Thee has thy father's own stubborn temper," replied Deborah angrily; but there the matter rested.

The wagon was ready and waiting; and Humphrey, stamping his feet, and drawing the muffler tight around his neck, looked dubiously toward the sea, which tossed and moaned restlessly beneath a low-hung, stormy sky; while the gulls, skimming along close to the water, uttered harsh cries of terror or warning as they fled before the chill east wind.

"It looks set for dirty weather, and that by noon of this day," said the farmer uneasily. "Molly, my maid, I don't feel right to leave you here your lone; yet you're a brave wench, and a stout one too, and Amariah will be back to-morrow."

"I'm not afraid, father. Why should I be?" replied Molly quietly, as she carefully arranged a hot soapstone in the bottom of the wagon for her mother's feet to rest upon. Her father stepped closer, and spoke in a lower voice: —

"The most that worries me is that money in the secretary yon. If it were not for that, I'd say shut up the house, and go stop at neighbor Hetherford's; but I don't like to leave so much in the house alone, and I don't like any but thee, my lass, to know of it. Reuben is a good enough fellow; but yet" —

"Don't be uneasy, father," interrupted Molly hastily; for Deborah's voice preceded her out of the house like a blast of the shrill east wind: —

"Mary, Mary! Surely thee has forgotten the elder-flower wine I was to carry to Friend Mehitable Barker, and the nut-cakes" —

"They're all in, safely, mother," replied Molly, and hurriedly continued in her father's ear, —

"Nobody will know of the money, whatever happens; and I will not leave the house until you return."

"God bless you, my faithful little girl!" muttered

the father, and turned to meet his wife, who staggered out of the house, her arms full of last packages, and allowed herself and them to be stored in the wagon by Humphrey's somewhat hurried movements, hurling back last charges at Molly all the while.

"Now don't thee forget, Mary, to change the water on the pickles every day, and feed the hens with hot food; and mind that Amariah looks well after the pigs, and see if thee can spin out all the rolls I have put in the top drawer; and be sure have Mercy Hetherford over to sleep with thee every night; and don't thee let Reuben stay after dark, and " —

But just at this point the horse and his driver came to an understanding, through which the wagon started suddenly forward, cutting short, the good dame's speech with a jerk.

CHAPTER VIII.

THE SPINNING-WHEEL.

A SOBER little smile flitted across Molly's lips as she noted the vivacious manner in which her mother turned upon her father, as the wagon drove away, and fancied the comments she would make upon the jerk with which her directions had been abruptly ended. Then shivering a little she entered the house, but paused on the threshold to look over at the roofs of some farm-buildings half hidden by the sand-hills.

"I hope Mercy will come before dark, and then Reuben needn't come with her. 'After dark,' says mother! With my will he'd never come."

And, closing and barring the front door, Molly passed through the melancholy "fore-room," as the parlor, sacred to visitors and solemn occasions, was called, to the great sunshiny kitchen extending across the back of the house, its wide latticed window looking southerly toward the sea, its porched door opening toward the east, and the family bedroom extending across the western end. Tabitha, the great tortoise-shell cat, came forward to meet her mistress, arching her back and mewing in a sentimental sort of way, which brought another smile to Molly's lips, as, stooping to pat her, she gayly said, —

"Why, Tab, surely you are never going to be lonesome, and so soon too! You and I are the garrison of the fortress, and must make a brave show, though it be with quaking hearts beneath."

She gave the cat her breakfast, and then busied herself in clearing the table, washing the dishes, and various household details, all performed in the rapid, noiseless, and thorough fashion of one who brings to such homely work the will, the mind, and the conscience that would fitly administer the affairs of a castle or a palace, had the individual been so placed.

Her active work finished, Molly drew the great spinning-wheel to the centre of the glittering kitchen; and humming cheerily a hunting-song, in which her father often indulged when alone with her in his boat or tossing the hay upon the meadows, she began the graceful toil, than which no sport was ever more becoming to lithe maiden form or shapely hands and arms.

The song had given place to a quaint old hymn, when a sharp tap upon the southern window made the spinner snap her thread, as she hastily turned to see a man's face pressed against the glass and smiling upon her. Not an unknown or alarming face, but yet a very repulsive face, — mean, sordid, cruel, with small gray eyes, too closely set, a narrow hollow brow, scant red hair, hardly perceptible in eyebrows and lashes, although straggling in patches over the cheeks and around the thin-lipped, deceitful mouth.

And this was the man to whom Deborah Wilder fain would give her only child, and that immediately.

As Molly recognized him, the song died from her lips, the look of placid content from her eyes; and, passing to the door, she slipped the bolt across it before she approached the window, and, opening it a little way, coldly said, —

"Good-morning, Reuben: have you a message?"

"Only that Mercy is coming over this afternoon. Shall I tie my horse, and come in for a little?"

"You know for yourself that my father said you were not to come in unless Mercy was with me: she does not appear to me to be here now."

"You are over-nice, Mistress Molly. Well, I only came to say to you, that after dinner I am going to ride over to the Corners; and, if you like, you may go too."

"But I don't like, thank you, Master Reuben, so that errand is soon done," said Molly scornfully; and Reuben's scowl did not improve his beauty, as he retorted, —

"You might at least be civil, mistress: what's amiss now, I wonder?"

"The weather is very much amiss for standing at open windows; so, if you'll excuse me, I'll e'en close this one, and go on with my work." And with a little laugh, as icy as the wind, she closed the casement, and turned the button securing it, then went back to her wheel without vouchsafing another look at the angry suitor, who went away muttering savagely, —

"Your mother will make you mend your manners, my lady, when she comes home: and, once we're married, I'll see what a little wholesome correction will do; I won't forget, never fear."

Ten minutes longer the spinning-wheel kept its rhythmic measure, as you may hear it in Mendelssohn's Lied; and then of a sudden Molly dropped the thread, and, clasping her hands together, stood with lifted head and steadfast eyes, while over her young face crept the look its lines would have taught a physiognomist to sometime expect there, although it might not be for years.

Joan of Arc resolving to give her young life to France; Charlotte Corday dedicating hers to Liberty; Anne Askew consecrating hers to God, — all these could recognize that look, and strike hands with one fit to be their sister; but like other great crises in our lives it passed unseen, unnoted, in silence, save as the girl's pale lips murmured almost inaudibly, —

"No! let what will come, I have made my mind: I will never be Reuben Hetherford's wife."

But the moments in which one remains on the pinnacle of a grand resolve are not minutes, and do not hold a second breath. Even as she spoke, a trouble began to shadow the girl's bright eyes, and dim the hero-light of her expression. Like a cloud, the prescience of conflict, and weary argument, and slow, crushing oppression, came over her, as she remembered her mother, who, for reasons of her own, had this marriage so much at heart, and who so well knew how to wear out her opponent in any struggle; and who never relinquished a point, though life was fretted away in fruitless opposition, as in the matter of her husband's religion. All this, and much, much more, passed through the girl's mind in that first prophetic flash; and then she set herself, with the dogged practicality inherited from her father, to consider the matter, point by point, as it would probably develop; and not so much from her own point of view as from her father's, whom she loved far better than herself, and had of late unconsciously taken under the protection of her own young strength and resolute nature: for the years which sharpened Deborah's tongue, and exasperated her temper, seemed stealing a little from the stone and iron of her husband's resistance; and a weary look was growing in his eyes, and a harassed wrinkle upon his brow, that made Molly's heart ache sorely when she noted them.

And in this matter she knew but too well that she herself should not be the only or even the chief sufferer; and here was the keenest grief, yet never a shadow of wavering. Did Anne Askew waver when she saw the rack, think you? or Jeanne d'Arc when she came to her funeral pyre? And this Molly was of their stuff, and could not shrink, though dearer than her own flesh was to become the martyr.

But it was with a heavy sigh that she at last drew her hand across her brow, and said, —

"Oh, poor, poor father! If only I could take it all, and all at once, and never see your dear eyes look so tired again! But it must go on. Yes" —

She sank into a chair, and sat motionless for a long hour; while the fire burned low upon the hearth, and the sparkle died out of the burnished pewter platters, and the wheel, but now so joyous, stood mute and motionless, and the cat ceased her purring, and moved uneasily about the room, muttering a discontented half-mew. Without, the clouds that all the morning had been trooping up from the under-world, and massing their forces far out at sea, found themselves ready to unmask their batteries, and with a shrill blast of onset swept down in a terrific whirl of wind and sleet and sand from the beach, all hurtling together against the window and down the wide-throated chimney, swooping the ashes from the hearth far across the floor, and into the cat's great golden eyes, until she arched her back, and spit and miauled in angry terror.

Roused from her revery, Molly looked about her for a moment abstractedly; then, with a visible effort at self-command, resuming her usual manner, she rose and went to the window, and saw that the storm had burst in snow and sleet, with every appearance of continuance.

"All the better. The Hetherfords will keep away," said she aloud, then, looking about her, saw that her careful father had supplied her with wood and water for twenty-four hours at least, and remembered that a man from the Hetherford farm was to look after the live-stock at the barn until Amariah's return with the horse and wagon next day. Then she swept up the ashes, prepared dinner for herself and Tabitha, and, when all was again in order, resumed her spinning, but not her song, — no, not even her hymn. Four o'clock, and the outer porch door was thrown violently open, the inner latch rattled, and a shrill voice cried, —

"Molly! Molly Wilder! Let me in! It's me!"

"Why, Mercy! I never looked for you in this storm!" exclaimed Molly, hastening to undo the door, and admit the whitened, dishevelled figure of a girl about her own age, but bearing too much resemblance to Reuben Hetherford for beauty, although his scant red locks had developed upon his sister's head into an abundant *chevelure* of deep auburn, the eyes to a pair of blue orbs twice the size of his, and his thin lips to a pretty, if somewhat shrewish, mouth. Still the family resemblance, the intention of the face, was too marked to allow Mary Wilder, at least, to admire it; and her manner, though courteous, was certainly a little cool, as she relieved her visitor of her snow-laden scarlet cloak and hood, and placed a chair for her beside the fire.

"So you didn't expect me?" began the visitor, drawing the long over-stockings from her feet, and extending them to the cheerful blaze. "Well, mother said it was as much as my life was worth to come out; and if you hadn't acted so silly when Reuben called at noontime, I needn't have come, for she would have sent him to fetch you over."

"How was I silly?" asked Molly calmly.

"Why, not letting him in, and running round fastening the doors and windows, as if he was a band of robbers at the very least. Ma'am says it's enough to put bad thoughts in a young man's head, when he wouldn't have had them himself."

"My father and mother both told me, while Reuben sat by last night, that I was not to have him in the house except while you were here, and even so, he was not to stay after nine o'clock. Your mother would not have me disobey my mother, I suppose," said Mary quietly.

"Well, I don't care, I'm sure," replied Mercy, with a toss of her head. "But she's going to send him over, the minute he gets back from the Corners, to take us both home on the sled. She says maybe we'd get snowed up here by to-morrow morning ; and, anyway, it's better for you to be over there nights while your mother is away."

"Your mother is very kind, but I shall stay here," returned Molly still very quietly, although a deep red rose began to burn on either cheek, and her lips closed a little tighter than their wont.

Mercy looked at her shrewdly for a moment, warming first one, then the other, of her chilled feet, then said, with a short, sharp laugh, —

"My ! Won't you and Reuben just fight when once you're married ! You're mighty proud of never giving in, but I guess you'll find your master then. I used to try to stand out against him sometimes, but I got sick of it."

"Why, what could he do to make you afraid of him ? " asked Molly a little curiously.

"Stick pins in me, pull my hair, pinch little bits right out of my arms, put things to scare me in the dark, set a dog on me, make mother mad, and lots of things beside. You'll find out if you undertake any high and mighty ways after you're married." And Mercy smiled delightedly at the prospect of the future. Molly smiled too, a smile half contempt, half conscious strength, and said, in her calm and even tones, —

"I shouldn't like to have my hair pulled, or my arms pinched, or to be made into a pincushion; and I think the best way to avoid it will be not to marry Reuben if those are his fashions."

"Oh! but you've got to marry him, you know," exclaimed Mercy, alarmed at the possible result of her revelations. "He'll be good enough to you, of course, especially if you don't contradict him. He thinks every thing of you."

"Hear the wind! It will be a dreadful night at sea!" exclaimed Molly, going to the window, looking out for a moment, and then partially drawing the curtain; but as she did so the cat jumped up in a chair, and, putting her fore-paws upon the window-ledge, looked out intently. Molly laughed blithely, exclaiming, —

"Well, Mrs. Tabitha, so I must leave the window uncurtained for your accommodation, must I? Well, there, you shall have a corner to yourself."

She adjusted the heavy moreen curtain in such a manner as to leave a small portion of the window uncovered, and then, drawing a little table in front of the fire, said cheerily, —

"And now we'll have our tea, and forget every thing beside. Mother made us a whole pantry full of goodies yesterday. She did not seem to think I could take care of myself at all."

"Did she make some of her pound-cake?" asked Mercy eagerly; for Mrs. Hetherford's larder was by no means so bounteous as that of Deborah Wilder, and Miss Mercy was both an epicure and a gourmand.

The pound-cake was produced, and cut into great golden squares; the nut-cakes, the snap-gingerbread, the pies, and the sweetmeats were all set forth; the rich cream-toast was steaming upon the table; and Molly had filled the two glasses with milk, — the innocent beverage not yet superseded in rural districts by tea or coffee, — when a jingle of bells, a stamping of feet, and the sharp rap of a whip-handle upon the door, announced a visitor.

"It's Reuben, come to take us both home!" exclaimed Mercy confidently: and the next moment proved her prophecy correct; for as Molly opened the door, the shaggy, snow-dropping figure of a man entered the room, and, removing the flapping hat tied over his ears, showed the mean features of Reuben Hetherford.

CHAPTER IX.

MOLLY ACCEPTS THE CONSEQUENCES.

WITH grave hospitality, untinged by any flutter of maiden delight in welcoming as guest the man whose life-long guest she may become, Molly Wilder received the new-comer, invited him to throw off his wraps, and to seat himself at the bountiful tea-table. Reuben accepted the invitation with alacrity; and having placed himself in the seat of honor,—at the foot of the table,—he asked a blessing, followed at once by a smile of bashful delight, as he added,—

"Seems almost as if we were married already; don't it, Molly?"

Molly made no reply: her whole consciousness seemed absorbed in the great resolve she had just made, and never for a moment forgot; and while Reuben, full of vulgar hilarity, heaped his own and his sister's plate with many a jest as to his generosity as a provider, and the bountiful table he loved to keep, and while Mercy, luxuriating in unlimited dainties, forgot all but their enjoyment, their hostess was watching both with dispassionate scrutiny, and figuring to herself a life wherein three times in every day she must confront that crafty and vulgar face, lighted as now by the greed of animal enjoyment, hear those harsh and uncultivated accents, and reply to jests that found no sympathy in her more refined sense of humor, or gossip that did not interest her. She was aroused from this revery by her lover's direct address : —

"You ought to have gone over to the Corners with me, Molly, there was so much news stirring, — about the fighting up in Canada, and all that. Say, I suppose you wouldn't let me go up there, and be a soldier, would you? not before we're married anyway, and after that I wouldn't want to go."

"Do you *now ?*" asked Molly, with a strong flavor of scepticism in her voice.

"Well, the pay is better than for farming, especially in the winter-time ; but maybe I'll make some money without risking your chance of getting a husband. They say, over at the Corners, that a big French vessel — a man-of-war — got driven up the bay by this gale ; you know how it's blown for most a week ; and the Johnny Crappos couldn't manage her, and she got ashore down on the Elizabeth Reefs, and just thumped to pieces there ; that was last night, — no, night afore last, and they've got 'em all prisoners down at the fort, — that is, most all ; but they think some got away : and they've offered a reward of twenty dollars a head for all that can be found and brought in before next Monday, when they're going to march 'em up to Boston to change off for some of our own men laid by the heels in Quebec. Now, if a fellow could find one of them lurking round, and get the twenty dollars, eh?"

"Would you sell a poor, trembling fugitive that trusted you?" asked Molly in a low voice.

"Would I? Wouldn't I, though?" chuckled Reuben, filling his mouth with mince-pie. "It would just be fun to lead him on, thinking you were going to hide him away safely, and once he was in the trap, phew! how quick you'd kick away the prop, and let down the door! And it ain't likely they'd be armed, so there wouldn't be any great danger."

"That's a consideration, certainly," replied his *fiancée* in so strange a voice that Mercy, whose capacity even for pound-cake and cream-toast was utterly exhausted, turned, and looked sharply at her for a moment, then exclaimed, —

"Why, Molly Wilder, what's the matter with you? You're as white as a sheet, and your eyes are like a cat's in the dark. If there'd been any thing to lay it to, I'd say you were awful mad."

"But as there isn't," said Molly, pushing back her chair.

"But as there isn't," echoed Reuben, also rising, "I think we'd better be going. You know, Molly, mother wants you to come over there to-night, and stay till the storm's over."

"Your mother is very kind, as I said to Mercy," replied Molly steadily; "but I cannot leave home."

"Oh, but you must!" retorted Reuben with easy positiveness. "Mother and I both think it's best, and mother won't let Mercy stay over here anyway."

"I am sorry, because in that case I must stay alone," replied Molly, still in her tone of calm and immovable decision.

Mr. Hetherford began to wax angry, and to exchange his lover-like tone for the surly and tyrannical one befitting his idea of the marital character and privileges.

"It's all waste time and breath for you to say any more about it," announced he at length. "You're a-going over to my house in just about ten minutes, and you may as well go with a good grace. A girl like you can't judge what's best for her; and, while your father and mother are away, me and my mother are the ones to say for you."

"I do not acknowledge the right at all, Mr. Hetherford, replied Molly coldly; "and, although very grateful to your mother and yourself"—

"Hang all that!" roared Hetherford: "I say you're to go, and you're going."

"I deny your right to command, and I shall not obey."

"I should like to know who has a better right to command a woman than her husband, or he who is soon to be her husband."

"You will never be my husband, Reuben Hetherford."

"Oh, pshaw! I've heard girls talk before."

"I never talk without meaning what I say. I have determined, fully determined, to break off my engagement to you, and I now do so. It is a thing altogether settled in my own mind, and your violence just now has only hastened the announcement of my purpose."

"Nonsense, Molly!" interposed Mercy, who read more shrewdly than her brother the signs of determination and strength in the face of her friend, and who wished to temporize if possible, and gain time to bring the maternal forces into the field. "Don't you and Reuben go to quarrelling to-night. Sleep over it, and you'll feel different in the morning; and, if you won't come over to our house for him, come for me. It's awfully lonesome for us two girls in such a storm as this, in this empty house; and, besides, I daren't stay when mother has sent for me. She'd be awful mad, and maybe come over after us herself. Do come home with me, and Reuben sha'n't say a word about it, anyway."

But Molly put her arms about the girl's neck, and, kissing her tenderly, repeated as firmly as ever, —

"I must stay here, Mercy; for my father and mother left me here, and I must obey them as you do yours. As for Reuben, I do not love him, and I could not make him happy or be happy myself with him; and it is much better the thing should end just here. I hope you will still be friends with me, Mercy, — you and all your house."

"As for that, I don't know," replied Mercy a trifle viciously, for her temper was getting the upper hand of her diplomacy. "I don't suppose we should feel just the same, any of us. But I don't believe we need spend much time settling all that, until your mother comes home, and we hear what she says."

"Yes: I guess she'll bring you to your senses, Mistress Mary," chimed in Reuben, whose face had for some moments presented a curious study of conflicting emotions, alarm and wounded love holding place inferior to a sort of cruel impatience, as if he longed above all things else to have this calm and haughty rebel in his power, and to try upon her fair person and disdainful spirit some of those arts of subjugation mentioned by his sister a little while previously. But, looking at him with a smile of superb contempt, she said very quietly, —

"It is of no use for us to talk more upon this matter, Mr. Hetherford. No human power can compel me to become your wife, and most certainly I never will. Neither will I leave this house; and, since Mercy cannot remain with me, I must remain alone."

"I wouldn't stay anyhow, after your using my brother such a fashion," exclaimed Mercy angrily. "I reckon you'll sing another song though, after your mother comes home. You'll be glad enough to eat humble-pie then, and maybe" —

"Hold your tongue," interrupted Reuben savagely, he being one of the many persons who cannot endure anybody's ill-temper but their own; and turning to Molly, with an attempt at her own quiet dignity, he said, —

"Well, Mary, we shall have to leave you, since you're so set on staying; and if I go out of your house this way I shall not enter it again without a good deal of urging. You had better think twice before you say the last word : you had better look well at the consequences."

"I have thought and I have looked, and I am quite

ready and willing to take all the consequences of my decision in both matters," replied Molly calmly ; and without another word Reuben Hetherford flung on his outer garments, and left the house.

CHAPTER X.

THE CONSEQUENCES.

IT is one thing to assert one's willingness to take the consequences of one's own action, and another to know what to do with them when they come. Molly Wilder was by no means tenderly attached to Mercy Hetherford: but she was her companion of infancy, she was the only girl she had ever familiarly associated with; she had tried to look upon her as a future sister, and she had always held a place of quiet superiority over her. When, therefore, she found her offers of assistance, in muffling her guest against the storm, angrily repulsed; when her efforts at placation produced only bitter retorts, or insulting silence; when she saw her late friend turn upon the threshold, and ostentatiously wipe the dust from off her feet, before springing into the sleigh Reuben had driven close to the step, — a pang such as she had never known in all her placid life stung through her heart. The only girl friend she had ever known repudiated and threw her off! By her own act, it was true: and not for one moment did the stanch heart waver in its determination; although, as in a flash of lurid light, she again saw the chance of many a bitterer pang, many a deeper wound, when her mother should know of her resolve, and should revenge the disappointment not only upon herself, but the dear father whom she loved better than herself.

She stood gazing out at the open door, the slow tears rising to her eyes and brimming unheeded over, while the sleigh was slowly turned, and so slowly driven out of the yard, that one might imagine the driver was granting time for even the tardiest of recalls; but none came, and it passed out of sight, leaving the ghostly sound of the snow-muffled sleigh-bells lingering for a few moments upon the night; and then no sight, no sound, but the white expanse of the level waste broken by spectral and snow-sheeted forms of familiar objects, and the hiss of the sleety snow as it smote the unshuttered windows, and heaped itself in fantastic wreaths and drifts about the lonely house.

A sudden dash of stinging sleet upon her face roused Molly from her abstraction; and with a heavy sigh she closed the door, shook the snow from her clothes and hair, and, re-entering the kitchen, shut the porch-door, and looked about her. The chairs hastily pushed back, the plates and knives and glasses around the table, even the wet print of feet beside the hearth, all told of late companionship and present abandonment; and for the first time a little chill of terror crept through the girl's healthy blood, and of a sudden she remembered Reuben's story of the escaped Frenchmen supposed to be prowling in the neighborhood. What sort of being a Frenchman might be, Molly did not know; but he was an enemy of her country if not of herself; and it was not so many years since the Wilders had left their English home, that they should have forgotten one of her prejudices, or ceased to feel her cause as much their own here in the colony, as there at the centre of government.

But Molly was constitutionally brave, and not at all given to imagination : so after a momentary glance at the prospect of invasion by a horde of desperate, fully-armed, and ruffianly men, probably black, or at least yellow of complexion, and murderous of demeanor, she set the subject aside, and going back to the door saw that it was securely fastened ; then taking a candle she went through the sacred and carefully-closed parlor to the front door, examined that also, recalled to mind the care with which her mother had looked to the security of every window in the house ; and, having thus convinced her reason of the unreasonableness of terror, found herself fully prepared for that sort of unreasoning and intangible terror, as impossible to combat as the flying shadows of the windmill sails.

"There is nothing to be afraid of," said she aloud, as she skurried through the dismal parlor, and closed the door behind her. A fluttering at the heart, almost depriving her of breath, mocked at her brave words ; and pressing her hand to her side she leaned against the door-casing, and, panting a little for breath, looked slowly around the kitchen. The familiar and homely scene re-assured her : upon the hearth sat Tabitha slowly blinking her great golden eyes at the fire, whose leaping blaze again made mirrors of the pewter platters ranged upon the dresser, turned the precious brazen kettle into a shield of pure gold,

and danced upon the jolly face of the tall clock in the
corner, just ready now to strike eight. The bountifully-spread table still stood as the convives had left
it, and, with the rich colors and picturesque abundance
of its viands, made a feature of the scene as attractive
in its place as the table spread by young Porphyro for
Madeline was in another.

"We're not afraid, Tabby, are we ? It's a deal
better to be alone than to have poor company: don't
you think so, puss?"

And Molly still a little fluttered, and not quite ready
for active employment, sank into the great leathern
arm-chair beside the hearth, and stooped to take the
cat upon her knee. As she did so a gentle tapping
upon the window attracted her attention ; and, turning
with a start she saw the face of a man, an utter stranger to her, pressed against the pane left uncurtained
for Tabitha's convenience, and looking fixedly at her.

CHAPTER XI.

THE FRENCH INVASION.

IN presence of real danger the terrors roused by imagination vanished at once ; and after a moment's steady contemplation of her unknown foe Molly rose, and, crossing the room to the great walnut-wood secretary mentioned by her father, she ostentatiously took from one of the drawers a clumsy pistol, such as was then in vogue, and, placing her finger upon the trigger, pointed it toward the window. The wild, white face was not withdrawn : indeed, a faint smile crossed the lips, and with a visible effort they uttered the one word, —

"Bread !"

Bread ! It was a history ; it was an explanation ; it was a fiat. The man who demands bread at the risk of his life must be in that extremity of need, which, like the presence of death, postpones every other consideration ; and Molly's brave yet tender heart would no more have dreamed of refusing such a demand than of deserting her father's death-bed. She threw down the pistol, and turned to the bountifully-spread table lying so tantalizingly before the eyes of the starving man ; then pausing, she muttered half aloud, —

"Drenched and shivering ! He will die out there, and yet "—

She turned empty-handed to the window, and, unbuttoning it, said gently, —

"You need warmth and shelter as much as food. Come round to that door, and I will let you in ; and when you are dry you may go sleep in the barn."

The wild eyes stared up in her face uncomprehendingly ; but as she pointed toward the door, and closed the window, the dimly seen figure moved away, and Mary hastened to undo the door, even despite a grotesque terror lest a troop of Frenchmen might be lurking without, and rush in behind this poor, starving wretch who probably feared them as much as she did. As she lifted the latch her fears seemed verified ; for with a swoop and a howl like that of demons or of Sioux warriors, the storm rushed down upon her, tearing the door from her hand, and flinging it wide, scattering the fire from the hearth, and so rudely ruffling Tabitha's fur that she set up her back, and spit, then slunk away with flattened ears and bristling tail, to hide beneath the settle. Molly, in spite of her lithe strength, staggered aside before that rude onset, and in so doing escaped a worse one ; for at the back of the blast, hurled like a stone from a catapult, came the figure of a man who, flung forward from the hands of the giant without, staggered headlong, and fell as if dead at Molly's feet. But at first she did not heed him : the fierce attack of the storm had roused the somewhat sluggish temper that had carried more than one of her yeoman ancestors to the fore-front of the fray, there to die if need be, but never to yield. Stepping aside from the prostrate form, Molly went to seize the shivering door, and with perhaps unnecessary vigor slam it in the face of the hooting wind, thrusting out the snow that would have prevented, with her feet. Then, slipping the stout oaken bar into its staples, she nodded triumphantly, and ran to throw back the blazing brands lying out upon the floor. Finally, as the renewed blaze sprang cheerily up, and filled the room with light, she turned to examine this waif thrown upon her hands by famine and storm. He still lay as he had fallen, his head and face clearly visible in the ruddy light; and as Molly glanced at them a sudden misgiving seized her mind: Who was this whom she had invited beneath that lonely roof, to whom she herself had unbarred the safe-shut door? this man, young, handsome, elegant, as she never had seen man before. Miranda-like she noted the clear, fine lines of every feature, the tawny gold of the thick-set hair, and the long moustache sweeping below the chin, the fine teeth gleaming between such haughty lips, and the white, smooth hand with its great amethyst ring.

Had a stranger such as this come to Mary Wilder's door in health and strength asking hospitality, she would, spite of storm and cold and hunger, have told him in her calm and gentle fashion that it was quite impossible for her to receive him, and he must go on; but now — here he was, and what was to be done but feed and warm and help him? But why did he not move?

At this point of her perplexed inspection, Molly started in horror: the left arm, upon which the senseless man lay, was doubled beneath him in a manner impossible to a perfect limb. Surely it was broken.

Raising the head and shoulders as carefully as possible, and resting them upon her knee, Molly drew out and straightened the wounded member; but gently as she did it the pain brought consciousness, and with a deep groan the wounded man opened his eyes, and after some wandering regards fixed them so piercingly upon the young girl's face that she colored deeply as she said, —

"You are very much hurt, I am afraid, sir."

"*Pardonnez-moi, mademoiselle : je suis fâchée* ——" murmured the stranger; and then his voice trailed off in an inarticulate murmur, and he was again insensible. These few words, however, had told the story, and completed the discomfiture of Molly's mind. The Frenchmen had come indeed; and this, chief perhaps of a band of desperate marauders, was lying here in the midst of her own kitchen, — nay, his head upon her knee. A thrill of mingled terror and excitement not altogether unpleasant sped along Molly's unused nerves, and sent a deep flush to her cheek; then laying the handsome head gently upon the floor she went to fetch a cushion to place beneath it, murmuring, —

"I must not let him die though he be my enemy; and my two arms are sound, thank God, and his is broken."

Then from her mother's cupboard she brought the bottle of strong waters, never used save in times of need, the hartshorn, the camphor, the flannels for rubbing, and all the simple arcana of domestic remedies which every skilful housewife of those days kept on hand, and well knew how to apply. Under this treatment the scattered senses once more returned, and the bold blue eyes again fastened curiously upon the girl's face, bending over him, and continued to watch her as she went to warm some broth left from dinner.

"It's lucky I didn't give you any more of it, Tabby," whispered she, as the cat rubbed appealingly against her feet, and the Frenchman, with a faint smile, added,—

"*Non*, Minon, *non !*"

"Here is some broth. Shall I feed you?" asked Molly, sitting down upon the floor beside her patient, who replied by opening his mouth; so, raising his head again upon her arm, she gravely and deftly proceeded to administer the food, which her patient received with both the eagerness of starvation and the restraint of civilization.

As she laid him back upon the cushion a frown of pain contracted the brows; and, glancing down at the wounded limb, he muttered some words in French, and then, turning to Molly, slowly said, —

"*Mon* arm, it is to break."

"Your arm is broken? Yes: I am very sorry, and yet more sorry that I know not how to help you," replied Molly sadly, her ready sympathy entirely repressing her somewhat dormant sense of humor. The stranger shook his head impatiently at finding himself unable to understand her fluent speech, and then, silently moving his lips for some moments as if conning some half-forgotten lesson, he said in the same slow fashion, —

"I am doctor, me. I can to make whole the arm the men to break."

"You are a doctor, and can set broken arms for people, do you mean?" asked Molly slowly. "But can you set your own? This one?" touching it as she spoke. The stranger listened eagerly, and with a smile, brilliant even through its wanness, replied, —

"Yes. To set, it is true. I do know so few English."

"So little English," corrected Molly, smiling in return; and from that moment the two began in the freemasonry of youth and necessity and mutual liking to invent a language, half very, very poor English, half signs and looks and inflections of voice, a little dashed with French whose meaning Molly guessed, and largely tinctured with that sort of magnetism by which some persons comprehend each other, they know not how.

In some one or in all of these ways the stranger soon made Molly comprehend that the broken arm must be attended to without further delay, and that splints, bandages, and other matters were to be provided; and Molly understood and obeyed all with a quick intelligence, delighting her patient, who told her in excellent French that she should have been a Sister of Mercy upon a field of battle. Molly, perceiving at a glance that this speech was a mere matter of expression, and not of direction, simply smiled in reply, and went on splitting pieces off a bit of planed board by means of a sharp little hatchet, which her guest presently remarked in French would have made a far more efficient weapon in her hands than the pistol with which she had threatened him.

Merely nodding her head good-humoredly at this second address without meaning to her ears, Molly proceeded to tear some strips from an old linen sheet, and to lay out some pins, a basin of warm water, soft towels, and finally, with a look of inquiry, to pour some of the Holland gin into a glass, and set it beside the other matters.

"Yes, my child, it will very likely be wanted, for this will be no painless matter," muttered the young man in his own language, as he sat upright in the easy-chair where he had hitherto reclined, and began to try to pull off his coat. Molly gravely and modestly proffered her help, and by slitting the sleeve of the broken arm from wrist to shoulder, the garment was removed; the waistcoat came more easily; then the young man with his right hand untied and removed his cravat, unbuttoned his shirt at the neck, and looked at Molly, who blushed scarlet, but steadily stood waiting to perform the services nobody else was there to render.

"*Une fille brave et pure comme un ange,*" said the doctor, rebuttoning his collar; and then pointing to the scissors upon the table, he gestured to Molly that she should cut away the sleeve of the shirt without removing the garment; she did it at once, and the wounded limb was laid bare. Molly uttered a little cry of dismay, for the bone had in one place protruded through the flesh, and the whole arm was bruised and wounded cruelly.

"Yes, it is to look sick," said the doctor, noticing her consternation. "The vessel went to wreck itself above the rocks. I in the water. The water so strong, so terrible, to hurl one into the rocks. My arm to go between this and that rock; the water to hurl me again, and my arm to stay there. What marvel that it broke me?"

His animated gestures, voice, and eyes made meaning of his oddly-chosen words; and Mary comprehended all, and replied softly, —

"God was very good to bring you alive out of such peril."

"God, — *le bon Dieu,* — yes! He is good always," replied the other, bending his head devoutly, while Mary began softly to wipe away the crusted blood from the edges of the wound. The patient watched her movements attentively, and said to himself half aloud, —

"A good nurse, a capital little nurse, but will she endure seeing the operation? She will lose her head when she hears the bones grate against each other, and then — Oh for one of my old comrades of the hospital, or even my dear abbé! Where is he now, I wonder? Food for fishes, or prisoner to those dogs of Englishmen?"

He ground his teeth, and Molly thought it was in pain.

"Do I hurt you? Do I touch you too roughly?"

asked she gently; and the courteous stranger smiled re-assuringly into her face as he replied, —

"Hurt me? Oh, never, never! It is you who are my good angel!"

"And now what next?" asked Molly, completing her task a little hastily, for these words were English without need of an interpreter.

The doctor looked at his arm, and shook his head.

"It will be difficult, it will be painful," said he in French. "She cannot do it, I will not ask it: I must try for myself."

He looked about him, and fixed his eyes upon one of the iron staples used to secure the bar across the door; then, partly by motions, partly by broken language, he instructed Molly to cut a strong band of linen, to tie it securely around the wrist of the wounded arm, and finally to loop it over the staple. Then with patient iteration and pantomime, he made her understand that so soon as the bone was pulled into place, whether he was insensible or not, she was to apply the splints and the bandages in the manner already explained to her, and secure them in place before attending to any thing else.

Molly, very pale, but bright-eyed and resolute, nodded comprehension, and watched as the loop of linen was laid over the staple; and the practised surgeon, manipulating the wounded arm with his right hand, began steadily to draw upon it, while great beads of anguish stood out upon his brow, and his teeth ground together in agony; then came the horrible grating of the fractured bone, and then the snap as the ends suddenly fitted into place.

"*Les eclisses,*—the wood!" murmured the patient, sinking into the chair Molly had pushed close behind him.

"Yes; I understand; drink a sip of this to keep you from fainting, and I will bind it up," said she, holding the glass to his pallid lips.

A few moments later the arm was properly secured and safely slung in one of Humphrey Wilder's great silk handkerchiefs; and then Mary opened the door of the bedroom, prepared the bed, and, coming back to her half-fainting patient, she took his right arm, laid it about her own Juno-like shoulders, and slowly rising, half lifted him to his feet, put her arm around his waist, and so led him to the bed and laid him upon it. Then she drew off his soaked and ragged boots and stockings, brought a jug of hot water, and placed at his feet, covered him warmly, and bending above him, as a mother might above her child, softly said, "Good-night! Our Father keep and help you!"

Then closing the door, she went to sit beside the fire, and cry her pure eyes almost blind in maiden shame and loneliness.

CHAPTER XII

THE ROSY DAWN.

IN the gray light of the next morning Molly Wilder roused herself from an uneasy sleep upon the settle beside the fire, smouldered now into a heap of warm ashes, within whose confines Tabitha crouched, purring sleepily, her head upon her folded paws. For a few moments the young girl lay staring about her, wondering at her strange situation, and vaguely recalling events so romantic and so utterly foreign to her usual life that at first she mingled them with her dreams; but when her eyes fell upon the coat hanging over a chair beside the hearth, the litter of bandages and splints upon the table, and the linen band still hanging from the staple, the whole scene of the previous night returned upon her; and, springing to her feet, she went at once to peep in at her patient.

He slept, but uneasily, for rising fever already tinged his cheeks and parched his lips; and, while Molly bent over him, he turned his head, moaned heavily, and muttered some words of which she only distinguished the name, " Valerie ! "

" It will be the name of his sweetheart, no doubt," said Molly to herself with a little pang of novel pain; and still she stood reading the unconscious face, and wondering if in the great world she had never seen, there were more men as noble, as handsome, as charming of manner, as this waif, so strangely cast by the waves at her very door, and yet not for her, but this Valerie, whoever she might be; and she wondered if Valerie, in her far-off stately home, would ever know and be grateful to humble Mary Wilder, the colonial farmer's daughter, who had nursed her lover back to life when else he might have perished.

From these unprofitable musings she was roused by a knock upon the outer door, so loud as to break the light slumber of the invalid, whose eyes flew open with a look of ready alarm.

"Be still, be very quiet; make no noise, for your life!" exclaimed Molly in a low and impressive voice; and then, running on tiptoe into the kitchen, she collected every article belonging to or betraying the presence of the stranger, and bringing them into the bedroom threw them down upon a chair, and closed the door. By this time the knock was repeated louder and longer than before. Molly glanced about the room, arranged her own dress a little, and went to open the door. A middle-aged man, with a round foolish face, set in a hay-colored beard just now full of icicles, stood upon the step, stamping, and slapping his hands, covered with great striped yarn mittens of Deborah Wilder's manufacture; for this was Amariah Coffin, the Wilders' hired man, and a privileged member of the household. Molly, who had feared Reuben Hetherford, or some messenger from that family, greeted the alternative with relief.

"Good-morning, Amariah! when did you get home?"

"Just now. Your mother was so scared at the wind last night, that she sent me off as soon as the horse was rested. I suppose she thought I could hold the roof on, or talk to the pigs and stop their squealing: they always have such a lot to say when the wind blows; some folks think it's because the devils were sent into them, and the old gentleman is always busy in a gale of wind."

"Well, I suppose you would like some breakfast pretty soon, wouldn't you?"

"Bless your heart, no, child! didn't you know I was to board over to Hetherford's while the folks are gone? Surely your ma'am told you."

"Oh, yes, yes! I had forgotten." And Molly blushed scarlet at her own pre-occupation of thought; but Amariah was already building up the fire, and did not notice her confusion, as he went on to say, —

"No: what I want is to make some warm porridge for the lambs, and get whatever you have for the pigs. If the hens' victuals are ready, I'll carry that out too, for it's kind of snowy for you."

An odd feeling of annoyance crept over the young girl's mind as these homely details of her daily life were pressed upon it, and she glanced unconsciously at the bedroom door as dreading lest they should penetrate within it; but in the next moment she took herself severely to task, and a feeling of honest shame at her momentary treason sent the blood again to her cheeks.

Yes, these matters of lambs and pigs and poultry were her life, and her father's and mother's lives ; and she was not going to disown them for all the handsome shipwrecked gentlemen the waves could ever bring to her. No doubt " Valerie " was a dainty lady who had never heard of such vulgar details, but that was not her affair. She should do her duty by this wounded man, nurse him and shelter him, and, when he was well, help him to escape from Reuben Hetherford, and all the other cowards who would betray and sell him, and then he would go back to his Valerie ; and she — well, at least, she never could be forced to marry Reuben Hetherford.

Amariah's rough voice broke in upon her revery with a laugh. " Well, Molly, I should think it was shearing-time by the way your wits are wool-gathering. Where's Mercy Hetherford, I say ? "

" Oh ! she didn't come ; or rather, she didn't stay ; " and then Molly hurriedly explained the occurrence of the previous night, while Amariah, who took a fatherly interest in all affairs of the child who had grown into womanhood under his eyes, listened attentively, one hand shading his face from the leaping flame, while with the other he mechanically stirred the porridge for his lambs, his goggling blue eyes fixed upon Molly's face.

" Sho ! " exclaimed he at last : " now the fat's all in the fire ; and won't ma'am be mad when she gets home and finds what a spot of work you've cut out for her ? Did you tell Reuben up and down you wouldn't have him ? "

"No matter about that. All is, Mercy won't be here to sleep or to help me, and I don't want you to ask any of them to come. I'm not at all afraid of being alone six days."

"'Cause, if you did," pursued Amariah sturdily, "I shall tell him not to take you at your word till after your mother gets home. She'll fix it."

"Amariah! Don't you dare to say such a word to Reuben Hetherford, or to say any thing about me in any way. It is surely no concern of yours."

"No consarn of mine, when I used to drag you both on one sled, and take you both up on Dobbin, and — O Gee — rusalem!"

This final exclamation was not, as might be supposed, the result of injured feeling on the old man's part, but of a great spatter of boiling porridge, launched from the unwatched kettle upon his wrist, and inflicting a burn painful enough to absorb all his attention for some moments. Molly, thankful for any change in the conversation, busied herself in spreading some of her mother's simple salve upon a cloth, and binding up the wrist as cleverly, if not as tremulously, as she had done the broken arm of the previous night. Amariah submitted gratefully, and, when it was finished, said, —

"There, now! That's better than new. You're a master-hand at comforting a fellow's hurts, Molly, and I'll do as much for you some day."

"Do it to-day, by promising not to speak of me to Reuben Hetherford, or to any of the Hetherfords," said Molly, so quickly that Amariah laughed aloud.

"Short accounts make long friends, you say," chuckled he. "Well, I'm a man of my word, and it's a bargain. Blow the horn if you want any thing. I'll come and shovel the paths, and draw some water, after I've done my milking and got my breakfast." And with this brief valedictory, Amariah took his bucket of mush, and went out to the barn. Molly slipped the bolt upon the outside door, drew a long breath, and hastened back to her patient. She found him wide awake and very feverish.

"Is it the English to prisoner me?" demanded he, catching Molly's hand in his burning fingers, and grasping it painfully.

"No, no," replied she soothingly, "it is a friend: we are all friends to you, and will prove ourselves so. You are quite safe here, and I will care for you."

"Foi de — what name are you, mademoiselle?"

"Mary, Mary Wilder, and your friend."

"*Marie, nom de la sainte vierge, nom de la foi, nom bel et bon.*"

"And what may I call you, my friend?" asked Molly, interrupting the feverish murmurings with her cool, clear voice, like a breath of morning air penetrating the close, warm room of an invalid.

"To call me, say you, Marie," replied the stranger, fixing his burning eyes upon her face. "They call me François *le baron — mais non, non! je n'ai pas le nom, la patrie, ou les amis*" —

"François, did you say?" asked Mary again, as she drew her hand from the detaining fingers, and smoothed the hair from the scorching brow. "Well, then, François, try to believe that Mary will protect you, and care for you until you are well, and keep yourself just as quiet and peaceful as you can. Do you understand, do you believe?"

"I believe in Marie, la sainte Marie," murmured François dreamily; and Molly softly went into the outer room to prepare such simple food as she knew was best for him, to contrive means for his comfort and security, and to go about her own homely duties, wondering the while at the strange new joy and light that had come into her life, transforming its dull monotony into an absorbing romance, and all at once enlarging its horizon, as if from a narrow valley she had climbed some sun-clad height, and found an unknown world lying at her feet, bathed in the glory of that light that never was on sea or shore.

CHAPTER XIII.

THE DAGGER OF REGINALD DE MONTARNAUD.

THE day went busily on. About noon, Amariah having dug a series of artistic paths in various directions, swept the snow from the wood-pile and chip-yard, drawn fresh water, and made the circuit of the house to see that all looked as it should, came into the kitchen to warm his hands, and have a word with Molly, who received him less cordially than usual, fearing that some sound from the bedroom might betray the presence of her charge, whose increasing fever rendered him restless and talkative. Fortunately, Amariah, being subject to earache in cold weather, had tied a red knitted comforter over the top of his head and under his chin; and while this garment no doubt added to his personal beauty, it seriously impeded his powers of hearing and his quickness of movement.

"Say, Molly," began he, after a brief account of the condition of matters under his charge at the barn and elsewhere, "have you heard any thing about those Frenchers that are lurking round Falmouth?"

"Reuben Hetherford said something about it," replied Molly carelessly. "Has he found them yet?"

"No; but I shouldn't wonder if he did, for he's

looking everywhere. He came over to our barn this morning, and hunted the mows as if he was looking for a stolen nest."

"He did? I wonder at his impudence, then! If he comes again I wish you would tell him that while my father is away I am in charge of his property, and that I don't allow any intrusions. Mind now, Amariah, I mean it; and I won't have Reuben Hetherford or any one else peeping and prying round the place."

"Sho, Molly, what's got into you to flare up that way about a trifle? I don't seem to know you to-day. I expect it's all along of getting mad with Reuben yesterday. Well, well, there's three things a wise man can't understand, and one of 'em is, the way of a man with a maid; but so fur as I see, the way of a maid with a man is contrarier yet. But say, Molly, I shouldn't so much wonder if one of them 'ere fellows was somewhere round these parts, after all. I wouldn't say it to scare ye, but I do wish that you'd go over to Hetherford's for the nights. I'd feel a heap safer about ye."

"What makes you think anybody is about here?" asked Molly, turning pale, and sitting down suddenly.

"There, now, you're scared; and that was just what I didn't mean to do. 'Tain't nothing, child, but" —

"Yes, it is, Amariah, and I want to know what. I am not at all frightened, but it is right that while father is away I should be told of every thing that happens about the place. Tell me, please."

There was an air of quiet authority in her voice that penetrated through the red comforter even to the old man's dull brain ; and he looked in some surprise at the handsome woman standing tall and straight before him, realizing, perhaps for the first time, how far she was removed from the little child whom he had coaxed, or frightened, or spoiled, or laughed at, a few years before. For a moment or two he said nothing ; but when he did speak it was in an altered voice : —

"Well, the fact is, Mistress Mary, that I saw footsteps round the well this morning that must have been made after the snow fell last night. Now, I don't suppose you went out there ; and there was nobody else in the house, you say."

"The wind blowing all night would have filled them up if they had been made before morning. Probably some one going by stopped to drink, or else "—

"They was made last night, and the water being spilt round the places froze right up ; and when I swept off the light snow this morning, there they was. They was made in the first part of the storm last night."

"Well, is that all ? "

The question was abrupt and impatient. We who know all, can understand that the girl's nerves were sharpened and alert to discover the extent of her danger as speedily as possible ; but Amariah only thought her peremptory and ill-natured, and answered dryly, —

"No, it ain't all. When I looked round the barn after daylight, I saw plain enough that some one had been there since I left yesterday morning."

"Of course there had. Reuben Hetherford put up his horse last night."

"I know he did. But it ain't very likely Reuben Hetherford raked down a lot of hay off the mow, and made a sort of bed in one of the empty stalls, and, when he'd done with it, kicked it under the oxen's feet and left it there. Now, who but a Frencher would suppose I bedded down my cattle with good English hay? Tell me that, will you?"

"Very likely father did it in his hurry of going away, or perhaps Reuben threw it down, and the oxen got it under their feet, or" —

"Well, then, 'Mary, Mary, quite contrary,'" exclaimed the old man in a passion, "what will you say to the knife I found in that stall? A thing such as murderers and house-breakers and Frenchers carry in their pockets to kill innocent folk in their beds! A knife with crinkle-crankles all over the blade, and a handle all fixed off with gold, and topped with a cross — a regular Papist cross — such as drove us all out of merry England to this savage country, where you can't so much as get a crop of barley off the sand and rocks they call land."

"Did you really find such a knife, Amariah?" asked Molly in a low voice.

"Yes, I did, child; and though I wouldn't have scared you by telling of it if you hadn't been so provoking with your perhapses and perhapses, I'm kind of glad the cat's out of the bag, after all; for now I reckon you'll have some sense, and go over to" —

"Where is that knife? Show it to me."

"I hain't got it: you'll have to take my word for it; and I haven't generally been called a liar."

"You haven't got it !   Where is it, then?"

"Reuben Hetherford can tell if you're o' mind to ask him about it."

"O Amariah ! have you given it to him?"

"Why, yes.   What's got into you, child?   I don't know you for the same since your folks went away."

"But what for?   Tell me all about it, do, good Amariah ! tell me the whole story."

"Well, if you won't be so scared, and look so white. Lor, child, you ain't so growed-up now as you was a while ago.   There, set down in your little chair, and I'll tell you ; though, come to think of it, there ain't such a sight more to tell.   I found the thing, a dagger they call it, I believe, in the stall where they had laid down for a sleep ; and when they went away one of 'em dropped it I expect.   So when I went over to breakfast, I carried it along, and showed it to Reub ; and he was dreadful worked up about it, thinking he'd catch the fellow right off, and get the bounty, — twenty dollars, you know.   And so he asked me to let him take it, and I did ; and as soon as breakfast was over, he came over and searched our barn, and then he rode off post-haste, and says he'll track the feller twenty mile but what he'll find him."

The story finished, Amariah began slowly to button himself into his great frieze coat, and to draw on the monstrous mittens which had been sedulously toasted during his stay upon the spears of the great iron and-irons.   Mary sat in her little chair mute and white ; her hands tightly locked upon her knee, her eyes steadfastly regarding the foolish round face of the old man. She was considering how far it was best to trust him, and whether he might prove a valuable ally. She knew his fondness for herself, and his honesty and singleness of heart ; but she also knew how incompetent his simple nature was to cope with the cunning and determination of Reuben Hetherford's, and she determined not to trust him, for the present at least.

So Amariah, much to his discontent, found himself allowed to depart with no token of relenting upon the part of his young mistress in the Hetherford direction ; and Molly shot the bolt behind him, and flew back to the bedside of her patient with the feeling of mingled relief and terror of a mother-bird who sees the predatory urchin pass by her nest, and knows not when he may return and rifle it.

François looked up at her with haggard eyes.

"He is burned in a fire ; he is too tight," murmured he plaintively. Mary read his meaning by intuition.

"Your poor arm is too tightly bandaged !" exclaimed she. "That is soon set to rights. O François ! I will do a great deal before I let them take you."

He did not understand the words, but he did the tone, and gratefully murmured in his own language, —

"It is an angel sent by the good God to care for me. Not a woman, — women are false and cruel, — women are Valerie."

She heard the name : she could not know in what connection it was spoken, and a sharp pain ran through her heart, and blanched her lips.

"Never mind !" murmured she, "I will nurse you

and care for you, and defend you with my own life, if need be; and when all is done you shall go and be happy with your Valerie."

The arm was cooled and bound up, the feverish face and neck softly bathed, the yellow hair, so strong and thickset that it seemed more like golden wire than hair, reduced to order, even the long moustaches combed and arranged, and then Mary stood looking and meditating. Fastidious neatness was part of her religion, both natural and revealed: besides this, she was an excellent nurse; and neither a neat-woman nor a good nurse would voluntarily select a very soiled and tattered shirt and a pair of military trowsers as the best and most comfortable costume for an invalid; but how was she to remedy the matter?

She went to the great chest-of-drawers at the end of the bedroom, and took out one of her father's capacious and comfortable vestments, carried it into the kitchen, and hung it over the back of a chair in front of the fire; standing beside it she looked down at Tabitha, who was just awakening from a nap, and softly said, —

"You'd do it, Tabby, wouldn't you?" And then covering her face in both her hands, she stood quiet a moment, and whispered to herself, —

"It is nought but selfishness to count the cost when one may help a sick and wounded man. It is not Molly who is to be thought of now, but François."

Then taking her scissors and the warm garment in her hands, she went back to the bedside, and saying very soberly, and in her mother's dialect, —

"It is right that thee should have some clean clothes, François;" she swiftly cut around the binding and down the other sleeve of the fragment of a shirt, raised the head and shoulders of her patient upon her strong right arm, and deftly threw the clean garment over his head, contriving to draw the loose wide sleeve over the broken arm without more pain than could be silently borne.

"And now I think thee can take off thy other clothes, and move to the fresh side of the bed, while I make thee some gruel," said Mary in a calm maternal voice, hiding so completely the quaking of her girlish heart, and the shame of her maiden modesty, that the young man looked up at her in quick surprise; but as his eyes met hers he read so well the doubt, and self-control, and pain in their calm depths, that he needed not to look again, and only replied gravely, —

"I thank you, mademoiselle: I can to do so."

So Mary closed the door, and, falling upon her knees beside Tabitha curled in the armchair, buried her face in her vari-colored fur, and wept a few hot sudden tears. One must have some sympathy, and Tabitha was a good confidante, for she never said, "I told you so," and never repeated what was said to her.

CHAPTER XIV.

MRS. HETHERFORD TAKES PITY ON MARY.

THE gruel was made and taken, the bedroom was arranged in its usual orderly fashion, all traces of the stranger within its precincts, except his actual presence, were carefully put away; and about three o'clock, Molly, a little weary at last, sat down beside the bed to rest, and watch the unquiet slumbers of her patient. The fever, a little subdued by the bathing and clean linen, had returned; and although the sick man slept, it was brokenly, and with incessant murmurs and tossings, which constantly threatened to disarrange the wounded arm, and make matters worse than in the beginning.

While Molly vainly sought by fanning, or re-arranging the pillows, or gently bathing the burning forehead, to still these restless motions, she was startled by a sharp and sudden knock upon the outer door.

" *Qu'est-ce que c'est!* " exclaimed François sharply, and starting up in his bed. Molly gently replaced his head upon the pillow.

" Keep very still ! Do not speak or stir," said she in a firm, low voice. "Some one is coming in, and must not hear you. There is danger if they do."

" Danger, danger ! *Les maudits Anglais,*" whispered François deliriously. Mary nodded without trying to understand, placed her finger upon her lips, and left the room carefully, closing the door, and drawing her great spinning-wheel across it. Then she hastened to open the outer door; and not too soon, for the visitor was knocking loudly and impatiently upon it. As she raised the latch, a much-muffled and irate woman pushed impatiently in.

"Mrs. Hetherford!" exclaimed Molly.

"Yes, it's me; and I didn't know as you were ever going to let me in. Were you asleep at this time of day?" asked the visitor, looking sharply around.

"No ma'am, but busy in another room. Won't you sit down, and throw off your cloak?"

"Well, I can't stay long. I've enough to do at home; but the fact is, child, I took pity on you, though you don't deserve it, and come over to give you some wholesome advice and oversight.'

"You are very kind, ma'am," replied Molly demurely, while the ghost of a smile flitted across her lips.

"Kind! Well, I think it is kind to come out such a raw-boned day as this, especially for a busy woman like me; but then I look upon you the same as I do on Mercy, and when you're married to Reuben you will be the same, you know."

"I told Reuben last night that I should never marry him," said Molly gently, but very firmly.

The matron tossed her head, sniffed contemptuously, and untied the strings of her green silk hood, of the shape called pumpkin, and possibly imitated from that national vegetable.

"I've heard of young folks falling out before now," said she, "and I've heard of their falling in again."

"But, as Reuben and I have not quarrelled, we cannot make it up," replied Molly. "I have always thought it was a mistake for me to have promised to marry him, and while I was alone yesterday, before he and Mercy came over, I made up my mind to break it off. I am not at all angry, and there is no chance of my thinking differently."

"*Marie, sainte vierge Marie!*" murmured a voice from the bedroom, plainly audible to Mary, but in Mrs. Hetherford's ears confused with a sudden screech from Tabitha, upon whose tail her mistress had trodden, as she lay asleep before the fire.

"Mercy on us! Why don't you turn that nasty cat out of doors? and how the wind whistles round this house!" exclaimed Mrs. Hetherford, turning from the fire to look about the room with half-formed suspicion of she knew not what. The mutterings from the bedroom continued, but less distinctly; and Mary, with a light laugh, drew her spinning-wheel a little way from the door, and began to whirl it busily, saying the while, —

"The wind makes a good deal of noise, to be sure, but I drown it with the sound of my spinning-wheel. Mother left me such a lot of rolls to yarn off, that I have not much time to get frightened. You'll excuse my keeping at work, I hope."

"Oh! you're very excusable," said Mrs. Hetherford in an offended tone, and drawing her cloak about her. "I'm a good deal in a hurry myself, and couldn't well leave to come over here; but, as I said, I took pity on you, more for your own folly than any thing else, and I run over to ask you once more to come and stay at my house till your mother gets back. It isn't suitable anyway for a girl like you to be all alone in the house, specially o' nights; and Mercy got mad when she and Reuben were here last night, and wouldn't come if I was to send her; and Reuben, he's took it to heart, what you said; and the only way to make things straight is for you to give up your will this once, and come along."

"I thank you very much, Mrs. Hetherford, very much indeed, but I cannot come," replied Molly, more coldly and briefly than she was aware of speaking; for her whole mind was absorbed in listening to the low murmurs so distinct to her own ear, and her physical powers were strained to the utmost in keeping up the incessant whirl of the wheel, which for the moment drowned all other sound. No wonder, therefore, if her reply struck short-tempered Mrs. Hetherford's ears as churlish and ungrateful. She rose at once, and, tying the pumpkin hood tightly under her chin, said, in a voice tremulous with anger,—

"Well, that's short and sweet, and to the point, Mistress Mary Wilder; and the next time I leave my work and come sneaking over here to coax an ungrateful minx to visit me, I guess you'll know it. I should think, at any rate, you might treat a woman old enough to be your mother with some little pretence of respect; but I suppose that isn't Quaker fashion. I don't know much about that kind of cattle, but I hear the courts at home are shipping them all out of the country. I hope there won't any more come over here."

"Didn't you know that Reuben has promised my mother that he will join them if I will?" asked Molly maliciously; and then, perceiving that the hood and her own anger had effectually closed the good woman's ears to any indefinite sounds, and that she was actually leaving the house, she abandoned the spinning-wheel, and, following her to the door, laid a hand upon her arm, saying gently, —

"Don't leave me in anger, Mrs. Hetherford, and forgive me if I spoke improperly to you. You have been very good to me all these years, and I do not want you to be offended now. Don't you know how many mince-turnovers, and cocked hats of gingerbread, you have made for me?"

"Oh! your mother can make 'em a sight better. Reuben told me so once."

"Yes, and never had another crumb of pie nor cake all that week," laughed Molly. "That was years ago, but I remember it perfectly. Come, auntie Hetherford, give me a kiss for old times' sake, and don't go away in anger."

"There, there! O Molly! I always said you'd be like sunshine in our house, and you'd be the making of Reuben; and now you say you won't. There, you needn't try to coax me round, for I won't be coaxed. If you want me for a friend you've got to give in, and come over to my house. Come now, be a good child, and say you will, and let Reuben drive the sled over for you before night. Say you will, now, that's a pretty one."

"I am so sorry, so sorry to displease you, dear kind friend; but I cannot, I must not. It is my duty to stay here, and I can do nothing else."

The pain of her kind heart in thus breaking off, as she knew she did, the ties of a life-time in familiar companionship and neighborly kindness, if not in real love, showed itself plainly in her face and in her voice; but the angry mother only felt the slight to her son, and the matron resented the young girl's resistance of her entreaties and effort: so with no reply save an indignant toss of the head, Mrs. Hetherford plucked her cloak from Molly's clinging fingers, and plunged out into the snow. At a little distance waited the sled on which she had come, with Reuben standing beside the horse's head. He looked eagerly toward the door as it opened, but, perceiving at a glance that his mother had failed in effecting a reconciliation, turned suddenly away, with no response to Molly's forced smile and salutation.

"And there go," said she aloud, as she closed and bolted the door, "almost the only friends I ever claimed outside this house, and now they are enemies. Had it not been for you, François, I could hardly have said Mrs. Hetherford nay, though I would never have married her son. Truly, Valerie may be a little grateful to me for my care of her lover."

CHAPTER XV.

THE PRIEST'S CHAMBER.

THE sleepless nights, the anxious days, passed on, stealing the color from Molly Wilder's cheek, the roundness from her form, the elasticity from her step, until the sixth morning arrived, and Amariah presented himself in the kitchen, fully equipped for a journey, and ready for any last words from his young mistress; but as he looked steadily in her face, his own shadowed with concern, and in his kindly, homely voice, and half paternal way, he exclaimed, —

"Why, Molly, child, how you have fell away, and how pale you look! You don't eat enough, I'll bet, though I've brought in two chickens, and as much as two dozen eggs, besides all you had in the house. I'm main sorry you fell out with Reuben, and so staid here all alone. It ain't no use to ask you to go over there for to-night?"

"Not a bit of use, Amariah. So you are going to start directly?"

"Yes, right away. I'll get over to Falmouth before night, and the stage will be along in the morning; so you can look for us to-morrow before dark. I've engaged Reuben's Hez to sleep in the barn to-night, so if you get scared you've only to blow the horn, same as you would for me; and he'll fetch in some fresh water in the morning. You've got wood enough?"

"Enough for a week, I should think," said Molly smiling merrily.

"And there's nothing more that I can do for you before I go?"

"No. Here is a little note for my father, and I want you to give it to him when he is alone."

"I understand; and I'll do it all right. Well, I guess I'd better be going. Good-by."

"Good-by, Amariah." And closing the door, Molly watched until the comfortable box-sleigh, well filled with blankets and rugs, drove away; and then, still like the mother-bird flying back to her wounded nestling, she hastened into the bedroom, and stood for a moment looking anxiously down at her patient.

"Yes, he is a great deal better," said she half aloud, and François, looking affectionately up at her, murmured in reply, —

"Yes, better, much of better."

"But are you enough better to bear moving?" asked Molly anxiously. "My father and mother are coming home to-morrow, and you must not be here unless you will trust them as well as me."

François shook his head, saying eagerly, "No, no! I can to trust no one but Marie."

"Then I must hide you. Will it hurt you very much to go through the cold house, and up into a cold garret? I am afraid it will."

"Tell again, my Marie: I not to understand."

So Molly, with patient iteration and gesture, explained her plan, and François at length understood.
In fact, even in five days these two had invented a
language quite their own, although compounded of
both French and English, besides that unwritten language previously mentioned, and used during some
portions of their lives by most persons, at least those
of sensitive organization.   But as our two linguists did
not reduce their invention to written characters, or
indeed seek to adapt it to popular comprehension, it
is impossible to transcribe it precisely ; and in relating
that François or Molly said thus and so, it is understood
that the language is not precisely their own, but rather
its interpretation.

Thus, then, after their own fashion, the two arranged
their plans, and chatted merrily and. happily until the
twilight fell, and Molly prepared a little supper for her
charge, watched him with maternal satisfaction as he
took it, then, making every thing tidy about him for
the night, sat down beside the bed, and began to sing
softly one of the old hymns her father still retained
from his early training in the Church.

François lay and looked at her for a while, and
then said, —

"I am glad you sing nothing gay, and I am glad
your voice is so deep and rich.   It is not in the least
like a bird-song."

"And why are you glad of that?" asked Molly in
surprise.

"Because I could not bear that any woman should
sing to me in a high, clear voice, trilling and soaring

like a lark, so sweet, so penetrating, so maddening."
He had run off into French in the last words, and
Molly drew away the hand he had seized in his.

"I suppose Valerie sang like that, and you could
not bear that I should try to imitate her," said she
impetuously, and so rapidly that François did not
understand a word, except the name.

"Valerie!" repeated he almost sternly, "what do
you know of Valerie?"

"Nothing. You have spoken the name in your
delirium, that is all. Pardon my freedom in repeating
it," said Molly coldly; and then she rose and went into
the other room, and never knew when Tabitha rubbed
against her feet, and purred her sympathy, for she was
staring through the uncurtained window with eyes that
saw nothing for the bitter tears that blinded them.

Suddenly out of the darkness shaped itself a face,
the mean repulsive face of Reuben Hetherford looking
steadily in upon her. A sharp terror seized upon
Molly's heart; not for herself in any case, but for that
helpless stranger whose life and liberty she had promised to defend to the uttermost. Could Reuben from
that angle see past her into the bedroom? Had he
heard voices? Did he suspect something, or was it
only herself for whom he was looking?

Not daring to answer these questions by an appeal
to himself, and yielding to the terror and repulsion of
the moment, more than to reason, Molly sharply drew
the curtain across the window, making sure that every
crevice was covered, and then flying to the door satisfied herself that it was securely bolted. As she did so,

a low rap upon the panel startled her, and Reuben Hetherford's voice called, —

"Molly, Molly Wilder! It's Reuben!"

But at the same moment another voice in the opposite direction called also, —

"*Marie! Chère Marie! Venez-ici de grace!*"

Running light and swift as a cat across the intervening room, Mary stood beside her patient's bed, and grasping his outstretched hand whispered, —

"Be quiet, be quiet, François, for heaven's sake! Some one is outside!"

Then back again to the door to say coldly and forbiddingly, —

"Is that you, Reuben? What do you want?"

But no one replied; and this sudden abandonment of his purpose, in a man so obstinate as Hetherford, alarmed Molly more than any persistence could have done; for it seemed as if, his suspicions having been in some way confirmed, he had retreated to take action upon them.

"I will not delay an hour after daylight," said Molly aloud as she returned to the bedroom; and then sitting beside François, her hand again in his, she told him of Reuben's visit, and of all the causes for her terror of him.

An hour later the farmhouse was quiet and peaceful; the innocent child sleeping rosily upon her hard and careless bed beside the fire, with Tabitha purring at her side; and the worn and wounded man of the world, of camps and battle-fields and courtly life, tossing restlessly upon his too luxurious bed, and dreaming now of Valerie hiding among the roses of the Provençal garden, and now of Mary bending over him with calm pitiful eyes, and hand of gentle ministry.

Morning broke, and Tabitha and Molly shook off their healthy slumbers just as François fell into his first sound sleep. Creeping on tiptoe to look at him, Molly covered him more warmly, closed the door, renewed the fire, and hung the tea-kettle over the merry blaze. Then she put the high fender in front of it, looked around the kitchen murmuring, "I am so glad Amariah is safely out of the way!" and, wrapping a warm shawl about her shoulders, tied the ends in a great knot behind after the picturesque gypsy fashion. Then she passed into the cold and cheerless front entry and up-stairs, followed by Tabitha, who ruffled her fur in expostulation at the change of temperature, but evidently felt it a duty to attend her mistress. From the upper landing ascended a narrow enclosed staircase ; and mounting this, Molly found herself in the garret, a great unfinished loft, dark except for a little square window at either end, and gloomy and quiet and funereal as one might expect of a place evidently used as the final resting-place of such objects as had fulfilled their uses below, and were now consigned to this limbo as an intermediate step to oblivion.

"A little scary up here, as Mrs. Hetherford says, isn't it, Tabby?" said Molly standing at the head of the stairs, and looking about her ; while Tabby, divining the presence of mice, began eagerly to prowl about the eaves, and sniff in the dark corners. Her mistress, meantime, softly humming one of the solemn melodies François had approved, began to remove a confused mass of lumber heaped behind the chimney, which, large and square and cumbrous, occupied great part of the middle of the place. Beyond it a rude partition of quilts and curtains divided off a little nook intended for Amariah's lodging, until Mrs. Wilder decided to banish him to the barn; and this screen still hanging made one wall of the hiding-place Molly had already in her mind contrived for the refuge of her prisoner. The chimney itself formed another side, the eaves of the house a third; and across the fourth, which was nearest the stairs, Molly re-arranged the old spinning-wheel, the boxes, the discarded tin fire-screens, and re-hung the ghostly garments from nails driven into the rafters in such manner that they seemed to keep watch and ward, like disembodied sentinels, over the approach to the hidden nest the young girl was so cunningly devising for her wounded nursling. The weakest side was that of the quilt and shawl partition, which Mrs. Wilder's restless spirit might any day lead her to remove, or at any rate to pull aside. Molly stood for some moments, her finger on her lip, looking at this screen, and meditating how to make it either more substantial or more inaccessible. Then a merry smile crossed her lips; and going to the truckle-bedstead in the corner, still left as Amariah had last used it, she dragged the great feather-bed off upon the boards, ripped it up with the scissors hanging at her side, and emptied the contents upon the floor in front of the screen, where they made a fluffy and unquiet heap not to be approached, especially by feminine skirts, without danger of suffocation to the intruder, and waste to the feathers.

"There, Tabby!" exclaimed Molly as she carefully turned the tick inside out, and then rolled it together in a downy and dusty parcel, "mother said she should have to empty that bed, and clean the feathers: so we've been smart, and done it for her, the first part, anyway; and she won't meddle with them before spring, I know."

Then, still smiling at her own exploit, Molly took a final survey of her arrangements so far, and went down stairs; where she found that the kettle had boiled over, and nearly extinguished the fire, and François had awakened, and was feeling rather abused at remaining so long unnoticed. A few bright words, a few deftly-rendered services, made him quite comfortable and restored his good humor, however; and as Molly turned away, saying with a sunny smile, "Now you shall have your breakfast," he caught her dress, and detained her to say, —

"You will to pardon my bad humor. The fault, it is yours, because that you to spoil me have: you are too much good to me, so unworthy."

"You were not ill-humored, only a little tired," said Molly gently; "and it is the greatest pleasure I ever knew to take care of you."

She blushed brightly as she spoke, and her calm eyes fell before the gaze François fixed upon them. He released her dress without reply; and, while she hastened away to provide his morning meal, the young man lay very quiet, his brow slightly knitted, his face troubled and thoughtful.

Breakfast over and removed, Molly cheerily said, —

"And now, François, you must be very patient and good, while I go and finish preparing your hiding-place. I have to make it comfortable now, and then we will see how we can get up there."

"Yes, you make a priest's chamber as they did in the old time, — for Huguenot to-day, for Catholic to-morrow," said François smiling. "Well, go then, dear child : I will be content."

So Molly again mounted to the dark and cheerless garret; and of the small space now so safely concealed from any but the most rigorous search, she soon contrived to make as cosey and comfortable a little nook as ever sheltered Huguenot minister or Catholic priest. The great mass of masonry composing the chimney, once thoroughly heated by the kitchen-fire, retained its warmth through the night; and Molly arranged the bed close beside it. Some skins of foxes and smaller game, which her father had shot and cured, made a soft and delightful carpet;. a chair and a little table were found among the lumber, and a candlestick and store of candles laid ready. Finally she brought a basin and jug, some of the fine towels her mother had made her spin, and had hired woven for the possible trousseau provided for thrifty maidens of that day, and the little looking-glass from her own room.

"There, that will do, Tabby; and now we will go and bring him up-stairs," said she, looking admiringly around when the mirror was hung, and all complete.

Tabby arched her back, enlarged the circumference of her tail, and purring approvingly followed her mistress down-stairs. They found François out of bed, looking very pale and exhausted, but partially dressed, and ready for departure.

"How brave you are, and how strong, to get up all alone!" exclaimed Molly admiringly; and then she brought a great soft shawl, and muffled him so far as he would suffer it, and some of her own shoes, quite large enough for his slender and patrician feet, and offered her shoulder to the uninjured arm of the invalid, who laid it caressingly about her neck.

"You are like Juno; no, it is Diana that you are," said he in French: "so fearless, so strong, so chaste, so unconscious of the Actæons of the world."

"Lean on me as heavily as you like, and be very careful with the stairs," replied Molly in English; and neither cared a whit for comprehending the spoken words, since the tone translated itself.

The priest's chamber was reached, the candle lighted, and the invalid carefully laid upon his bed, when a thundering knock upon the front door resounded through the house.

"It is danger!" exclaimed François: "they know of me, and they will perhaps do harm for you. Let me to them, and I will swear you know not that I here am."

"No, no, François! all will be well without that," replied Molly hurriedly. "Only keep very, very quiet, and, even if we come up here, make no noise unless you are actually discovered."

Then blowing out the candle, she went out, paused to arrange the pile of lumber a little more carefully, took a final view of every thing, hurried down stairs, and locked the door at the foot ; then, flying to the bedroom so lately vacated, stripped the clothes from the bed, and finally, running back to the front door, she unbolted and opened it. Upon the step stood Reuben Hetherford, and a man whom Molly remembered to have seen at the Corners, but whose name she did not know.

CHAPTER XVI.

THE SEARCH-WARRANT.

GOOD-MORNING, Mistress Mary Wilder," said the stranger, with grave politeness; for Reuben, like Judas Iscariot and other celebrated traitors, hung back in shame at the treason he yet was determined to effect.

"Good-morning, sir," replied the girl briefly: "may I ask your name and errand, an' it please you?"

"My name is John Dibley, and my errand to search for an escaped prisoner, suspected to be concealed in this house."

"And why should you so suspect, Master Dibley?" asked Mary, with a steady glance at Reuben, who, stung into speech by its contempt, hurriedly exclaimed, —

"There is no use in denying it, Molly. I saw last night, when I looked in at the kitchen window, — I saw you stoop over some one in the bed, and I saw a hand holding your dress as you turned away, and I heard a voice not yours."

"People who look in at windows and listen at keyholes are very apt to get their stories wrong," replied Molly calmly. "If you mistook my cat Tabitha for a Frenchman, and her white paw for a hand, and have brought Master Dibley over from the Corners this cold morning to arrest the poor puss, I can do no less than show her to him. — Master Dibley, if you will come in, I will lead you through every room in this house, and deliver up all the Frenchmen you may find. Master Reuben Hetherford shall keep watch on the outside, lest some of them escape ; or, if he prefers, he may stare in at the kitchen window. Inside the house I have my father's orders not to admit him."

Mr. Dibley looked foolish, but stepped inside the door, which Molly immediately shut and bolted.

"I — I — kind of brought Reuben along as a special constable — a — h " — stammered he.

Mary stopped, with the door of the parlor in her hand, and turned round upon him, while the morning light, streaming in from behind, seemed to magnify and irradiate her form, and touch the dusky lights of her coronal of hair into gleams of red gold, until she looked like a crowned queen scorning the invader of her realm.

"Do you know my father, Master Dibley?" asked she quietly.

"Yes, mistress : he is an honest and honorable man."

"And do you think he or his household would harbor those who were enemies of the colony, or of the king?"

"No, mistress ; and yet " —

"And do you know that I, one weak girl, am all alone in this house, keeping it safely until my parents shall return? and do you suppose it likely that I should admit and hide a Frenchman, or any other man, in their absence?"

"That is what I said to Reuben Hetherford. I said, says I "—

"But why did you come, then? And why, above all things, should you bring that man to help you, as special constable or any thing else? Don't you see, sir, that all he wanted was the chance to offer me this insult and slight? We two have quarrelled, after being troth-plight lovers; and that, as you may see for yourself, is reason enough for all this moil. I warrant, now, he asked you to make a special constable of him?"

"Well, yes, Mistress Mary, he did," confessed poor Dibley, glancing longingly at the front door; "and now that you tell me all this, I see that the youth has been too hasty, and I, perhaps, too ready to believe him. So I take your word that there is no one in the house but yourself, and "—

"Nay, nay, sir, you shall not do so! Since you and your special constable are here, and, it may be, a whole posse more in ambush round the house, you must e'en go through with it, and look at least into every room. I must tell my father, when he returns, that his daughter was cleared from the suspicion Reuben Hetherford has brought upon her."

"Nay, mistress, be not so angry. I comprehend the matter now, and I am fully satisfied "—

"So am not I, then, Master Dibley; and I do insist upon your following me. This is the parlor; and as you see, except in the drawers of that secretary, there is no place of concealment. Here is the kitchen; and there upon the hearth sits Tabitha, my companion and bed-fellow since my parents' departure. No doubt, Reuben Hetherford may have seen me bending over and petting her, and even seen her paw holding my dress; for we have been guilty of such follies in our loneliness, have we not, poor Tabitha? Here, then, is the bedroom; and I crave your pardon not to have arranged it more fittingly since I arose. I was not expecting company so soon. Here is the door of the cellar: and, I pray you, step a little carefully on these damp and rotten boards; my father has talked so long of mending them! Lo, you now! You have fallen, and I am afraid hurt your leg! Be careful, I beg; for the potato-hole is close beside you, and you may easily slip in."

"I have!" cried the unhappy constable, stumbling headlong into the little pit toward which Molly had artfully led him: "if you held your candle so that I could see, it were better than to give tardy warning of danger."

"Our cellar is but a dark and cramped place for a visitor," replied Molly meekly: "had I known that you were coming, I would have lighted it with more than this one poor candle. Here is father's cider-barrel, and here the pork, and here"—

But Mr. Dibley was already limping up the broken staircase, muttering his satisfaction; and, with a faint smile upon her lips, Molly followed him, and in spite of his resistance insisted upon conducting him upstairs, where she threw open the bedroom she usually occupied, the unfinished one opposite to it, and then laid her hand upon the garret door, saying, —

"Now, here is the garret door locked! But wait here, an' it please you, and I will look for the key. Surely mother would not have carried it to New Bedford with her, would she?"

"It is useless, it is quite useless, to look for it, Mary," exclaimed the constable, trying to prevent her from going down stairs: "I am quite and altogether satisfied, and have been so from the first."

"But so am not I, Master Dibley," persisted Molly, "I have been suspected of harboring enemies of my country; and I want you to be able to say that you have thoroughly searched this house, and found only Tabitha besides myself. I will go and look for the key; and, if I cannot find it, I will draw the staple, and so take off the lock."

As she spoke, she slipped past the reluctant constable, ran down the stairs, and into the kitchen, where she looked carefully around her, thought she distinguished Hetherford's figure outside the window, and for his edification began rummaging the drawers, boxes, shelves, and every sort of receptacle in the room. Suddenly she heard Dibley's heavy feet creeping down the stairs; and, snatching the key from the box where she was looking at that moment, she rushed out, and confronted him with it.

"At last, sir!" exclaimed she: "I have searched through all mother's boxes, and here it is. Now come up again, please, and we will look."

"If your garret is as grewsome an abode as your cellar, I do not believe even a Frenchman would hide there," said Dibley, smiling grimly; for Molly's bright

face and cheery tone made him ashamed of churl-
ishness.

"It is not much better," said she, unlocking and
throwing open the door: "I will go first to show you
where the loose boards are ; for, if you fell through, it
might prove a worse affair than the potato-pit.   This
way, please."

"Thank you, my dear child ; but I can see every
thing from here," replied Dibley with paternal kindness, and wholesome fear of the loose boards.   "That
is a lot of household stuff out of use, I suppose."

"Yes.   Shall I pull it down for you to see that
there is nothing behind it?"

"No, no, maiden: I am satisfied, I tell you.   I
could see if there were a mouse hidden in the place.
I can make my affidavit to have searched the house
from garret to cellar, more especially the cellar, and to
have found nought therein alive but one fearless
maid and one tortoise-shell cat."

"Yes, remember the cat above all, since she may
be the Frenchman Reuben Hetherford espied through
the window."

Chatting and laughing merrily, the two descended
the stairs, Molly locking the door behind her, and so
down to the front door. Upon the step waited Reuben
Hetherford as if he had never moved. Molly regarded him with cold and wrathful eyes ; and in spite
of his effort to slink behind florid Mr. Dibley, turning
to bid an apologetic good-by, she had a last word for
him : —

"My father will know how to thank you for this

good turn done to his house and daughter, Master Hetherford ; and be sure he shall know all your kindness so soon as he is at home."

Reuben made no reply, and the two departed. As the sound of their sleigh-bells died away, Molly locked the door, and, going into the kitchen, threw herself upon the settle in as near to a fainting condition as she had ever known. She did not cry, she did not moan, or laugh, or speak, only lay upon the wooden bench, white and still and mute as a snow image, all the life and warmth gone out of her, and only the sense of a terrible fatigue remaining. Tabitha, who had restlessly promenaded the kitchen for some time, looked up at her with eyes narrow in the morning sunshine for a few moments, then leaped softly upon the end of the bench, and walked carefully up the length of the recumbent figure until, reaching the head, she curled herself upon it for a nap. The contact roused Molly, who, smiling feebly, rose to her feet, saying, —

"I must not stay idling here, while he is making himself sick with anxiety. Come, Tabitha, let us go up."

CHAPTER XVII.

AND VALERIE?

ABOUT sunset the jingle of bells and the sound of voices announced the arrival of the travellers; and Molly, running to the door to receive them, was startled at seeing her mother, much muffled and covered with rugs, lying in the sleigh, with her husband holding her head upon his lap, and Amariah sitting on a firkin to drive, as the seat had been removed.

"What has happened? What is the matter with mother?" demanded she, running out into the snow, and peeping over the edge of the box-sleigh.

"Mother has a bad cold and a touch of rheumatism, — that is all," replied the father cheerily; while poor Deborah herself only moaned inarticulately. Amariah, however, was ready with his explanation : —

"She felt it her duty to ride on the outside of the stage-coach, and exhort some ribald fellows, who only laughed at her; and so got cold, and has a rheumatic fever to pay for it."

"Peace, Amariah!" exclaimed his master sternly. "When your opinion is wanted it will be asked; and meantime help me lift your mistress, and carry her into the house."

But this operation was a severe one; for the least

movement was so painful to the unfortunate woman, that she constantly begged her husband to abandon the attempt, and he as often complied, until at last Molly suggested lifting the blanket upon which she lay, and so bringing her in. This plan succeeded a little better; and in a few moments poor Deborah was laid in her own bed, and Molly was carefully and affectionately attending her. But, even in the midst of her sincere grief and care for her mother's sufferings, the young girl found time to note and smile a little at the odd fortune which in two successive days had given her two such diverse patients to attend in the same bed, and each so unconscious of the other's proximity. Diverse in every respect, as she soon found; for in proportion as François was gentle, patient, grateful, and cautious of letting his needs be known to his nurse, Mrs. Wilder was fractious, complaining, and requiring, so that when Molly at last came out to put the finishing touches to the meal her father had nearly prepared by himself, she looked so pale and tired that he said tenderly, —

"You are very weary, my child. You must have some one to help you, now that mother is laid by."

"Oh, no! thank you, father dear. I am very strong, you know, and after the first it will not be so hard."

"You do not look so very strong now, my lass," persisted the father, softly smoothing the nut-brown hair with his great palm. "It was too much for you to be so long alone, and so worried. Amariah told me of your falling-out with Reuben; and I heard over at the Corners of his malice in accusing you of harboring a Frenchman, and bringing Dibley here to search my house. Of a truth I shall have a word to say to friend Reuben."

"I was not frightened of John Dibley, father, and there is no harm done," said Molly with a gallant attempt at carelessness, as she met her father's steadfast eyes.

"No, you were not frightened, I well believe, my stout-hearted wench," replied he proudly. "But you were angered and shamed to have your discretion so called in question. They did not know my maid when they fancied she would harbor strange men unknown to her father, or willingly deceive him in any fashion."

As he spoke, Humphrey Wilder drew his daughter toward him, and tenderly kissed her brow. The caress was unwonted, and put the last touch to the tumult of emotion in the young girl's heart. Sinking upon her knees at her father's side, she burst into a passion of tears. It was the first time since she was a little child that he had seen her so moved ; and, pressing her head to his breast, he soothed and chid her as if she had still been one.

"Why, there, then, my moppet, what ails thee? Tell father all thy little troubles. Fie, fie ! thee shall not sob so, and spoil thy pretty eyes. What is it, child?"

"Nothing, father dear, nothing but — but I am so tired, and I have been so put about with all these things," sobbed Molly, clinging for a moment close to that great loving heart, never cold or silent to her, and then shrinking away with the remorseful consciousness that she was keeping a secret from the father who so entirely trusted her, and allowing him to accept a tacit denial of the charge so truly brought against her by Hetherford.

Remorse and shame dried the tears that tenderness had caused to flow ; and, wiping her eyes, Molly sprang to her feet, and hastily moved out of reach of the caressing hand whose touch seemed liked a brand of infamy to her excited mood.

"I have been growing nervous in this last week, I . am afraid, father," said she smiling wanly ; "but I shall try to do better now that you are at home."

"You are tired, child," replied her father tenderly, "and now get thee to bed and rest. I will do all that thy mother requires until morning. Sleep and rest, and waken my own bright-eyed little Molly."

Glad to escape the loving scrutiny of those calm eyes, Molly paid a short visit to her mother's bedside, saw that she was quite comfortable, and apparently almost asleep, and then retreated up-stairs to her own room. Waiting there some moments to make sure that her father would not summon her for some last message or charge, she blew out her candle, and, lighted only by the moonlight shining in through the window above the front door, unlocked the garret-door, and softly crept up the stairs. She found François awaiting her with eager curiosity ; for the sounds of the arrival, and of Mrs. Wilder's removal from the sleigh to the bedroom, had reached his retreat, but all without explanation. Moreover he had now become

so accustomed to the constant companionship of his
gentle nurse, and so interested in the conversations
they constantly kept up, that he had been very lonely
for some hours, and was disposed to be a little peevish in consequence.

Molly perceived the mood, and with ready tact
soothed it away by a few soft and half-caressing words
and touches, before she began the story of the arrival
and her mother's illness; which she narrated in the
detailed and minute style so comfortable to an invalid.

But the quick ear of the listener noticed a change
in the voice, a weariness in the manner, and a hidden
care in the look of the girl's face; and, when she had
finished all her little story, he took her hand in his,
and said, —

"And what else, sweet one?"

"What else, François? What do you mean?"

"Tell me what lies behind all this? The *arrière
pensée* we call it; and I know not how to say it in English, nor yet in our new language."

"Well, I will tell you, François!" exclaimed the girl
vehemently. "I cannot endure the idea of cheating
my father another moment. He has heard of the
search, and he said they did not know me if they
thought I would deceive him; and he looked into my
face, and my silence told him a lie if my tongue did
not. I never lied before since I was a little child;
and I feel so guilty, so mean, so base! François, I
cannot do it!"

She twisted her hands together, and clinched her
teeth to keep down the rising emotion. Not twice

in one day should such weakness master that calm and assured mind ; not twice in one day should man look upon Mary Wilder's tears. A brief silence ensued, and then François coldly asked, —

" And what do you intend to do, mademoiselle ? "

" To tell my father that you are here, and trust to his good heart and discretion. That is, I should do so if I only thought of my own wishes ; but I promised you that I would not tell any one."

" You did promise so, and I believed you."

" Believe me still, then ; for I have not betrayed you by word, or look, or silence."

" You are only preparing to do so."

" Not without your leave, François. I cannot take back or break my promise if you hold me to it ; but you will not be so cruel, will you ? "

" Oh ! rest content, mademoiselle : I hold you to nothing that your so sensitive conscience holds wrong. Betray me if you will, and as soon as you will. I dare say the jails are comfortable enough in your little town of Boston ; and I may be exchanged, or the war may cease, before I am very old. Go and call the respectable Monsieur Wilder as fast as possible, I pray you."

And, awaiting this event, François threw himself over upon his other side, with small care for his broken arm, and lay with his back to Molly, silent and forbidding, as if counting her already an enemy.

She sat very still, and looked at him ; the feeble light of the candle showing the wan whiteness of her face, the brightness of her fixed eyes, and the hands so tightly clasped upon her knee. Three long minutes ticked themselves away upon the watch hanging at the head of the bed; and François, unable to endure the utter silence, threw himself back into his former position, looked keenly at the statuesque figure beside him, and mockingly asked, —

"What! not gone yet, mademoiselle?"

"You are wrong and cruel to treat me so, François!" exclaimed Molly, in a voice sharpened by pain and the sense of wrong: "I have not showed myself so weak or so treacherous as you seem to wish to think me."

"It is needless to remind me of my obligations to you, mademoiselle. I am crushed beneath their weight already, and only wish there were a possible way of repaying them."

"And you think I am taunting you with your obligations, as you call them?" exclaimed Molly in a tone perilously near contempt: "how little you know me, and I thought we were so well acquainted! A traitor, a liar, and mean enough to recall my own services to one willing to forget them! Can I do any thing for you before going down stairs?"

"To call your father?"

Molly turned away with no reply but a look of indignant reproach; and François caught her dress.

"Stay, Marie! You can do something for me."

"What is it? Do not hold my dress, please."

"You can forgive me. I have been cruel and unjust; I have tortured you who are so kind and patient with me; I have been unmanly, childish, I know not what. But it is you who have spoiled me; no one, not my mother, not any one, has been to me as you have been; and I repay you thus! Say that you forgive me, Marie."

"Yes, I forgive you," said Molly wearily.

"Not that way, not so coldly and sadly! Give the bad child the child's kiss of forgiveness here upon his brow; ah, do! sweet Marie!"

"No, François! you are not a child, and I cannot treat you as one,—not in that way, at any rate."

"Then treat me as a man, and kiss me because I love you, Marie, darling Marie, my Marie!"

He seized her hand, and tried to draw her toward him. She did not struggle or resist, only standing in all her calm stateliness of form, looking down upon him, she said in quiet scorn,—

"And Valerie?"

CHAPTER XVIII.

DR. SCHWARZ.

THE next morning, when Molly at length succeeded in finding time and opportunity to carry up her patient's breakfast without observation, she found him grave, courteous, and rather formal.

She had expected eager questioning as to her possession and knowledge of the name she had used at their last interview, and whose sound had so astonished him then that he had let her go without another word; but, instead of this questioning, she found herself confronted by a certain polished reserve, that air of high breeding at once the most intangible and the most effective of weapons, in the hands of those who have the right to employ it.

But Molly, in her way, was as proud as our friend the baron in his, and, replying to his polite speeches as politely, she performed her wonted services with her usual faithfulness and dainty nicety; and, in setting aside some portion of the breakfast to serve as lunch, remarked that she might not be able to come up again before the noontide dinner, as she should be busy with her mother in all the time possible to spare from the house.

"I am truly grieved to be so much trouble," replied

François courteously, " but I trust it will not be for very long. I think I shall attempt my escape to-night or the next night. My arm requires attention which I cannot give it, and it is as well to risk imprisonment as the loss of a limb, and perhaps death."

If he thought to startle her out of her calm by either of these announcements, he did not succeed; perhaps her pale face grew a little paler, her quiet voice a little more calm, but she only said, —

" I am indeed grieved that your arm is worse. A doctor is coming this morning to see my mother, and if you choose to trust him " —

" A thousand thanks ! Will you permit me to remind you of my wish for absolute secrecy? "

" I only mentioned the matter. I did not intend to do any thing without your permission."

" Then if you will be so very good as to do nothing at all ! "

" Certainly. I must leave you now. Good-morning."

" *Au revoir*, mademoiselle."

And as Molly closed the door at the foot of the stairs, and turned the key, her prisoner said to himself, —

" Valerie de Rochenbois would never make so stately a *dame du château* as this country girl. François, *le baron de-rien-de-tout*, is not the idiotic pride of birth washed out of you by all these waters? "

Entering the kitchen with her little tray of dishes, Molly was met by her father, hastily coming in at the porch door, but apparently too much absorbed in his own errand to notice that of his daughter, whom he eagerly accosted.

"Here is the doctor, Molly, to see thy mother. It is not the man I sent for to New Bedford, for he was away, as Friend Haslow writes to me; but another, very good also. He is a Dutchman, and his name is Schwarz, Peter Haslow says. Here he is."

The stamping of snowy feet upon the step announced that Dr. Schwarz had followed his host from the barn, where their first interview had taken place, and where he had lingered to watch Amariah's attentions to his horse, whose wet coat and heaving sides told that he had travelled long and vigorously. Molly regarded him with some curiosity; for she could have counted upon the fingers of one hand all the strangers who ever had come beneath that roof since her remembrance, and this Dutch doctor seemed not the least peculiar among them. A tall, stout figure, muffled in many coats, capes, and comforters, a mass of sandy hair floating upon the shoulders, and mingling with a shaggy beard of the same color, a monstrous pair of green glasses: these were her first impressions of the new doctor, who, in answer to Wilder's greeting and presentation to his daughter, replied in fluent but strongly accented English, —

"I kiss your hands, dear mees. Is the lady your mamma no better yet?"

"No better, I am afraid," returned Molly, glancing at the speaker in some surprise, and wondering if the German-English was always so like the French-English, to which she had grown accustomed. "Will you come in and see her now?"

"Directly, dear mees. May I take off the coats first, here at the fire?"

The coats removed, the doctor warmed his thin, dark hands before the blaze, casting curious glances about him, from behind the green goggles, as Molly rather felt than saw.

"Now, then, we are ready, if you please," said Dr. Schwarz suddenly; and Molly led the way into the bedroom, where the invalid was eagerly expecting him. Standing silently beside her mother, the girl listened intelligently to the clear questioning, the rapid conclusions, the assured diagnosis, of the new physician, and settled in her own mind that here was a very different, a much more advanced, practitioner than Dr. Crake at the Corners, or even Dr. Pilsbury, the magnate of New Bedford, for whom her father had sent before arriving at home.

"It is rheumatic fever that attacks your mother, mees, and danger of the lungs also," said the doctor, rising from his seat beside the bed, and leading the way into the kitchen, where Humphrey Wilder impatiently awaited his verdict.

"Danger of inflammation of the lungs, do you mean?" asked he, catching the last words.

"Yes, my friend. She should be watched for the next two days or so, very carefully."

"By a doctor, do you mean, sir?" asked Molly.

"Precisely, mees. It may save a life to her, to receive certain remedies in season."

"And cannot you remain with us for the space of two days?" asked Wilder anxiously. "I will pay you any thing in reason for your time and pains."

Dr. Schwarz hesitated, coughed violently, and walked to the window and back. Molly, watching him attentively, asked herself what motive this utter stranger could have for playing a part among simple country-folk, not rich enough to attract cupidity, and with no secrets in their lives worth any man's investigation; and yet some instinct of her nature warned her that this man had entered her father's house with a purpose other than the avowed one, and that, in spite of his apparent reluctance, he had every intention of remaining. The suspicion was confirmed when he turned around, and, looking at her, said to her father, —

"Well, yes, Master Wilder, as they call you, I will see the good wife past her danger. I am not in practice anywhere, so am not tied; but in passing from New Amsterdam, where I live, to Boston, I staid at New Bedford, and introduced myself to your Dr. Pilsbury there. I cannot go back to New Bedford and here again: so, if you wish it much, I will remain two days and nights."

"We shall esteem it a great favor, truly," said Wilder calmly. "Molly, you can prepare a bed for Dr. Schwarz, can you not? Perhaps in the parlor."

"He shall have my room up-stairs, father," said Molly quietly; "but you had better make a fire in the parlor, where he may sit meanwhile."

"Not so, not so, my friends," interposed the doctor hurriedly: "I shall go to walk directly. I have a passion for the country and the open air. I shall see as much of it as possible while my patient needs me not. No parlor, no fire, no seclusion, for me, if you please. In the house I shall find myself most happy in the sickroom, or here in this admirable kitchen."

"Sit here, then, in my armchair, friend, and tell me how you of New Amsterdam like to become Englishmen," said Wilder heartily; and, as the two men settled to masculine talk, Molly went quietly around the room preparing dinner, attending upon her mother, and listening to every word, and watching every motion, of the mysterious stranger.

"He may be Dutch, but he understands French," said she to herself, as she caught a "*Pardieu!*" unconsciously let slip in the heat of discussion.

The midday meal was served and eaten; and Dr. Schwarz, after a brief visit to this patient, declared his intention of taking a long walk, and proceeded to muffle himself accordingly. Molly watched him with the same quiet attention she had bestowed upon all his movements, and was a little startled when he suddenly turned upon her, as her father preceded him out of the door, to ask, —

"Well, and what do you think of the doctor from New Amsterdam?"

"I have not yet made up my mind, sir," replied the girl, in her grave, unmoved manner.

"Take advice, then, my charming mees, take advice upon him," muttered the doctor as he passed her; but Molly breathlessly detained him, while she demanded, —

"What do you mean, sir? Advice of whom? Of my mother?"

"Not so much of her, perhaps, as of those who have seen the world, who know how a Dutch doctor should appear; who — how should I know? A young lady has always a friend of whom she takes advice."

He went out as he spoke, leaving Molly in a bewilderment of doubt, hope, fear, hesitation.

"At any rate, I must take François his dinner," said she to herself; and, first seeing that her mother was comfortably settled for a possible nap, she hastened to arrange the dainty bits reserved from the family repast upon her little tray, covered with a clean napkin, and carried them to her prisoner.

He met her with a conciliatory smile, and, taking the tray from her hands, laid it down, saying, —

"It is not to eat that I am in haste, but to see you, my Marie stern and sweet."

"And I have news for you; but I cannot stay many minutes, for my father will be coming in, and my mother may need me," replied Molly, replying with her eyes to the tender smile and the loving words. "Do you know Dr. Schwarz?"

"*Le docteur Schwarz?* No; and I hope he knows not of me."

"I think he does, or at least suspects." And then Molly, in her clear, brief style, related all the events of the morning, not forgetting her impressions, the French exclamation, and the mysterious counsel given by the doctor as he left the house.

François listened to all attentively, and, when the story was finished, remained for many moments silent, his head between his hands in his favorite attitude of reflection: at last he said, —

"You are always right, dear Marie. This man is a spy; one of two: first, a friendly spy, who looks for me to do me well; next, an enemy spy, who would prison me for twenty dollars. Either it is one whom I know would look for me if he were himself free, or it is one sent by this Ayterfor"—

"Hetherford, François."

"*Eh, bien!* it is all one; but it may be of him, and it may be—well, and what next, my Marie?"

"That is what I want to ask you. I have arranged that he shall sleep in my room, and the door of that is close to the foot of these stairs: now, cannot we contrive that you should see him as he comes up the stairs?"

"Surely, surely, and yet—say to me one time again, how does he look?"

And as Molly patiently recapitulated the description of the stranger's odd physique and costume, François, listening attentively, shook his head.

"Still it may be a disguise," said he in French, and then, seizing Molly's hand, continued to her,—

"Now, see, dear little one. You give me the key: I go down, and sit on steps at the door inside. This man come up, and I hear his talk with—will it be you?"

"My father, I suppose," said Molly, blushing a little.

"True, true, your father. Well, the risk is the more, but no matter. I shall look, and I shall listen: if it is my man, it is well; if not, no harm. You understand all this, *cherie?*"

"Yes, François; and if it is a friend he will help you to leave us," said Molly heavily.

"If it is he I hope, he will do me good to my arm," suggested François; and Molly's face grew bright and hopeful, as he had fancied it would.

150   *A NAMELESS NOBLEMAN.*

"Yes, François; and if it is a friend he will help you to leave us," said Molly heavily.

"If it is he I hope, he will do me good to my arm," suggested François; and Molly's face grew bright and hopeful, as he had fancied it would.

CHAPTER XIX.

LOYALISM AND LOYOLAISM.

IN the barn Dr. Schwarz found, as he had expected, Amariah, diligently doing nothing; and, slipping a bit of silver into his hand, said cordially, —

"Come now, my fine fellow, and show me the walk I ought to take."

"Thank'y, sir. Why had you ought to take a walk?"

"That's another thing; and you have not studied physic, have you?"

"Well, I dunno."

"It is British and it is rustic to ask questions, and to evade replies; but nevertheless I wish to walk, and, if you are the good fellow I think, you will show me the way."

"Oh, well! I don't mind a walk, though you couldn't well miss of the way so long as you saw this house, or Hetherford's over there."

And Amariah, who had lounged to the door of the barn, nodded toward the snow-covered roof and stone chimney mentioned as the only ones in sight. The doctor regarded them attentively through his green goggles.

"And that is Hetherford's, is it?" asked he. "And

who is Hetherford himself?   Let us walk that way as
well as any other."

"All right, master," replied Amariah placidly; and
as the pair strolled along the snowy track the old
fellow, who dearly loved the sound of his own voice,
gave his attentive listener a brief sketch of Reuben
Hetherford's history, including his futile courtship of
Molly, and his revengeful attempt to annoy and
mortify her by bringing a constable to search the
house while she remained alone in it.

"Frenchmen!" interrupted the doctor at this point.
"But are there, then, Frenchmen about here?"

"Sho!   You must have seen 'em, or leastways heard
tell of 'em in New Bedford!" exclaimed Amariah
sceptically.   "Why, it was town's talk there."

"Well, but New Bedford is not here.   What has
been seen of them here?" asked the doctor; and
Amariah, nothing loath, told of the footsteps beside the
well, of the disturbance of the hay, and of the knife
or dagger in Reuben Hetherford's possession.

"Now, but that is curious if true," said Dr.
Schwarz.   "Is not that the man going to his barn
now?"

"Yes, that's him.   Want to see him?"

"Oh, no! it is as well to hear your story as to hear
it from him; and yet — yes, let us turn in and speak
to him a little.   Say that I am the Dutch doctor of
New Amsterdam who cures your mistress.   I cannot
speak so good as you, friend Amariah."

"That's a fact," replied Amariah complacently.   "I
never see a Dutchman that could, and I've seen as

many as half a dozen in my day. You talk as good as any of 'em."

"Yes, we all talk the same, I know," replied Dr. Schwarz, with a little inward chuckle ; and then they entered the barn, and Amariah repeated his lesson very faithfully. Reuben received the stranger civilly, having already heard of his arrival, and was easily led into talk of the late shipwreck, the escape of some of the prisoners, and his own attempt at their recapture. Dr. Schwarz listened admiringly, contriving by artful questions or remarks to draw out all of information or rumor that Hetherford had to give.

"These French ! these French !" exclaimed he at length, as the well began to give token of going dry under such diligent pumping. "They have forever been the enemies of the Dutch, and more than ever now that our stadt-holder has married your princess, and Holland and England are one, and France the enemy of both. Oh, I know them, I know them well, the murderous villains ! Why, they are not content to kill a man outright, but needs must poison their swords and daggers, so that even a scratch, ever. to grasp the handle in your warm palm, is death by torture. Oh ! I have seen it, I have known it in my own country."

"Sho ! You don't say !"

"There, now ! Listen to that !" exclaimed Reuben and Amariah in one breath, as they pallidly stared into each other's eyes.

"I told you I found that knife in Wilder's barn," faltered Reuben ; but Amariah's fright was not sufficient to allow this statement to pass unquestioned.

"No, you didn't find it, nuther!" exclaimed he. "I found it, and you took it away from me; and now, if you've got pizened along of it, I dunno as I'm to blame."

"Well, I don't want it any longer. You can have it back as soon as you like," said Reuben miserably. "And I hope no harm's done yet. Could you tell if you saw it, doctor, whether it was poisoned, or not?"

"That depends, my friend. There are poisons and poisons, you know. I have studied these matters very much, but I cannot always be sure. Show me, and I will tell you."

"All right. I've got it here in my drawer." And Reuben, going to a rude standing desk where he was in the habit of keeping account of his hay and other crops, unlocked it, and produced the dagger we first have seen in the gardens of Montarnaud. As the eyes of Dr. Schwarz fell upon it, he made a slight movement of impatience, and extended his hand; then checking himself, said carelessly, —

"Yes, it is French. I see that at first."

"Well, look at it close, and tell, if you can, whether it is poisoned," insisted Reuben, pressing it into his hand. The doctor scrutinized it solemnly for some time, blade, hilt, and especially the wavy lines arabesqued upon its surface.

"Ha! Do you see those words, my friend?" exclaimed he suddenly, thrusting the dagger under Hetherford's eyes, and pointing excitedly to the half-obliterated Latin motto beneath the crest of the Montarnauds.

"I thought that was writing, but I couldn't quite make it out," said Reuben, trying to look wise, and only looking scared.

"Probably you do not read Arabic," suggested Dr. Schwarz considerately.

"Well, no, I don't know as I do."

"Then of course you would not read here, as I do, 'I carry the message of the cobra.' That means that the blade is so imbued with the venom of the deadliest serpent of India, that its merest scratch is certain death. And you, unhappy man, have had it lying in that desk among loose papers, and I know not what! How can you be sure that you are not already wounded?"

"Wounded!" shrieked Reuben, minutely surveying his red and callous hands; "I don't see any thing, but—here, you look, doctor!"

"First, let me put this evil thing out of harm's way," replied Dr. Schwarz, carefully folding the dagger in a handkerchief. "You do not want any thing more to do with it, I presume?"

"Ludamassy, no! Here, what's this on my left thumb? ain't it a wownd?"

"Why—yes, it does look like one. Does it burn and sting with sharp thrills of pain?"

"I—don't—know. I never thought about it till now."

"I dare say you will feel it to-night; and if you do you must wrap it in a poultice of rye-meal, with an onion outside it, and keep it very warm until morning. I don't believe it is poison; but, if it should be, that will be the best thing to do: nothing will do much good, I am afraid."

"Oh, Jehoakim!   A pretty night's rest I'll get, watching for my death, may be," groaned poor Reuben, as pale as death, and already grasping his scratched thumb with despairing energy.

"But I hope it is not of the dagger that you are hurt," suggested the doctor, already upon his way to the door, having achieved his errand.   "I shall hear in the morning from our good Amariah that you are quite well, I hope; and I will carry away the dagger, and destroy it in a way that none but *medicos* understand.   It is not safe to leave it in the world."

"I don't want to see the hateful thing again, nor I don't suppose Amariah does, either: do you, 'Riah?" asked Reuben, gazing at his thumb.

"Well, I'd like to try it onto a fox, or a woodchuck, or some of them vermin.   I'd like to see how it works," replied Amariah meditatively; but the doctor indignantly turned upon him in the interests of humanity, —

"What! you desire to torture some poor innocent creature, and see him die in agony for your own curiosity!   Now, fie upon you, Amariah!   I had thought better things of you!   No: I shall destroy the dagger so soon as I come at the means, and it shall not do more harm to nobody in this world."

Silenced, if not convinced, Amariah followed his guest, who, already satisfied with the walk he had so clamorously demanded, was striding down the snowy road toward the Wilder farm.

CHAPTER XX.

THE DOCTOR PROBES A LITTLE.

AMARIAH ! It is time you were milking ! " called Humphrey Wilder's placid voice from the barn as the two men approached ; and Mr. Coffin, nonchalantly obeying the summons, left the doctor to proceed to the house alone. Coming in from the dull and chilly twilight of out-of-doors, the kitchen with its clean-swept hearth, brilliant fire, and odor of cleanliness, looked a little paradise of content ; and Tabitha seated squarely in the middle of the rug before the fire, her shoulders up to her ears, her eyes half closed, her paws tremulously sheathing and unsheathing their claws in the fulness of her delight, seemed the ruling genius of the place.

Dr. Schwarz stood looking about him with a smile for some moments, and then throwing aside his wraps, approached the fire, saying, —

" A poor shipwrecked fellow might be very well contented here, to be sure."

The door toward the front of the house hastily opened, and Molly Wilder entered softly and swiftly ; but at sight of the motionless figure beside the fire hesitated slightly, and colored a little. The keen observer behind the green goggles smiled also.

"I have startled you! You thought to find the room empty as you left it. You were careful not to make a noise to let the mother hear you," said he quietly.

Molly regarded him uneasily, and made no reply. The doctor smiled again, and followed her to the other end of the room.

"Have you taken my advice?" asked he softly.

"What advice, sir?"

"I advised you to seek help in forming an opinion of me, me, myself: I advised you to describe all that I say and do, me, the queer Dutch Dr. Schwarz, late of Leyden, Holland, and see what one thinks of me."

"I — I do not understand," stammered Molly.

"Fie, now, my dear young lady! that is not worthy of such honest eyes, and so brave a mouth! See, I will tell you a secret if you will keep it for me."

"I do not know that I ought to keep it."

"Yes. It harms no one; it concerns no one but me, and another, and perhaps you a little."

"I will try to keep it."

"I trust you. See this dagger!"

He suddenly drew it from his pocket, and laid it upon the dresser against which she leaned. Mary flushed scarlet with surprise, but said nothing, nor offered to touch it.

"You have seen that before?" asked Schwarz.

"Never."

"But it was your servant who found it in this barn."

"I know that he did, but I never saw it."

"Truly! Well, this knife belongs to a dear friend

of mine who is lost. I am here to search for him; since, by some stories I heard at New Bedford, I judge that he is somewhere here concealed. Now, I ask nobody to betray a secret they have promised to keep. As I trust you now, so he may have trusted you; and you would be burned alive sooner than betray a trust. See how I read your face! But still if that man, my friend, knew that I am here, knew that I am ready to carry him away to a place of safety, he would be very glad. If one could find him, and place this dagger in his hands, and say, ' The friend who once before brought you this, now sends it to you, and is waiting, as he waited then, to help you,' — if one could say that to this man, I think it would be doing him good service."

Without a word, but with a long and steady look into the face so near her own, Molly took up the dagger, wrapped it again in the doctor's handkerchief, and placed it in her pocket.

"Molly! Molly! Where's that man? I feel a deal worse," cried the invalid from the bedroom.

"Here, madam, and coming so soon as the hands are duly warmed," replied Schwarz, returning to the fire; but Mary detained him.

"Are you really a doctor?" demanded she sternly: "you are not surely daring to trifle with my mother's life!"

"No, no, good child, a thousand times no," replied the stranger warmly: " I am not indeed a physician by diploma; but I have studied much in helping my friend to study, for he is truly an accomplished physician, and I am utterly competent to cure the excellent mother. — Now, madam, I come."

CHAPTER XXI.

THE JOY OF MEETING.

SEATED beside his patient's bed, and gravely listening to all her maundering complaints, Dr. Schwarz nevertheless saw and heard with a smile of good-humored malice Molly's quiet exit from the kitchen, and made himself so agreeable to her mother that the good lady never remembered to peevishly call, "Molly, Molly, I say! What is thee about?" as she had done nearly every five minutes of her waking hours since she had been ill.

By and by the door opened as quietly as it had closed, and Molly's light step was heard moving about the kitchen, in attendance to her ordinary duties. Dr. Schwarz wound up his rambling description of the manners of Dutch mothers very briefly, and, strolling into the outer room, placed himself in the young girl's way with an air of expectation; but she surveyed him with calm and abstracted gaze, and when he ventured softly to·say, "Well, what of the dagger, my child?" she sweetly and innocently replied,—

"Oh! I have just put it safely away. Did you want it again so soon?"

"No, no, but"—

"Yes, mother! Excuse me, sir, but my mother calls."

Nor could the doctor find another moment for private speech with this artless and simple young creature from that moment until about nine o'clock, when Humphrey Wilder, after fully enjoying a prodigious gape, said to his guest, —

"When you would like to go up-stairs, doctor, I will show you your bedroom."

"Now, if you please, directly," exclaimed the doctor with much alacrity: "I will but say good-night to my patient, and leave her in your hands until the morning, unless some change occurs. The baths of hot spirit may be continued" —

"That reminds me, Molly," interposed her father, "to ask how you could have disposed of more than half that case-bottle of strong waters? I got your little billet by Amariah, asking me to fetch some more, and I did so, but" —

"Hush, dear father! Do not worry mother with hearing of these domestic mishaps," murmured Molly, laying her hand upon her father's lips, and coloring a little angrily as she felt the keen eyes of Dr. Schwarz steadfastly regarding her through the odious green goggles.

"A mishap! What! did you spill it?" persisted Wilder, whose mind was of that honest order which, not entertaining many ideas at once, does full justice to each as it comes forward.

"Why, after a fashion, yes, father," said Molly, with a short laugh. "But no more on't now, I pr'ythee; for our guest is waiting, and I would look once more to his lodging before he goes up-stairs."

"I doubt not that all is well prepared already, maiden, but perhaps there is some final touch that might not be given until the moment of my appearing on the scene, so in God's name go and give it; and if, like a fortress, you have a signal, a watchword for the night, let it be for this time, 'An old friend!' Say that, as you make those last preparations up-stairs, and all will go well."

During this somewhat mysterious speech Wilder had obeyed a summons from his wife, who desired a pillow raised a trifle, and then replaced exactly as it was before, and now stood, candle in hand, patiently waiting while Molly fled up the stairs swift as a young deer, and the doctor went to pay his parting visit to his patient.

"All is ready now, father," announced the girl, re-entering the room, her cheeks lightly colored by some strong emotion, but her eyes fearless and bright as they met the doctor's shrewd gaze, while, with the courtesy of that age, he raised her hand to his lips in saying good-night.

"A brave girl, an heroic girl, fit to be the wife of a noble, and the mother of heroes — if the noble only thought so," muttered the doctor, following his host up-stairs, and on the landing pausing to look keenly about him, and say aloud, —

"You have quite a large house, Master Wilder; many rooms not always in use, I perceive."

As the accents of his sonorous voice resounded through the silent spaces about him, the door of the garret stairway opened silently a very little way, and an eager eye peeped out. Schwarz saw it, and said nothing: Wilder did not see it, and, going forward into the bedroom, complacently replied, —

"Why, yes, it is a pretty good house, doctor. You see, when we built, nigh twenty years ago, Molly was a baby, and we hoped that God would send us more children; so we framed the house to accommodate them. But He did not see fit so to do; and we have never finished more than this, which is Molly's bedroom. But when she marries our neighbor, Reuben Hetherford, he is to come here to live; and they will finish off the other rooms, and inhabit them. That is, always, if God so wills."

"But this Hetherford is a mean fellow, and a coward," objected the doctor. "It is he who brought the constable to search thy house and insult thy daughter. I heard of his boastings and threats in the matter, and of the knife he had found, and all the silly story, before I came to Falmouth."

"I know, friend, I know," replied Wilder with a slow and puzzled look upon his honest face. "That is a matter to inquire into, and verily I am prompted by nature to be exceeding wrathful; but this marriage is a matter long settled, and Deborah, my wife, has set her mind upon it, and when her mind is set she does not often give up her way; and"—

"But, friend, every man should be master of his own house, and every father should guide his own child; and surely you never will allow your wife to sacrifice this fine girl to a wretched little spy, who— But we shall speak more of this to-morrow if you will:

it is too cold to keep you standing here ; so good-night, my worthy host, good-night."

"Good-night, friend.   It is but a cheerless room surely ; and yet my little Molly sleeps here the winter through."

"Then I should be ashamed to speak of the cold," said the doctor, smiling grimly ; and candle in hand he followed his host to the landing-place, saw him well down the stairs, heard the door into the kitchen close, and then without looking round he said aloud, —

"So the *mot d'ordre* for the night is ' An old friend,' and the countersign should be " —

"Constant and true," replied a voice close behind him, and the next moment the friends were locked in each other's arms.

"Have a care, *mon baron*, or this stupid candle will set thy curls on fire ! " exclaimed the abbé, whom we will no longer thinly disguise as Dr. Schwarz ; and a mutual laugh relieved the emotion which with two women would have dissolved in tears.

"Have a care yourself, *mon abbé*, or they will hear us ! " whispered François. " Let us go into your room : for, if the invalid ·should be worse, they might come to seek the doctor, and you can hide me away ; but if you were up-stairs in my priest's chamber " —

"Then it was up-stairs that you were hidden all the time," interrupted the abbé. " Come, my son, let us get into the bed, and cover all but our noses ; then, while they are slowly freezing, we will relate and listen to every thing. This frightful cold congeals my very ideas."

"And yet you are tolerably protected : even the top of your head and your chin are covered with more than their natural thatch," laughed François, plucking at the tow-colored wig and beard. "I never cherished very profound regard for thy nose before ; but, truly, I am compelled to love it now, for it is the only morsel of thy real face left uncovered."

"If it will make thee happier, thou shalt see the whole," replied the abbé, pulling off wig, beard, and goggles, and displaying his own close-cut black hair, well-shaven chin, and dark Provençal eyes.

"Ah, that is better!" exclaimed his pupil, attentively regarding him by the light of the flickering candle. "Why, abbé, thou art a comely fellow, now that I look at thee closely. I never noted it before."

"I can believe it," returned the abbé in gentle sarcasm. "Thou hast been so occupied in admiring thyself, thou hast had no eyes for me until now."

"Would not one think we were two girls fresh from our two convents, instead of men who have oftener faced death than the looking-glass?" laughed the baron ; and then the two friends, without disrobing, hid themselves from the freezing atmosphere, beneath the mountain of home-spun blankets and woollen comforters with which Molly had piled the bed.

"And now, friend, for thy story first," said François affectionately. "And, to begin with, where didst thou find thy disguise?"

"The wig and beard were bought for last carnival-time in Rome, and the coats and mufflers from a worthy trader in this fair land," replied the abbé complacently. . "When we packed our mails to leave the Holy City, I put up the wig and beard, thinking another carnival might find us poorer than we then were, and less able to buy the means of amusing ourselves. I did not think they would serve in so merry a frolic as we had the other night, with the ice-cold waves on one hand, and these blood-thirsty, or rather dollar-thirsty, provincials on the other. Well, to go back to the time when we reached Ghent, and found that the Dutch, instead of our dear allies, had become our sworn enemies, and joined themselves with our hereditary foes the English : you remember how you said that, although you never would set foot in France again, you would go to the other side of the world and fight her battles ; and so we attached ourselves to the poor ' *Vainqueur*,' so terribly vanquished by the winds and waves of Buzzard's Bay, as they call the gulf where we were wrecked. You being ranked as surgeon, and I as chaplain, we each were allowed our luggage ; and I brought along the Roman chest without unpacking it. When, out here, the captain quietly told us that the ship was unmanageable, and, if we escaped death among the rocks toward which we drifted, we had the cheering prospect of a prison or a platoon from the natives, who, like all colonists, were more bitter in the quarrel of their mother-country than she was herself, you will remember that we went down to our stateroom to select such matters as would serve us best if we arrived on shore alive. You took your dagger, your silver spoon and fork, your dressing-case, and some clean linen ; I took all the money remaining to us, or, rather, to you " —

"It is all the same thing, my dear abbé, go on," —

"My breviary and this wig, for I rapidly reasoned thus : We two are not to be drowned yet, I feel it : we are then to be prisoners ; if so, we are to escape ; after escape, nothing is more necessary than a good disguise ; here it is, *allons donc !* and I put it in the pocket of my breeches.   You see, my baron?"

"I see.   And then?"

"And then the ' *Vainqueur* ' went to pieces among the rocks, and some of us saw you swimming like a merman toward a little cove, and hoped you reached land safely ; but just then our captors came off in boats, and picked us who remained undrowned off the wreck, agreeably mentioning, in some barbarous imitation of French, that we were prisoners, and would be shot if we attempted an escape.   I am, as you know, a priest, and not a soldier ; so I submitted with such grace as I might, but was careful not to let it be discovered that I spoke English, lest I should become important enough to be looked after more closely than the rest.   Happily, no one betrayed me ; and our captors evidently did not think a slender, beardless fellow, in half a shirt and black breeches, very much of a prize, and did not even search me. We were taken to some log-cabins and mud-walls called a fort, and waited there several days, while a man rode to Boston and back for orders ; and while they searched the country for you and two or three other poor fellows who swam toward shore, and may or may not be drowned or beaten to death upon those accursed rocks.

"Finally, four days ago, they marched us out *en route* for Boston, their principal village or town, I believe; and on the road I succeeded in giving them the slip, and hid in a barn, and behind hay-ricks, and in the woods, until the search for me was over, and the convoy passed on. Before this I had bought a coat and a muffler of a countryman, in whose house we stopped to rest on the first day; and now, after all was quiet, I came boldly out into the road, having first, you understand, assumed my disguise, and took my route for this place."

"What! Running back to the prison you had just escaped?"

"Running back to the friend who would not have deserted me, had the cases been reversed."

"It is true, it is equal. None the less, I thank you heartily. Go on, if you please."

"Well, I came to a town wherein stood a tavern, and to the tavern I boldly betook myself; and, being questioned with the solemn impertinence characterizing these savages, I replied that I was a Dutchman of New Amsterdam, named Schwarz; and, being demanded my profession, I said physician for want of a better."

"'Oh! going to visit Humphrey Wilder's wife,' suggested the landlord, who headed the inquisitorial tribunal. I nodded solemnly, and waited to hear more, for a whole chorus of women broke in; and, by good use of my ears, I soon found that this goodman Wilder and his wife had passed through the place in the morning, she very ill and he very scared, and that he had mentioned sending to New Bedford, a place some forty miles from here, as I understand, for a physician ; and then they again demanded of me if I were coming in his place. At a hazard I inquired, —

"'Did not Master Wilder mention the consultation of physicians to be held over his wife's case?'

"'No ; but I dare say Dr. Pilsbury does in his letter,' says my landlady, producing a letter from her pocket.

"'Oh, there is a letter!' exclaimed I, holding out my hand so confidently that she put it into it at once ; and I as unhesitatingly pocketed it, saying, 'I will go over to Wilder's directly, then, and carry the letter myself; for, since my brother Pilsbury has written, he will not come at once.'

"The argument was unanswerable to the slow bucolic mind, and although my landlady gasped a little she did not object : and I at once proceeded to hire a sleigh and horse, averring that I had left the stage-coach a mile or so from the town, for the purpose of visiting a friend ; but, as three mouths opened to require the name of this friend and a description of his house, I stopped them by demanding in turn the details of some hints I had heard thrown out in the Wilder matter, and, above all, what they had to do with the French prisoners of whom I had heard, and upon whom I expended a good Hollandische oath or two ; for, you know, hatred of the French is at this moment the strongest bond of union between the Dutch and English.

"Then I heard the whole story of this rascal Hetherford's suspicions and discoveries, and of his calling upon the law to aid him; and then the constable himself, who drank a grog there at the moment, told his part of the story; and from the whole I easily understood that you were actually hidden here, and that this good girl with the calm, strong face was concealing you. Then, for the first time, I resolved to come to this house to see the sick woman. Before that, I had no further intention than to secure a vehicle and some pretence for driving round the country, in hopes of coming upon you in some way. But all this Hetherford and constable matter made it very easy for a man trained in the Seminary to understand the whole plot in an instant, especially when I gathered that Mademoiselle Marie was all alone in the house for several days, and also nights, after our shipwreck.

"So, making a long story short, I opened and read good Dr. Pilsbury's letter of regrets that he could not come, and at the bottom wrote, in an excellent imitation of his crabbed script, a postscript recommending Dr. Schwarz of New Amsterdam. I came, I saw, and I conquered; for I am here with you, my baron, and the horse in the stable waits to carry us away when and how you will."

"To carry us away!" echoed the baron, in a tone so unexpected that his companion turned to look at him in the darkness, and said, in a half-offended tone, —

"One would say you were sorry to go, my baron!"

CHAPTER XXII.

AND THE PAIN OF PARTING.

AND now I will tell you my adventures," exclaimed François, not replying to the semi-accusation of his friend; and, plunging with some precipitation into the history already so well known to us, he rapidly rehearsed it, dwelling very little upon the part concerning Molly, and a good deal upon the insolent intrusions, as he described them, of Reuben Hetherford.

"But he is the betrothed husband of this young woman," remarked the abbé dryly, "and naturally feels an interest in her connection with a handsome young man whom she hides in her bed-chamber."

"Betrothed! What nonsense you talk, my dear Despard!" exclaimed François a little imperiously. "Mademoiselle Marie had already broken any such ties before I had the honor of meeting her."

"Nevertheless her father told me to-night that she was to marry him," persisted the abbé.

"She will not, then," replied his friend so sullenly that the abbé thought it best to defer some remarks not likely to be well received just then; and only said with a good-humored laugh, —

"Well, we need not settle every thing to-night,

since I have arranged to stay here another day and night; and in the course of to-morrow we shall see how it is best to manage our departure. Meantime let us sleep a little. Will you remain here for the rest of the night?"

"Thanks, no: I have a charming little priest's chamber above there, and will leave you undisturbed in this."

"Good-night, then; and do not forget to thank God who has so favored us thus far," said the priest.

"I do not forget, *mon père*," replied his former pupil a little coldly, and went his way.

The reverend Vincent de Paul Despard rolled himself comfortably in the bed-clothes, and, addressing himself to sleep, murmured cynically, "I have loved him fifteen years or more, and saved his life half a dozen times; and she has known him one week, and already puts me to the wall. Well, *mon petit baron*, I have seen you in love several times before this."

The next day passed in the quiet farmhouse much after the usual manner, that is, to outward seeming; but for three persons beneath that roof this calm exterior covered a whole world of emotion, peril, and uncertainty. When Dr. Schwarz appeared at breakfast it was with a more inscrutable face than ever; nor did he attempt any private conversation with Molly, who could not yet know with certainty whether he was the friend for whose advent François had so eagerly hoped. The somewhat brief and silent meal finished, and the doctor's first visit paid to his patient, he accompanied Mr. Wilder to the barn; and Molly sped up stairs with the breakfast-tray so difficult to prepare without observation.

François received her gently, but somewhat sadly, and, without waiting for questioning, said, —

"It was he, the friend for whom I hoped."

"And is his name really Dr. Schwarz?"

"Names are of little consequence, dear child. Neither he nor I have any in particular, — to-day one, to-morrow another. *Fortune de guerre*, my girl; and he has come to carry me away."

"And you are glad to go, I suppose?"

"Who would not suppose so, Marie?"

The reply was no answer; and Molly felt it so, and busied herself silently in her arrangement of the little breakfast-table. François watched her for some moments, then suddenly seized her by the hand; but, as he opened his mouth to speak, a shrill sudden noise resounded through the house, and Molly, starting, cried, —

"'Tis mother's call. I left all the doors open, and gave her a stick and a brass kettle to beat upon if she needed me. I will be back anon."

"Send Dr. Schwarz up, meantime, if it please you, sweetest," called François after her; and for once Molly was not displeased to find the burly figure of the doctor standing sentinel before the kitchen-fire.

"Will you go up-stairs for a few moments, sir?" asked she in a demure whisper as she passed him.

"Does Monsieur le Baron send for me?" inquired Schwarz in the same tone, and with a smile of good-humored malice at thus winning from the prudent girl a confession of the secret she had so jealously guarded up to this moment.

"'Those who seek, find,'" replied Molly passing into her mother's room, and meeting as best she could the invalid's querulous questioning and complaints.

Dr. Schwarz meanwhile had strolled out of the room and up-stairs. François was on the watch for him; and, first of all, insisted upon taking him up to his own snuggery, there to admire the various devices and thoughtful attention to his every need, managed by Molly out of such slender resources and scanty space as she could command.

Then the two descended to the door at the foot of the garret-stairs, and there held their conference in such wise that in case of interruption, each could escape in the direction of his own room without delay or noise.

"First of all, let me see this arm of thine, *mon baron*," said the abbé. "Yes, yes, it needs the lancet, and some fresh bandaging; and fortunate is it that those same pockets of mine held our case of surgical instruments and a few drugs. Steady, now, my friend; there! I would I could call upon the fair Molly for some warm water, and a little help; but we will make it do with a drop of *eau de vie* to take off the chill. Now, there, all is comfortable, is it not? and you can sit very well in the corner of this stair, and get a little color back to your lips before we talk."

"Thanks, good friend. I did not use to be so squeamish over there in the *Pays Bas*."

"You have been pretty well knocked about of late,

mon baron ; and ten days or so of close imprisonment, in that coop above there, are not strengthening, although possibly delightful.

"And now for our plans. I think that in the earliest dawn it will be well for you to leave the house, and secrete yourself in a little lonely cattle-shed, or it may be barn, which I will presently show you from the window of my bed-chamber. Then, directly after breakfast, I shall leave this place, and, arriving opposite the cattle-shed, pause to attend to my harness. You will jump into the bottom of the sleigh, cover yourself with the fur robe, and an instant later when the sleigh emerges from behind the building, I sit erect and alone upon the bench as before."

"The barn will hide all this from the windows of the house, you are sure?" asked François meditatively.

"Quite. I just took a little exploratory tour in that direction."

"And where do we go after this?"

"To Canada, my friend, as straight and as speedily as the necessity of concealing ourselves from the official eye will permit. We have plenty of *louis d'or*, and some English broad pieces. When one horse gives out we can buy another ; and so with the help of a good deal of pardonable lying, which I take upon my own conscience, we will get through admirably."

François sighed. "To-night !" murmured he in a melancholy voice. The abbé made a movement of impatience, and suddenly said, —

"By the way, Monsieur le Baron, let me congratu-

late you on your birthday, although a week or so gone
by. Is it possible that it is seven years since we merrily kept the twentieth in the dear old Château de
Montarnaud? Do you remember how the tenants and
vassals all flocked to the château to drink the young
baron's health, and to hope that he would marry some
noble lady, and come to live among them?   And perhaps you may yet, *mon baron.*"

"Never, *mon abbé*," interjected François.

"And Mademoiselle de Rochenbois," pursued the
priest musingly, "how lovely she looked that day, as
she placed the olive-wreath upon your head, and bent
to whisper I know not what in your ear."

"Enough, Perè Despard, enough!" interrupted the
baron. "You are very subtle, and you have only my
own interests at heart; but you cannot influence me
thus. As you have reminded me, I am to-day a man
twenty-seven years old, and for the last seven of those
years a soldier of fortune. The story of those years
has altogether effaced the pride of birth, the appetite
for adulation, the hope of adorning the proud name
bequeathed to me, — yes, even the memory of Valerie
de Rochenbois, whose name I speak to-day for the
first and the last time since we turned our backs upon
the land that holds her, and speak it simply to show
you that I can do so. No, abbé, you are very clever;
but it is not thus that you will move me."

"Then are we to pack three persons into yonder
little vehicle, and so make sure of discovery, imprisonment, and perhaps death, at the hands of a Puritan
mob?" asked Despard sullenly.

"Wrong again, my abbé. I will not take my wife away from her father's house until I have a home of my own to offer her."

"Your wife, monsieur!"

"Not yet, but so to be, *mon prêtre.*"

"*Eh bien!* When the war is well over, no doubt we shall travel back from Canada to find our rustic *bonne-et-belle,* and no doubt she will have waited for us; and the golden age will come back to adorn our nuptials. Pray celebrate them in the summer-time, that all the sheep and pigs, not forgetting Amariah, may wear wreaths of roses."

"*Cher abbé,* you are very angry, and it seems to me are forgetting yourself a little. Suppose we separate for an hour or so; and, when we both have our tempers more under control, I have a further proposition to make to you."

"Pray excuse any want of deference I may have shown, Monsieur le Baron, either to you or to the fair Dulcinea del Toboso, who " —

The violent closing of the door in François' hand cut short the priest's apology and comparison; and with a wrathful smile upon his lips he went down-stairs, and posted himself doggedly at the bedside of his patient.

"The sooner they get together, and settle the manner of our triple suicide, the better," muttered he in French; and Mistress Wilder turned feverishly on her pillow to ask, —

"What are you saying, doctor?"

"That you are surprisingly better, madame. Now

please to tell me how many times in your life before this, you have been ill."

Five minutes later, Dr. Schwarz smiled at seeing Molly steal quietly out of the kitchen.

CHAPTER XXIII.

THE BETROTHAL.

CREEPING softly up the stairs in a reluctant fashion, most unlike her usual decisive step, Molly paused outside the screen covering the entrance to the "priest's chamber," and timidly peeped through before entering.

François sat beside his little table, his chin in his palm, his eyes set in such earnest meditation that he had not heard her light approach. Evidently some thought deep and painful, leading to some momentous resolve, was stirring at his heart,—some thought that drove the color from his cheek, drew his brows together in a heavy frown, and set his lips so sternly that the tawny moustache writhed sardonically. Suddenly he straightened himself; and with an airy gesture of contempt, as of flinging some bauble from him, he exclaimed aloud, —

"*Adieu, la belle France! La belle Valerie! Toutes les bagatelles de mon enfance! Voila une belle paysanne*" —

Part she understood, part she guessed, and with a gesture as haughty as his own she turned to go away; but the light rustle of her garments caught his ear, and springing forward he pulled aside the curtain, and, seizing her hand, drew her toward him so confidently, almost rudely, that she released herself, saying cold-ly, —

"What is the matter, François? I came only to ask what provision I shall make for your journey. You will need food, for you must avoid the publics in this part of the country; and you must have plenty of warm clothing, and " —

"I need and must have something far more valu-able than food or clothes, *belle et chère* Marie," inter-rupted François, attempting to put an arm about her waist; but, drawing back, she said yet more coldly, —

"Your pleasure in quitting this poor place, sir, puts you beside yourself. What is this that you wish for, then?"

"O Marie, be not so coy, so chill! Do not trifle in these few last precious moments. You know very well, sweet one, what it is I want: it is you, my darling, your own dear, stern, yet most tender, self. Marie, you love me, do you not?"

"You take too much for granted, sir; and I like not this style of talk, hidden away here in my father's garret. The man who woos me must do it openly."

"But, Marie, you know how that is impossible. If I come down these stairs, and declare myself to thy father, what choice do I leave the good man but either to deliver me with my friend up to government, or brand himself forever as a traitor, forfeiting land and liberty, nay, it may be life, it he lets us go? Will you destroy your father as well as your lover and his best friend, Marie?"

"No, I will not do that," said Molly tardily; and a look of perplexity softened the rigor of her brow. The man saw his advantage, and pushed it : —

"You would rather sacrifice yourself, dear saint: but that you cannot do without sacrificing at least one life with yours; for I swear to you, Marie, I swear it on this crucifix," — and, drawing from his breast the golden and jewelled crucifix his dying mother had hung there, and which had never left his neck, the young man pressed it to his lips, and held it in his hand as he continued, — " yes, I swear upon this sacred emblem that I will never leave this place again until you have not only given me heart for heart, Marie, but have promised to become my wife when I shall claim you."

"O François! Wicked, foolish, unkind! How dare you so take the name of God in vain? Think what you say! Suppose I do not give these crazy promises and assurances which you have no right to demand, what will you do? Spend the rest of your life here, pr'ythee?"

"Spare your scorn, *ma belle :* I speak no more than I mean, and can carry out. What will I do, say you? Not stay here, in truth! I am tired of playing a rat's *rôle*, and hiding in a garret. Why, truth of me, Marie, I am growing afraid of your Tabby already. No, if I once am convinced that Marie refuses my love, and scorns my offer of marriage, I will not indeed leave this garret, since I have sworn not, but I will come out and dance a gavotte upon those loose boards yonder, and company myself with so blithe a song, that not only your venerated father, but Amariah, whom I really long to see, and Tabitha, and perhaps madame your mamma herself, will come rushing up to see what demon has taken possession of their house.   Then I shall say that I have hidden myself here quite altogether with nobody's knowledge, but that I find voluntary imprisonment as bad as involuntary, and, besides, desire most ardently to visit the village of Boston, and so give myself over — what! O Marie, Marie, forgive me, sweet, forgive me!"   For Molly, hurt, frightened, perplexed, above all beset by a new and nameless sorrow gnawing at her heart by day and night ever since the baron's flight had seemed imminent, suddenly broke down, and, sinking into a chair, laid her pretty arms upon the table, and her face upon them, and began sobbing, not noisily, but in the deep grieved fashion of a loving yet reticent heart, wrung beyond endurance.

Before that sight and sound, the bitter mockery of the young man's mood fled away like fog before the west wind, and left the clear depths of his better nature open to God's dear light.

Kneeling beside the weeping girl, yet not daring to touch her, save a timid finger upon her arm, he pleaded his cause: I know not how, she knew not how, yet so successfully that after a little the noble head rose slowly, and the brimming eyes met his with a smile so shy and proud, and withal so sweet, that the lover's arms fairly quivered in their longing to grasp and claim that loveliness, yet dared not stir, lest the dear smile should vanish.

"Marie! I love you, I love you dearly! Will you be mine honored wife?" whispered he; and Molly, still smiling yet unbending, replied, —

"Why, that is better, François! At first you would have had me confess to loving you, and now it is you who say you love me."

"Yes. I was wrong at first. O child! you are cruel, you torture me, it is not worthy of you: you are not of the women who play with men's hearts, and fling them away; you are strong, you are brave, you are noble. Be worthy of yourself in this moment, Marie. Answer my true, deep love, truly and honestly."

He said no more, but rose to his feet, pale and eager, yet with a sudden dignity upon him which Molly had never felt before. The blood of generations of nobles, of men who loved honor better than life, and women who armed their husbands and sons for battle, and held their castles against the foe in their absence, was stirring in his veins; and not even for his life's love would he longer sue, or brook trifling or hesitancy. Molly looked at him; and the perception, subtler than thought, told her all this, told her, too, that on that moment's truth and courage hung her own and another's happiness for a whole life. She, too, rose; and standing bravely before him, though her face burned rosy-red, and her voice choked almost into a sob, she said, —

"I will not trifle, I will not hide the truth: yes, I do love you, François."

"Now God's blessing on you, my brave, sweet love!" exclaimed the baron, putting his arm about her, and pressing the kiss of betrothal upon her lips, yet immediately releasing her, and saying, with a tender authority in his tone, —

"Now, then, *bonne-et-belle*, sit you there; and since we have but one chair in our *ménage*, I will sit upon the stool beside you, and let us arrange for our wedding. And first of all, dear love, I have no name but François."

"Nay, François, I must confess to having surprised one of your secrets. I know your name already."

"You know my name! How then, mistress?"

"Do not be vexed, but your friend all unconsciously betrayed it. He asked, 'Does Monsieur le Baron wish to see me?' Now I know that *monsieur* in French is answerable to master in English, so *le baron* remains for your name. Master LeBaron they would call you here."

The cloud of annoyance passed from the baron's brow; and with a quizzical smile he replied, —

"Your wit is too shrewd for me to gainsay it, pretty one; and I confess myself vanquished. Then, since my name is Master LeBaron, will you be called Mistress LeBaron, and that at the time I am about to propose?"

"O François! no need of settling that yet. It will be many a long day before the war is over, and you can come back," said Molly with a sigh.

"So many, sweetheart ('tis the prettiest word in all your language, Marie, and I have so often longed to say it to you), so many days until the war is over, that we will wait for none of them, not one. We will be wed this very night, before I leave the house."

"Nay, now, François, I shall be displeased. again an you take that tone. It is but folly to speak of it, besides."

"Wait now, my *fiancée*, and listen, and be not so ready to decide matters on which I have thought for days."

"But, think as hard as you may, François, you cannot make me think of playing traitor to my father so."

"Nay, child, what traitor? If I come back here with means of supporting you, with a position as a physician, and with a constant though weary heart, and we told your father we had been affianced since so many years, and you assured him that you loved me well, and would wed none but me, think you he would consent?"

"I know he would, for he too loves me well."

"With father-love, yes. It is I who will show you what is a man's love for his wife, my Marie. But hold, I will not be tempted from my point. He would consent, you say. Well, then, what harm in giving our betrothal the sanctity and safety of a priest's blessing? It is but the ceremony that I ask, not one kiss of your dear lips unless you give it willingly. Only let me feel, in going out to face danger, hardship, and death, that the sweet saint who prays for me, as I know Marie will pray, has a wife's right to be heard above; and that, come what will of change or chance to her or me or others, she is still my own true wife whenever I can claim her. Only God and our two selves and the priest will know; but I shall go out, and you will stay here, both of us armed for our separate fight as no uncertain contract could ever arm us."

He was silent, keenly watching the face of the young girl drooped in anxious thought. He saw that her own heart fought on his side, and, like a wise general, did not interfere with the action of his allies. At last she said dreamily, —

"And I tried so hard to be a truthful girl, at least."

"And do not you owe truth to your husband, promised or actual, more than to any other man? And will not this be the strongest possible safeguard to your truth?" asked the lover almost harshly. "You know how your mother wishes you to marry this *scélérat*, who would sell my head for twenty dollars; and you know how she will urge you, and how you may be all but forced into it, especially should she in dying make it her last petition, or should your father die, and leave you alone in her hands. And, if you *cannot* marry him, is it not stronger than if you simply will not? At any rate, it lifts a load from my heart in leaving you, Marie, if that is something."

"That is, indeed, almost every thing. But my father! I cannot, cannot deceive him, François. I will not!"

"Four and twenty hours after I am gone you shall tell him, if you will. Sooner than that, he might feel bound to give the alarm. You shall tell him, or indeed anybody else, after that time, that you are a wedded maiden, waiting in her father's house until her husband can claim her."

Another pause, and then Molly said again, —

"But the minister, Mr. Watkins, couldn't come without every one knowing."

"And he need not come," replied François more gayly; for well he knew the proverb of the fortress, and the woman who parleys. "We want no Vatkins here, for we have a consecrated priest beneath the roof already."

"What, Dr. Schwarz?"

"You call him so, sweetheart, but he is a priest. I will not say his name; but his title is Monsieur l'Abbé, and he can marry us so that none but the Pope himself can undo the knot."

"Then he is a Papist; and you, François?"

"I too, Marie. Did you not know it?"

"I guessed it the first day, when — when I saw that thing about your neck."

"My mother's crucifix, Marie: she hung it there, praying with her dying lips that it would shield her boy from harm to soul and body; and of a truth, soldier of fortune though I am, and rough life though I may have led, I believe that prayer has done its work; and no sin beyond repentance has stained the soul, and no great harm, though many a danger, has befallen the body. Marie, as I lay there on your cruel shore, my arm mangled between those rocks, and death already clutching at my heart, I found strength to put that crucifix to my lips, and call upon the Son of God for aid in my extremity. The next wave, instead of beating the breath from my body, lifted me, and carried me high upon the beach. I was saved."

"Oh, thank God, thank God, François!"

"Yes; but I think my appeal, and the blessed crucifix, and my mother's prayers moved the good God then," said François simply; and Molly, looking into his brave, earnest eyes, felt a moment's vague regret that she had not been reared in this positive, comforting faith. So it was answering herself, rather than him, that she said,—

"But I can never become a Papist."

"Poor child! How little you know the joy that you scorn! frightened from it by the bugaboos men have set up. But I will never constrain you, sweet wife, nor even argue with you: religion shall be one of the things we will put away, and never speak about. I am not afraid for you, my saint."

"One of the things? What else, François?" asked Molly in a troubled voice; but François answered firmly,—

"All my life, sweetheart, until the night I tapped upon your casement, including him whom you call Schwarz, and one whose name you have twice pronounced, but will never speak again if you would spare me pain. Canst curb thy woman's curiosity, thy wifely rights, so far?"

"It is not curiosity, François; but you ask very much. I give you my whole heart, lay open my whole life. Your kiss is the first, man save my father, ever laid upon my lips."

"And I can give you no such sweet assurance, Marie. I am seven years your senior in years, seven times seven in experience of the world, and a rough, bad world too. I give you no freshness; I can make you no confidences of the past; but, from this day out, I give you my life, all and entire. I give you my love, my faith, my honor, my all. Perhaps one woman in a thousand is strong enough in herself to give such perfect confidence to her husband; and I believe you to be that woman, Marie. Am I right? Will you trust me so entirely? Will you be my wife?"

And Molly, laying her hands in his, and raising her calm eyes fearlessly to meet his scrutiny, simply said, " I will."

CHAPTER XXIV.

GRANDMOTHER AMES'S CURTAINS.

THE great eight-day clock in the kitchen struck twelve with all the resonance and deliberation so clearly distinguishing the midnight from the noonday voice of any responsible clock ; and as the sound died away in the supernatural stillness, also sure to follow the stroke of midnight, the door leading from the parlor to the kitchen opened very gently, and Molly's pale face peeped out and listened anxiously to the quiet breathing of the invalid, accompanied by the more positive demonstrations of the husband sleeping on a cot beside her bed.

Truth to tell, Dr. Schwarz had assured his patient a good night's rest by a judicious soporific ; and Humphrey, like most hard-working healthy men, needed no coaxing to his ten-hours' slumber.

"God bless them both, and forgive me !" said Molly under her breath, as she re-closed the door, and turned the button upon the inside. Then raking open the fire, with which, rather to her father's surprise, she had indulged herself on retiring, she lighted a couple of candles by aid of one of the coals, put some wood upon the embers, and looked shyly about her ; for this was Molly Wilder's wedding-day, coming up so still and cold from the wintry sea; and all alone in the dim chill chamber she was to make her bridal toilet. But how? She had no pretty clothes, no ornaments or coquetries of the toilet, for her mother's asceticism and the lonely life alike discouraged such frivolities: but François had jestingly bade her make herself beautiful for his eyes, since there would be no others to admire her; and she fain would do so.

But again, how? Ever since nine o'clock, when she retired to her extempore couch upon the parlor-floor, Molly's mind had been actively exercised in recalling all the traditions of brides, their costumes, and their manners, that ever had come within her knowledge. The only one she had seen with her own eyes was at a meeting of Friends she had attended with her parents: and that one was about forty years old, and wore a skimpy dress, cape, and bonnet, all made from the same piece of drab-colored silk, and, by way of ornament, had decked herself with such an air of stern resignation and determination, that Molly, on the way home, innocently inquired of her mother if Friend Hannah Trimble were married against her will, that she looked so sour over it; and Deborah, yielding with a grim smile to the fascination of bridal gossip, replied that it were shrewder to ask that question of Phineas Coffin, since every one knew Hannah had wed him whether he would or no.

"But do all brides look like that, mother?" persisted the child; and her mother, plunging still deeper into worldly talk, proceeded to describe a bride and a wedding she had seen in the parish-church at home, where the lovely Lady Anne was arrayed in flowing white satin robes, with garniture and veil of ancestral lace, and a crown of orange-blossoms upon her head, a bevy of noble maidens at her side, and troops of village children to scatter flowers in her path.

As old memories came back, Deborah's cheek flushed, and her eyes sparkled; but Molly still appeared dissatisfied. "But that was a lord's daughter marrying a lord," objected she. "How do people like us dress? How were you dressed yourself, mother?"

Deborah smiled a little, and looked slyly at her husband, who grinned sympathetically back at her; and then she said with an odd softness in her voice, —

"Why, there was a time about it, child. Thee knows I was a Friend already, and should by rights have dressed like Hannah Trimble to-day: but thy father, there, set his hard head against it, and would have his bride come to him in white, as a pure maid has a right to do; and at last my people gave in, and my father himself bought the white cambric for my dress; and when I was to leave the house he stuck a white rose in my hair, and said it matched my neck; and we walked to your father's parish-church, and were married just as well as Lady Anne herself. I have the dress saved by for thee, child, when thee is grown. The body will be a deal too little, but the skirt will make thee a fine petticoat for best. But there, enough of this worldly talk. — Humphrey, did not thee think the Spirit moved me mightily in meeting yesterday? Did thee like what I said?"

Molly remained obediently silent, but rested not by

day nor night until the white cambric dress was given over to her own keeping; and the skirt, lengthened down by several inches and freshly laundered, now hung over a chair ready to serve at its second bridal.

"All in white, as a pure maid has a right," repeated Molly to herself, as she looked at it, and touched it reverently. "Yes, I will be in white, sure enough; but what white?"

She opened the closet-door where all her wardrobe hung since yesterday, and stood, a finger upon her lip, contemplating the well-remembered garments in silent perplexity.

That new stuff dress of Quaker brown, so ugly in its fit, and clumsy in fashion? No, indeed. The striped blue and white linsey-woolsey, or the yet shabbier gray and black? Oh, no! The homespun linen for summer wear, and the striped short-gown and petticoat, and the "cooler" for hot weather of India chintz, brought from England in the emigration? Not one of all these was of the slightest value now; and Molly shut the closet-door with a sigh, and looked about her. But refusing is not choosing; and when the closet-door was closed, Molly had shut away her entire wardrobe, and stood looking about her with such an air of dejection and perplexity, that, much as we condemn her stolen marriage, we fain must pity her a little, all alone here in the silence of midnight, so forlornly struggling to provide some little beauty and fitness for that nuptial hour, around which fond mothers ordinarily heap their tenderest cares, and smiling friends their most assiduous attentions.

Even the resolute determination for a white dress
had something of pathos in it; for it sprung from the
unconscious protest the maiden soul was making
against what might seem unmaidenly even in his eyes
for whom the sacrifice was made. "As a pure maid
has the right," she whispered to herself again, as, taking a little wooden box from a drawer, she sat down to
turn over its but too familiar contents. Such poor
little bits of finery! So useless, so ugly! One longs
to re-create that fair form and bright maiden head
from the dust of two centuries, and pity and caress
and comfort it at least. Two centuries and more ago,
and yet how close akin to yon young girl's heart was
this whose story her descendant so lovingly tells to-day!
The world is born new every day, yet always the same
dear old world.

Ah! One item for the toilet at last. Here are
some yards of white ribbon bought for a bonnet-
trimming of that peddler last summer, and not yet
used. That will do for — well, something; but the
recollection of the peddler has suggested another
idea, — an idea at the same time so audacious and so
delightful that Molly stood for a moment with clasped
hands and blazing cheeks contemplating it in the air
before venturing to approach more closely. Then,
laying the box back in the secretary-drawer, she drew
from the very remotest corner of that receptacle a
parcel wrapped in silver-paper, and carefully pinned;
and, seating herself, slowly unfolded and unrolled a
web of delicate bobbinet lace, bought in much fear
and trembling at the expense, by Mistress Wilder, of

this same peddler, who professed to have himself imported it from Holland for the especial use of feminine Friends, who used it for those formally folded yet not ungraceful neckerchiefs forming part of their regulation costume. The purchase made, and the peddler gone, Deborah's heart, at once thrifty and ascetic, sorely misgave her for her self-indulgence; and, carefully laying aside her lace, she confined herself for some months to the coarsest and poorest of the muslin kerchiefs with which she was already supplied. Molly, who had watched and smiled at this little comedy, had from time to time tried to persuade her mother to wear the lace, or else allow her to do so: but piety forbade one of these courses, and prudence the other; and the coveted snare lay fresh and crisp in its rustling paper, all ready to entangle the footsteps of the incautious maiden who approached it.

"A bridal veil, and of the choicest, if only I dare use it!" murmured Molly, unwrapping the lace, and letting it float over her two hands as she held it above her head, and glanced shyly into the black depths of the mirror, whence she half expected to see her mother's angry face confront her.

"But I will be so very, very careful of it, mother dear, if only you will lend it," whispered she, turning toward the partition behind which lay her mother's bedroom.

Reverently laying the lace upon the backs of two chairs, Molly once more gazed around the room, seeking inspiration from the familiar surroundings. The secretary? Nay, she knew the contents of every one of its drawers, and no bridal dresses were among them. The closet? It had been ransacked. The cupboard above the fire? Nothing there. The triangular beaufet, or, as Molly had always heard it called, the bo-fat, in the corner? It contained some precious bits of china and glass, and the silver teapot that had been her father's father's, but nothing to meet the present need. The chest? Molly's eyes dwelt upon it long and meditatively, as if by clairvoyance reviewing through the closed lid the manifold objects she had so often seen displayed. The chest itself was a curiosity, and nowadays would be a treasure; for it was of dark English oak, quaintly carved, and adorned with old brasses, such as we vainly imitate to-day in lacquer-work. It had belonged in the Wilder family long before Humphrey himself joined it, and had "come over" with him, if not in "The Mayflower," at least in one of those later vessels which actually brought so many of the chattels attributed to the freight of that remarkable little brig. But, although the chest was old, the country was as yet too new to value it for its age; and even Molly considered it more as a convenient receptacle for household stuff not in frequent use, than as an heirloom; and she mentally went through its treasures with mournful negation of each one, until she murmured to herself, "and grandmother Ames's curtains." Then she stopped, flushed a little with some sudden thought, swiftly crossed the room, and, kneeling before the chest, lifted the heavy lid, and burrowed in its contents. Finally she dragged up from the depths a great parcel, carefully pinned up in linen, with a paper pasted upon the outside, inscribed, "Grandmother Ames's Curtains."

Carrying the package nearer to the light, Molly unfastened it, and rapidly took out and unfolded the contents. They were such as are to be found in many an old family chest to-day, perhaps carefully preserved as monuments of the industry and task of the women who have gone before; perhaps tossed aside and forgotten, and merely retaining their places in the land of the living because no one takes interest enough in them to destroy them. For grandmother Ames's curtains were a full suit for three windows and a bedstead, of fine India muslin, and all wrought by her own fair hands with festoons and wreaths and scattered bouquets of such flowers as may have bloomed in Eden, but never upon the vulgar earth; with wondrous scrolls and arabesques, and such wanton freaks of needlework as the inspired composer of music may indulge in upon his piano, or the accomplished "skatist" perform upon the ice before an admiring crowd. Grandmother Ames was a swift and diligent needlewoman, and these curtains had been the great achievement, the *magnum opus*, of her life; and at her death they were solemnly bequeathed to her daughter Deborah, constituting with one feather-bed, and one scarlet broadcloth cloak and hood, a fair and equitable fourth of the Ames inheritance. Molly Wilder had often seen these curtains, and admired them with that sort of vague awe inspired by the Bayeux tapestry, or a patchwork carpet said to contain ten thousand bits of cloth, or any other enormous and utterly useless waste of human life and industry: but to-day they aroused a new and vital interest in her mind, and one certainly never contemplated by their artificer; for in all those yards of wrought muslin, a little tarnished by years, but still of a very delicate creamy white, the maiden saw the vision of a wedding-dress, — a vision not clearly defined as yet, hardly more indeed than a bright possibility, but still something to set her cheeks to glowing, and her eyes to flashing, and her fair bosom to panting with delight and impatience. The curtains must not be cut, of course; and how else could they be shaped? Again and again Molly took up the separate pieces, and examined them, busily murmuring the while, —

"These six long window-curtains will make the skirt, sweeping the floor like that Lady Anne wore when mother saw her married: nay, I will use two for a round petticoat, and the other four shall make the train. Ay, that goes swimmingly; and for the body, why not this headpiece of the bed-curtains?" She held it out at arm's-length, and surveyed it with that intuitive appreciation and speculation in her eye, answering in the feminine genius to the fine frenzy of a Galileo or a Mitchell searching for the possible planet or comet science has taught him to expect in defiance of all the usual beliefs of man. It was a long, scarf-shaped, or rather cape-shaped, piece of muslin, some three feet broad in the middle, and perhaps six or seven long, designed to hang inside the two head-posts of the old-fashioned bedstead, and to delight the eyes of its occupant or occupants, since no one out-side could catch a glimpse of it.

"Let me see, let me see," murmured Molly busily; and, hastily arranging the more substantial part of her toilet, she adjusted the skirt and train, and then, taking the head-piece, laid it over her shoulders like a shawl, crossed it upon her bosom, and tied the ends behind in a great knot, the soft and fine fabric lending itself readily to an arrangement impossible with any thing more substantial, and Molly's stately and statuesque figure bearing off grandly that style of classic drapery which on most modern figures is so overwhelming and unbecoming. The edge of the fichu thus arranged covered the upper part of the arms; and the days had not yet arrived when the sleeve became an indispensa-ble part of the dress, being at that time ranked more with gloves and masks as part of the out-door costume, to be tied on when about to leave the house, and laid aside on entering it. So Molly, gazing into the dim mirror, felt no dismay in observing that the round, white arm was uncovered from the elbow down, or that a soft and creamy bit of neck was to be seen between the folds of the fichu, blending admirably with the stately throat above, and suggesting sweet possibilities below.

Then Molly loosened her chestnut hair, coiled it afresh, and laid over it the web of lace, suffering one end to cover her face, and binding it around with the fillet of white ribbon in unconscious classic accord with the style of her robe, and in perfect harmony with her own Juno-like beauty.

Finally clasping her hands, and dropping them in front of her, she stood for a moment looking at herself in shy approval and astonishment; for never had mirror given back to her an image like this, and yet it was herself. Her own gray eyes, but when so soft and dewy in their brightness? her own mouth, but when so tremulous and tender in its dreamy smile? her own cheeks, but when so charmingly colored? even the wide white chin looked soft and loving tonight; even the little ear blushed pink with sweet emotion; even the bright hair lay more softly upon the brow, and coiled more crown-like upon the queenly head.

Yes, she saw that she was lovely, for she had quick appreciation of all loveliness: and she used the knowledge as her noble nature and pure heart prompted; for, still gazing in the mirror, she said, "It is because François loves me, that I look like this; and how can I thank God enough for sending him to love me, and for making me comely in his eyes!"

So she fell upon her knees, and had not yet arisen, when the clock struck three.

It was her bridal hour.

CHAPTER XXV.

THE WHOLE TRUTH, AND NOTHING BUT THE TRUTH.

THE clock struck three; and, quietly opening the door into the front hall, Molly stole through the passage and up the stairs; her white robes shimmering ghostily, her light foot noiseless as Tabitha's, who, having with round grave eyes watched the progress of the toilet, now accompanied the bride, somewhat as the "milk-white doe" escorted Lady Clare, seeking Lord Ronald's tower.

The door of Molly's own room stood open, and her lover, advancing to meet her, took both hands, and, raising them deferentially to his lips, murmured, —

"My brave, true love!" and so led her into the room where stood a tall swarthy stranger, at sight of whom Molly stopped in astonishment; but her lover re-assured her: —

"It is your old friend Schwarz, Marie: he was in disguise, that he might the better help me. Now you see him *au naturel*, that is all. I would present him to you if I dared, but it is better you never hear the names in which our enemies still may search for us; so call him, if you will, Monsieur l'Abbé, or perhaps *mon père* Are you content? Can you trust me in all?"

"I have trusted you, and I will always trust you, François," said Molly with such sweet gravity of meaning that the lover's cheek was tinged with delight as he ardently replied, —

"And you shall never repent your noble confidence, my Marie: I promise it to you *foi de — foi d'un gentilhomme. —* Now, *mon père.*"

The abbé, who remained so grave and silent that one might say he had but little relish for his duty, opened the wave-worn little book in his hand, and began to read the service in a voice hardly above a whisper, yet so sonorous and full in its intonations that the Latin words, falling for the first time upon Molly's unlearned ear, seemed the language of some strange, beautiful land of romance, wherein she walked as in a gorgeous dream; and surely romance could hardly have hoped, in this wintry wilderness, to find material so fitting as this dim chamber, with the sombre priest hurriedly muttering his full-mouthed Latin phrases, the beautiful bride in her quaint costume, the stately bridegroom gazing at her so ardently, and Tabitha, who, seated in the midst, fixed her gleaming eyes on each in succession with true Satanic intelligence.

"*La bague, mon fils,*" muttered the priest; and François, slipping from his finger the great amethyst Molly had admired when her future lover lay wounded and half dead at her feet, placed it upon her finger, and held it there while he repeated after the priest some words whose meaning Molly could only guess.

"Kneel, my children," said the priest in English, and, as they obeyed, he laid his hands upon their heads, and, in a firmer and heartier tone than he yet had used, bestowed upon them the apostolic blessing, which, in the belief of both men, conveyed a positive gift of good far beyond a charitable wish; while Molly felt the tears start to her eyes in gratitude for she knew not what.

"Monsieur and Madame LeBaron, allow me to offer my warmest felicitations, and hopes for your happiness," said the abbé, as the new-married pair rose to their feet; and in pronouncing the new name, adopted since morning by his friend and pupil, the priest allowed a twinkle of humor to kindle his dark eyes, and a tone more jocose than solemn to penetrate his deep-toned voice.

But Molly could not appreciate the joke; and François had no mind for it, being occupied in admiring his bride.

"And whence this charming costume, so richly wrought, and yet so virginal in its simplicity?" asked he, touching the embroidered edge of the fichu as it lay upon Molly's arm. "Is it not the Indian muslin that our fine ladies abroad are so pleased to wear?"

"I believe so. Do you like it?" replied she with a flush of pleasure, and a dimpling smile at the jest she in turn had all to herself.

"But whence did it come all of a sudden, as if the fairies had decked thee for thy bridal?" persisted François a little curiously. Molly hesitated for half an instant, and decided not to disillusionize her bridal robe by bestowing upon it the homely name of window-curtains; and, in thus deciding the first ques-

tion arising in her married life, she gave no unimpor
tant clew to her whole future course ; for truth-telling
wives may be divided into two broad classes, — those
who tell all the truth, and those who tell nothing but
the truth : to our mind, and to Molly's, these latter are
the wisest, and even the truest to the spirit of their
marriage-vow. It was the first time the question had
been presented to her, and there was no time for
reasoning ; but intuition, deeper than reason, decided
it at once, and it was not half a minute after the
baron's question before his all-unconscious baroness
replied, —

"And how do you know but the fairies did deck
me for my bridal? You told me yourself it was the
mermaids who brought you here in the first place for
my " —

"Nay, say it out, sweetheart, — thy husband. Say
it for me once, dear wife. Lay thy coy arms about
my neck, and give me the kiss I will not take without
thy leave, and say, 'This for my husband François,
from Marie his wife.'"

Smiling and ashamed, she did exactly as he bid her ;
and he, holding her close to his heart for one sweet
moment, and then gazing reverently into the deep,
true eyes lifted to his so bravely yet so shyly, felt a
sudden burden of responsibility, almost of remorse,
fasten upon his heart, at knowledge of the change he
had wrought in this fair and pure life, and how its
whole future lay in his hand.

"God so deal with me, as I with you, my wife ! "
whispered he ; and she for answer kissed him yet
again, then released herself from his embrace.

"I am sorry, my friends, but I must remind you of the time," said the abbé dryly. "It is all but four o'clock; and our friend Amariah is very matutinal, not to mention our worthy host, who sometimes, as he tells me, rises before the dawn."

"Yes, yes. François, you must go at once," exclaimed Molly, her firm mind springing back to its balance upon the instant. "I drew the bolt of the front door before I went to bed, and the hinges are well oiled, so that it will open noiselessly. The basket of provisions is in the parlor, and the extra wrappings are here."

"Most thoughtful of wives, and so young in that sweet character!" exclaimed François uxoriously. "Yes, all is ready but my will; and that I think will never say, ' It is time to part.'"

"I pray you, do not forget the moccasins I gave you to put over your boots, or the extra stockings. One's feet are so cold after some hours in a sleigh."

"I will not forget, Griselda."

"And thy poor arm," pursued Molly, not caring to inquire who Griselda might be, or have been; and her earnestness and persevering adherence to the matter in hand roused François from his dreams of delight, as no personal responsibility would in the least have done.

The abbé also showed himself, in this emergency, to be no less a man of affairs than a priest and a physician: he thought of every thing, generally finding, to be sure, that Molly had thought of it beforehand, and laid down the whole plan of the escape both for François and himself so clearly that there could hardly occur at any point one of those dreadful breaks in the chain of connection, by which many a captive has, just in the moment of deliverance, found the road cut from under his feet, and been helplessly remanded to a bitterer captivity than ever. He had even taken occasion, in the course of the day, to go in and out of the front door several times, so that whatever footprints might appear upon the hard frozen snow should be attributed to his feet. Softly opening the door, he pointed out this fact to the baron, bidding him be careful to tread exactly in the same track; but the caution was unheeded, for, as the last barrier between the captive and liberty was removed, he turned back to his captivity and his jailer with a clinging love, such as he had not yet known, and, clasping Molly in his arms, whispered,—

"Sweet wife! I cannot leave thee thus. Shall I stay, and risk all, or will you come with me?"

"Neither, François. We knew that we did but join to part. Be strong, dear husband, and let me be strong; for you are a man, and should show me the example."

"And so I will. Good-by, darling: God be with you, and keep you! Do not doubt me, even though years should pass. So sure as I live, I will come to claim you."

"I should never dream of doubting it," said Molly in some surprise: and then they clung together in one of those embraces whose passion is all pain, for the sorrow of parting strikes its bitterness through the sweet of love, and the sweet makes the bitter all the more pungent.

It was Molly who, at the last, unclasped her husband's arms from around her neck, and gently pushing him toward the door whispered, —

"Go, dear, in the name of pity, go!"

"Yes, *mon baron*, it is madness to delay," murmured the abbé impatiently; and François, without a word, with but one more lingering kiss, allowed himself to be led to the door, which presently closed behind him, but not until the last cautious echo of his footsteps had died upon the frosty air. Then the abbé turned, and looked shrewdly at Molly. She was white as her dress, and leaned heavily against the door-casing with closed eyes, from beneath whose lids great tears were slowly forcing their course. Light as a cat the priest mounted the stairs to his own room, and presently returned with a little flat silver cup, part apparently of a pocket-flask.

"Drink this, madame!" whispered he peremptorily. "Drink, if but one sip, to your husband's safe journey."

"Oh, if I could insure it thus!" replied Molly; but she took the cup, and smiled, and whispered something, and quaffed the contents, never knowing whether it was sea-water or good French brandy: to her it was a pledge to François, and that was all.

"And now, madame," pursued the abbé, receiving back the cup with a smile, "I recommend that you take off and put away this beautiful dress, and, after hiding all signs of unusual confusion, get a little sleep before the day breaks. I shall do so, for it will be many a night before we shall sleep so securely again."

"The advice is good, sir. Good-night."

And Mary went into her own room, where the dying fire still shed a warm and dusky glow, fastened the door, and drew aside the window-curtain. The intense, brooding darkness of the hour before dawn was over all the earth; but beneath it the snow shot up a sullen and sepulchral gleam, as in the darkened chamber of death the shrouded form in its cold white vestments cannot be hid.

Mary shuddered, and dropped the curtain, then fell upon her knees whispering, —

"Eye of man can see him not; but thou, O God, thou to whom the night is as the noonday, oh, watch him and keep him and save him, and bring him back to me!"

CHAPTER XXVI.

THE MAIL-BAG OF THE "CIRCÉ."

NEWS, news, *cher docteur!*" exclaimed a gay young officer of artillery, looking in at the open door of a little barrack-chamber wherein the regimental surgeon sat reading and smoking.

"And what news, *mon capitan?*" asked he a little languidly. "Have the Hurons captured·a party of Iroquois? or is it the Iroquois who have annoyed the Hurons this time? or "—

"Nothing of the sort; but news that may take us all back to *la belle* France, leaving the savages to fight out their own squabbles, and murder these Jesuit fathers, who hunger so furiously after martyrdom, at their leisure. A brigantine from home, just anchoring below the citadel; and here comes the chaplain to confirm my report."

"What! You have already heard the blessed news of peace, Capt. Reynier?" asked a mellow voice as the chaplain entered the room.

"What, peace! Is it true, then? Has the mail come ashore?" And, without waiting for reply, the young man dashed out of the room and down the stairs.

"News of peace, eh?" asked Dr. LeBaron still

languidly, still indifferently, as Père Vincent closed the door, and came to seat himself beside his friend.

"Yes, doctor, and other news also," replied the priest in a voice of suppressed emotion. "I have a letter."

"A letter ! But how did any one know of your whereabouts or your identity?" asked the doctor sternly. "That is, any one but your religious superiors," added he more gently. " Is the letter from one of your fathers?"

"No, but still from a priest. You remember Père Noailles, who went home invalided a few months after our arrival in this place?"

"Yes. Surely, Father Vincent, you did not betray our identity to him?" demanded the surgeon angrily.

"Not at all, my son ; the worthy priest and myself never exchanged six words about you in our lives, or, indeed, many about myself individually. I found him a man of rare discretion and reserve ; and, although we spent many hours in close communion, I do not know at this moment what was his name before entering the church, or his birthplace, or family condition, — in fact, no more than he does mine."

"Well, and he has written to you?"

"Yes, a most interesting account of the Oratorian College, and the Lazarist Fathers, who are doing great work in the provincial towns."

"Ay? Well, that is all good," replied the surgeon politely indifferent.

"But the good father encloses another letter in which you may take more interest," pursued the priest, taking a folded paper from his pocket. "It is from my sister Clotilde, whom you may remember."

"But, abbé, how could you write to your sister, as I suppose you did, without betraying your whereabouts and mine also?"

"Very easily, as you shall see : I wrote to my sister, mentioning neither date nor residence. For any thing to be gathered from the letter, the writer may have been resident in Japan or Nova Zembla. This letter I enclosed in one to my spiritual superior, to whom, you know, as a member of the Society of Jesus, I am obliged to report myself at stated periods, — knowledge as impossible to spread beyond its authorized limits as that obtained in the confessional. I asked him to transmit this letter to my sister through a certain priest, her confessor, and to desire him to write at her dictation a reply. This, given by the confessor to his and my superior, would be transmitted to Père Noailles, and by him enclosed to me. My somewhat complex plan worked as smoothly as most complex matters do when committed to Holy Church for guidance ; and here is Clotilde's letter. Will you look at it?"

"Thanks ; but you shall tell me any thing in it that especially interests yourself," replied the doctor in a voice full of meaning and warning.

The priest laid the letter upon the table at his friend's elbow, and rose, saying, —

"You had better read it for yourself, and in solitude. We shall meet at supper if not sooner." Then he went out, and the doctor resumed his book and his pipe, reading steadily down one page, turning the leaf and beginning another, with no consciousness of a single word or line, while the eyes so steadily fixed upon the printed page were far more conscious of the sidelong reflection upon the retina of that unfolded sheet upon the table than of the object immediately in front of them. Suddenly, with an impatient gesture, the surgeon tossed the book upon a bed at the other side of the room, flung the pipe upon the table, and, striding to the window, stood staring down upon the wonderful landscape at his feet, where the blue waters of the St. Charles dance down to lose themselves in the more turbid flood of the St. Lawrence, and both together flow majestically onward to the sea, laving the broken and picturesque shore, circling around the storied islands, and opening one of the great highways by which first France and then England found their way to the heart of the New World. Magnificent as was the view, even more so then than to-day, and competent as were the educated eyes of the surgeon to read and comprehend its charm, they roved over it now as blankly as they had over the printed page of one of his most-valued medical treatises; even the sea-worn and battered brigantine, anchored almost at his feet as it looked, her decks and rigging swarming with men, while a whole fleet of Indian canoes plied back and forth between her side and the pebbly shore, lay unseen before the eyes whose blank gaze rested only upon a *simulacre* of the table behind him, with that open letter lying in the middle. But, as the stern gaze never faltered, this homely vision slowly faded away, and clear in the summer air rose another, wavering and hovering between the gazer and the undulating tops of the evergreen forest across the river, whither now his eyes were directed, — the fair vision of a stately château, gray with ancestral honor and glory, with a garden at its feet where color and perfume and warmth and delight mingled in one sensuous dream of beauty and enjoyment, and, in the midst of a drooping tree, a form —

The doctor turned, muttering a savage malediction upon his own folly, and snatching up the letter devoured its contents with hungry eyes : nothing there written could be so dangerous as the imaginations it suggested unread.

The first part was simple and quieting as need be ; mere homely details of Clotilde's own experiences, — how she had married, and been a mother, and now the child and the husband both were dead ; and she, living with her married brother for a while, but meaning to go to service again so soon as madame should come back from Paris and take her ; and then with all the rambling inconsequence of an illiterate writer followed these passages : —

" But you did not know that before I was married I was at the Château de Montarnaud for a while after the old count was dead, and Count Gaston de Montarnaud came to the property, and took possession ; and when he went away he would not take madame to Paris ; they said, because she flirted so with the great lords there, but at all events he left her. And the housekeeper recommended me to mend the countess's laces, for you know the nuns taught me to do it beautifully, and so I went ; and when she knew I was your sister, she made me sit always in her bedchamber, and talked with me hours at a time. She tried so hard to make me tell where you were, that, if I had known, she would surely have got it from me; but I only could say how you wished so much to go to see our Saviour's tomb at Jerusalem, and I thought you might be in some monastery there. But she said, in an angry sort of way, she did not believe it; and then she asked, did any one go with you? but how could I tell when I did not know? So day after day we talked: and, brother, I can tell you what I fancy you want to know, though you did not exactly ask; but it is quite true that Madame la Comtesse would rather be Madame la Baronne even to-day. I would not say *it* if the count were still alive; but, now that he is nicely killed by the gentleman whose wife he carried away, it is no harm. And if you know where our dear master the baron is, I wish you would tell him he has only to come home and marry her, and be Comte de Montarnaud, unless the little Mademoiselle Thérèse is her father's heiress (I do not know, and Father Jacques says he does not, how that would be); but at any rate, when I saw the countess, not two months ago, only a few weeks after the count's death, she asked me, with her handsome face all flushed and bright as a young girl's, if I had not yet heard one word from my brother; and I know what I know. Yes, yes, brother! I know full well that she has never ceased to love him; and now she is free, and handsomer than ever, and rich, and a morsel for the daintiest master. And she promised that when she came back from Paris, whither she must go to settle the count's affairs, I should come and live with her again, and be *gouvernante* to Mademoiselle Thérèse, who is four months old, poor little darling."

And then Madame Clotilde's letter wandered off again into personal details; and, having read it to the end, the doctor slowly folded it, laid it upon the table, and stood looking gloomily down upon it.

"Say, Victor, what is the name of the brigantine?" asked a merry soldier voice below the window. And another replied with a laugh,—

"'Circé.' She comes to tempt us all to desert this barbarous solitude, and get a passage back to France; don't you see?"

"The 'Circé,'" echoed Dr. LeBaron, with a cynical smile. "Yes; but only fools believed in Circé twice."

At the mess supper-table the doctor and the chaplain met again; and, when the meal was finished, the priest followed his friend from the room and up to his own quarters. As he opened the door, the latter turned, and quietly said,—

"Will you come in, and take your letter, abbé?"

The abbé silently complied, took the letter, and without glancing at it, or asking if it had been read, put it in the pocket of his *soutane*, and said,—

"I have not quite emptied my budget of news yet, my friend."

"No? What remains?"

"I am going home. I am recalled by my superior. Will you go with me?"

"What, to France?"

"Yes: why not?   Your father and your brother are dead: if Gaston's child dies, you are the heir of your father's estates, as well as your mother's, for such were the terms of her marriage settlements. You have worn out by time and travel all bitterness or pain of association, and may settle peacefully down, either beneath your vine and fig-tree at Montarnaud, or the apple and pear trees of Normandy, to live out your life in your own country, and among your own people; for you are, after all, a Frenchman, and nothing can deprive you of that proud inheritance."

Wily abbé!   He never alluded to the widowed and regretful Valerie; for he was sure that the letter had done its work, without need of further help.

The doctor, striding up and down the narrow chamber, listened attentively to the end, and, as the abbé's voice died away, stood with his back toward the room, staring blankly out of the open window at the starless sky and unseen shore.   Suddenly he turned, and, without approaching the other, said slowly and distinctly, —

"I do not think my wife wishes to live in France."

"Your wife?   Mademoiselle Marie Wilder?"

"No, Madame LeBaron, as she herself named her future husband."

"My dear baron, I have got one more piece of news for you, — news which has waited two good years, and to-night is to be produced."

"It seems a day of revelation, *mon abbé;* but I do not think your last news will stir me more than the first.   What is it?"

Father Vincent rose from the chair where he had thrown himself, and, approaching his friend, laid a hand upon his arm, and looked earnestly into his face. It was grave, attentive, and expectant, but not so agitated as the priest would have had it. He was a skilful musician, but the instrument did not respond as he had hoped.

"My son, you were but a child when your father placed you in my charge; and since that day your welfare and improvement have been, after my vocation, my dearest care."

"I believe it, *mon père*, and have been always, as now, grateful and reliant."

"I am now to tell you of a step I took for your sake against your own pleasure, and perhaps against my duty. At any rate, I am led to expect that my recall is due to the confession of this step, which I made by letter to my superior; and I may have severe penance to undergo on my arrival with him. Meantime you will perhaps be angry; and yet you will see upon reflection that I sacrificed myself for you, since I knew at the time that I was liable, both to your anger, and to ecclesiastical censure for my act, and yet " —

"For Heaven's sake, abbé, have it out, and let the explanation come after the matter to be explained! What have you done?"

"Rather, what did I leave undone, my son! I will tell you in one word. I did not actually marry you to the girl whom I but now styled with intention Mademoiselle Mary Wilder. The words you repeated after me were no more than those of solemn troth-plight, and those which I muttered afterward were but one of the penitential psalms.   I knew that you were to leave her immediately; I knew how unlikely it was that you would ever return; I had seen you in love, more or less, three or four times already; I knew that, if you ever should return, it would be so easy to complete the ceremony I had begun, or to procure dispensation for you from the vows of betrothal you had assumed; and I deceived you for your own good, *mon baron*, — for your own good.   You have done no wrong to any one; and you stand there at this moment a free man, — free to return to your estates, to your home, and to — any wife you may choose to wed.   No law of God or man forbids."

"No law except one you do not comprehend, as it seems, my poor little abbé; and no wonder, since probably it was not taught in your father's shop.   I mean the law of honor."

And, with a look of withering scorn, the doctor was striding from the room, when the priest seized him by the arm, and said in a broken voice, "No, no, *mon baron:* you shall not go until you forgive me.   It was for love of you, in your interests, I did it.   What other motive could I have?   It seemed so unlikely you should be desirous, even if you were able, to consummate so unsuitable an alliance, after years of absence had destroyed the romantic illusions under which you then acted.   It seemed so possible that just what has now happened should happen: that you should become heir to the estates, and return to possess them; and what could you do with a low-born rustic for your wife?"

"Enough, enough, abbé! Let go my arm. Nay, then, here's my hand, old friend. I do believe thou didst it for my good; but it was a terrible mistake, and one that cannot be too soon rectified. Still, I was wrong to throw thine honest father's shop in thy teeth, and I crave forgiveness for the ungentle taunt. But for the rest, — first move the rocks on which this fortress stands, and then try again, if you will, on my determination: it is the firmer of the two. Shame on me to confess it, there was a moment when the Devil tugged hard at my soul, and filled it with sights and sounds and memories of long ago, — memories so alluring, that, man-like, I half regretted that I was fast bound to another life. But I never once dreamed of the dastard course you would have had me pursue — but there, then, I will not be angry. Our ideas differ in such matters, *mon père,* — differ from the cradle. You are a priest; and it is one of your mottoes, I believe, you Jesuits, that the end justifies the means: but we others, you know, we, too, have our watchword of ' *Noblesse oblige ;* ' and my mother taught me those words, and somewhat of their meaning, as soon as I could speak. We both must live after our traditions, *mon père ;* but I forgive you heartily, and crave your forgiveness, and only trust your superior may not be too hard upon the irregularity, as we must call it."

"I don't know," muttered the abbé ruefully, as the doctor in his white heat of excitement walked to the window, and leaned out for a moment into the cool darkness of the night. "To be sure, there was no mass: it cannot be called a sacrilege ; but — the superior is very severe, and it *was* irregular."

"And now," resumed the baron, returning, "my next step is to get my discharge; since peace is declared, that can be no difficult matter: and then southward, so fast as horseflesh will carry me, to claim my wife; for wife she is in the eye of God already, and shall be so in the eye of man so soon as she may be made so."

"You will find no priest there; and a marriage by one of those snuffling Huguenot ministers is no marriage," said the abbé half triumphantly.

"Then it will be a civil ceremony before a magistrate," replied François coldly; " and perhaps that is better, for I hold that the religious service has been already performed sufficiently to satisfy all requirements. God is true, although His priests may palter with his truth. And I doubt not the honest intention of the two who thought themselves wed that night is stronger in His eyes, than the deceitful informality of the ceremony."

"You are very severe, *mon baron.*"

"I am afraid it is my nature, *mon père.* Yet here is my hand again, and we part firm friends."

"But I must return to France all alone; and, when I left it, I swore never to part from you if I could help it," said the priest mournfully.

"Yes; but now you cannot help it, nor can I," replied the baron steadfastly, and left the room.

CHAPTER XXVII.

THE BUNCH OF GRAPES.

IT was toward sunset of a lovely day in June that a stranger rode slowly into the town of Plymouth, — old Plymouth, Plymouth of the Pilgrims.

Do you know the Plymouth of to-day, — the quiet, sleepy little town, with its few drowsy lions, and its little store of relics? and have you, you who have either risen above the pride of ancestry, or claim some other lineage than that of Mayflower Pilgrims, — have you made the little round of these, and gone away wondering why you ever came hither, and what anybody finds in Plymouth to draw them there year after year; and why her children, wheresoever they may wander, turn so eagerly back, in body may be, at any rate in heart, to the old Rock, as year by year the 22d of December comes round, and they say to each other with shining eyes, —

"It is Forefathers' Day in dear old Plymouth."

Have you wondered why it should be thus? and do you still wonder? Well, I cannot tell you; but the gray old sphinx of a town knows the answer to that riddle, and several others, and tells them, too, to him who has ears and heart to listen, and eyes wherewith to see the sights she will show in the dim twilight on

Burying Hill; or when the moon throws strange shadows upon the midnight streets; or when at high tide, the gray fog shutting off all else, one hears the lapping of the waves upon the beach, and remembers with a thrill of awe that sea and sky and fog and sandy beach are unchanged and unchangeable for all the changes of two hundred and fifty years.

Oh! to a child of the Pilgrims, with their blood warm at his heart, their names his proudest boast, their calm strength and unconscious grandeur of life his greatest ensample among mortal men, — to such an one the genius of the old town is neither silent nor chary of her gifts; for him in those still hours she recalls the noble forms of Bradford, and Carver, and Standish, consulting with the venerable Brewster, as they stroll along the shore, how food shall be procured for the well-nigh starving community, how the savage foe shall best be conquered into a friend, and the faithless friends in England be made to fulfil their compact; or again she shows the same men, leaders, gentlemen, and scholars though they were, toiling up the steep ascent of Leyden Street, bearing their burdens with the rest from the seashore to the common-house whose site is still lovingly remembered; or, going a little farther back, she shows the desecrated Rock restored to its lonely dignity, and beside it the clumsy boat of " The Mayflower " whence the Pilgrims step with solemn thanksgiving upon this the threshold of their new home, whose magnificence they do not yet suspect. And not the men alone : for beside the stately and elegant Carver, already governor of the colony, stands Katharine his fair dame; and Standish leads his Rose, and Priscilla Mullins makes way for the young matron, little guessing how soon that place might be her own; and John Alden gazes at Priscilla, and thinks how fair she is; and Warren and Winslow and Howland are there, and Elder Brewster's fair daughters, Love and Ruth, and many another maid soon to be a wife. And then, as the scene changes, one sees the stern, rough soldier Standish, and Bradford the statesman and scholar, and Carver the aristocrat, attending the sick smitten down by the pestilence of that first winter, nursing them with the patient tenderness of women and the strength of men, until they had buried more than half of their company upon the hill beside the shore; planting their graves with wheat, that the Indians might not see how many there were. I wonder, when they eat bread of that grain, if they did not remember, "Except a corn of wheat fall into the ground, and perish, it bringeth forth no fruit."

Well, one must linger no longer, but, passing on some threescore years, come to the Bunch of Grapes. It was the tavern of Plymouth then, and for a century later, — a long, low-browed building, the upper story overhanging the lower by a foot or so, with a great carved and gilded bunch of grapes hanging from each corner of the projecting story. A quaint old house, and with plenty of stories of its own which we may some day rehearse together; but just now we must be steadfast to the summer evening when LeBaron rode up to the door, and sat waiting for some one to take his horse, and bid him welcome. But a moment's observation showed that all was not well with the Bunch of Grapes and its inmates. The latticed windows all swung wide to the sweet summer, and the doors stood hospitably open: but neither rosy landlord, nor buxom landlady, nor smiling waiter appeared to welcome the guest; and the two or three old topers seated upon the bench beside the door seemed too much absorbed in some wonder-fraught gossip to do more than casually stare at him, and then back to their whispered dialogue. Glancing impatiently at them, the doctor threw himself from his horse, and rapped sharply with his whip-handle upon a panel of the stout oaken-door; but, as if this had been the signal for some dire catastrophe, a dismal shriek resounded through the upper chambers, followed by such a rapid succession of shrill screams, cries articulate and inarticulate, sobs, and peals of maniacal laughter, that the listeners gasped for breath, and turned pale even to their gorgeous noses.

"Why, what is this? What is doing here?" demanded Dr. LeBaron, seizing by the arm a trembling lad in a white apron who now appeared at the door of one of the lower apartments.

"I — I don't know, sir; but I guess it's missus," replied the lad, bursting into blubbering sobs, and rapidly withdrawing to the seclusion of the bar.

"What is the matter up there?" repeated the doctor in his most peremptory tones, as he strode to the outer door, and collared a man who stood peeping fearfully in.

"Why, you see, sir," returned this individual, gently

sliding from the inconvenient grasp, and settling his neck-gear as he spoke, "Dame Tilley has got to have her leg cut off; and, poor soul, she takes it to heart a bit."

"Oho, that's it!" exclaimed the surgeon, his curiosity rapidly changing to professional interest. "And why must the good woman lose her leg?"

"All along of a bad knee that the doctors can't cure, sir; and they be afraid it will spread, I believe."

"What, the knee spread? Surely, that were a novel mischance!" exclaimed the doctor, smiling. "And so the amputation is now in progress?"

"Anan."

"They are cutting off the leg just now?"

"Why, the doctors be up there; but I guess they haven't buckled to't yet. There's not been time."

"Who are the doctors?"

"There's Pilsbury from New Bedford, he's the main one; but old Dr. Coffin from Sandwich, and Hallowell, our own doctor such as he is, they're up there helping. Lord! how she do screech! I'll lay they're a-cutting into her now."

"She's in an hysteric fit. They won't handle her that way," muttered the doctor uneasily; and then, opening the door of the bar-room, he peremptorily beckoned forth the tapster, who was solacing his grief by a tankard of small beer.

"Here, Jacques, come here and get this shilling for yourself," ordered he; and Jacques, whose name was Zebedee, came at once, a subdued grin struggling oddly with fright, terror, and beer, upon his countenance.

"Now go up-stairs as fast as you can, and tell your master that a surgeon of the army is here, who would like to help at the operation if he will permit, and ask him to beg permission of the worthy surgeons already on the field."

"Yes, sir." And Zebedee, spurred to intelligence as well as haste by the shilling already in hand and the hope of more to come, did his errand so well that in about two minutes he returned with the landlord at his heels, his honest face pale and troubled, and his voice broken with emotion through the professional cordiality it mechanically assumed in greeting a guest of evident social consequence.

"Zeb told me you were an army-doctor, sir, and had kindly offered to " —

"Yes, yes, my good friend : it is hard for you, but these things can be made less painful sometimes by dexterity and practice. Perhaps I may be of some use ; as I have, I suppose, amputated hundreds of limbs where a country practitioner has one. Bring me up, if these gentleman consent."

"Lord ! yes, sir ; and, if they didn't, I'd rather put my poor woman into your hands alone, than theirs ; for Dr. Pilsbury he's old and fumbling, and so's Coffin ; and Hallowell knows more of cows and horses than of humans. This way, sir."

He opened the door of the large front room, where, upon a bed drawn into the middle of the floor, lay the unfortunate woman, her face flushed and swollen, her long black hair floating wildly, her hands clenched, and her eyes roving from face to face of those crowd-

ing around her bed, more with the hunted and fero-
cious look of a wild animal at bay than of a suffering
patient in the hands of physicians whom she trusts to
relieve and save her, even through the agency of
sharpest pain.

Consulting together in whispers around the table,
where some surgical instruments were boldly displayed,
stood the three doctors, — two of them the red-faced,
gray-haired, hard, and well-grooved country practitioner, who, after a youth of bewildered experiment
and doubt, has in middle or later life settled upon a
narrow round of treatment and drugs, and adapts all
cures to them. The third, a younger man, who, without making pretence to a diploma or an education,
did what he could, and as he could, to relieve the
ailments of his townsmen and their cattle, stood
listening deferentially to the opinions of his superiors,
offering an occasional hesitating remark, to which the
magnates scarcely paid any attention. A mob of
women — servants and neighbors, the mother of the
sick woman, and her sister with a baby in her arms —
filled the room, and surrounded the bed, almost to the
exclusion of the air for which the poor fevered creature was panting.

"If it was a dumb creetur, now," Hallowell was
saying as the landlord re-entered the room, " I should
say there wa'n't no need of cutting on't off at all.
Squire Watson's cow had a bad leg last winter, and I
doctored it, and cured it, and she's a well cow to-day ;
but then " —

"But then, you must remember, Master Hallowell,

that it's not a cow we are talking of, but a human," interposed Dr. Pilsbury with some acrimony; "and one kind of treatment won't answer for both. What I say is, that woman's leg is to come off: and, if she won't consent, we'll just strap her down, and take it off without her consent; and that quickly, for the light's going, and my eyes are not what they used to be."

"Good-evening, gentlemen. Will you allow me to look at your patient, and add my poor experience to yours in conducting the operation?"

At sound of this calm, harmonious, and cultivated voice, the somewhat heated and excited practitioners turned, and surveyed the new-comer with surprise and a little professional jealousy.

"Good-evening, sir," said Dr. Pilsbury at length. "You are an army surgeon, landlord Tilley says."

"Yes, of the royal army, and naturally of some little experience," replied the new-comer; and then, without waiting until his rival should gather self-possession to inquire, "Under which king, Bezonian?" he approached the bed, and courteously waving aside the throng of women, and murmuring to the patient, "Permit me, madam!" he deftly turned aside the clothes, and examined the suffering member, whose wrappings had already been removed in preparation for amputation.

The three practitioners drew near, and looked on with jealous attention; and the sick woman, calmed and comforted, she knew not how, by the look of that powerful and assured face, and the touch of hands fine as a woman's, and strong as a ploughman's, said, with a long, quivering sigh, —

"O doctor, if you could only save it to me ! I'm but a young woman, and a stirring one ; and if so be I've got to die, I'll die : but I won't live a cripple, to hobble round on crutches like an old granny ; I won't, I won't, I won't !"

Her voice rose to an hysterical shriek, and her clenched hands beat furiously upon the counterpane.

" She's going off again ! " cried one woman, and, —

" Now, Betty, Betty, don't 'ee, don't 'ee, that's a good lass !" added another ; and the mother, asserting her privilege, elbowed her way to the front, sharply exclaiming, —

" Now, Betty Tilley, be done with that, if thou knows what's good for thyself ! Come, then, ar'n't you ashamed to be such a baby, and these good folk all here to see thee have thy leg off like a brave woman, and " —

" Nay, then, mother-in-law," broke in the landlord : " sure it is no time to be flouting at the poor thing, and scolding never comforted a sick woman yet."

The mother-in-law replied, the other women chorused, the baby began to scream, and the patient to cry hysterically, and toss herself about in the bed sobbing, " I won't, then, I won't, I won't : I tell ye all there'll be no show, for I won't have it off."

LeBaron looked at Dr. Pilsbury, and saw that he had lost his head, and knew not what course to pursue ; at Dr. Coffin, who feebly followed the example of his superior ; and at Mr. Hallowell, who, abashed by

Pilsbury's reproof, no longer ventured to hold any opinion at all.   In this emergency he seized the landlord by the arm, and drew him out of the encounter, where he was rapidly getting worsted by the nimble tongues of his opponents, and sternly demanded of him, —

"Do you know that all this is killing your wife?"

"Ay, but what's to be done, sir?   You see"—

"Turn every human creature out of the room except those three doctors, and keep the house quiet."

"That I'll do, if you'll stand by, and see that they don't hack and hew at my poor lass while I'm away, and she screeching that they sha'n't."

"No one shall touch her to-night, at least, — I'll promise you that.   Come, now, out with every one of them, in the twinkle of an eye!"

Then, leaving this somewhat difficult task in the willing hands of the landlord, the surgeon returned to the side of the raving woman, and, taking both her hands in his, sat down on the edge of the bed, and said, in a calmly assured voice, —

"Now you are to be quiet, dame, do you hear?"

Gradually, beneath that firm grasp and firmer eye, the contortions of body and frenzy of mind subsided into languid moaning and tears; and then the doctor, gently smoothing the hair from the poor corrugated brow and hot cheeks, said gently, —

"Nothing is to be done to-night but to rest and refresh yourself, dame.   Will you be good, and try to sleep?"

"And know my leg is to be cut off in the morning?" whimpered the woman. "If you would say that it could be cured, I'd sleep gay and well."

"Come, then, now that you are quiet, and the room is still, I shall look at it once more, and we shall see what we shall see, madam."

Once more he examined the limb minutely, repeatedly, thoroughly yet gently, and then, laying the clothes over it, turned, and beckoned his colleagues to follow him from the room. Outside the door they found the landlord standing sentry, with a stout staff in his hand.

"I said I'd crack the head of the first one that came up those stairs without leave, doctor; and I'll do it too," exclaimed he valiantly, and addressing the latest comer as the acknowledged head of the consultation.

"And you did well, my friend," replied LeBaron gravely. "Now go in there, and speak calmly and gently to your wife, but talk as little as may be. I will see that no one comes up stairs."

Then leading his companions a little farther from the door, he; turned and, laying a finger lightly and impressively upon Dr. Pilsbury's breast, he said, —

"That leg can be saved. It must not be amputated."

"Nonsense, man!" blustered the old doctor. "The woman will die if the leg don't come off. It shall come off!"

"It shall not come off, if the landlord takes my advice, and I think he will," replied LeBaron firmly.

"Very well," exclaimed Pilsbury: "I throw up the case."

"And I take it," calmly returned LeBaron.

CHAPTER XXVIII.

DAME TILLEY'S LEG.

"THEY want you out there, Tilley," whispered Mr. Hallowell in the landlord's ear; and leaving the subdued and silent vet. beside his wife's bed, the landlord went into the passage, and, was confronted by the red and furious face of Dr. Pilsbury, who exclaimed in a voice thick with anger, —

"Look at here, Tilley! are you going to let this man, a stranger, and nobody knows who, take charge of your wife? or am I to do so? We can't both; and if he stays, I go, — that's all."

"The fact is here, my good friend," interposed the cool voice of the other, before poor John Tilley could stammer out any reply at all: "this gentleman is sure that it is necessary to cut off your wife's leg to save her life; I am equally sure that it is not, and that I can, if not interfered with, save both leg and life. Shall I try?"

"I'm sure, gentlemen, I'm sure you're very good, both of you; and I am loath indeed to offend Dr. Pilsbury, that every one calls such a fine doctor; but poor Betty, she's so set against losing the leg, — and if this gentleman is dead-sure he can cure it, and is an army surgeon, and used to these things" —

"Oh, I see, I see, goodman!" interrupted Pilsbury, pushing rudely past LeBaron, who retreated with a courteous bow: "you'd rather have this fellow, whose name even you don't know, and so save my fee; for I suppose he'll take his pay in beer" —

"One moment, if you please, my dear doctor," interposed LeBaron quietly: "professional brothers should never forget the courtesies of their clique. Allow me to offer my card. If you care to glance at it, I should be glad to show you my diploma, and commission as surgeon in the French army."

"Oh, a Frenchman!" exclaimed both the doctor and the publican in a breath. The surgeon gravely bowed.

"Yes, gentleman, a Frenchman."

"Well, Tilley, if you're going to give over your wife to be murdered by a French quack, you're not the man I take you for," said Pilsbury, putting his nose in the air so as to bring his spectacles to bear upon the card in his hand.

Goodman Tilley looked bewildered; and glanced first at the irate yet triumphant face of the long-known and venerated Pilsbury, then at the calm, handsome, and slightly sneering one of the stranger and the Frenchman. At last he said in a hesitating and reluctant voice, —

"Well, Dr. Pilsbury, I suppose I'll have to ask you to — no, dang it all, I won't neither! I like this man's looks, and I believe he knows what he says, and can do what he promises: and as for Frenchmen, why, it's peace now 'twixt us and them; and if it wa'n't, and if he was the very Old Fellow himself, horns and hoofs and all, and could save Betty's leg I'd let him, so be he didn't meddle with her soul."

"Well, I can promise so much," replied LeBaron, heartily grasping the hand of the honest landlord laid in his; "and I will undertake the case in the interests of humanity, if you will agree on your side, that I shall pay my reckoning at this inn like any other guest, and shall receive no fee, but that this gentleman and the others shall be paid whatever has been promised for their services."

"Why, that's handsome, and more than they could ask," replied Tilley in a tone of evident relief. "And if you'll go in and speak to Betty, sir, I'll follow the doctor, and give him a good glass of strong waters before he starts, and talk him round a bit. As for old Coffin, it don't matter; and our own man, Hallowell, isn't of much account anyway."

The landlord hurried away; and Dr. LeBaron returned to the bed-chamber, where he found the veterinary examining the limb, and the patient regarding him with suspicious and uneasy glances.

"If you please, doctor," said the new-comer very courteously, taking the bed-covering from the other's hand, and drawing it over the limb, "the case has, I believe, been confided to my charge, and I will attend to it."

"Oh! certain, certain, doctor," replied the vet. obsequiously; "and if, as I gether, you think it can be cured instead of cut off, why, I'm of your opinion too, and wanted to say so; only they wouldn't hearken to me,

being an onlarned man, but with a good nateral gift
for physic and such matters."

"I shall be glad to speak with you to-morrow morning, at eight o'clock, if you will do me the honor to
call," replied the Frenchman with exquisite urbanity.
"But just now my only object is to quiet my patient,
and give her a good night's rest."   And, hardly knowing how or why, the worthy vet. found himself going
down stairs with two vague impressions struggling in
his mind, — one, that the new doctor was a very skilful
and also agreeable man ; the other, that he should have
liked to stay longer in his society, and wondered why
he did not.

Presenting himself next morning at the appointed
hour, Master Hallowell found himself courteously received by the new doctor, and called not so much to a
consultation, as a clinical lecture at Dame Tilley's
bedside, where he received in a scant half-hour more
instruction on the subject of the knee-joint and its
peculiar temptations to disease, than he ever had
gathered in his life before.

"And there will be no need of amputation?" asked
he timidly, as the two retired from the sick-room.

"Amputation!" exclaimed Dr. LeBaron contemptuously.   "It should never have been mentioned in the
case.   The clown cuts down the cankered tree : the
gardener cures it, and enjoys the fruit."

CHAPTER XXIX.

THE DARK HOUR BEFORE DAWN.

DEBORAH WILDER never quite recovered from the rheumatic fever in whose grasp we left her, but rose from her bed a decrepit and feeble imitation of the tireless and restless woman who had lain down upon it. All the rest of the winter and spring she led a mummy-like existence, swathed in red flannels, night-caps, and felt slippers, and hovering over the fire, while everybody else was panting for a breath of fresh air ; and although in the heats of summer the foe released his hold for a little while, and the poor victim tried to stir about the house and resume her manifold duties, it was soon evident that both strength and ability were gone for a while, if not forever, while the power of fault-finding and dictation flourished more vigorously than ever upon the ruins. Strong and brave and sweet as was her daughter's nature, the year succeeding her mother's illness tried it to the utmost, and might have broken it down at last but for the occasional half-hour by day or night when the girl stole away to sit in her little hidden priest's chamber, and dream over every word that had been spoken there, every look and caress that faithful memory reproduced, and to dwell upon the sweet vague hopes of the future, when François was to come to claim her, and she should persuade him to remain at the farm and make all her duties light by advice and sympathy, while he himself should achieve a wonderful reputation by his medical skill, and in time become as famous as Dr. Pilsbury himself. Then she settled how his room should be arranged, and, shyly glancing at the possibility that it might be her room as well, deeply considered the subject of furniture and ornament, and resolved that for the first few months, at any rate, Grandmother Ames's curtains should be applied to their original use ; and, having dressed the bride, should afterward decorate her bridal chamber.

Then the poor child would take from her bosom the amethyst ring, symbol of her mock-marriage, and kiss it, and admire it, and remember how she first had seen it on the cold wet hand of the half-dead man she had brought across her father's threshold, and nursed back to life and love.

There had been a crest cut upon the ring ; but by some strange accident, as she imagined, a piece had been chipped from the face of the gem in such a manner as to quite obliterate the device. Nor would Molly have been the wiser had it remained : for her education in the gentle art of heraldry had never been so much as begun ; and sable, argent, gules, and azure, passant, séjant, rampant, and couchant, were words conveying no meaning to her ear.

But the ring had belonged to François ; he had himself placed it upon her finger, and called her wife in doing so ; and the Kohinoor itself would not have tempted her to an exchange.

So life went on in the farmhouse by the sea, with much hard work, very few enjoyments, no society, a deal of pain and suffering to the mother, and through her to the daughter, until all minor discomforts and annoyances were put to flight by one terrible blow, as the smoking of the kitchen-chimney is forgotten when a thunderbolt tears through the house.

Soon after noon on a fearfully hot day in July, Humphrey Wilder was brought in from the hay-field by four men, speechless, senseless, dying. The sight of him thus, quite upset the poor wife's little remaining strength of mind and body; and Molly was glad to accept Mrs. Hetherford's offers of counsel and help. The stricken man lingered through that day and night, and in the next night died. Molly never left his side, taking mechanically such food as Mrs. Hetherford brought to her, but neither sleeping nor resting for a moment.

In the last few hours he recovered consciousness; and then his daughter, kneeling beside him, said, —

"Father dear, I have somewhat to tell you. Can you listen? Will it tire you too much?"

"Nay, child, speak. Unburden thy conscience while there is yet a little time," whispered the dying man; and then Molly, in briefest phrases and with no excuses, told the story she should have told upon her wedding-day, but had not, partly from maiden shyness, partly from shame at her own duplicity, partly that she thought it would be another burden upon her father's mind. Yet, now that the strange illumination of death shone upon all around her, keen remorse at having even by silence deceived this beloved father seemed more impossible to bear than even the grief of his departure.

Wilder listened, his dim eyes fixed upon her own, until the faltering voice ceased in one wild sob, and the petition laid with tears and kisses upon his hand : —

"Oh, forgive me, father! Forgive me before you die!"

"Nay, child, did you doubt my forgiveness, that you tarried so long to claim it?" gently chided the father. "I guessed a good deal of this, and many a time I would have spoken, for I saw how it fretted thee to deceive thy mother and me; but, shall I tell thee, Molly, although I would never have chidden thee, I thought perhaps 'twas no more than thou didst deserve to so chide thyself, and I let thee go on for a while. And then, if I knew, I must have told thy mother, for, Molly, I kept no secrets from her; and she might not have been so tender with thee.

"Yes, child, I partly knew. I saw thee carrying food to the garret, and I heard of the hue and cry after the Frenchman; and I knew if one were here I ought to give him up, and I shut my eyes. And when that doctor came, I knew such tow-hair never grew on such a black-a-vised face as his; and I heard two men's voices in the night; and that last night, when on stroke of midnight you opened your door, and looked out into the kitchen, it wakened me, and after a little I got up softly, and peeped through the door, fearing I knew not what, only I never doubted you, Molly, never. And peeping so, like that Tom they tell of, I saw my maid making herself brave in a white gown, and I knew it meant a wedding, and I knew not what to do; but still, my child, I trusted thee so wholly that I kept still, and sat there by the kitchen hearth, my face in my two hands, till I heard the front door open and shut, and I said, —

"'It is not my girl that has so left my house. No: I will trust her, I will trust her yet; for if she is false, then it is time for me to die.' And I waited on, and waited on, until my own sweet maid opened the door, and said, —

"'There, Tabby, go if you will, and see you tell no one.'"

"Oh! I remember that too, father, but I never saw you."

"No: your eyes were too blind with tears; but I saw you, my maid, and I saw the heart-break in your face for days after that as you looked at me, and looked at me; and I punished you, poor lass, by never giving you the chance to speak, until you left wanting to.

"But there, all is past now, and I am past. And, child, I forgive you freely, and I bless you and wish you well; and for your sake I can forgive him too, although that is harder, for it was through him that my girl committed the only fault worth mentioning in all her life. But I forgive him now, Molly: tell him I forgave him, and you too, poor child, you too. Let us speak no more of this. Tell me how thy mother bears this blow."

So they talked the night away; and in the gray dawn the grand, brave heart ceased to beat, the soul

departed as calmly and trustfully as it had lived, and
Molly Wilder wept her bitter tears of self-reproach and
loneliness beside her father's corpse.

Self-reproach! Ay, there is the bitterness of the
grave, there is the sting of death, not for ourselves,
but as we kneel beside the quiet face that will turn no
more toward us, even upon its death-pillow; the still,
still lips that answer not, though our plea for forgiveness burst our own heart in its intensity; the eyes,
whose glance was our light of life, and now so solemnly closed for us and all the world. Oh! be
warned, be warned in time : let not the sun go down
upon your wrath; speak out your penitence while yet
it may avail.

After this night came a time in Molly Wilder's life
which she never spoke of when it could be avoided,
and never thought of without a shudder; for, though
the gold come forth from the furnace seven times
refined and purified, the passage is none the less terrible, and the dross is not burned away without fierce
and consuming pain to the pure metal that remains.

Deborah Wilder had, after her own wintry fashion,
loved her husband very dearly; and his loss, added to
her own physical condition, completed the work disease had begun. She took to her bed, and to weary
alternations of a little worse and a little better, but
never well enough to be less than a constant care and
fatigue to her patient nurse, at whom she fretted and
scolded and complained incessantly. Besides this,
came the work of the house and such farm matters as
pertained to the house; and finally, when harvest-time

was at its height, Amariah came one night to his young mistress to confess that he was no longer what he once was, and felt that the work of the farm, especially at this season, was quite beyond either his ability or his strength, and was already ruinously behindhand; concluding by advising her to accept an offer, transmitted through him from Reuben Hetherford, to get in the harvest, and finish the autumn work of the farm, for half the crops.

"Half the crops, merely for gathering them in! Does the man take me for a fool?" blazed out Molly in most unwonted wrath. "Tell Master Hetherford, with my compliments, that I shall be in far sorer need than this, before I make such a bargain as that, or any bargain indeed, with him."

"But how shall we get in the rye, Molly?" persisted Amariah: "the wheat is ruined already by yesterday's rain, and the oats are dropping every day."

"Get help from Falmouth. Hire a man, or two men, and get in the crops just as father used to show you how."

"But how will we board the men, and you worked to death already?" whined the poor old man.

"Not to death; for I can do yet more, and not quite die," replied his mistress bravely. "Go down to-night, and see if your sister Susan will come and stay with me until Thanksgiving time, to care for mother and to help in the housework."

So two men and a woman were hired; and when the crops were gathered, and her hirelings dismissed, Molly easily reckoned that it would have been many dollars cheaper to have allowed the whole harvest to decay as it stood, and oh, so great a saving of labor and vexation to herself!

"And when spring comes, who is to do the planting?" whispered she to herself in dismay.

Spring came, and found Amariah so disheartened in spirit, and so feeble in body, that Molly willingly accepted the resignation he timidly offered; and, having steadfastly looked her position in the face, concluded, that, acting as her mother's agent, she had no right to decline the offer renewed by the Hetherfords, this time in the mother's name, to carry on the farm for the ensuing year for half the gross profits. Mrs. Wilder, being consulted, gave a peevish consent, and from that day out worried and fretted incessantly at the waste and ruin she foresaw; and for once saw truly, since Hetherford was only restrained in his skinning system, by the hope of ultimately possessing the farm and its heiress, whom he had never ceased to desire and to persecute.

At last poor Deborah Wilder's weak and unsavory taper went out altogether; and she not so much died, as ceased to complain or fret. Molly could not sorrow as she had for her father; and yet, standing beside her mother's shrouded form, a new and strange desolation settled down upon her heart with an exceeding weight and bitterness, as she remembered that she was an orphan, without one relative, so far as she knew, this side the Atlantic, and none upon the other whom she had ever seen or cared for. Homeless, too; since Mrs. Hetherford had already explained to her the impossibility of her remaining alone in the farmhouse, and invited her to come and stay with them; giving the other half the crops as an equivalent for her maintenance, during that year at least.

And it was two years and three months since François had bid her good-by; and in all that time she had not heard one word from him. "And perhaps will never hear!" whispered this spirit of creeping gloom, so new, so dreadful, a visitant in the girl's bright heart; but the heart was yet strong enough to rebel at such domination, and cried out bravely, "Then it will be because he is dead. If he lives, he will come."

"And why should he not be dead?" persisted Despair. "Your father, so strong and stalwart, is dead; your mother is dead; you have yourself felt as if Death stood very near, and beckoned you to follow him. Why should not François be dead?"

"Because God is good, and loves me, and I trust in him," moaned the child aloud; and, falling on her knees at the side of the quiet figure of the dead, she tried to pray, and could only moan, —

"Help me, O my Father! help me, or I perish."

Then came the funeral; and when it was over they led her to that new home, which to her never could be home; and in the gloaming she stole away, and went back to the old house, and up to the priest's chamber in the roof; and there, beside the pallet she never had removed, she at last was able to weep the tears that could not have fallen in that strange and dismal new abode, and so wept away the load that all day long had crushed her brain and heart.

Coming down stairs after a while, she stood in the room where her father had died, and where she herself had made that stolen bridal toilet; and as that night came back in every detail, the heavy eye brightened, and a tinge of color crept to the cheek and lips, and a long breath lifted the load upon her lungs. Then, still following in her memory the progress of that night, she went and unbolted the front door, and opened it. No snowy pathway stretched before it now, but a carpet of clover-turf; and the great white-rose bush beside the step nodded its stately head toward her own, and a cloud of incense floated from each pure chalice upward to the sky.

A horseman rode slowly past the little corn-barn, in whose shelter François had found his last refuge; but she did not heed him, for she was burying her tearful face in the white roses that she held in both hands, and finding strange comfort in their wordless whisperings. The traveller looked at her, however; and then he leaped from his horse, and came across the bit of greensward, and, as she looked toward him with startled and affrighted eyes, held out both his arms, and said, —

"My wife! My darling!"

"O François! You have come, you have come!"

CHAPTER XXX.

A BRIDAL PROCESSION.

MRS. HETHERFORD and her son sat in the star-light upon the back stoop of their house; he with his hat dragged down over his eyes, his elbows upon his knees, chewing a bit of stick in a manner so vicious as to suggest he would willingly have so destroyed some enemy. She, slowly rocking back and forth in a wooden chair, which creaked at each vibration with a peevish and weary sound, was knitting in the dark, and eagerly narrating the events of the evening. A few rods away the great gray sea thundered upon the sands, scorning in its changeless might the restlessness and helplessness of the men who call themselves its master.

"So just as I got to the door, with the horn in my hand to blow for supper," pursued Mrs. Hetherford, "what should I see but my lady Molly marching up the path, as grand as you please, with this fine gentleman beside her, good-looking enough, I'll give in, but phew! prouder than Lucifer himself, and walking as straight and smart as if the ground wasn't quite good enough for him to walk on. Up they come, while I stood kind o' dumbfounded with the horn in my hand; and Molly says, says she "—

"'Mrs. Hetherford, this is Dr. LeBaron, a gentleman to whom I have been troth-plight for some time. My father's last words were to wish that he soon might come to claim me, and here he is. We shall be married in the morning at Squire Drew's, and go directly to Boston.' Then he took off his hat, and made a bow like as he was making fun of me, and I courtesied, like a fool, just as I would to a lord in the old country; and then I recollected where we are, and who Molly is, and all, and I said, kind of patronizing,—

"'Well, well, you've stole a march on us, Molly. What do you expect Reuben will say? But come in, both of you, and have some supper.' But upon that my lord drew himself up as if I'd taken a liberty, and bowed again, and said something to Molly, and walked off; and she explained how he was going to sleep over at her house, and she'd found enough left for his supper out of the things set out for the mourners to-day. So that's all; and I must say, of all the disgraceful "—

"Shut up, mother," dutifully interposed her son at this word: "there's nothing disgraceful that I see. If Molly's promised to the man with her father's consent, and now is going to marry him, who's got any thing to say? As for the rest, if he's too proud or too fine to come inside my house, all the better, says I: let him sleep or lie awake where he will, so long as Molly's safe up-stairs here. Let 'em marry as soon as they like; but this is what I've got to say,"—and, breaking out of his enforced calm, Reuben sprang to his feet, and, lifting hand and face to the starry sky, he swore a black and bitter oath that before she died Molly Wilder should be his wife.

"Let her marry this man," repeated he, "let her marry six men if she will, but I will be the seventh, so help me God or the Devil, I care not which "—

"Hush, hush, Reuben!" exclaimed his mother, rising also in horror; but, dashing aside the hand she would have laid upon his arm, he strode away into the night, flinging back the warning, —

"And mind you don't say disgraceful of her again, mother: for in flinging dirt at her you fling it at me; for, so sure as she lives, she yet shall be my wife."

"Then, God help her!" muttered the mother, out of the bitterness of a wounded mother's heart; and, indeed, she had much to bear with this son, whom during his infancy she had ruined by indulgence, and who now repaid her in the customary fashion, especially during the last two or three years, when Molly's open aversion and avoidance had doubly imbittered his temper. Mercy, too, had married, and removed to some distance, leaving the widowed mother sole recipient of the abuse formerly shared between the two; so that, altogether, we must pity Dame Hetherford not a little, as she sees her hope of a sweet-tempered and helpful companion for her lonely days snatched away as soon as granted.

Molly, meantime, sitting at her window above, vaguely heard the murmur of voices, but cared not for them. She was listening rather to that solemn voice of the sea, voice familiar to all her life and all its needs, and telling now of the sad, grave life of the last years finished and put away, and the bright, sweet day dawning with to-morrow's sun. She loved him so, and she trusted him so! Without a question, hardly an answer, she had heard his plans, including a marriage before a magistrate to obviate the necessity of relating the first marriage; and her words, as they left the old house forever, were the keynote of her life, —

"I trust you, François, as my father trusted me."

Early the next morning Dr. LeBaron rode up to the door of the Hetherford mansion; and Molly, who had risen with the dawn, came down to meet him, already dressed for her journey. At her invitation to enter, he simply smiled and shook his head; and Molly went to seek her hostess, whom she surprised peeping at the stranger from behind her bedroom-curtains.

"I am going now. Won't you say good-by, aunty?" asked the girl, clinging to the one poor apology that was left her for the home-love and home-life that suddenly loomed so largely before her eyes. Quite to her surprise, Mrs. Hetherford turned, and, putting her arms about her neck, said with a hearty kiss, —

"No: I won't say good-by; but if you're bound to be married this morning, I'll go along too, as far as Squire Drew's, and show that if your own mother is dead, there's one that feels like a mother to you, and always means to, wherever you go."

"Will you really? Oh, thank you, thank you, dear aunty! and I am very sorry if I was short or cross with you last night; but I thought you would never take to it kindly, and "—

"And you were bound to have your own way whether or no, just as you always did," interposed the dame, who was acting partly under instructions, partly from a real, although very gnarled and twisted, affection for Molly.

"But one thing is sure," pursued she, when the two had kissed again, and each had wiped her eyes : "you are not going away without your breakfast, you nor your young man neither. Reuben was away at daylight to the ma'shes after salt hay ; and we three will have a cosey little meal, and then I'll have old Dolly saddled, and we all go to the squire's together."

So Molly, clinging still to this phantasm of a home and a mother, went out and tenderly besought her lover to yield his pride, as she had done hers, to this old woman's pleasure and hospitable wish, and come inside the house, and partake of the morning meal.

François listened, patted her cheek, smiled, and — yielded? Oh, no ! but calmly said, —

"My darling, I told you that I never should set foot beneath that man's roof, nor will I ; and as for eating his bread — pah, it would choke me !"

"But his mother — it is she whom I wish to please ; and I have no mother, François, and it is so strange and sad for a girl to go to her husband with never a woman's face to kiss good-by upon !"

"Well, child, let her come with us if she will. I do not say nay to that ; and go you in, and eat and drink at her table, and play at mother and daughter with her if you can. I will wait."

"No, no, François. I will come now."

"Nay, I have a project. When I went to saddle my horse this morning, I found a silly old man patting and feeding him, who presently let me know that he was Amariah, of whom in the old times I heard so much; and he, it seems, had already scented out my presence, and tottered over here from his home, wherever it may be, to look after us; and, among other confidences, he intrusted me with his intention of making a fire in the dear old kitchen where I first saw you, and preparing himself some breakfast. He spoke of plenty of fresh eggs in the barn with a chuckle of satisfaction, arising, probably, from the memory of many a stolen feast upon them; and I remembered your innocent surprise one day when no eggs were forthcoming for your invalid's breakfast. Well, with plenty of fresh eggs and some other matters which Amariah will forage for, I shall construct an omelet which will make the few remaining hairs upon that old man's head stand erect with wonder and awe. You remember my telling you how to make an omelet?"

"Yes, and my notable failure. But I will try again if you will teach me."

"And, that I may be a worthy teacher to so fair a pupil, I will go immediately, and perfect myself in the operation." And, doffing his hat, François leaped upon his horse, and rode away, leaving Molly half vexed, half gratified, and saying to herself as she re-entered the house, —

"Always so gentle and so courteous, but always having just his own way, and never mine!"

An hour or two later a little cavalcade set forth from Dame Hetherford's door, consisting of that worthy woman herself, decked in an antiquated robe of green silk, with a structure upon her head called a calèche from its resemblance to the hood of the vehicle of that name; after her the lovers, he riding firm and square upon the big black horse which had brought him from Boston, and she upon a pillion, bashfully supporting herself by an arm around his waist. Finally came Amariah, bestriding a blind and halt old steed which he had borrowed for the expedition, and urged along by incessant thumps and whacks.

"My love," said François, lifting her from the pillion at the squire's gate, "I trust that you rest content. You have not gone to your nuptials without a bridal procession."

"We only needed Tabitha to make it perfect," replied Molly with a little laugh half a sob. "Dear old Tabby! she saw the real marriage, and ought to have lived for this; but I am going to have her daughter sent after me as soon as we have a home."

CHAPTER XXXI.

THE VALUE OF A DOCTOR.

AND how is my good friend and patient, Mistress Tilley?" asked Dr. LeBaron, as he drew rein before the Bunch of Grapes, and saw the landlord joyfully come forward to meet him.

"Marvellously better, doctor, marvellously!" replied the publican, beaming all over with delight, "and wearying for a sight of you. Why, sir, I have a will to be jealous in hearing nought but your name upon her lips from morn till night, and when will he be back, and how many days are gone so far, and praises of your looks, your voice, your ways" —

"Spare me, good friend, spare my blushes," laughed the doctor, springing to the ground, and helping his companion to alight. "And if you will give my wife and me room in your pleasant house we will abide to-night with you, and I shall see good Mistress Tilley, two or three times at least."

"Your wife, sir! Aha! The gossips will be at rest now, for they could not make it out why you were travelling down the Cape only to come back again in a week or ten days, as you said; but it is all the better, all the better."

"All the better for me, no doubt; but for whom

else?" asked the doctor in some surprise, as he led his wife on through the low-browed hall into the parlor, so cool and shady in the summer noon, with its sanded floor, and dark old furniture, the asparagus-boughs hanging from the great beam running through the middle of the ceiling, the nosegay of roses in a bow-pot upon the hearth, and the floating muslin curtains across the windows.

"Who beside myself is all the better for my marriage, good mine host?" asked the doctor again, as the landlord, smiling and bowing, would have here left his guests.

"Why, sir — but I may not tell: it is yet a secret, but soon to be known to your worship, that is, when " — and stammering and bowing and tumbling over his own toes, John Tilley contrived to get himself out of the room, and closed the door behind him.

"It is some present, or perhaps a feast, planned for my return, and wherein my wife now shall share," said the doctor, as he helped Molly to undo and lay aside her riding spencer and hat, and then deftly and gravely arranged her bright brown hair, a little dishevelled by the wind.

"I wonder how my darling's face would look under the towering head-dresses worn by the fashionable dames abroad just now," said he, taking the round chin in his hand, and seriously regarding his wife's fair face. But she somewhat sharply withdrew a step, and coloring vividly said, —

"Content yourself in the beginning, François, with the simple country girl whom you have wed. She will never be a fashionable dame, or look like one."

"So jealous lest I should regret mine own act, little one, and so sharp in reproving the fault that was not, except in your own fancy!" said her husband gently. "My Mary is not one of the women of fashion whom I detest; but she surely is the sweet and gentle and docile wife whom I have loved so longingly, and sought so carefully, is she not?"

"You are gentler born than I, François, and must teach me to amend my rude ways and blunt speech," replied Molly with proud humility, and her eyes filling with tears.

"I can teach thee nought half so important as nature has taught thee already," whispered her husband, kissing away the tears, much to the delight of Margery Sampson, the landlady's sister, who, standing with the door in her hand, announced smilingly,—

"Mistress LeBaron's bedroom is ready, if she cares to go to it."

"Ha, pretty Margery!" exclaimed the doctor, turning around without the least embarrassment, while Molly's tears were dried by fiery blushes, "and how goes the world with thee, child? And is the dame ready to see me yet?"

"Oh, yes, sir! and more than ready; and she bid me ask if you could look in upon her now for a moment."

"Indeed I will, Margery, if you will take my wife to her own room. Your sister is where I left her, I suppose."

"Yes, sir: you know the way. Come, madam."

The delight of a woman in the society of her favorite physician is one of those amiable weaknesses of the sex at which men may marvel and sneer, but which they never need hope to eradicate, since it springs from two very feminine traits, — the love of talking about one's self, and the delight of relying upon masculine strength and skill in directions where the domestic authorities are obliged to confess incompetency or feign superiority. The father, husband, or brother sets down that peculiar feeling at the nape of the neck, that odd buzzing in the ears, or that tendency to tears and pettishness in the early morning, to imagination, nerves, or some other "glittering generality" of contempt; but Dr. So-and-so listens gravely to all the symptoms, asks questions, recalls former interviews, pays a little compliment, assures the invalid that she is too delicately constituted to bear any rough or careless treatment; and finally shakes twelve little powders into twelve little papers, numbers them carefully, — for mind of man refuses to contemplate the mischief ensuing from the irregular consumption of those powders, — and retires leaving his patient soothed, cheered, and already far upon the road to recovery. She has her three dollars' worth, and the unsympathetic monster who has to pay it is justly mulcted for his unfeeling conduct.

So Dame Betty Tilley passed a charming half-hour with her doctor, as she already styled LeBaron; and then he was called to tea, and still lingered over that pleasant meal when Goodman Tilley, appearing at the door, solemnly announced, —

"Master Bradford, Master Howland, and Master

Southworth, selectmen of the town of Plymouth, request the pleasure of Dr. LeBaron's presence in the parlor of this inn."

"Request the pleasure of my company!" exclaimed LeBaron, starting to his feet, and carrying his hand to his belt, as if seeking a weapon. "And for what? The war is over, peace is declared!"

"And it is an errand of peace that brings them here, as you shall see," replied Tilley, still in the solemn and impressive manner of a herald negotiating between high and mighty powers. The doctor glanced at him, then at Molly, who had turned very white; and then, tossing his head in the careless and haughty fashion habitual with him, he strode out of the room, and across the passage to the twilight-parlor where his guests awaited him.

They rose to meet him, and stood steadfastly regarding him for a moment without speaking,—three grave, responsible, thoughtful-looking men, worthy successors of the fathers whose names they bore, and the mantle of whose dignity still covered their descendants. Bradford was the first to speak; and after mentioning his own name, and those of his associates, he said,—

"You are called Dr. Francis LeBaron, sir?"

"Yes, Master Bradford."

"And are a surgeon of the French army?"

"Again, yes, gentlemen; although at a loss to understand the reason"—

"I crave your pardon, sir; but before speaking will you listen to the message we, the selectmen of the town of Plymouth, have been charged to convey to you, and in that message you will find the motive of what seems to you impertinent meddling."

"By no means, Master Bradford, and gentlemen. I am but astonished that so humble and individual as myself should have excited any attention at all in this respectable town, or that its selectmen should trouble themselves to inquire aught concerning me."

"They probably would not, sir, except for a need in the town which you possibly may supply," returned Bradford with a cool composure, equalling, at least, the slightly arrogant tone of the baron, whose steely eyes flashed suddenly upon the speaker, as he moved a chair towards him, and courteously said, —

"Will you seat yourselves, gentlemen? I am most happy if in any manner I can oblige you, or the town, more than by removing myself from it."

".That remains to be proven, Dr. LeBaron. We have all known, and in a manner witnessed, through the eyes of Phineas Hallowell, your skill and good judgment in the matter of Dame Elizabeth Tilley's leg; and he says that you showed him sundry papers proving your claim to the rank of physician and sur- geon accredited by the European schools, and ranked as such in the French army."

" Excuse my interruption, messieurs the selectmen ; but I would be distinctly understood as *not* having shown my diploma, certificates, and commission to the good cow-doctor in proof of my claims, as you phrase it ; for I make no claims, or give any man the right to question my statements. I come here a traveller, and

a stranger; I find a woman about to be mutilated by
— well, by unwise practitioners; I interfere in the interests of humanity and science, and cure her. Afterward, in discussing foreign colleges, and modes of
education, with Master Hallowell, I show him certain
documents as matters of interest to a man having
some slight acquaintance with physic. That is all;
and, if there is some one else sick in the town, I shall
be happy to render my services again in the same fashion, but must decline to submit to a previous cross-
examination at any hands."

John Bradford allowed a decorous moment of silence to intervene, and then replied, his cool and
measured tones following the rapid and somewhat
heated utterance of the Frenchman, as the chill north
wind sweeps in to fill the vacuum left by the burning
air exhaled from the face of the desert, —

"It is ever unwise, young man, to resent an injury
not offered, or to reply to a question not yet asked.
If you will hear me out, my errand is briefly this : —

"We have here in Plymouth no educated and competent physician, and we wish for one. Your skill has
already been proven; and your education and rank
may be proven by the exhibition of the papers shown
by you, from whatever motive, to Phineas Hallowell.
This being settled, we are empowered by the town to
invite you to remain among us as our surgeon, physician, and apothecary. The town offers you a tract of
twenty-five acres of land wherever outside the village
you may select it, and a house-lot on the main street,
with assistance, if you need it, in building a house

thereon : you will have such fees as are usual among us, some of them paid in money, but more in produce ; and you will receive a cash salary of ten pounds, by the year, for attention and physic for the town's poor."

" And that is quite as much as, if not more than, we do for our minister," said Constant Southworth, breaking silence for the first time ; while John Howland stirred uneasily in his chair, and cleared his throat as if to audibly indorse his companions' statements, but, thinking better of such waste of words, relapsed into his usual golden silence.

Dr. LeBaron looked from one to the other of those gray and impassible faces, and felt a certain respect and deference arising in his mind, such as the presence of kings and emperors had not always evoked in it. He bowed courteously to all three in succession, and answered in the same tone, —

" First and always, messieurs, I have to thank you for the confidence in my poor skill, and also in my moral and social standing, implied in this invitation, which is so unexpected that I must beg a little time to consider of it, and to consult my wife, who accompanies me, and must have her voice in the choice of a residence for life. I had intended to settle in Boston, but have made no binding arrangements there, and — shall I see you again in the morning, gentlemen ?"

The selectmen looked at each other, silently rose and stood, their rock-like faces turned upon LeBaron as he first had seen them, while John Bradford quietly replied, —

"We shall be here at eight o'clock of the morning, and trust to find you ready to accede to our offer."

CHAPTER XXXII.

A TREATY OFFENSIVE AND DEFENSIVE.

PUNCTUALLY as the clock struck eight the next morning, the three selectmen entered the parlor of the Bunch of Grapes; and before the sound of their footsteps in the passage died away, Dr. LeBaron followed them, looking very handsome, and a little supercilious, in the bright June morning, for he carried a roll of papers in his hand, and felt that he presented himself on approval. The selectmen gravely saluted him, and waited in silence for a reply to the questions already sufficiently stated. The baron unrolled his papers upon the table, and said, —

"Will you take the trouble to glance at these, gentlemen? Here is my diploma from the University at Bologna, this from the Medical School at Vienna, this certificate of ability from the Physicians' College, London, and this is my commission as surgeon in the French navy."

In perfect silence the worthy selectmen placed their spectacles upon their noses, carefully read each document from end to end, with the exception of the commission, which, being expressed in French, was only intelligible to Bradford, while the crabbed Latin of the others was familiar enough to all.

The inspection finished, Bradford took off and folded his spectacles, and having looked earnestly at his colleagues, who gravely replied by answering looks, he said, —

"These papers are perfectly satisfactory, Dr. Le-Baron, in all points save one. They are made out simply in the name of Franciscus, except the commission, where the title is *le docteur* François. Your name, I understand, is LeBaron."

"Worthy Master Bradford and gentlemen," replied the doctor, "we have arrived at a point foreseen by me since I first understood your errand, and one past which we may possibly never go, however much I may regret losing your friendship and countenance. I am, as you perceive, a man of no nationality, educated in Italy, in Germany, in England, in the school of the world, — in one word a cosmopolitan. I have no name except that of Francis, Latinized by one set of my acquaintance, Gallicized by another, Anglicized by the third. To this name I add for convenience' sake that of LeBaron, which may or may not belong more than another to me. Here you have all of my history that you will ever possess; and from this day forth I shall answer no man's questions, even as patiently as I have yours. If, under these conditions, you care to have me settle among you, and act as the physician of your bodies, I am ready to accept the offer made me last night."

"One question more, Dr. LeBaron, before we close the contract," replied Bradford, after a brief consultation with his associates : "what is your religious belief?"

"That from which your fathers fled. I am a Roman Catholic," replied LeBaron briefly and sternly.

A slight movement of undisguised horror told the feeling with which this announcement was received, and again the three consulted in whispers; while the baron, with an angry flush upon his high Norman cheek-bones, rolled up his papers and put them in his pocket. Presently Bradford turned toward him, and in his grave yet benevolent voice said, —

"You have rightly said that our fathers fled to this bleak and arid soil to escape the corruptions and tyranny of the Roman Church; and we, their descendants, hate and dread it as we should. Nevertheless, even as in your own art it is sometimes permitted to employ deadly and loathsome poisons for the healing of disease, and the skilful physician can turn even the tongue of the adder and the venom of the toad to more advantage than an unlearned man can the pure and pleasant remedies of nature; so it is permitted to us to use your skill, regardless of your religion,— that is, if you will accede to certain conditions."

"As what, gentlemen?"

"That the silence you propose, with unnecessary asperity, to maintain in regard to all your worldly affairs, shall extend to those spiritual as well. That you shall never mention to any person beyond us three, your religious beliefs or opinions, or in any manner inculcate or teach them, even in your own household. The matter will be a secret confined to ourselves, and hence no scandal shall arise. We must also stipulate that you shall, as often as convenient, attend divine service in the meeting-house on Sunday, and instruct your family so to do. And in concluding, I pray you, sir, not to resent this plain speaking, or this somewhat rigid stipulating upon our part, since we act, as it were, in the place of fathers of the family among whom we invite you to dwell. And while we are amply willing to intrust the bodies of our children to your skill and judgment, we would anxiously insure against peril to the souls which are so much more to be valued; even as men, while lighting a fire in times of pestilence to purify the air, hedge it about with jealous care lest it consume their homes."

"In truth, Master Bradford, you are a plain speaker, and I know not whether of two courses to pursue: to wish you all a very good morning, call for my horse, and ride away, relieving this good town of its present dangerous association with a noisome and loathsome poison, tongue of adder, venom of toad, and destroying fire, all which similes you have used in describing me, — or to give you my hand, call you the only honest man I ever saw, and accept your offer on your own conditions."

"The latter is the wiser and more Christian course, doctor," said Bradford smiling grimly.

"Say you so? Then I adopt it," exclaimed Le-Baron frankly, and courteously suiting the action to the word. "But allow me to tell you, friend, that your medical education is far behind the light of modern science. We no longer use powdered adders or steeped toads for medicine; and, indeed, it is much doubted whether the toad possesses either the venom or the jewel attributed to him by the ancients."

" Indeed ? Well, doctor, we shall be ready to learn of you in all matters physical ; and by God's grace you may learn of us some of those great and awful spiritual truths which startled our fathers from their sleep beneath the claws of the great and terrible dragon of Popery."

" Hold, good Master Bradford ! I have in turn one condition to impose before the bargain is sealed."

" And what is that ? " asked Bradford anxiously.

" That no one shall seek to corrupt me to Protestantism. Let the silence on the subject of religion be mutual."

" Friend, I stand reproved," replied Bradford humbly ; and so went his way, followed by his colleagues.

CHAPTER XXXIII.

THE ROSE-GARDEN OF PROVENCE.

AGAIN at Montarnaud, again in the summer garden where the flowers bloom as freshly and as gayly as they did twelve years ago; where still the fountains tinkle, and the birds sing, and the sweet winds come and go with kisses on their breath. The château is even more imposing than of old; for the revenues of Rochenbois have come to fill the empty coffers of Montarnaud, and the old house has been restored, amplified, and embellished, until it hardly knows itself. Time the Destroyer has given way to Time the Perfecter everywhere; and not a change is to be seen that is not an improvement. But stay : what shall we say of the lady reclining in this garden-chair beneath the shade of the fragrant oleanders, one of whose petals has fallen so charmingly upon her dusky hair? What have twelve years done for her whom we left a girl of sixteen in all the glory of her morning loveliness? The cheek could hardly be more colorless than it was then ; but one seems to feel that the blood no longer pulses so rapidly beneath its creamy surface, and the merry mouth has learned to fold itself more immovably, perhaps more scornfully ; the wealth of lustrous hair is coiffed more artificially than in the old time ; and the large dark eyes move more languidly, and hardly care to raise their slumberous lids at every call. The toilet is no longer that of a careless girl, but perfect in its taste, art, and befitting richness. In fact, we have here the handsome and elegant *dame du grande monde ;* and the Valerie who perched in the branches of the oak, and teased her nurse and governess, is gone forever. And yet one must change his half-breathed sigh of regret at this loss into one of astonishment and delight, as he catches sight of a little fairy form chasing butterflies among the roses ; a little atom of life and light and motion, looking, with her floating gold-bronze curls, her glowing cheeks, and parted lips, her dancing eyes, and swift aërial motions, more like the creation of some wonderful magician, a fairy caught and clothed with some elemental and unsubstantial body, than a child of ordinary earth. And this is the little Thérèse, heiress of Montarnaud and Rochenbois, only child surviving of Valerie's loveless and disastrous marriage. Up and down the garden paths skims the child, swift as a swallow, uncertain as the butterflies she chases : and after her toils a young woman, her comely face warm with wrath and sunshine, for she wishes of all things to seat herself in some cool and shaded nook to spell out a note just handed her by one of the servants, in the handwriting of her dearly-loved brother, whom as yet she has seen but once since his return from foreign travel, and who is to visit her, with the consent of Madame la Comtesse, this very day ; but, in chasing this restless little sprite up and down, she cannot even find time to read what may be the announcement of his arrival.

A figure in clerical costume appears at the head of the steps leading from the terrace down to the garden; and Madame Clotilde, as she is called, utters a joyous exclamation, —

"It is he, my dear brother, mademoiselle!"

"Can he catch butterflies?" asks the little lady, and then adds in a tone of disgust, "Why, he's a priest too! I wish somebody but priests would come here. I like soldiers better: I wish mamma did."

Madame Clotilde approaches her mistress, and joyously announces, —

"My brother, madame. May I leave mademoiselle with her nurse, and take him into the house?"

"No: fetch him here, and take Thérèse to the other end of the garden," languidly replies the countess. "The heat and her voice have given me a headache, and perhaps Père Vincent's conversation may amuse me for a while."

So Clotilde, with a decided pout and frown upon her pretty face, goes to meet her brother, and delivers the lady's mandate, adding a few words of muttered complaint on her own part, at which he gently smiles, murmuring, —

"By and by, my child, by and by."

Then he approaches madame, who does not disturb herself except to smile graciously, and wave her hand toward a chair close beside her couch. The abbé bows profoundly, seats himself, and studies his companion with sidelong imperceptible glances.

"It is a long time since we met, monsieur l'abbé," says Valerie in a tone of courteous indifference.

"And yet nothing is changed except for the better here at Montarnaud, madame."

"That is as one thinks. Twelve years leave their mark wherever they pass." And a gloomy shadow crosses the countess's beautiful face, as if those twelve years suddenly stood between her and the sun. But, rallying immediately, she inquires absently,—

"And where have you been all these years, monsieur?"

"In many places, madame. I have visited nearly all the countries of the world."

"Indeed! You must have seen many curious things. And where did you remain longest?"

"I can hardly tell, madame; for it has seldom been an unbroken year in any one place."

"And were you never homesick, abbé?"

"Sometimes,.I confess, madame; for there is no spot of earth so charming or so dear to me as France."

"Then, why did you not return sooner?"

"I had work to do abroad, madame."

"Oh! you were sent upon some mission by the Church?"

"We priests do nothing except under direction, madame."

"And you are never allowed to travel alone, I am informed," said the lady carelessly.

"Madame forgets perhaps that I am not a Regular," said the abbé with an air of explaining every thing.

"Well, then, you *did* travel alone?" demanded the countess petulantly.

"Sometimes, madame."

"And other times who was your companion?"

"One is always meeting friends and associates, madame. From Rome to Vienna I travelled with Père Clement, a pupil of Père Condren, and a very holy man. Then in Ghent I met with the venerable Père Bourdaloue, and we travelled to Geneva; and"—

"Yes, yes, I understand; but I meant rather to inquire how long you held companionship with my husband's brother, le baron François. You went abroad in his company at first, if I remember."

"He is not in France now then, madame?"

"That is what I am asking you, monsieur."

"Excuse me, madame; but it is I who must ask news of you in such matters. I am so new an arrival on French soil that I have hardly yet seen any one."

Madame la Comtesse clenched the costly fan in her right hand until the pearl sticks broke with a light crush audible to the priest's ears. Then she sat a little more upright, and said,—

"Monsieur l'abbé, I need a chaplain here at Montarnaud. The duties are very light, not interfering with any other appointments he may hold, and the salary is something very considerable to a priest meriting my approval. Would the post suit you, do you think?"

"Admirably, madame, if I receive permission from my superior to accept it."

"And who is your superior?"

"I have so many, madame! The general of our Order first, no doubt: but, as I am attached to the Cathedral at Marseilles, I am under the authority of the bishop of that diocese as to the disposal of my time; and, if madame pleases, I will lay her very flattering proposal before him to-night, and, having permission, will accept " —

"One moment, monsieur. Before we settle the chaplaincy we will finish our conversation upon other matters. Where did you tell me you parted from the baron François, who left this house in your company?"

"It is quite true, madame, that the baron left here in my company upon the night of the unfortunate quarrel between him and the Vicomte de Montarnaud, and remained for some days with me in Marseilles; but since that I have no news to tell of him."

"Nothing? *En passant,* I have news for you of Mademoiselle Salerne. She is a rich widow now, and probably in need of a confessor. I must get her to keep house for me while I am in Paris this winter; and, if you are chaplain, you will look after her, I hope. Meantime, what were you saying of my brother-in-law?"

"Madame, the last time I had the honor of mentioning my pupil's name to you was in conveying a *billet-doux* from him to you after his flight from this house; and on that occasion you very properly reprimanded me for meddling in matters unbecoming my profession, and threatened to report me to the Comte de Montarnaud, then alive. That reproof has had so salutary an effect upon me, that I believe I have absolutely lost my memory in all matters except those pertaining to the Church. I cannot, for instance, recall at this moment any thing whatever in connection with

the baron François beyond your refusal to reply to
that *billet-doux*."

"Is it possible, my dear abbé? This is a misfortune in which I am compelled not only to sympathize
but share, since with so fatal an infirmity as loss of
memory, you could not perform the duties of chaplain,
and we must relinquish the idea."

"So I supposed, madame."

"You are quite sure that you cannot conquer this
treacherous memory, at least in one direction?"

"Unfortunately, I am quite sure, madame."

"Such a pity! Adieu, then, monsieur. I will not
detain you from your sister longer. She has so few
opportunities of seeing her friends, poor thing, since I
do not approve much visiting or receiving among the
persons in my employ."

The abbé bowed profoundly, and withdrew; mutter-
tering between his teeth as he once more brushed the
roses of Montarnaud from their stems with the skirt
of his *soutane*, —

"These aristocrats are terribly monotonous! They
have only one little set of insolences, and all use them
the moment they cannot have their way in every
thing."

It was one of the unheeded mutterings heralding
the wildest storm of anarchy the world has ever seen :
it was called the Reign of Terror.

CHAPTER XXXIV.

THE RESTORATIONS OF THE CHAPEL.

AMONG other advantages of Madame la Comtesse de Montarnaud's frequent residences in the capital, she had become acquainted with her country neighbors, and chiefly with the sprightly and fashionable Marquise d'Odinard *née* d'Aubigney, who had married a fair estate about as far from Marseilles on the one side as Montarnaud on the other. In Paris the two young women were inseparable, and in the country visited each other when nothing more amusing presented itself. In one point, however, they had hitherto found but little sympathy; for Olive d'Odinard, young, rich, pretty, and spoiled, found a certain piquancy in varying her worldly pleasures with some of those ascetic observances already coming into vogue at court, where the rule of Madame de Maintenon was replacing the gay sovereignty of de Montespan; and the most frivolous votaries of fashion made a point of weeping during the sermons of the elegant preachers, on whose lips still rested the fires kindled by Francis de Sales, Bourdaloue, de Condren, Vincent de Paul, and the rest who illuminated this cycle, and so powerfully revived the dying faith in France.

But Valerie, although she would fain follow every

fashion of the court, could not endure the weariness besetting an untrue religious life; and, when urged thereto by her friend at certain periods, would sometimes declare that there was no king ready to marry her as there was for Madame de Maintenon; sometimes that cards, stupid as they were, were less wearisome than prayers; and sometimes that priests always sent her to sleep before she had time to profit by their eloquence.

But in the night succeeding her futile attempt to corrupt the Abbé Despard's loyalty to his friend, Valerie suddenly remembered that Olive had invited her to dine on the following day at her house in company with Père Roussillon, coadjutor of the cathedral in Marseilles; and the marquise had urged the invitation by the remark that Père Roussillon was precisely the man to work her friend's conversion. Valerie had jestingly declined this invitation, but now resolved to accept it, nodding confidentially to herself in the darkness as she did so, and then falling asleep with the smile of an approving conscience on her lips.

The next morning found her silent and thoughtful; and about noon, having made a careful toilet, she entered her coach, and arrived at the Château d'Odinard about three; the marquise being so ultra fashionable as to dine at that hour when on her own estate, although in Paris obliged to conform to the court hour of one.

"You see that I have come, *ma chère*," said the guest, embracing her hostess with effusion; "for I found myself so *triste* without you after yesterday. Besides, I want to consult your Père Roussillon"—

"O Valerie! about your conscience?" exclaimed Olive, clasping her hands in rapture.

"No, dear," replied Valerie dryly. "About a much more interesting matter, the restoration of the chapel at Montarnaud. It is quite in ruins; and I want it made just as lovely as yours here at Odinard, and then I will have a chaplain and daily mass. Now, I hear that the coadjutor understands ecclesiastical architecture *à merveille*, and I thought I would consult him. Am I right?"

"Admirably right, *ma mie*. Yes, indeed, Père Roussillon understands all this sort of thing as nobody else does. The restorations at the cathedral were all his work. The bishop put the whole thing in his hands; and, truth to tell, the dear bishop is not half so learned a man as his coadjutor, although of course more holy."

"Why more holy?" asked Valerie in surprise.

"Just because he is a bishop, I mean. Is not his holiness the Pope more holy than — well, this Père Despard, for instance, who has just been made assistant at the cathedral? I was so vexed on Saturday to find him in the confessional! He said Père Roussillon was ill, and had sent him in his place."

"Père Despard is assistant to the coadjutor, is he?" asked Valerie carelessly.

"Yes. But he is nobody. Come up-stairs, and let Pauline arrange your head-dress a little. How lovely you have made yourself to-day!"

When the ladies returned to the *salon*, Père Roussillon had already arrived with some guests, and was

presently seated beside Valerie at the table, much to
his satisfaction as well as hers; for Madame d'Odinard
had spoken so often and so earnestly to her confessor
of this altogether worldly yet altogether charming
friend of hers, and expressed such an ardent wish for
her conversion, that the worthy coadjutor, not a little
bitten with the zeal for proselytism so current just then
in France, felt a considerable desire to try his powers
on this rebellious daughter of the Church.

But the good and simple priest was no match for
the practised woman of the world whom he aspired to
lead, and very soon was himself led, all unconsciously
no doubt, but very docilely, into precisely the paths
where she had intended he should tread. The restorations of the chapel were thoroughly discussed; and
it was Père Roussillon himself who proposed to visit
Montarnaud the next day, and make further suggestions
on the spot; and Madame Montarnaud promised to
present herself very, very soon at the cathedral, not
only to admire the restorations on which the good
coadjutor justly prided himself, but to perform the religious duties which she owned, with the innocent self-
accusation of a child, had been sadly neglected; and
then dinner was over, and the company adjourned to
the garden to make Watteau pictures of themselves in
the twilight; and presently the priest again found himself beside the fair convert, who evidently only needed
proper guidance to do such great things, and by and
by was insensibly led into talking of the missions in
Canada, a subject in which, as all the world knew, he
was deeply learned and warmly interested. Espe-

cially he waxed eloquent in praise of Madame de la Peltrie, that young, wealthy, and attractive widow, who had found it joy to devote herself and all that she possessed to the actual toil and privation of this mission, who had built churches and convents in the wilderness, taught the Indians, nursed the sick, encouraged her fellow-laborers, and now recently died upon the scene of her glorious career, leaving a terrible gap in the heroic band still lingering on the shores of the St. Lawrence, although well-nigh discouraged.

"I wish I were a woman like that," said Valerie in bitter admiration, as she listened to the priest's glowing periods, and for a moment she really did; then returning to her own life with a little shrug and sigh, she said, "What vivid pictures you draw of all these things, *mon père!* You have been in Quebec, or at least spoken with some of these heroes?"

"I have never been allowed to go, although always desiring it," said the priest. "But I have spoken with many of our returned missioners, and lately have talked much with my new assistant, Père Despard, but just returned from Canada."

"Ah, yes, Père Despard," said Valerie carelessly. "I used to know him very well in the old days at Montarnaud. And did monsieur my brother-in-law interest himself in all these good and pious works?"

"Indeed, I fear not," replied the priest absently; and then suddenly recognizing his indiscretion, he glanced somewhat severely at the Eve beside him, and coldly said, —

"I crave pardon of madame. I answered at random and without listening to her question. May I ask madame to repeat it?"

Madame could not immediately reply; for her lace flounce had caught on the twig of a holly-bush, and such costly lace must be dealt tenderly withal. By the time it was released and she stood upright again, miladi's *rôle* was taken, — the admirable but most delicate *rôle* of audacious frankness. Looking straight into the somewhat threatening eyes of her companion, she laughed lightly, and said, —

"I have surprised your secret, *mon père!* and you are angry at me, and no wonder! It was very bold, very irreverent, and you shall put me to penance the very first time I go to the cathedral; but I did so want to know if that poor boy were alive, and where, and how. My companion of childhood, my husband's only brother, the heir after Thérèse to all our estates! Was it not reasonable that I should desire to know?"

"Most reasonable, madame; but why not ask honestly for the information, supposing I had it?" demanded the priest reprovingly, yet softening.

"Ah, *mon père!* do not set me bad examples, then, by trifling with the truth. 'Supposing you had it!' but I already knew you to have it: I saw the Abbé Despard but yesterday; and, although he would not give me the intelligence I asked, himself, he let me understand — But there, my heedless tongue will bring me into new mischief. At any rate, I know that you know all about my poor brother, and that you feel bound to keep the secret, although as it was not told you in confession it can be no sin to reveal it; and so, neither wishing to give you the pain of refusing me, nor the temptation to betray a confidence, I just surprised you into a confession which does away with all need of further reticence. Say you forgive me, *mon père*."

The coadjutor shook his head and frowned, yet smiled in such evident amusement that Valerie saw that the day was hers, and went on, —

"And it is in your interests, *mon père*, as a pillar of the Church, as well as in mine as a relative, that I wish to find and influence this misguided boy. My poor little Thérèse is but a puny child; and should she die unmarried François inherits all the property of Montarnaud and Rochenbois; and after him again comes Berthier de Montarnaud, his cousin, and a bitter Huguenot."

"A Huguenot!" echoed Père Roussillon, in a voice as if he said, "A boa-constrictor!" Valerie nodded significantly.

"Yes, indeed, a Huguenot of the Huguenots, who would sell every thing that could be sold of these fair estates, and pour all the proceeds into the hands of these heretical and blasphemous Genevan ministers. Is it not worth while to do something to prevent this?"

"Is it not, indeed!" echoed the priest: "madame, you alarm me incredibly, and I fully forgive the little ruse by which you surprised my knowledge of your brother's whereabouts. Still, I do not feel at liberty to give you one word further of information without the knowledge of Père Despard, and his permission to repeat — Stay, if he would .himself speak to you, it might be better, would it not?"

Valerie smiled maliciously. Really it would not be bad to have this insolent priest, who had so coolly refused to give her the information she sought, forced to come and give her yet more; and she somewhat eagerly replied, —

"Oh, yes, *mon père!* Give him your orders to tell me all that I desire to know, and bring him with you to-morrow to Montarnaud."

"I can hardly give Monsieur Despard orders in a matter of this sort," replied the coadjutor coldly, for something in the malicious tone repelled and warned him. "For I am neither the Bishop of Marseilles, that is to say, his ecclesiastical superior, nor am I his confessor and spiritual director : but I will represent to him the great benefit possibly to be gained to the Church by openly imparting any information concerning his late pupil to the relatives of that gentleman; and — in short, madame, you may expect the abbé to accompany me to Montarnaud to-morrow."

"Thank you, thank you, *mon père,*" replied the countess, feeling that she had better push the matter no farther. "And now tell me something more of Madame de la Peltrie, whom I absolutely feel tempted to imitate."

CHAPTER XXXV.

THE DOCTOR'S DRESSING-ROOM.

THE piece of land for the doctor's house was allotted by the town, and the tract of woodland apportioned; but when the question of building the house arose, it was found that the new citizen had not only ideas of his own, but the means of carrying them out. So far from accepting assistance from the town, he proved himself a more liberal and indulgent paymaster than the mechanics employed had ever met, and so courteous moreover, that these men, all of them worthy and responsible townsmen, found no derogation from their dignity in obeying his orders.

Some little gossip arose, however, as the new house approached completion, and still more when it was furnished and ready for occupancy; for, although the principal rooms were arranged much after the usual fashion of the time, and filled with the best part of the movables from Molly's own house beyond Falmouth, there were two rooms forming a wing or L, devoted to her husband's sole occupancy, and furnished after his own taste, partly from Molly's stores and partly from articles purchased in Boston where the doctor made occasional visits, although none of the gossips could ascertain whither he went. The lower of these rooms, connected with the main body of the house by one door, and with the street by another, was Dr. LeBaron's office, library, and smoking-room; and from it a narrow, enclosed, winding stair led to a room above, called his dressing-room, opening into his wife's bedroom; the latter a large and well-furnished chamber, adorned with the famous curtains wrought by Grandmother Ames and serving as Molly Wilder's bridal dress. The doctor's dressing-room, although containing various matters not considered essential by his stern and ascetic townsmen, might, however, have passed without comment, but for one article appearing there on the very day when the house was pronounced ready for occupancy, and whose presence, discovered by Desire Billings, the young woman who had undertaken to help Mistress LeBaron in her household duties, was before bedtime known at nearly every fireside in Plymouth. This was a hammock, a new and substantial hammock, probably bought in Boston on the doctor's last visit thither, and swung by his own hands to iron staples, inserted during the building of the room, in the solid oaken beams at the corners, proving, as Desire shrewdly pointed out, that this arrangement was no sudden caprice or fancy of the doctor's, but a deliberate plan of life.

"And is it furnished with bedclothes?" asked the gossip to whom Desire first confided her discovery. That discreet young woman screwed up her mouth and slowly nodded.

"There's a hard pillow; what it's made of, I don't know, but not of good live-geese feathers like those in the rest of the house; and there's a couple of black things that maybe pass for blankets, and there's a sort of a rug to lie on. If you call that 'furnished with bedclothes,' why, I don't."

"And he'll leave that poor young woman's bed for such a pig's nest as that!" exclaimed the gossip; and then she and Desire Billings flew in opposite directions to spread the news and the conjectures.

The next day Dame Priest called upon the doctor's wife; and after various professions of friendly interest, and matronly readiness to aid the young wife by counsel or sympathy, she asked to be shown over the house. Molly, a little proud of her new dignity and possessions, complied with friendly alacrity, and displayed the pretty parlor, not half so dismal as that which had originally contained most of the furniture; for Dr. LeBaron had insisted upon a wide, sunny window filled with boxes of flowering plants, and had provided two or three good pictures to ornament the walls, and advised in the less formal arrangement of the furniture. On the other side of the front door was the more usual sitting-room, with Molly's work-table, an open fireplace ready piled with light wood for the first chilly evening, and some comfortable chairs, as comfort was then understood.

"And this door?" demanded the visitor, laying her hand upon the latch of the one her topographical instincts told her was that of the study containing the secret stair, as it was already called.

"Oh! that is my husband's office," said Molly calmly; "and I think he is there now, so we will not

disturb him.   Here is our little dining-room ; and here
the kitchen, which you see Desire keeps so nicely it
is the best room in the house.   Then, will you come
up stairs ? "

" I don't care if I do," replied Dame Priest, whose
whole visit had tended to this point.   So up stairs
they went, looked into the guest-room, with its chill
and formal appointments ; into the sunny little bedroom devoted to Desire Billings ; the great unfinished
kitchen-chamber, where already a modest little pile of
undesirable furniture represented its future use as a
lumber-room ; and finally Mistress LeBaron, with an
effort to hide her own delight under an assumption of
carelessness, threw open the door of the room over
the sitting-room, and said, —

" This is my own room."

" Yours and the doctor's, you mean, my dear," corrected the elder matron ; and Molly pleasantly replied, —

" Why, of course.   It would not be mine at all if it
were not his ; for I should not be his wife."

Margery Priest stared a little ; for the sweet security of love thrilling in Molly's voice was inharmonious
with the unhappiness she had come prepared to
probe.

" Well," said she reluctantly at last, " I'm glad
you're so comfortable, dear ; and this is really a beautiful setting-out.   What nice furniture, and what lovely
curtains !   Did you do them yourself ? "

As she asked the innocent-seeming question, Dame
Priest approached the bed closely as if to examine the

needlework, and glanced shrewdly between the curtains; but the smooth and unwrinkled exterior told no tales. Evidently the fortress was not to be surprised, or taken by siege; a *coup de main* must be attempted; and without saying a word Dame Priest turned, and raised the latch of the door answering to that of the study in the room below. It was fastened inside, and her vigorous tug resulted merely in the sharp tingle of her own fingers as they slipped from the latch. Molly smiled and said nothing; but having gone so far, the inquisitor threw discretion to the winds, and boldly inquired, —

"Where does that door lead, Mistress LeBaron?"

"To my husband's dressing-room," replied Molly briefly.

"And does he keep it locked against you, poor child?" demanded the dame compassionately.

"No; for I never tried to open it," said Molly, turning to leave the room; but her visitor detained her by a grasp upon her arm, while she said, —

"Child, you need not try to hide it from me, that am a woman old enough to be your mother, and have married girls of my own. You've married a foreigner, French or German or Italian, — some say one, and some another; and now he's treating you as those men always do treat their wives, having his separate bedchamber, and separate doors to let in nobody knows who all, and you his lawful wife locked out. It's a shame, I say; and if there's no one else to take your part, you poor motherless child, I will; and I'll speak to that man myself, and tell him he's town-talk already, with his hammocks, and his dressing-rooms, and his secret staircases, and private doors; and you just as sweet and pretty a wife as any man need ask!"

She paused, more from failure of breath than of words, and, putting her arms round Molly's neck, planted a vigorous kiss upon her cheek, finding it impossible to reach her averted lips. The young wife received the caress, and released herself from the embrace gently but decidedly.

"You are really very kind, madame," said she in the calm, sonorous tone from which her voice seldom varied; "and if you would like to speak to my husband at once, I will bring you to him."

"Well,—I'm ready. I never gave way before prince or potentate yet; and I'm not in terror of any mortal man," asseverated the dame, considerably startled at this prompt acceptance of her offer, and not a little aghast at the idea of direct collision with the doctor to whom she had never spoken. But without further parley, the doctor's wife rapidly led the way down stairs and through the sitting-room to the door of the office, which she opened without hesitation. Dr. LeBaron sat in a leathern arm-chair beside the open window, looking into his newly-planted garden, reading a foreign newspaper, and spoiling the sweet summer air with the fumes of a pipe.

As his wife and her guest appeared, he rose, laid aside the pipe, and bowed with somewhat ceremonious politeness. Molly at once explained her errand.

"Dr. LeBaron, this lady is Mistress Priest, whom I believe you do not know. She has somewhat to say to you ; and, as it also concerns me, I will, if it please you, stay and listen."

"May I offer you a chair, madame?" said the doctor, placing one for each lady, and then seating himself with grave professional attention. Margery Priest felt herself daunted far more than when she had encountered a drunken Indian in the woods, and only preserved her scalp by personal prowess. She glanced from the doctor's handsome, haughty, and expectant face, to the severe and threatening features of his wife, colored scarlet, cleared her throat, and desperately began, —

"Well, you see, doctor, your having that hammock has made a good deal of talk ; and I thought, Mistress LeBaron being so young a woman, and an orphan as I understand, I might speak to her as I would to a daughter of my own. I'm sure I feel like a mother to her already ; and so I thought I'd speak to her, and — and " —

Her voice died out in a little nervous gasp ; and Dr. LeBaron waited gravely, politely, but in vain, for the end of the chaotic sentence. At last he said, —

"I fear, madame, I hardly understand you as yet. You feel like a mother to Mistress LeBaron, for which she and I are deeply grateful; but why that amiable feeling on your part involves the displeasure of the town at my owning a hammock, is not plain to my dull mind."

"Why, you have a separate room, and a private door, and a secret staircase !" exclaimed Dame Priest, clutching her departing courage with both hands, and speaking very loud.

"True, madame, and then?" asked the doctor in a tone of silken courtesy.

"Why — why — well, but you're a married man, aren't you?"

"Happily I am, madame."

"Well then, doctor, to speak out plain, we think here in Plymouth that married men have no need of any room except their wife's."

"And you have been selected by the town officers to convey their mind to us?"

"Oh, no! I don't claim any thing of the kind. I only came in a friendly way, to tell Mistress LeBaron that — that" —

"That you felt like a mother to her. Ah, yes! I understand," said the doctor gayly. "But it is the fashion in most countries, madame, for the mother, when her daughter is married, to make over her guardianship to the husband, at least until he proves himself unworthy of the trust. When my wife feels me to be thus unworthy, I doubt not she will apply to you without delay for comfort and protection. Might I ask you to wait for that day before again putting yourself to this trouble?"

"Yes, sir," replied the dame, bewildered at a speech sounding so deferential, and yet, as she dimly suspected, so baffling in its meaning.

"And now," pursued the doctor, "since you have mentioned my poor little domestic arrangements, allow me to show them to you. This door, opening upon the alley at the side of my garden, is what you mention as the private door, I presume. It is intended for the use of my patients; and I think it is better than for them to pass through my wife's sitting-room to arrive at the office, do not you?"

"Why, yes, doctor, I suppose it is."

"Very well. Then here is the secret staircase, opening by this door without other fastening than a latch, and obvious to every one entering the office. Will you go up?"

Without reply, Mistress Priest climbed the steep and narrow stair, and through a door at the top passed into a small room, containing many objects she had never before seen and at which she stared open-mouthed. Dr. LeBaron gravely pointed them out:—

"This, madame, is a dressing-case of foreign workmanship, and more usually found in older countries than here perhaps; still, not dangerous to the public peace or to household morality. These are shaving-brushes and razors; these are called tweezers, and this is a flesh-brush to be used in a dry bath; those are English boot-hooks, and this is a powdering apparatus. Here is the closet for my clothes, and this for my boots"—

"Well, there's the hammock anyway!" exclaimed Dame Priest triumphantly, as she pointed at the obnoxious article slung across one end of the little room, and neatly furnished with the bedding described by Desire Billings.

"Yes, madame, there is the hammock anyway, as you justly observe. Pray, madame, did you ever swing in a hammock?"

"I? No, indeed, doctor."

"In that case, madame, you have no idea of the salubrious and recuperative effects of its motion ; sedative yet exhilarating, monotonous yet not stultifying " —

"I don't know what any of those long words mean," interposed Mrs. Priest sullenly.

"Then, madame, you can never understand why I keep a hammock in my dressing-room," replied the doctor gravely. "Mistress LeBaron has studied the subject, however, and may explain it to you."

"Does she ever get into the thing?" demanded Mistress Priest eagerly.

"Whenever she chooses," replied the doctor with gravity.

CHAPTER XXXVI.

THE DEAD THINGS THAT WILL NOT SLEEP.

A YEAR passed by, — a year of sweet content to Mary LeBaron, of revolution to her husband; for in every day of it he laid aside some jot or tittle of the old life, and by just so much adapted himself to the new. Molly silently watched this process, and with rare self-control made no comment, either upon what was laid aside, or what assumed. In the very dawn of her married history she had comprehended and accepted her part in her husband's life, and there remained content. He had told her that from his past she was forever excluded; and, remembering Lot's wife, she never looked back. She soon understood also that all comment upon his looks, spirits, or especially his silences, were unwelcome, and after a little she never made them: she found that all assumptions as to his nationality came under the forbidden head; and she soon said that she "did not know," when asked if her husband were a Frenchman; she perceived that he abhorred giving account of his movements during absence, or even of mentioning what persons he might have met, and she never set up that domestic tribunal before which so many good wives nightly arraign their husbands. Quick in all his perceptions, LeBaron was not slow to notice this silent submission to his wishes, and as silently rewarded it by a large admixture of respect and admiration in the love he never had ceased to entertain for his wife. He was none the less reticent certainly, and the spaces of his life wherein he chose to be alone remained closed as rigorously against her as all the rest of the world: but there were pleasant paths of daily life wherein he delighted to walk beside her; there were hours of happiest intercourse wherein he fed her mind with knowledge gathered in many a foreign clime, or from books of which she had never heard. He thrust aside for her the narrowing walls of seclusion and inexperience, and gave her, through love of him, that liberal education credited to the lovers of fair Lady Mary Montague.

In fact, the LeBarons were an exceptionally happy couple; and yet a weaker woman would have been miserable in Molly's place, and a less self-contained man would have shown upon the surface the pains and struggles with which the citizen of the world cramped himself into the narrow sphere of the village doctor. True, this sphere was always and rapidly enlarging, as the fame of the thorough-bred, daring, and intelligent surgeon spread through the country-side; so that after two or three years his practice extended, so to speak, over a radius of at least a hundred miles, since his advice was sought from that distance in cases of difficult surgery or mysterious disease. Among his townsmen, and those who saw him most constantly, but one opinion was ever heard as to his skill, his industry, or his benevolence; but at least two very varying opinions were held and proclaimed as regarded his social character and behavior, — one class of persons finding him brief, sharp, self-asserting, even insolent of demeanor; others complaining that he ridiculed their alarms, and laughed at their symptoms; while the poor, the humble, the timid, and the unfortunate declared themselves healed more by the doctor's patient and tireless sympathy, courteous attention, and charitable remembrance of all their needs, than by his physic; and the fourth and smallest class of persons, those who showed themselves reasonable and considerate, courteous and delicate, said that if there was but one gentleman in the American Colonies, that gentleman was Dr. LeBaron.

It was in the third year of his marriage, and the second of his son's life, that the doctor was summoned late one evening to attend a sick man at the Bunch of Grapes. He went at once, and first encountered his stanch friend and partisan the buxom landlady, who greeting him heartily, said, —

"Yes, doctor, there is a gentleman up-stairs who wants you. He came in 'The Nautilus,' just down from Boston with a cargo of groceries and English wares. We have some first-rate Hollands and some white sugar aboard, if you are wanting any at home: and when Cap'n Storms came up, this passenger came along too; and the cap'n he said he was a Boston gentleman, that being but poorly had tried the sea-trip for his health, but could not abide the living on board, and so was e'en worse than when he started, and thought he would land and go home that way; but when he got to my house, he asked had we never a doctor in town; and I, — well, though he is indeed a gentleman, and a man of substance, too, I could not but laugh in his face, and say after him, ' Never a doctor, quotha ! Why, sir, didst never hear of the great Dr. LeBaron, who ' " —

" Now dame, dame, have I not forbid thee, time and again, to cackle over me after that fashion? I'll take thy leg off yet, if thou art so disobedient."

—" ' The great Dr. LeBaron,' says I, ' who is sent for to New Bedford, — yes, and to Boston itself, — when there is a matter passing the skill of their own doctors and you ask, have we never a doctor !' So says my gentleman, ' Then send for him in Heaven's name, and let him cure this horrible feeling at my stomach if he can.' And so I says to Zeb, ' There, man, finish your supper, and run round for the doctor ;' and so " —

" Yes, yes; and he's up in the best bedroom, I'll be bound?"

" That he is, doctor; and " —

But the doctor was already out of hearing, and tapping peremptorily at the door of the best bedroom, the same where we were first introduced to the medical faculty of Plymouth Colony during their famous consultation over Dame Tilley's leg.

" Come in," said a muffled voice; and entering at once, Dr. LeBaron approached the bed, whereon lay a man, covered with blankets, but fully dressed, who rose at his approach, and looked him in the face without speaking. The doctor returned the look, at first

with curiosity, then with some other and more powerful emotion, — so powerful, in fact, that it suddenly
blanched his handsome face to a dull ashen hue, as he
quietly said in French, —

"It is you, then, *mon abbé!*"

"Yes, *mon cher baron*, it is one of the oldest, and I
really think the very warmest, of your friends. What
joy to find you alive and well!" And with real emotion the abbé embraced his former pupil after the effu-
sive style of his nation and his epoch. The doctor
rather submitted to, than returned, the embrace, and
suddenly sat down. The abbé looked at him keenly
for some moments, then said, —

"You are not glad to see me, *mon baron.*"

"Truth to tell, abbé, you enter my present sphere
of life in so comet-like or meteoric a fashion that I
am a little afraid of you."

"Has three or four years sufficed to do away with
all the old system, and establish a new one, in which I
have no place?" asked Despard in a tone of real
grief. LeBaron sadly shook his head.

"I had hoped so. At this moment I am not sure.
I have tried hard enough to forget."

He lapsed into gloomy reverie; and the priest
looked at him with curiosity and impatience, trying to
gauge as rapidly as possible the changes that time had
wrought, and the most accessible present point of
approach. At last he said, —

"My friend, I have one distinct errand to you. In
fact, I am sent as part of my penance for a very
serious fault, to make a certain acknowledgment to

you; and this would have brought me, even without my earnest desire to see you once more."

"And this acknowledgment is"—

"Briefly this. I told you in Quebec that I had not married you to Mary Wilder."

"Yes; but we have been married since."

"Not by a priest, not in a church, I hope!"

"No, by a magistrate."

"I am relieved, for the sacrament must not be profaned by repetition; and you were really married by that hasty midnight service, garbled and shortened though it was."

"And did you know it when you tried to persuade me to turn my back upon my wife, and return to France to marry another woman?" asked the doctor sternly.

"No: at least I was uncertain; and I am confident now, as I was then, that such a ceremony, the marriage not being consummated, could have been set aside without trouble. But still it was a marriage, consented to by the parties, and witnessed, if not regularly conducted, by a priest; and I have been severely censured, both for trifling with the sacrament, and for leading you into doubt as to the validity of your marriage. You will pardon me, *mon baron ?*"

"The more readily, friend, that your temptation never took hold upon my will for an instant. The only effect of the doubt you suggested was to make me submit very gladly to the civil ceremony, which was desirable at any rate for the public satisfaction."

"And you are happily married?"

"Most happily. I am sorry that I cannot invite you to my home to witness my felicity; but my wife would recognize you, and not for the world would I let her suppose the dead past could find its resurrection in her home."

"Does no ghost from out those early years ever confront you, then?" asked the priest meaningly. The doctor laughed somewhat cynically, and replied, —

"Well, yes. My boy is the image of my father; and I could not refrain from a *bon mot* in that connection, whose humor has hitherto been confined to my own breast. I have named the boy Lazarus, as one called from what I fancied a sealed tomb."

"A ghastly jest, and not too reverent, my son," replied the priest severely. "And what have you to say upon the matter of religion?"

"Nothing, *mon père*, except that I am no renegade."

"That is at least something, and I have news for you in that direction. What do you think of a tiny yet vigorous shoot of the venerable faith planted even in the town of Boston, that stronghold of the Puritans, those schismatics of the schismatical Church of England, to whom the altar is an abomination, and even the blessed crucifix a mere idolatrous emblem?"

"And you are the gardener of this daring bit of transplantation?" asked LeBaron sceptically.

"Under God, and my superiors in the Church, yes; and already there is a fair and promising beginning. We own a house, and in that house is a chapel, and to that chapel resort a few of the faithful, whose num-

bers shall yet increase; and we have the germ of a
school and of a hospital supported by the willing
work and ample means of certain Christian ladies,
not regular sisters of any order, but devoted for a
time to these good works."

"But is this allowed in Boston?"

"If the least suspicion of our true character arose,
I suppose neither sex nor age would prevent our all
being hanged beside the Quakers who were executed
the other day for their religious opinions."

"Then you live in secrecy and constant danger."

"Yes. Has the Church ever avoided danger, or
counted the lives of her servants more highly than
the harvest of souls they may gather into her fold?"

"It is true, father; and yet these people among
whom I live, and those of Boston whom I know, are
a·God-fearing, moral, and charitable people. Is it so
needful that all men find heaven by one road? Is
there not a gate for the Gentiles as well as for the
Jews?"

The priest started from his chair in horror, and,
grasping his pupil by the shoulder, cried in a voice of
unfeigned emotion, —

"My son, my son, it had been less grief to me to
see you in your coffin than to have heard such a question from your lips! The taint of heresy has cor-
rupted a soul made glorious by the Lord for his own
service. The unbelieving wife hath stolen away the
faith of the believing husband unequally yoked with
her" —

"Hold there, father!" interposed the doctor warningly. "Bring no third person into this matter if you would hold to the truth. I have never exchanged a word upon the question of religion with my wife, since she was my wife ; nor do I deserve the censures you are so ready to heap upon my head. It is true that I have learned toleration, even from this intolerant people, who could far less easily forgive my faith than I their heresy ; but so far as my own belief goes, it has never swerved one line, one hair's breadth, from that which you yourself taught me in the first dawning of my reasoning powers."

"*Mon baron*, will you give me proof of that declaration?"

"My word needs no proof to establish it ; but for old affection's sake I will give any proof within reason, of my loyalty to the Church."

"Then, come to Boston during this next month, and spend a day and night at our mission-house."

"Gladly, if that is all ; and what is more, you shall confess me, and I will hear a mass and receive the sacrament once again."

"That was in my plan, you may be sure ; and now let us have a little chat upon worldly matters, for I leave here early to-morrow morning."

CHAPTER XXXVII.

A CRUCIAL TEST.

IF for some days after his evening visit to the Bunch of Grapes, Dr. LeBaron was a little more moody and silent than his wont, a little more given to late sitting over his books and papers in the office, or long rides over the sandy and desolate country roads, Molly did not question him as to the cause, and only contrived to make the house and her own society the more attractive when he showed a desire to seek them. The baby-boy, so quaintly named, occupied a good deal of his mother's time also; and Molly had learned to live her life without too much effort at understanding or controlling it, so that her husband found almost every day fresh cause for admiration and appreciation of the love that could let the beloved object alone, and the patience that was neither dullness nor sullenness. One day he came to her as she sat cooing and laughing to the child, who, fresh from his bath, was struggling manfully in her lap against the primal curse of clothing, hung over her for a moment, then, with one kiss upon her lips and another upon the cheek of little Lazarus, he said, —

"Sweetheart, I am going to Boston, and shall not be home for three days. I have arranged with Hallowell about my patients, and sent forward one of the horses to the Halfway House, so I shall make the journey in one day each way, and be home on Monday evening. You are content?"

"Of course, François, as content as I can be when you are not beside me. You might have let me pack some clothes, though."

"I have all I wish in my saddle-portmanteau; so good-by, love, and have a care of young master."

"I shall have nothing else to care for until his father comes home," said Molly, hastily wrapping the child in a blanket, and following her husband to the door, where his great black horse, called Centaur, stood pawing and neighing in his impatience to be off. The doctor mounted, and, turning in the saddle for a last good-by, sat for a moment looking in loving admiration at the mother and child standing in the dark doorway, the morning sunshine touching the red lights of her bronze hair into a golden aureole, and shining pleasantly upon her calm and matronly beauty, the pure and steady radiance of the eyes uplifted to her husband's face, and the unconscious grace of her stately figure; in her arms lay the noble boy, his baby face turned with grave attention upon horse and rider, and one hand masterfully clutching a stray lock of his mother's hair. A fair picture, and a winsome one, thought Dr. François LeBaron, loosening the rein, and allowing the great black horse to launch powerfully forward; and as he rode through sun and shade, the picture journeyed with him over sandy plain, and fragrant pine-forest, and long stretches of half-settled country, until at noon he broke his fast and changed his horse at the little inn known for more than a century later as the Halfway House between Plymouth and Boston.

At night he arrived in the latter town ; and, having placed his horse in the stable of the old Exchange Coffee House, he set out on foot to find the place to which Father Despard had directed him. But this was not so easy a matter as it sounds to us of to-day : for the streets were neither numbered nor lighted, and many of them not even named ; so that it was not until more than an hour of rambling through the crowded and irregular district now known as the North End of Boston, that the visitor knocked at the door of a large house standing in its own garden a little way from the street, and so dark and forlorn in appearance as to suggest the death or absence of every living creature within its walls.

After a long delay, the door was cautiously opened so far as an inside chain would allow, by a man, who gruffly asked, in an Irish accent, —

"What's your will, sir?"

"Is Master Desmond within?" replied the visitor, using the *alias* assumed by his friend while dwelling in the camp of his enemies.

"I'll see, sir." And, leaving the door unlatched but chained, the servant retreated, and soon returned, followed by another dimly-seen figure, who civilly asked, —

"Do you wish to see me, sir? I am Master Desmond."

"And I, Dr. LeBaron," replied the guest.

"My dear friend, is it really you!" exclaimed the master of the house, letting fall the chain, and throwing wide the door. "You will excuse our precautions, but "—

"Not a word, not a word, my friend," interposed the guest heartily. "I understand that the Church Militant naturally intrenches herself, and "—

"Hush, my dear fellow, not a word, I beg of you, until we are safe in my sanctum! To be sure, Patrick O'Donoghue, who opened the door to you, is stanch and loyal, an importation of my own from his native Ireland; but one never knows — walls have ears: but here we are, as safe as in the Quirinal." He opened the door of a small room, only to be approached through two others, and displayed a cosey retreat, warmed and lighted in this chill October evening by a small wood fire, and well supplied with books, comfortable furniture, and a round table covered with the preparations for supper.

"I am just in time, it seems," said LeBaron, smiling, and rubbing his hands. "I remember that as no one knew how to fast more rigidly than yourself, abbé, so no one better understood how to feast, or could manage to do so on more slender materials."

"You flatter me, my son; and yet why should not a Religious study how best to utilize the abundant gifts of Providence? Do you remember the ragout I once made from an amiable and unfortunate cat when we were upon our retreat into Canada?"

"Do I not? And the soup from the bones the farmer's wife had thrown out her back door."

"Yes. But here comes Patrick with our supper; and here is Father Pinot, my coadjutor and assistant, who will be glad to see you after having heard so much of you."

The younger priest, a vivacious and agreeable companion, bowed courteously: a short Latin grace was said, and the three men sat down. It was years since LeBaron had found himself so nearly in his native element as to-night; and he abandoned himself to an hour of convivial enjoyment very different from the staid feasts at which he was often called to assist in the town of his adoption, or even from the pleasant but simple and brief meals at which he and Molly sat habitually in their own house. Here the cookery was delicate and refined, purely French in its character, and accompanied by French wines; the service was admirable; and the two priests, laying aside for the moment all that is severe or ascetic in their profession, showed themselves in the light of cultivated and experienced citizens of the world, quick, witty, apt at quotation or allusion, and with a range of conversation not to be found among more quiet and homely folk. It was even a luxury for LeBaron to speak freely in his native language: for his English, although scholarly and sufficiently fluent, was always a little formal, and often spoken with consciousness of the effort at mental translation; for it is a rare and ultimate stage in the acquirement of a foreign tongue when one's thoughts shape themselves to its idioms, and Dr. LeBaron never fully reached it.

A clock upon the mantle struck the half-hour after

eight; and Father Pinot, glancing at his superior, grew suddenly grave and silent. Despard nodded slightly, and pushed back his chair.

"You will join us in the chapel for compline, at nine o'clock; will you not, doctor?" asked he of his guest, who had begged him to use no title but this.

"With pleasure, if you will show me the way thither," replied he, rising from the table.

"Oh, it is not time yet! Father Pinot and I have some preparation to make; and it is our rule not to allow any festivity to exceed an hour's time. If you will remain here, and amuse yourself with a book, Patrick shall summon you at nine, or a few moments earlier."

The priests left the room; and LeBaron, not caring to read just then, threw himself back in his chair, and sat staring into the fire, his mind filled with chaotic thoughts, memories, and associations, until a touch upon his shoulder and Patrick's rich Milesian accents recalled him to the moment and the occasion. Following the man through a passage, opening behind one of the bookcases, he presently found himself in a small and richly ornamented chapel, cunningly devised, as he afterward found, to appear from the outside like a rough addition to the house, without windows or exterior doors. Quite half this room, divided from the rest by a light bronze screen or railing, was occupied by the altar and chancel, within which stood the two priests, attended by a boy-acolyte who was busily lighting a censer in a little sacristy opening into the chancel. Outside the screen, with LeBaron, knelt

Patrick and several women dressed in semi-religious robes, their heads covered by veils.

The service began; and as the words and intonations familiar to his childhood and youth fell upon the ears of the guest, as the odor of incense reached his nostrils accompanied by the silvery clank of the chains of the censer, he covered his face with his hands, and, bowing his head, wondered if this were indeed a vivid dream, or if it were not rather true that the past bleak, bitter years of exile had been the dream, and this was reality.

From this reverie he was roused by the softly-chanted strains of the vesper hymn in which he had joined so many times at Montarnaud; and, listening eagerly without raising his head, he seemed to hear again the pure and penetrating tones of the voice with which his had so loved to chime in those not-yet-forgotten years, — that voice so peculiar in its *timbre,* so deadly sweet in its fearless heights, so caressing in its depths, that when Molly Wilder first sang to him in the lonely sea-side farmhouse, his greatest pleasure in hearing her had been that no tone of her voice resembled that voice. And now it seemed close beside him: its subtle charm piercing his very brain, and sending the blood tingling from heart to finger-tips and back again with sickening force and tumult.

> " Ave Maria, Maria sanctissima !
> Ora pro nobis, ora pro me !"

sang the voice; and surely it was no vision, no memory, that could sigh out the familiar words in that tender, loving tone, so vividly recalled, so never to be forgotten. Slowly and unwillingly LeBaron lifted his head, and looked toward the little group of women kneeling at the other extremity of the screen; but the veils hid all the faces, and even the outline of the head and shoulders : and, as the last words of the hymn died upon the fragrant air, all bowed low their heads, awaiting the benediction.

When LeBaron raised his, he was alone, except for the servant who stood patiently awaiting him. Following, without noticing that it was through another passage than that by which he had entered the chapel, LeBaron presently found himself in a small and dimly-lighted room, where beside a marble figure of the Madonna stood a veiled woman; her black robes contrasting vividly with the cold whiteness of the statue upon which she leaned as if for protection and confidence. As the disturbed and already suspicious visitor stood looking at her, while the door silently closed behind him, the woman swiftly advanced a step, and knelt at his feet, throwing back her veil as she did so, and lifting her beautiful, passionate face to his in mute and anguished appeal for pity and forgiveness.

LeBaron started, and quivered all through his form, as quivers the lion when the hunter's spear reaches his heart; but he did not speak, and it was she who presently murmured, —

"François ! Have not you one word for me, after all these years ?"

"What word, Valerie ? What is to be said between us two ?"

"Forgiveness. I betrayed and denied you when you had the right to expect my loyalty."

"It is forgiven long ago."

"Forgiven coldly and formally, but not forgiven as you used to forgive my faults, François! Not forgotten."

"Yes, — forgotten."

"Your voice does not sound so, François; and I know every tone of the voice for whose sound I have so longed, so pined."

"Yes, forgotten, Valerie, but not easily. You and your falseness became indissolubly one in my memory, and to forget one I was obliged to banish both."

"And I am forgotten!"

The words wailed out upon the quiet air like the cry of the spirit denied the entrance to Paradise, and LeBaron felt a great and terrible pity stealing over his heart. Involuntarily his hand extended itself toward that bowed head, and words of gentlest soothing rose to his lips; but with a mighty effort he folded his arms across his breast, and, moving a step away, said gently and coldly, —

"Pray rise and seat yourself, Valerie. I have already assured you of my forgiveness if you care to have it; and, as my brother's wife and widow, I may think of you with interest and well-wishing. All else was ended for us when I left France."

"Say, rather, when you fell in love with another woman!" exclaimed Valerie, springing to her feet, and confronting him passionately. "For, after all, it is only you who have been false to our early love: I never pretended to love Gaston, I never pretended to have forgotten you."

"Do not make a boast of it, madame," replied LeBaron sternly. "If you married a man consciously loving another, and then cherished the love your own act had made guilty, let shame keep you silent upon both scores."

"François! François! Have you no pity? And I have wearied so for one look, one word; and now you are so cruel!"

"It is you, Valerie, who are cruel to both of us. Child! Do you suppose my heart is ice or stone? By this day's work you have destroyed for me the quiet of months, years perhaps. Cruel! What cruelty could you have devised, had you been my bitterest foe, more subtle than thus to come, and with every accessory of our purest and best association, force back upon my memory and my heart the images, the feelings, the bereavements, that I have spent years in uprooting and throwing aside, though in doing so I have shaken my nature to its depths? It is you who have shown yourself cruel, insensate, selfish."

"You still love me, then, since I can make you suffer! O François!"

And, gliding to his side, she laid her hand upon his folded arms, and looked up in his face, her eyes humid, her lips parted, the subtle fragrance of her hair and dress floating around her in an atmosphere of intoxicating languor. He did not move hand nor foot; nor, though his face grew deadly pale, did his eyes flinch from the full regard of hers. At last he slowly said, —

"Love you, Valerie de Montarnaud !   Love you ! There is not a woman on earth whom it would be so impossible for me to love."

"Oh ! "

"Yes, it hurts you; and I am sorry to pain you. There are not even in my heart those poor dregs of love that make us enjoy the pang we can inflict upon her who has deceived and betrayed us. I do not even hate you, Valerie : after this, I do not even care to avoid you. I thank you for the work of this last five minutes; for you have put forth all your art to re-kindle the fire whose ashes I had feared to disturb, and you have shown me that they are wholly cold and dead.   Are you content?"

" Content ! " repeated Madame de Montarnaud in a tone of withering scorn, " yes, for I see that your peasant wife has dragged you utterly down to her own level.   I cannot love a man who is no longer a gentleman."

" If it soothes your mortification to speak disparagingly of me, you are very welcome to do so, madame. As to my wife, it is better that you should not speak of her at all; since she is a woman far above your comprehension, very far above my deserts. Pure as the angels, true as light, unselfish and devoted and loving, and with a strong, brave heart that only needs to know the right to follow it, she is not of those among whom you chose your life, madame, nor have you the ability to gauge her. But with her, and with her child, lie all my hopes in the future, all my joy in the present; for I love and trust her as I never could have loved and trusted you, Valerie, even had you been true to me."

He left the room, nor did she seek to detain him. In the study he found Father Despard, who waited for him with ill-concealed anxiety. LeBaron looked at him sternly and reproachfully.

"What was the motive of your plot?" asked he, leaning upon the mantel, and looking down upon the priest, who sat designedly in the shade.

"Simply this, my son," replied he fluently: "I am in this place as a propagandist: my only motive is the nurture and spread of our holy faith in this new country. Madame de Montarnaud is also absorbed, body and soul, in this good work; and it is her money which largely supports the mission. Now, you are the heir, after her child, of most of her property; and it is certainly desirable that you should be consulted as to its disposition. Again, you are a Catholic, detached from the influences and rites of the Church; and it is most desirable that you should be led to join with us who represent her, however feebly, and should be brought into charity and sympathy with your fellow-laborers. Now, Madame de Montarnaud felt that you were not in charity with her, and fancied that by a personal interview your differences might be adjusted. I knew, that, if I warned you of her presence, you would not visit me; and I consented to this little *ruse*, by which I brought together two of my children, temporarily estranged, and joined them once more as co-laborers in the holy cause which must to all of us be so much dearer than any personal prejudices or wishes. Was I wrong, my dear pupil?"

"If your explanation is perfectly sincere, father, I should say that you were not so much wrong as — pardon me — stupid ; and *that*, I had never supposed to be one of your failings. You probably knew beforehand, as well as I know now, the nature of the explanation likely to ensue between Madame de Montarnaud and myself ; and had not my heart been guarded by a very vivid and very honest love for my wife, I can hardly tell the extent of the mischief likely to have sprung from your amiable and innocent little device. As it is, no harm is done, unless, — and it would be an odd bit of retributive justice on your head, *mon père,* — unless Madame de Montarnaud finds her zeal for mission-work suddenly cooled, and goes back to France, carrying her money with her."

"H'm !" ejaculated the priest starting a little, but after a moment re-settling himself placidly as he replied, —

"Fore-warned is fore-armed, my son. I will terrify madame by letting her see that I dimly suspect a motive in her zeal which she has never dared to confess to me."

"And now, father, I will to bed : we will have a long talk to-morrow after mass ; and I shall set out upon my journey home as soon as sunset allows me to travel, — as soon as Sunday is over, that is."

"What, you yield to these Puritan edicts !" exclaimed the priest contemptuously.

"If I did not, I should taste Puritan discipline," replied the doctor tranquilly : "besides, father, you must remember, as I have just been telling Madame de Montarnaud, that this land is now my land, and this people my people."

"But never their God your God, I hope, my son," replied the priest solemnly.

"Is there, then, more than one God, my father?" asked LeBaron significantly.

CHAPTER XXXVIII.

THE BELLE ISLE.

AND so thé years went softly on in the quaint
town beside the sea, until Lazarus LeBaron was
a fine, stout lad of thirteen years, with his father's
stalwart Norman figure, and his mother's calm and
steadfast eyes. And still it was Time the Perfecter,
and not Time the Destroyer, that left his mark upon
Molly LeBaron's face and form, changing her girlish
comeliness to the stately beauty of her matronhood,
giving through the expansion of the mind, and greater
intelligence of the feelings, depth to the eyes, mobility
to the mouth, and a greater range of inflection to the
voice; while the peaceful and regular life, the calm
temper, and constant sunshine of her home, con-
served the delicacy of her complexion, the youthful
roundness of her outlines, and the smoothness of her
brow.

So thought her husband, idly watching her as she
moved around the room arranging little matters,
flecking away specks of dust, painting the lily of spot-
less cleanliness with yet an added lustre.

"Yes, doctor," she was saying, "I really think a
voyage would do you great good. You have been so
overworked through this sickly September; and, at any

rate, our cruel winters always tell upon you. Remember the cough you had last year "—

" Yes ; I took cold when I was six years old, and that was the result," interposed LeBaron, in the grave, quizzical tone in which he met so many of his wife's solicitudes, and to which she now dryly replied, —

" I dare say. It was unfortunate ; but still, now that you have so good a chance to make a trip to the Havana and back, and cost you nothing, for Capt. Pinot said before that he would take you at any time for the pleasure of your company "—

" Ay, but, my dear, Capt. Pinot never had my company long enough to find out that there is no pleasure in it. Would you have me cheat the worthy mariner?"

" Ah, Francis ! don't torment me, when I'm trying to persuade thee to do thyself a service, and not to think of how I'll miss thee, dear." And throwing down the duster, Molly came, and, crouching at her husband's side, laid her folded hands upon his breast, and raised her fair face to his with an irresistible gesture of entreaty and devotion. LeBaron stooped, and kissed her tenderly, then smoothing away the hair from her brow, looked long and earnestly into the clear, good eyes steadfastly upraised to his. It was a minute or two before either spoke ; and then he said very gently, —

" Molly, thou'rt a fair woman, and better than that thou'rt a good woman, and strong and brave as thou art sweet. I would I were a better man for thy sake, dear wife."

A lovely morning glow stole over the noonday beauty of the upturned face ; and then it hid itself upon his breast, and the arms crept up around his neck, and never a word came from the fond tremulous lips, and never a word was needed.

The door was suddenly thrown open ; and a bright, handsome boy stood on the threshold, opened his eyes a little at the unwonted sight, yet with the tact of all the Montarnauds went straight on with his message as if he saw nothing : —

"Father, Capt. Pinot has come ashore, and bid me ask if you would come off to the ' Belle Isle ' to see a passenger of his, a gentleman, too ill to come ashore, — a nobleman, and very rich."

"Yet not noble enough nor rich enough to keep himself in health, nor cure himself when ill," remarked the doctor, always on the lookout to cut down any aristocratic weeds springing in his son's character.

"No ; but the captain spoke as if he were a very great man, and he's not over civil generally."

"Hah !   Very great — that might mean dropsy ; and not over civil — that may be spleen," said the doctor musingly, as he stepped into the office, and changed his coat and shoes. Lazarus colored a little, but glanced at his mother, whose calm eyes were fixed on his, and remained silent.

"Come to the wharf with me, my boy," said the doctor presently emerging.   "Perhaps you can indulge in the dear delight of going off to the brig."

"That's what I like !" exclaimed the lad gayly ; and down the steep of Leyden Street they went, and along the wharf past Pilgrim Rock, distinctly recognized but not specially honored in those early days, to where the captain's gig, manned by two sturdy Jack Tars, lay tossing up and down on the gay October waves.

The captain himself, a bluff yet civil Breton, stood impatiently watching the doctor's approach, and, after a hearty grasp of the hand, and greeting in the foreign yet fluent English necessary to his traffic, gestured toward the boat, saying, —

"Let us go then, let us go! This monsigneur of a passenger of mine is in such a thousand devils of a hurry always. Will young master go aboard? It 'is most admirable. Quick, then. Oars!"

"So your passenger is ill. Is it of the sea?" asked the doctor tranquilly, as the boat shot away from the wharf, and pursued a course, very like that of a rocking horse, toward the brig.

"Not altogether," replied the captain, lowering his voice to a confidential tone. "He is old and very rich, and he once was young and very rich; and one naturally pays in one's latter years for the gayeties of ones earlier years if one has been immoderate."

"You are a philosopher, captain."

"Well, one sees the world as one travels around it; and one finds time for thinking between Bordeaux or Marseilles and Boston or Plymouth."

"It is true, my friend. And our invalid's name?"

"The Marquis de Vieux."

"I don't like marquises, they're unlucky to me," muttered the doctor rapidly; but Lazarus heard him, and remembered the words later.

" And he's going to Hayti, is he ? "

" Yes : he has great estates there, and has made up his mind that the climate of the tropics is just what he needs to make him a boy again. Expects to find the fountain of youth, you know, doctor."

And the worthy Pinot laughed uproariously at his own jest, but sobered sufficiently to whisper just as the boat grazed the brig's quarter, —

" Better be a little careful with your patient, doctor : he has the devil's own temper, but he's enormously rich, and can afford it. Why, there's enough gold and silver in one shape and another aboard here to buy up yon little town of Plymouth altogether."

" My good Pinot, you mistake," replied LeBaron quietly. " 'There is not enough to buy even the poor doctor of Plymouth."

An hour later Dr. LeBaron, pale, silent, and abstracted, descended the side of the " Belle Isle," and was rowed ashore without speaking a word. As he and his son climbed the steep street toward home, however, he stopped, and, with a hand upon the boy's shoulder, turned to gaze thoughtfully down at the French brig gently tossing upon the incoming tide, and from that upon the bright face of the lad turned wistfully up toward him. But, educated in the strict discipline of the age, Lazarus asked no question until his father, smiling in his grave way, said, —

" Well, boy, what is it ? "

" I don't know, father ; only I wish the ' Belle Isle ' had not put in at our harbor this trip."

" Say you so, Lazarus, say you so ! " exclaimed his

father in a tone more thoughtful than the boy's words seemed to warrant. They walked on in silence; but just at the angle of the hill, before reaching home, the doctor again laid hand upon the boy's arm, and asked, —

"Lazarus, art man enough to care for thy mother and the home affairs some three months or maybe four?"

"I'd try, father."

"Why, that's thy mother's own boy. 'I'll try' means more with her, and maybe with her son, than the strongest 'I will' of most others. Go now, we'll look for thee at dinner-time."

In the pleasant sitting-room, with the door open to the office so that she could see the doctor's leathern arm-chair beside the garden window, sat Molly sewing busily, and softly singing one of the psalms with which St. Paul bade men make merry. Her husband, coming in, stood for a moment to watch her, then seating himself, and trifling with her work-basket, said, —

"And so you think, Mistress Molly, that I had better go to Hayti in the 'Belle Isle'?"

Molly grew pale, and the psalm died off her lips; but raising a brave face, she replied in a voice as brave, —

"Yes, Francis: it will be for your health, I am sure."

"But what then if I stay four months, until February we will say?"

"Four months, Francis! Is it best for you to do so?"

"That is for Molly to say.   There is a sick old man on board the 'Belle Isle,' sick and whimsical, and very rich.   He is all alone but for two servants, and he has quarrelled with all his kith and kin.   He is going to his estates in Hayti, and he will die there before spring: that is a confidence, my wife."

"You needed not to tell me so," said Molly proudly; but her husband only tapped her lightly on the cheek, a favorite caress, and went on.

"Well, this droll old gentleman, who calls himself, I know not what, marquis I believe, has taken, at first sight, so violent a fancy to the poorhouse doctor of Plymouth Colony, that he must have him to go on the voyage, and establish him on the estates.   That would take two months or so; and, as I foresee that he will find himself altogether worse so soon as he leaves the sea, he will cling to me as the last hope; and, if there is no other physician at hand, I can hardly leave him just at once.   So we must put the absence at three to four months; and my marquis of Carrabas will give me in advance, here in my hand, Molly, three hundred louis d'or, equal to three hundred pounds sterling, — as much money as I can earn in this dear Plymouth of ours in three years, even reckoning the ten pounds by the year for the care of the poorhouse."

"I have seen for a long time, Francis, that you were chafing at your narrow bounds; yet do not mock at the home where we have been so happy."   And just a little tinge of resentment colored the wife's cheek, and rang through her gentle voice.   LeBaron looked keenly at her, and laughed in an unmirthful fashion.

"You answer your own mind, and not my words, wife," said he. "Well, what think you of my lord marquis of Carrabas and his three hundred pounds?"

"I think you will go with him."

"Nay, then, by all the saints in the calendar, my Grizel, I will not go with such a sending."

"How, what, — what do you mean, Francis?"

"Why, such a patient face, and such a mournful voice, and such an air of resignation." And LeBaron, half vexed, stood looking down at Molly half wounded; and neither spoke, until Desire, showing a flushed face at the door, inquired, —

"Is the doctor at home? Well, then, shall I put dinner on, and be done with it early?"

"Yes, if it is ready, and you are ready, doctor," said the mistress in a tone of relief; and so they sat down, and before the meal was over Molly cheerfully said, "I must be busy now in looking over your summer clothes, my dear, and seeing what else you need. It will be all summer in Hayti, I suppose."

"It is the best of summers where you are, sweet," replied her husband; and so the question was decided.

Four days later the "Belle Isle" sailed out past the Gurnet; and Lazarus, standing beside his mother on Burying Hill to watch the old brig out of sight, suddenly inquired, —

"Why did father say marquises were unlucky to him, mother? What is a marquis?"

"I think they are more unlucky to us than to him, Lazarus," replied Molly, turning with a sigh to go down to the village where already the shadows lay cold and dark.

CHAPTER XXXIX.

MARQUISES ARE UNLUCKY TO ME.

"THE packet is in from Boston, mother; and now sure there will be a letter from father, won't there?" and Lazarus, standing close at his mother's side, kissed the glossy head so often drooping as now over the work in her lap. She looked up eagerly enough at his words, and answered with a smile, —

"God send it may be so, my boy! Almost three months, and the 'Belle Isle' never heard from."

"But then you know Capt. Pinot did not mean to make this port on his return voyage, mother."

"No; but I thought we should hear. Well, — it may be now. Go down to the wharf, Lazarus, and see if the mail-bag has come ashore."

"Kiss me, mother, before I go."

"Why, there, dear child. But all is as God wills Lazarus."

Half an hour later, when the boy returned, his mother came out of the doctor's dressing-room; and her face was very pale, but very radiant.

"There is no letter for us, mother; but Master Bradford bid me say he had news that he would give you for himself presently. He was talking with a stranger man who came down in the schooner, — a sailor, I think."

"Now God help us, my boy! If he had good news, kind Master Bradford would have said it out. Stay here, Lazarus, — I may want you, my son, to help me bear what is coming."

And turning back into the little room, so altogether her husband's, Mary LeBaron shut her doors about her, and sought for strength where she had so often found it, and should yet so often seek it.

Lazarus gently tapped upon the door. "Master Bradford is down stairs, mother."

"I will come." But when she entered the room, and gave her cold hand to the venerable man, and fixed her great asking eyes upon his, it was down his cheek, not hers, that the tears flowed fast; and it was his voice that scarce was audible for emotion, as he said, forgetting all his careful preparation, —

"'The Lord giveth, and the Lord taketh away,' my daughter."

"Blessed be the name of the Lord," replied the white lips of the bereaved woman; and, sitting down in the nearest chair, she covered her face for a moment, then said in a strangely hushed voice, —

"Tell me as quickly as may be, good friend. I can bear it better to hear it all out at once."

So subduing his own emotion, Master Bradford told how the "Belle Isle" had encountered in the Bahama waters the craft of a famous buccaneer of that time and locality, named Black Beard, who, from his lair in one of the inlets of the island since called New Providence, sallied forth, now to attack some vessel whose freight he had reason to suppose valuable, and now to make raids upon the mainland, his ravages extending as far north as the Carolinas.[1]   Either from information or by a shrewd guess, none could now say which, Black Beard had decided that the " Belle Isle " was worth his capture on this occasion, and had lain in wait for her, taken her by surprise, slaughtered most of the crew, and having thoroughly stripped her, not only of the treasures of the poor marquis, but of every other valuable, had secured her crew and passengers, living and dead, below hatches, set fire to the brig, and sailed away, leaving her to consume and sink.

One of the sailors, sick in his berth below at the time of the attack, had crawled out of one of the portholes, secured a floating spar, and in the confusion and smoke of the onslaught contrived to float out of the immediate vicinity of the pirate before any one had leisure to discover or pursue him ; and after a night and day in the water was picked up by some natives from one of the other islands, who would have sold him to Black Beard as a slave, had not he fortunately effected his escape, and worked his way to Massachusetts Bay, where he hoped to find some French vessel returning home.   Telling his story to the governor, who two hundred years ago occupied more the position of father and guardian of the colony than the governors of to-day do or could, he was sent on to Plymouth Plantation, there to give by word of mouth the heavy news so important, not only to Dr. LeBaron's family, but to those of two other townsmen who had taken passage on the " Belle Isle."

Such in brief was the news that the kind Bradford, then ruling Plymouth, had come to give as best he might to LeBaron's widow; and, having given it, to kneel and pray beside her that God would give strength to endure the loving chastisement His own hand inflicted.

Molly listened to heavy news, eloquent prayer, and well-spoken consolation, with the same set white face and fixed, unseeing eyes for all. When the somewhat puzzled magistrate rose to go, she rose too, and, holding out her hand, said gently, —

"I thank you very much, Master Bradford, and will you kindly excuse me to any of the neighbors who may speak of coming to see me before to-morrow? I had rather be alone."

"Will you not see the elder?"

"No, if it please you, sir. I had rather be alone."

"Then you shall, poor child; and none shall take offence if Desire denies you at the door."

And we, too, will leave her alone.

CHAPTER XL.

MOLLY HOLDS THE FORT.

NO doubt our Puritan and Pilgrim ancestors possessed affections and sentiment like ourselves;
but these graces of life were, in the stern first century
of their experience on the sterile shores of New England, made so subservient to the iron principles upon
which their commonwealth was founded, the tastes
of the individual were so constantly sacrificed to the
well-being of the community, that small evidence of
even ordinary feeling appears upon the surface of
their records. Notably is this the case in the matter
of second marriages; for from the first landing of the
Pilgrims, or rather from the first winter when so many
marriages were dissolved by death, it seemed to be
received as a grave political if not moral duty, that
grief for the dead should be postponed to care for the
living; and the widowed mourner should, after the
briefest possible widowhood, take another partner, and
raise up children for the Lord and His people.

· Rose Standish had not lain many months in her
grave when her husband applied for the hand of Priscilla Mullins; Dorothy Bradford had hardly settled
herself to her wave-rocked slumber before the governor sent over seas for fair Alice Southworth, his first

love, to come and be his second wife. And all through the records of those early days we find the marriages following the burials so rapidly that the funeral meats might have been at least lukewarm for the marriage feast.

In view of this state of things Mary LeBaron was not scandalized, although much grieved, when her dear old friend Bradford called upon her one autumnal day, about a year after her husband's loss, and premising his errand with some kindly commonplaces, to which she replied in her gentle, absent fashion, came to the pith of his errand in this direct style : —

"I have come to-day, my dear child, to give you some counsel which I do earnestly desire you to follow. I would see you married again, as St. Paul advises the younger widows ever to do ; and I have a good and suitable husband to propose. One, too, who has some sort of a claim upon you, in that you once were troth-plight to him, and broke the bond for no other reason than a maid's idle fancy. I mean Reuben Hetherford, Mary."

"Reuben Hetherford has spoken with me, good father Bradford, and I have given him his answer," replied Molly quietly, but with a little color rising to her cheek, a little light to her eye. The patriarch smiled, and lifted a gently deprecating hand.

"I know it, Mary : I heard it all from Hetherford himself ; and it seemed to me you had shown him less than your usual gentleness. I hardly knew our dove-like Mistress LeBaron in the scornful dame whose words he reported."

"It is like him to try to set you against me, sir, you who have been my best friend since — but I will not contradict him. Believe me a shrew an you will, father; but let me, in all reverence to you, say again, as I said to him, I am the wife of one man, and that man Francis LeBaron. And though God has in His righteousness removed him from my sight, from this world even, he is none the less my husband; and I can no more take another than can Dame Sampson because her husband has gone voyaging around the world."

"But, mistress, you will not make yourself more faithful or more righteous than the fathers of our colony here" — began the governor rather severely; but Mary, putting her hands together, raised them in such meek deprecation of his anger that he paused irresolutely, and she took advantage of his doubt to put in her own plea.

"Nay, father, be not displeased: say that I am but a poor, silly woman, and let me go my way, looking only to your honorable guardianship for protection and counsel; for in very truth Reuben Hetherford could never fill your place in those respects. I shall be no charge to any one; for when the money my dear husband left in your hands is gone, I can sell my farm near Falmouth, and I think already of opening a little dame-school here in my own sitting-room; there are many who would trust their children to me; and I may dismiss Desire, and there are other economies — in truth, father, I need no man to care for my affairs except yourself."

"But the lad, Mary! Lazarus surely needs a father."

"He has one, sir; and one of his daily lessons is to learn to be what that father would have him. I may be all unfit to train him, but Reuben Hetherford shall never be master over Dr. LeBaron's son."

"Pride, Mary, and bitterness and prejudice and perversity. Those are the good gifts you would give your son, are they?" asked Bradford severely.

"Better those than cruelty and treachery and falsehood, the goodly blossoms of Hetherford's nature," replied Molly, in so undaunted a tone that the governor rose in much displeasure, and would have left the room but for the fair, soft woman suddenly replacing the self-asserting matron who opposed him but now, and who clasping his hand in her own long, smooth fingers raised it to her lips saying, —

"Nay then, nay father, but I will not have you leave me so. Did not you promise to be a father to the fatherless and to the widow? and have not I given you the love and reverence of a daughter? Forgive my obstinacy, and do not altogether break my heart by going away in anger."

"Well there, then, child, there. Kneel down and take my blessing. I was vexed, no doubt; but, after all, God himself guides such as you, and I need not to meddle. Hetherford shall not persecute you, nor shall any one."

So that danger went by, and the winter passed. Mary opened her dame-school, and dismissed Desire, but, besides her household duties and the care of her little ones, found time to carry on the lessons her husband had begun with his son, and which were already far beyond the most advanced branches of the village school system. The governor occasionally examined the lad, and looked at his books, generally making the mother's heart flutter before he left her by prophesying, that, in a few months more, master must be sent to Boston, or perhaps to the new college at Cambridge, to finish his education, already outgrowing a woman's grasp.

After one of these examinations and prophecies, the widow's candle burned very late o' nights for a long time; and her sweet, steadfast eyes grew red, not with weeping only, but with poring over Latin and even Greek grammar and lexicon, and puzzling algebraic signs, interpreted finally more by intuition spurred by love, than any colder mental process.

It was the next morning after one of these visits, and one of these vigils, that Molly received a visitor admitted by Lazarus, who came to call his mother, and take her place in the little school while she received him. A tall, dark, handsome man, the top of his head bald or shaved, and the black hair beneath a little gray, although the firmness of the muscles and clearness of the eyes suggested that mental toil and hardship, rather than age, had added the silver threads. He stood in the middle of the parlor as the widow entered, and gravely bowed, remaining silent until she spoke.

"I remember you very well, sir, although I have not seen you since the night of my marriage, and do not know your name. But as his friend"— And then, a sudden thought striking her, all the gentle calm of her manner broke up in a most unwonted whirl of agitation, the soft color fled her cheek, the eyes filled, the lips quivered, and, hardly able to command her voice, she gasped, —

"Oh! You are his friend! You know all — you were with him before I knew him — he would — do you know — O sir! is he — is he alive?"

"Ah, madame! If he were, you would not have seen me stand here, here in his home so silent and so sad!" replied the abbé in real emotion. "I loved him, madame, not as you, I do not claim it, but I loved him more than ever I loved mortal before or since, and the news of his fearful death has changed the face of all the world to me."

But Molly hardly heard the loving tribute, so touching when offered by a man to the memory of a man. The sudden hope, the deadly revulsion, were too much for strength already sorely taxed ; and, sinking suddenly into a chair, she grew so white that Despard would have called for assistance, had not she found strength to whisper, "Wait!" and then, summoning her indomitable will to fortify her exhausted energies, she sat upright and said, —

"Excuse me, sir. It was a foolish idea. Nobody would have known it sooner than I if my husband had been alive. When did you see him last?"

"About two years ago, madame. A little before he sailed for Hayti."

"Where? You were not here, surely?" asked Molly a little sharply, a little jealously. The abbé recognized the tone ; and his own became confidential as he replied, —

"No, madame : I have had some business in Boston during the last few years, very delicate and peculiar business ; and it was, above all, desirable that nobody should discover my identity. My dear doctor sometimes visited me : but you know his sense of honor, and his loyalty ; he promised to tell no one, no one at all, of my affairs, and so no doubt felt himself debarred from mentioning me to one who doubtless shared all the secrets of his life, not so defended."

He looked inquiringly and a little watchfully at Molly, who raised her head, and met his eyes fully and almost defiantly ; and when she spoke her voice was clear and cold as the north wind whistling past the windows.

"You are mistaken, sir : I was agreed with my husband that all his life before we met should be to me as it had never been. You belonged to that life, and you were never mentioned between us after the first evening of our re-union. I do not even know your name, and I do not desire to know it : the secrets my husband living kept from me are doubly sacred to me now that he is gone. I am not even sure, pardon the discourtesy of the words, but I am not at all sure that it was well for you to visit me to-day ; for I do not think he would have bidden you hither had he been alive."

Despard remembered his visit of fourteen years before to the Bunch of Grapes, when Dr. LeBaron had declined to admit his guest to a sight of the domestic felicity he boasted, and was silent. Molly continued, —

"And yet I cannot be sorry to see one who knew and loved him whom I hold so dear. You are kindly welcome, sir." And as she gave him her hand, the conflict of feeling, the glow of tenderness, the doubt, the eyes brimming with tears yet not overflowing, the tender, tremulous mouth, despite the true, firm voice, all combined to make so fair a picture of her face, all told so clearly of the great loving heart, and the powerful will, and the inflexible honor, and the truth before God and man, that made up this woman's character, that the priest, no mean judge of human nature, no tyro in the nature of women especially, forgot, in reading that noble page outspread before him, to release the hand he held, or to make reply to the words he hardly heard, so that it was the widow herself who, with a little added dignity, presently said, —

"Sit down, I pray you, sir, and tell me if you will what brought you to our little town."

"Pardon my stupidity, madame. I was but thinking that my friend had indeed shown his usual rare discernment in the selection of his wife. My errand? It is one that since I have seen you I am almost afraid to unfold; and yet, the strong mind, the noble self-command I see, should give me confidence that their possessor will not allow any excess of maternal fondness to resent " —

"What!" demanded Molly almost sharply. "You speak of my son, of Lazarus? What do you know of him?"

"Only that he so wonderfully resembles his father in face, form, and voice, that I am sure he must in mind also; while his mother's calm and truthful eyes give steadiness and purpose to the whole."

"Yes,—he is very like his father.   And then?"

The abbé smiled a little.   The idiom caught from LeBaron's French-English mode of speech pleased him.

"And then, madame," replied he gayly, "it would seem well fitting with the rest, that the son so like his father should be trained as was his father, and by the same hand.   It cannot infringe upon the privacy you so nobly respect, for me to say that I educated François from his early boyhood, and you know how I succeeded."

"Master Bradford, our governor, and all the men fit to pronounce on such matters here, will have it that my husband possessed more learning than all of them together," said Molly in proud simplicity.

"The worthy gentlemen show themselves fit for their honorable office," replied the abbé with a bow. "Well, then, madame, all at a blow, I petition for the privilege of educating the son as I did the father. You believe me competent?"

"Oh, yes, sir! fully competent, and the advantage to my poor boy would be untold; and indeed it would be a most fitting thing that the father and son should learn of the same lips; and I thank you most kindly for the thought, but"—and Molly's fluent words suddenly checked, and the color left her cheek as she slowly added, "but are you coming to this place to live, sir?"

"God forbid!" and the abbé imperceptibly crossed himself in horror.

"Then how could it be?" demanded Molly reproachfully.

"Surely, madame, Boston is not so very far from here," replied the priest, not daring yet to announce the whole intention of his visit; but Molly's rapid instinct forestalled him.

"You do not mean even Boston," cried she: "you would take him away! You have come here to rob me of my son!"

A swarthy red showed for an instant upon Despard's sallow cheek; and suddenly adopting a new tone he replied, —

"Well, yes, madame: my plan, or rather the plan of those who have a certain authority to arrange your son's destiny, is more extended than I at first announced; and, had you been a weaker woman, I might have waited some months before revealing the whole" —

"Spare all pretences, now at least, good sir," interrupted Molly more bitterly than she often spoke, "and tell me, as briefly as you may, who pretends to have any authority over my son, except myself; and what is the worshipful plan they have conceived?"

"Briefly, then," replied the abbé, stung by her scorn almost beyond his usual self-command, "the relatives of your late husband are of a very different rank from that the boy at present moves in; and as he will be heir to certain estates, or rather is now the actual possessor of" —

"Hold there, sir, if you please, and remember my caution against betraying the confidence my husband, somewhat riskily as it seems, reposed in you.   Besides, it matters not what claims my boy might have anywhere but here; for here is the only home his father desired to claim, here the only relatives his son will ever own.   It seems needless to speak further of what brought you here, does it not?"

"Perhaps, madame," replied the abbé, now thoroughly out of temper, "perhaps even your marvellous wisdom will allow me to judge for myself of my own affairs; and I insist, before accepting my dismissal, upon clearly stating that I come with offers of a thorough education, of a handsome fortune, a distinguished name, and a most suitable alliance for the young gentleman of whom we speak, upon the one condition of your resigning him into my hands; and it seems to me, courtesy apart, that a woman strong and sensible as yourself, a mother tender and self-sacrificing as yourself, would think twice before refusing such advantages for her son.   What but sheer selfishness and self-will should induce you to prefer for him the life of poverty, obscurity, and immolation, which is all these sands and pine forests have to offer?"

"Nay, sir," replied the widow, with a smile cold and fine as the edge of a razor, "they have for him what they had for the men whose graves you find on yonder hill, what they had for the man whose name I bear, and whose wishes are my law: they have freedom, — freedom from tyranny, freedom from corruption, freedom from other men's control.   My son will live in the home his father preferred to all the riches, honors, and alliances of which you speak, and which

I shall forget just as soon as I possibly can, sith it was not his pleasure to tell me of them. You have my last answer, sir."

"Then nothing remains but to bid you a fair good-day, and a long adieu, since we are not likely to meet again," said the abbé angrily.

"Most unlikely, I should judge. Good-by, and go in peace, my husband's friend," replied Molly, in her usual tone of gentle gravity.

CHAPTER XLI.

LETTER FROM THE ABBÉ DESPARD TO MADAME DE MONTARNAUD.

MY DEAR DAUGHTER,—In reply to your last somewhat impatient letter, I will simply say that I have done my best, and all that is possible, to carry out your wishes, and that I have failed, and the plan must be abandoned. As for your idea of kidnapping the boy, for it amounts to that, it is absolutely out of the question; and I rather wonder at your suggesting it to one you profess to reverence as your spiritual father. I told you of my interviews with Hetherford, and the dowry I promised in your name if he married the widow and relinquished the boy, although, in point of fact, he needed no inducement to either course. I also suggested his interesting the governor of the colony, who is madame's great friend and adviser, and taught him various arguments he should offer to that gentleman. This negotiation failing *in toto*, I saw the lady herself, and have given you the result of the interview in a letter you had apparently not received at date of your last. Probably you have done so before this time. That woman should have sat upon a throne, or led an army. She was so completely mistress of the situation in our encounter, that I retreated from her presence in a state of humiliation more wholesome than agreeable, and my meekness ever since has been most edifying. In all seriousness, my daughter, your schemes for this lad are absolutely impossible of execution; and we must marry Mademoiselle Thérèse to some noble *sieur* of Languedoc, who will add her name and title to his own, and at least keep the estates out of the clutches of the

Huguenot. *En passant,* our good and· pious king, advised no doubt by Madame de Maintenon, seems dealing somewhat strenuously with *ces messieurs* since the revocation of Nantes. Well, we must not allow human sympathies and weakness to blind us to the true interests of the Church; and I sometimes wish that these people among whom I labor to so little effect, and who in their own country are styled Malignants, could be transported to France, and there dealt with after the fashion of Vendée. And yet I know one fair, soft creature who would see the flesh cut piecemeal from her bones, and the bones wrenched asunder by wild horses, before she would give up her faith or her will or her son.

With this, goes a letter to my superior, asking a leave of absence, if not an abandonment of the mission. It does not prosper, and would not, as I believe, even in worthier hands than mine. If the people were without a faith like savages, or in the way of comparing their own sterile belief with the full and satisfying creed of the true Church, as in the Italian countries, or in fear of death and poverty as now in France, there would be hope; but to ask these smooth-faced, prosperous rogues to give up their worldly standing and sanctimonious public prayers, to risk life and goods, and the respect of men, for a faith which they have always known and deliberately abandoned, is, as you saw while here, an almost hopeless undertaking. I could hardly wonder at your abandoning the task, and cutting short your emulation of Madame de la Peltrie before reaching her glorious end. Remember, however, that it is only by the way of the cross that we reach the crown.

And now, my dear daughter, I will say adieu, hoping that it may also be an *au revoir;* for if my permission to depart arrives by return mail, you will see me as soon thereafter as wind and wave will carry me. I struggle in vain against the very human desire to see my own dear home and friends once more, and the spiritual longing to join again in the stately and venerable service of my beloved cathedral.

With my blessing and constant prayers, I am as always, dear daughter,

Faithfully your father,

VINCENT DE P. DESPARD.

When Madame de Montarnaud read this letter some four or five weeks later, she quietly refolded it, nodded her head twice or thrice, and murmured, —

"I suppose *le bon Dieu* made these men to develop the superior intelligence of the women. We never quite know our own powers until we find it necessary to remedy their blunders."

CHAPTER XLII.

ON BURYING-HILL.

IT was the chill gloaming of a November day; a leaden sky hung low above the flat and lifeless sea, crushed by its weight, and reflecting its color; the skeleton trees shivered in the wind moaning fitfully out of the east, and slowly bringing in a great fog-bank to lie like a shroud over the face of dead Nature, — a chill, defying duffle mantle, or robe of fur, and sending a shiver through even the stoutest frame; while the old wives, comforting their frosty noses and withered fingers at the blaze snapping upon every hearth, cried, —

"Hark to the fire treading snow! It will be a shrewd night on the coast. God keep the sailors!"

"They signalled another brig off the Gurnet just before dark," reported goodman Priest, as he stood beside the chimney, and stirred the logs with his heavy boot.

"Another? Oh, yes! 'The Messenger' from Boston came in this morning," replied his wife. "Well, if the brig's skipper is a prudent man, he'll stay off the Gurnet till morning light, and not risk Brown's Island and Dick's Flat in a night fog."

"Pity but he had thee there to guide him, dame,"

replied her husband with a chastened smile ; and the dame retorted, "And if he has no better headpiece on's shoulders than thee, Diggory, he needs me."

Creeping in, and creeping up, the fog has reached Burying-Hill, and goes stealing along between the rows of stones marking the streets and alleys of this city of the dead, already more populous than the town below, hanging dankly upon the funereal ever- greens set here and there about the graves, and seem- ing to wither away the last freshness of the grass crouching beneath its tread. And here, at the highest point of the hill, the fog finds a fit subject for its clinging, crawling possession. Beside a gravestone newly set, yet with no mound at its foot, crouches a woman clad in deepest mourning weeds, her head en- veloped in a muffling veil between whose folds showed a wild and woeful face, — a face where pride and pas- sion had fought with grief until all its beauty was lost in scars of conflict, and the great gloomy eyes, once its charm, burned like the fires whereby upon a stricken field men seek the bodies of the slain.

Quiet and impassive as the dead around her she crouched there ; but it was not in the gentle resigna- tion of hallowed grief; the volcanic throes were for the moment exhausted, yet only gathered strength for a new outburst. On that face, as on that of Milton's Satan, one read that so long as the deathless spirit en- dured, so long it was that of a rebel against God ; never should it arrive at His peace.

At a little distance, his back turned to the silent mourner, stood a man, his hat pulled over his eyes, his arms folded, his face, gray as the sky and the sea and the fog, bent downward, his mind so lost in gloomy thought·that the present scene and companionship were forgotten, and he did not hear the light tread of a woman, who, climbing the little footpath among the graves, passed close behind him, and approached the stone with the sable figure crouched beside it.

This woman also was in mourning, but of a less exaggerated sort than the other; and the close little hood, concealing nearly all her hair, left exposed a face white, and thin, and grief-worn indeed, but still and holy as the effigies of a saint. Tears and vigil, and prayer without ceasing, had indeed wasted away the roundness and much of the comeliness of youth, but had left in its place a radiant loveliness, a solemn and thrilling beauty never seen save on the faces of —"they who, with their Leader, have conquered in the fight;" faces from which men "take knowledge that they have been with Jesus."

Approaching the stone with her quiet tread, she presently stood unperceived beside the other, who, with her face buried in her hands, was now sobbing heavily. Mary Wilder looked at her a moment in grave surprise, then, laying a hand upon her shoulder, softly said, —

" Friend, why dost thou weep beside this stone?" The crouching figure sprang to her feet, drew the veil across her face, and haughtily demanded, —

" What is that to you, madame?"

" Much," replied Molly patiently. " For this stone is placed here in memory of my husband, as you may read; and one who mourns beside it must have known and loved him, and so is dear to me."

"Oh! You are the peasant whom he chose to style his wife!" exclaimed Valerie in a tone of biting contempt, as she swept the veil aside, and looked her rival in the face. A little color crept into Molly's cheek; but her voice remained patient and sweet as she replied, —

"I was indeed his wife, madame, — both was and am, for death has not broken the bond; and that I was his wife in sight of God and man, this gentleman can testify, sith he it was who married us."

"This lady is indeed the widow of our friend, my daughter, and should be so treated," replied the abbé, who had approached at the sound of voices, and now stood beside his charge. For reply Valerie pointed contemptuously at the stone, and said, —

"Why, see! she does not even know his name. Francis LeBaron she styles him. Pr'ythee, madame, what do you call yourself?"

"By my husband's name, as wife and widow should. I am Mary LeBaron."

"But, good woman, that is no name, as even you must know. What other name had he? What was he called before, as I have heard, you yourself invented this absurd title, name, whatever you choose to call it?"

A puzzled look disturbed the calm of Mary's face: the color deepened, and her eyes turned wistfully from that angry and contemptuous face to the stone, whereon was rudely inscribed, —

> " To the Memory of
> DOCTOR FRANCIS LeBARON
> Phthycian & Chirugeon
> of Plymouth Plantation.
> He was lost at sea off the Bermudas
> Nov y III. 1690
> And this stone is raised to his memory by his
> Wife and Son."

The sight of the beloved name seemed to re-assure her; for if without anger, it was with much dignity that she turned her eyes again upon the face of her opponent, and said, —

"I do not understand you, madame; and I do not care to inquire your meaning. If my husband chose to forget his earlier history, and begin his life from his arrival in this country, he had a right to do so. If he chose to conceal that history even from me, the wife whom he loved and trusted far beyond her deserts, I will not have another hand withdraw the veil he chose to draw. This gentleman knows my resolve in this matter: he may explain it further; and as methinks it is ill proving our love and honor to him who is gone, to wrangle over his headstone, I will bid you a fair good-night, and go my way."

"Good-night, madame," replied the priest, removing his hat, and bowing courteously; but the high-bred lady of the politest court in Christendom contemptuously turned her back, and made no reply.

Poor human nature! No gilding and no lacquer are permanent enough to hide its deformity at some moments of a passionate life. The only safeguard against ugly exposure, sooner or later, is to change the whole groundwork of the fabric, to replace the original material with one not perhaps so highly polished on the surface, but sound and fair throughout.

CHAPTER XLIII.

A PROVENCE ROSE.

MOTHER must not stay up on the hill in this fog and chill," said Lazarus LeBaron, throwing down his book, snatching his hat, and putting a ing down his book, snatching his hat, and putting a fresh log upon the fire where already the kettle softly sang of evening cheer and domestic comfort. Hurrying along through the village, whose twinkling lights and ruddier streams of fire-blaze showed that the folk were generally gathered about their hearthstones, the lad began to mount the hill already dusky with night as well as fog, when he heard a blithe young voice just out of sight singing a little French nursery rhyme, —

> " Tous les vaches de Picardie
> Sont nommée Marie, Marie ;
> Donnez-moi du lait, chérie ! "

And then exclaiming in the same language, —

" Well, Marie, is there anybody up here but messieurs the dead men, do you suppose ? "

" But no, mademoiselle," replied a coarser voice. " And who knows but they may attack us for disturbing their repose ? Let us return to the inn, and await madame there as she bade us."

Lazarus, taught by his father and the French sailors who pervaded the port in those days, understood the language easily, but was a great deal too shy to use it on his own account; so hastening his steps a little, he overtook the speakers, and said in English, —

"Are you looking for somebody on the hill?"

"*Ah, ciel!*" exclaimed the merry voice; and Lazarus could now see through the gloaming how fair and bright a face went with it, before, lapsing into a ceremonious tone and very careful English, the young lady continued, —

"You are but too good, sir; and if you will graciously tell us if a lady is up here among the graves. A boy said so below there, but it is so gloomy here."

"A lady, do you say?" asked Lazarus, his eyes fixed upon the flower-face so different from any thing he ever yet had seen. "My mother is here; but you do not seek her, I fear."

"Your mother! No; but it is my own that I want," exclaimed the girl, flashing out a smile. "Two lambs, each crying for its sheep mamma."

Lazarus laughed too, and said something, he knew not what; for he was thinking that the dark velvety pansies in his mother's garden-plot were almost as rich as the eyes laughing into his, and that new broken cocoanuts were not so white and fine as those little teeth laughing with the lips.

"Come, mademoiselle," interposed the nurse, her sharp black eyes peering into the fog on every side, and her French mind divided between delight in "assisting" at even so mild an impropriety as this interview, and terror lest it should be discovered. But her young mistress was French also, and, fresh from her convent and a tedious sea-voyage, found it very pleasant to chatter there in the twilight with a tall lad whose fearless blue eyes so plainly told his admiration, and upon whose downy cheek glowed a color fair to see and unknown to southern France. So they prattled on, these two, speaking of Heaven knows what, and never guessing at the tragedy going on among the graves above them, or of the tangled life threads they might so easily smooth or still further complicate, until upon their gossip broke a clear cold voice, saying, —

"Son! Are you looking for me?"

"O mother! — yes, — that is, — this young lady is looking for her mother. Did you see her?"

With a strange look of anger upon the face ordinarily so sweet and still, Mary LeBaron turned, and fixed her eyes upon the girl, who, smiling timidly, replied to the look in her pretty accented English, —

"Yes, madame. My mother and her chaplain, they went out from the inn, and asked the path to the cemetery to see some memorial of which the landlord told them; and I go to seek them because it is so lonely at the inn. You will perhaps have met them above there."

"She married, then, and you are her daughter?" asked Mary, her thought taking words almost unconsciously.

"Married! But yes, madame, since it is my mother of whom we speak," replied the Montarnaud so haughtily that Lazarus colored afresh, and, drawing closer to his mother's side, took her hand in his. Recalled to herself, Mistress LeBaron glanced at her son, then again at the girl, bowed her head in grave courtesy, and simply saying, —

"There is a lady on the hill, and a priest with her;" she moved decidedly away, Lazarus perforce accompanying her, although with a backward look so wistful that a faint smile crossed his mother's face in seeing it; but neither spoke until close to the garden gate, when she said, —

"Lazarus, do you remember your father's saying that marquises were unlucky to him?"

"Yes, truly, mother."

"And did not his words prove sooth?"

"Only too fairly true, mother."

"And did he not bid you heed me when he should be gone ?"

"Ay; and do I not, sweet mother?"

"You have been better than the best so far, my boy; but there comes a time, — and I was called a good daughter, too, but I was found wanting when that day came to me, — all I would say now, my boy, is this, marquises are unlucky to all of us, as well as to our head; and his words were not only a prophecy, but a warning.   Yon maid is fair?"

"Passing fair and winsome, mother."

"Well, she and her mother and her priest and all belonging to her are of the marquises; and your father bids you, through me your mother, beware of her and all of them.   Avoid speech or look or any association if you would obey him, and avoid the curse of rebellious children.   Do you understand?   Will you heed?"

The light of the fire within struck through the casement, and fell upon the speaker's face ; and Lazarus almost forgot to answer for wonder at the terror, the pleading, the agitation, pictured there : never in all his life had he seen it so stirred ; and it was not until his mother's cold hand closed sharply upon his, and her voice demanded, "Well ! Have you no word for me?" that he replied, —

"I cannot tell your meaning, mother, nor why my few words with that fair young lady should so move you ; but to obey my father, and please you, are more to me than all the maids with dark eyes and white teeth who ever walked : so be content, mother, I will not go near her or any of them, or speak to them, an I can help it, while they stay in Plymouth. Does that please you?"

"'If you can help it,'" repeated the mother dubiously ; and Lazarus laughed out as he replied, —

"Why, yes. You would not have me turn and run, like the tailors from the kyloe cow, if I chance to meet these folk, and they ask me the way hither or yon? I need not do so, though they be marquises twice over, need I, mother?"

"Why, no, I suppose not ; and yet — you know the word of Holy Writ, — touch not, taste not, handle not. But I trust you, my boy, now that you know my will and his will. I trust you never to deceive me," and then, as Lazarus pushed open the gate, and hastened to undo the door for her to enter, the widow whispered bitterly to herself, "as I did my father and mother."

CHAPTER XLIV.

WHEN THE FOG LIFTED.

THE fog, brooding heavily all night over sea and shore, lifted with the sunrise and the turn of the tide, allowing the cautious skipper of the brig, reported by Dame Priest as lying off the Gurnet, to make out his landmarks, and assure himself of sufficient depth of water to steer clear of the dangers of the harbor, whose intricate channels were not yet buoyed out. The pale autumn sunshine lay broad on Burying Hill, touching the doctor's headstone with melancholy light, and throwing its long shadow westward across the vacant grave that should have been his. In the village below, a note of decent merrymaking already resounded; a sort of glee befitting men who daily prayed to be delivered from the damnation they and all men deserved, and who, even in praying, grasped a loaded musket in one hand, haply to discharge it before the orison ended at prowling beast or more dangerous savage.

But to-day, instead of Fast and penitential exercises, the governor had ordained a feast of thanksgiving for the bountiful crop (as Plymouth crops go), the peace and safety of the colony, and God's continued favor to these His peculiar people. It was holiday at the dame-school; and although the widow and her son could not join in even the sober mirth of their neighbors, nor would accept any invitation to their houses, Mary thought good to notice the day, not only by hearty thanksgiving for the protection and comfort assured her by the Guardian of the widow and the fatherless, but by a little feast, principally adapted to her son's tastes and fancies. The doctor, partly because he was a Frenchman, partly because he had travelled much in lonely places, partly from natural propensity, had his own ideas and a fair stock of knowledge in matters of the *cuisine*, and had amused himself by imparting them to his wife, and encouraging her to experiment and sublimate in the art least æsthetic, but most essential to domestic comfort, of all the band. So it was just in the act of putting a chicken-pasty in the brick oven, while the fine fat pullet already revolved before the fire at the end of a string fastened to the ceiling, that Mistress Le-Baron was interrupted by a sharp rap upon her front door, and, as Lazarus was out of the way, must go to open it herself, her fair face flushed, her round arms bare, and some tips of bright brown locks peeping from beneath her widow's cap, and curling with the warmth of the neck and temples they caressed. Certainly the widow never looked so well in her attire of ceremony; and yet a certain womanly vexation dyed her cheeks yet brighter, as opening the door she found the lady of the hill, and the priest, upon the doorstep. Gravely saluting them, she hesitated for a moment; but seeing that they plainly intended to enter, she bade them do so, and pushed open the door of the sitting-room, where a Thanksgiving fire blazed upon the hearth.

"I do but hope Lazarus will not come home," thought Mary, following them in, yet was half-ashamed of the ungracious thought when Valerie, throwing back her veil and holding out both hands, said, —

"Will you forgive my rudeness of last night? I was so distressed and *bouleversée*, what you say upset. I did not sleep all night for need of your pardon, and, besides, *mon père* here scolded me so much, he is so great a friend and admirer of yours. Say that I have your pardon, dear Madame LeBaron!"

"Surely, if you need it, madame," replied Mary, allowing herself to be kissed on either cheek, but not returning the caress. "I may have been wrong myself: at any rate, I bear no ill-will. Will you sit down?"

"Yes, indeed : who would not sit in this so charming room? especially, madame, as we have much to say to you, much to implore."

Mary bowed yet more coldly, and seated herself in her own chair, — that chair beside the work-table, and commanding a view through the office-door of the leathern arm-chair where the doctor had been wont to sit looking out at the pretty garden behind his house, and smoking a meditative pipe. But in these sad days the office-door was always closed, and Mary had made Lazarus put a button upon it to prevent the children opening it in her absence. It was her only luxury, poor soul, to steal away sometimes, and, closing the doors about her, sit and weep in that old chair the tears she never suffered to interfere with her own duties or her boy's cheerfulness. And you may be sure every thing in that room remained the same that it had been on the day when LeBaron saw it last, and no speck of dust was allowed to gather there.

"And now, dear Madame LeBaron," began Valerie with the smile of Versailles upon her lips, but a haggard anxiety in her eyes too natural to be controlled, "we have a very, very great favor to ask of you, and a proposition to make ; and O madame ! for love of him we both mourn, in memory of him, in reverence to him, do not refuse me. It is my life I ask of you ; but that is not much, it is my child's happiness, the welfare of a great estate, the benefit of the Church of Christ " —

" Be careful, be careful, my daughter," muttered the abbé, fixing his keen eyes upon the face of his penitent, who calmed herself by a great effort, and continued more quietly, —

"You saw my daughter last night, madame ? "

" The young gentlewoman I met upon the hill ? "

" Yes. Is she not pretty, well-mannered, modest ? "

" As well as I could determine in a moment's seeing, she was all these." But the assenting voice was cold and hard as the stone above the doctor's empty grave.

"Well, madame," pursued the eager voice of the other, while the priest's keen eyes watched every word, " I, too, have seen your child, your son, the son of — François " —

" You have seen him ! Where ? " demanded the widow in a tone of mingled terror and displeasure.

"Content you, madame," replied the visitor with a gesture of haughty derision, breaking through the conciliating courtesy of her manner, — "he has not disobeyed your command to avoid us. The abbé met him, and would have brought him to me, but he would not come; so, finding that he was bound to the church, the — the " —

" The meeting-house we call it, madame."

" Pardon !   The meeting-house, — well, we went there ; and I sat as near the boy as I might, and studied him.   O madame, it is his father's noble head and stately form again !   It is a marvellous likeness."

"Yes, he is very like, but not so comely as his father," said Mary softly.

"Well, then, madame," pursued Valerie, joining her hands in passionate entreaty, " oh, then, madame ! by that dear father's name and memory I implore you, let your boy stand in his father's place. Suffer him to resume the name and rank of his noble ancestors, to inherit their estates, and to wed with his — with my daughter, the *demoiselle* you saw last night, and whom, if you will, you shall see again, and question as you will, satisfying your maternal heart that she is all any mother could demand as her son's wife.   I do not tell you her name or mine, because you have said more than once you would know nothing save what your husband told you ; but I can assure you, monsieur l'abbé, whom you trust, he will assure you, that the rank, the wealth, the position, I offer your boy are those that any noble of France might accept with joy ; and so far as we can, and preserve your husband's secret, we will give proofs " —

"It is useless, it is but waste of words and hopes and feeling, for us to talk more of this," interrupted Mary, her lips white, her brow drawn with anguish. "I cannot, for one moment, think of this plan of yours with aught but horror and shame. To sell my boy! To send him back to all from which his father fled! To set at nought the years of struggle and endurance with which my husband bought release from the life to which he was born, and which he trained his son to scorn and dread! I will not tell you, I will not betray the secrets of that dead heart by showing even for this, the story that I read there; but I know, I know as if he were here to tell it, that I speak my husband's will when I say that his son had better die and be buried on that lonely hill above there, than to go back to the luxury and vice and soul's death of the life from which his father escaped even as by fire.

"I speak for my husband, I speak for myself, when I say, No, never, to your proposition, and do most earnestly beseech that it may never in any form be repeated. It has been too much urged already."

"Obstinate" — began Valerie, her haughty anger flaming out at last; but the priest grasped her arm, commanding her to silence by a look, while he smoothly said, —

"One more word, dear daughter, before you turn us out. Your son is now nearly fifteen years old, is he not?"

"Quite so."

"And so manly of his age that his own judgment should count for something in a matter so closely affecting himself. Will you not consent that we should lay the matter before him; in your presence if you will?"

Mary hesitated for a moment, and in a sudden mental picture saw the boy's flushed and eager face as he spoke last night with that fair maid upon the hill, and turned so reluctantly homeward; but the next moment the serene light of truthful love crept back into her eyes, and she quietly said, —

"You may ask him — in my presence. But I know not where he is."

"He passed the window a little while ago, and looked in," replied the abbé eagerly. "And since then I heard the window of that room," pointing to the study, "open very softly. I fancy our young friend will be found there."

And the abbé did not quite restrain a smile of appreciation of his triumph. Mary caught and read the smile with one glance of her eye, and proudly saying, —

"My boy would not be worth the struggle we make if he were an eavesdropper. Look and see!" — she unbuttoned and threw open the office-door, glanced in, then with a stifled cry staggered back and fell into her accustomed chair, covering her face with her hands.

"Poor woman! She caught him in the act," murmured the abbé; and Valerie, with a smile of contemptuous triumph, swept past him into the little room, uttered a loud shriek, and fell senseless to the floor.

"Great heavens!" exclaimed the priest, following her, and halting petrified upon the threshold.

There, in the leathern chair, beside the open window looking to the garden, sat François LeBaron, his arms folded, his head bowed, his eyes fixed upon the figure of his wife where she crouched rather than sat, her ghastly face and wide eyes directed toward him with a look of love and horror and suspense.

And yet she was first to recover self-command, and rising painfully, to approach him step by step, her white lips forming some noiseless phrase, her hands outstretched toward him, who, dead or living, must ever be dearest of all God's creatures to her heart. As she reached the door he rose, and came toward her, unheeding Valerie's prostrate figure in his path.

"Mary! Wife!" was all he said, and she was in his arms; and Despard went to raise Valerie, and support her to a couch; and then arose the confusion of broken phrases, and interrupting voices, and half replies to half-heard questions, which take the place of conversation at such a moment. But presently the doctor's voice rose distinct from the confusion; and the tones were cold and clear, and perhaps a little mocking, — a tone more familiar to the guests than to the wife, or son, who had softly entered the room.

" Pardon for the annoyance I have caused you, my friends. Nothing was farther from my intention than the *coup de théâtre* I have effected, and I confess to not a little annoyance when the door so suddenly opened; but now " —

"Yes, but how come you within? You who are dead! You whose stone we have wept over! You whose widow wears mourning weeds!"—demanded

Despard, his cynical humor already struggling with the honest emotion of his heart.

"It is a history, my friend, and I do not just now feel in an historical mood," replied the doctor impatiently; for the presence of these ghosts from out the past irritated him, and he longed to be alone with the wife to whom he would have spoken so differently. "Quite in brief, then, I arrived in a brig from New Orleans an hour since, I met my son upon the wharf, I sent him before me to prepare my wife for my appearance, wishing, of all things, to prevent startling or annoying her, and to avoid a scene. The boy saw guests through the window, and ran back to tell me; I bade him go softly through the garden window into my office, and unbolt the door to me; he did so, and I seated myself, partly to calm some inconvenient emotions of my own, partly to wait until my wife should be alone. So sitting, I heard enough to make out the proposition with which you, madame, have honored us, and to coincide perfectly with my wife's decision. As she justly said, she spoke for me and for herself, yes, and for the boy too, although, that you may never resume the idea, you shall ask him for yourself, and now. There he is."

But Valerie, revived by the care Mary had forgotten her own emotions to render, shook her head, her mournful eyes fixed upon François, who met them steadily and without emotion.

"Speak you then, abbé," resumed the doctor. "There is my boy: what would you of him?"

"If I might talk quietly and more at length with

Monsieur Lazarus"—began the abbé; but the doctor impatiently interrupted, "You may: you shall leave no loophole for the future, only you shall promise solemnly to reveal nothing at present hidden, or stay— pardon me, *mon père*, but I had rather, on the whole, make the proposition myself, and here and now. Listen, Lazarus! you told me of the young girl you met last night, and of this lady and gentleman speaking to you this morning: that young lady is daughter of this lady. She is, as you say, beautiful, she is very rich, very highly born and educated; and her mother, for reasons I do not choose you to know, unless you accept the offer, wishes you to marry this demoiselle, her fortune, and her title, which would become your own. She and this gentleman will take you with them to their home, and give you every advantage and luxury possible to procure, and I make no doubt will treat you with all courtesy and kindness; possibly affection, but of that I am not so clear. This is a fair picture of what you offer, abbé, is it not?"

"Yes, my doctor, fair, but very inadequate."

"You hear, Lazarus. The abbé means that I have only given a bald outline, which you may fill in with all the glowing additions you fancy, especially in the direction of the young lady. The reverse of the picture is, that from the moment you leave this place for this object, you become an utter stranger to your mother, to me, and to our home. You become for me, merely a part of the association I have struggled for twenty years to clear myself from, and to forget. Your name, your country, your life, will all be hateful to me, and my only effort in your direction will be to forget your existence. My wife, do I speak your mind, as you but now did mine?"

"Yes, Francis, in all things."

"Then, my boy, you have the whole thing before you, and you are to give your reply without fear or favor."

"Pardon," interposed the abbé, "but if the young gentleman were to have a little time to consider. We do not leave this until to-morrow: will you permit that he have the night to think of it, perhaps to visit us this evening?"

The doctor hesitated, casting an uneasy glance at the boy, whose fair face and honest eyes were turned intently toward his mother. It was she who spoke, and it was with a smile of proud confidence into her son's face, —

"If you will have my opinion of it, my husband, I would say yes. I will trust Lazarus to go there."

"Very well," replied the doctor, looking from one to the other. "You will not forget what I have said, my boy?"

"Not a word, father."

"And you are quite sure that I say no more than I mean, and will carry out?"

"I am quite sure, sir. You always do as you promise, and so does my mother, and so will I."

"Ay, say you so?" and the father well pleased held out his hand, which Lazarus grasped manfully, and looked across at his mother, leaning upon her husband's shoulder in rare disregard of the presence of spectators.

"And I, for my part, promise," continued the doctor, "that neither my wife nor I will say another word upon this subject in presence of the boy, until after he has given you his answer at nine o'clock to-morrow morning; and he shall be with you this evening, on condition, always, that my secret is religiously kept. Do you promise for yourself and the ladies, abbé?"

"I swear it, doctor."

"That is finished, then." And Dr. LeBaron so plainly wished the interview also to be finished, that Valerie indignantly rose to go; but Despard, preventing her, said in his genial fashion, —

"But after all, *mon docteur*, how came you alive?"

"Ah, yes! I forgot. This devil of a pirate — excuse me, ladies, but he really was just that — had, as it seems, assured himself of the list of passengers on board the poor 'Belle Isle;' and as he had especial need of a physician and surgeon at his charming country-seat, he gave command, before boarding, to look out for me, and secure me alive. It was done by means of a blow from the handle of a cutlass upon my head, which floored me like an ox " —

"Francis!"

"Nay, Molly, 'tis all well long ago, silly child. When I opened my eyes it was on board the pirogue; and the same night I was landed upon the island of Monsieur Black Beard, where two or three of his wives nursed me until I was well enough to nurse them, and to set the leg of a young ruffian, son of Black Beard, and already a greater villain. They watched me well, and kept me safe for a year and over, when I managed my escape by a boat to a neighboring island, then to another where fishing-craft sometimes put in for water, from there to New Orleans and home. Will that do for a very weary man?"

"Perfectly; and as madame is an invalid, and needs rest, we will, if you please, say *au revoir*, and return to our lodgings. We shall see you this evening?"

The doctor bowed profoundly in reply to Valerie's profound courtesy; but neither spoke, neither offered a hand, neither sought the other's eyes. It was such courtesy as only flourishes upon the grave of dead, dead love.

Another moment and the visitors were gone; and as the door closed, the doctor turned to his wife, his face aglow, his arms wide open, his voice broken with love and longing, as he cried, —

"My wife, my darling, my own!"

It was Lazarus who interrupted that moment of paradise; and he opened the door to say in his grave and sonorous tones, —

"Mother, the pullet is roasted to a turn, and I have taken the pasty out of the oven."

"Yes, yes, I will come!" exclaimed Mary, her face all aglow as she extricated herself from her husband's arms, and followed Lazarus to the kitchen.

The next morning about ten o'clock, Master Lazarus again entered the sitting-room. His mother sat in her own chair, looking over a little pile of clothes, remnant of the doctor's ample outfit. He sat in his leathern chair beside the garden window of the study, smoking his pipe, and narrating his adventures in a tone of whimsical gravity all his own. As the boy entered he became silent, and looked at his wife : she, less self-conscious, looked at her son, her soul in her eyes. Lazarus came close to her side, laid his arms about her neck and kissed her tenderly, then, going to his father, slipped a shy hand into his saying, —

"They've sailed, father ; and the gentleman bade me say good-by to you for all of them ; and the lady added, 'And tell him we shall trouble him no more : he is safe.'"

"And the demoiselle? What said she?" asked the father grimly. Lazarus blushed scarlet, and slid behind his father's shoulder as he muttered, —

"She said nought, — but — she gave me this !" And the boy just showed a knot of carnation ribbons, then hid it in his breast. LeBaron smiled a little sadly, and, patting the child's, shoulder said, —

"Well, well, it's all over, then, is it?"

"Yes, father, quite all over."

"There, then, go to thy mother, and she'll comfort thee as mothers can. You have done well, my boy, and escaped right easily."

"Sit down and listen to father's story of the pirate, Lazarus," said Mary quietly ; and the lad obeyed.

CHAPTER XLV.

GOOD-BY.

PROBABLY François, *le baron de Rien-de-Tout* as he once styled himself, in all his chequered life enjoyed few things more than superintending the uprooting of his own monumental stone, and erecting it afresh in his own garden, precisely opposite the office window and leathern chair; and many was the quiet hour he spent, pipe in mouth, gazing dreamily out upon it, a placid smile upon his lips, a humorous twinkle in his eye.

And, final proof of his wife's devotion and womanliness: few things annoyed her more than this habit, and yet she never spoke of it.

Valerie's last promise was kept. Never more came tidings over sea to disturb the quiet of that simple home, the hard-fought peace of that strange, nameless life; never flew butterfly or humming-bird from the rose-gardens of Provence to the bleak· shores of Plymouth Bay, but the pure breath of ,the Mayflower perfumed those barren shores, and heart's-ease bloomed in Mary's garden-plot, nor failed as the years went on.

Lazarus married, nor once alone; and his second wife was daughter of the Bradfords: many children sat around his board, and went out into the world carrying the new name of LeBaron; but the fairest, the best-beloved, the nearest to her father's heart, of all the girls, was his daughter Thérèse; and it was his whim, or one of them, — for this Dr. LeBaron, like the first, was whimsical and reticent, — to like to see her dark hair decked with carnation ribbons.

On the crest of Burying-Hill stands to-day, just where Dr. François uprooted his mistaken memorial, another stone, of black marble, and stately even in its decrepitude: it bears the inscription, true this time, although not all of the truth: —

Here lyes y Body
of
DOCTOR FRANCIS LEBARON
A natyve of France and Physician
of Plymouth.
AD 1704